Praise for the Deadly Series
by Jaycee Clark

"Ms. Clark . . . has you sitting on the edge of your seat, reading furiously to find out what happens next. The suspense resonates throughout . . ."

— Love Romances

"*Deadly Shadows* is a well-written, riveting tale filled with fascinating characters and an engaging storyline."

— Romance Reviews Today

"*Deadly Ties* . . . blends suspense, romance, and danger into a thrilling story."

— Romance Reviews Today

"*Deadly Obsession* is the third book in the Deadly series and is an absolute must-read!"

— Fallen Angel Reviews

"*Deadly Games* is a suspenseful, action-packed, and thrilling story that kept me on the edge of my seat. Another excellent romantic suspense from Jaycee Clark."

— Joyfully Reviewed

"Jaycee Clark's Kinncaid Brothers series is hot hot hot and *Deadly Secrets* is no exception."

— Goodreads

Books by Jaycee Clark

Angel Eyes
Firebird
Talons (coauthored with Shannon Stacey, Mandy Roth, Michelle
      Pillow, and Sydney Somers)
Black Aura
Ghost Cats (coauthored with Mandy Roth and Michelle Pillow)
Ghost Cats 2 (coauthored with Mandy Roth and Michelle Pillow)
Ghost Cats: Revenge
Phoenix Rising II (coauthored with Donna Grant and Mandy Roth)
The Dream
Deadly Shadows
Deadly Ties
Deadly Obsession
Deadly Games
Deadly Secrets
Deadly Beginnings
Hunted

Deadly Secrets

Jaycee Clark

BEYOND THE PAGE
PUBLISHING

Beyond the Page Books
are published by
Beyond the Page Publishing
www.beyondthepagepub.com

Copyright © 2013 by Jaycee Clark
Material excerpted from *Deadly Beginnings* copyright © 2014 by Jaycee Clark
Cover design by Dar Albert, Wicked Smart Designs

ISBN: 978-1-940846-11-8

Acknowledgments

There are so many to thank. First and foremost, the brainstorming/ reader/critiquing/editing crew: Renee Meyer, Patti DuPlantis, Sydney Somers, and Kristie Clark Messer—thank you all for reading through this, for all the emails, all the encouragements, listening to me obsess and stress. To Syd and Kristie, thank you for all the many, many, *many* conversations about character motivations, plot twists, and whatever other detail I was being neurotic about in whatever version I was working on at the time.

Have to give a huge thanks (and readers, you should as well) to Mandy M. Roth for making sure Quinlan stayed alive in *Deadly Games* way back when I wrote that book rather than the original idea. Plus, she's always believed in me and my ability to tell this story if I'd just "shut up and write it."

To Heidi Fedak, thank you for answering my questions about the Gulfstream V and flight times.

To my medical crew: Aunt Toni, Vanessa Shirley, and Jessica Cross, thank you for answering all my medical questions and not thinking me too weird when asking the best way to . . .

For my law and law enforcement questions, thanks to Boyd Clark and Uncle George.

Any mistakes made are wholly and completely mine.

Quinlan's been a journey to write for me in so many ways. Must thank my editors extraordinaire Jessica Faust and Bill Harris for keeping me on track, putting up with my neurotic self, and making this book shine.

And last but not least, a monumental Thank You must be shouted out to the readers. Without you guys, Quinlan would still be languishing in various files and the Kinncaids would be known only to me.

Acknowledgments

Thank you for all your support! You guys saw the potential in Quinlan and his story before I did.

Thanks, as always, to my wonderful boys for understanding when Mom has to write.

This one is for my sister,
Kristie Clark Messer,
baby of the Clark Clan.

Prologue

New Mexico, two years ago

He waited until the patient's breathing leveled out.

"This is insane," she whispered beside him.

His attention was settled on the woman on the operating table. No one would ever know. They never ever did. That was the beauty of it all, or part of the beauty of it all.

So fucking easy.

Her swollen stomach was already an orange brown from the Betadine. He watched the monitors, the computerized screen showing not only the mother's heartbeat but the baby's as well. He listened to the soft swishing to make sure the baby's heart rate stayed within a safe range.

"Is everything ready?" he asked, already thinking ahead to a phone call he needed to make and the happy parents-to-be.

"Of course." She sighed. "I don't like these."

He was tired of listening to her complain. A shrewd bitch, but too soft too often in his opinion. "These are never pleasant. Just don't think of it. Remember, this little one will bring in fifty thousand. And it's not like anyone will miss the bloody mother. If you could even call her that."

The woman next to him said nothing as she rearranged his tools. He heard her moving the instruments around on the metal tray.

The mother's heart rate was a little high, but that didn't concern him.

He picked up the scalpel, steadied it, and quickly made a lateral incision on the very pregnant belly. Blood welled in the wake of his sharp object.

Normally, he was obscenely careful in performing this operation, but it wasn't as if he had to worry about the outcome. The mother had become a liability. He gripped both sides of the incision, prying through fat tissue and muscles, feeling the tissues rip under his force. At the uterus, he slowed, took a deep breath and concentrated. He heard the mother's erratic heart acceleration. With a precision born of practice, he carefully cut through the extended womb. The babe within squirmed, shifting beneath the tissue. The infant's heart rate swished louder in the quiet room.

In seconds, he had the baby out of the confines of the uterus. A boy, which he'd already known. Quiet squeaks filled the air while he suctioned the mucus from the babe's mouth. Then the small eyes blinked open. The cord still pulsed.

He puffed out a relieved sigh. "He's a big one."

She looked at him over the top of her mask and he read the disapproval mixed with greed in her eyes. The greed always won, always.

She clamped off the cord, her surgical gloves squeaking on the instrument, and clipped it.

"What of her?" she asked, motioning toward the woman.

He ignored the question. "We don't need any more complications. Someone will come in and take care of her. Here, get the babe ready. We've three buyers to choose from."

The operating room was filled with the newborn's cries and mewls as she wiped him off and rubbed him gently, talking softly.

He took a deep breath and pulled the mask down. "Healthy little boy, aren't you then?" he asked, rubbing a finger down the small upturned nose.

He reached over and pressed an intercom button. "Send Kevin in."

She kept her attention centered on the babe; a head full of dark black hair topped the little pink head.

"Beautiful little guy, don't you think?"

She nodded. "He's healthy. Weighing in at . . . roughly eight pounds thirteen ounces."

Music still played; slow strands of Handel waltzed around the room.

"Apgar's good," she muttered, noting and jotting down other details of the baby's health.

He nodded and reached for his cell phone. He hit the speed dial and waited. The voice on the other end picked up. "You better have come through for the amount on the table."

He smiled. "You worry too much. Pick a buyer. Healthy dark-haired boy."

There was a pause on the other end, then a sigh. "Good. No complications?"

He shook his head, part angered that the question was asked to begin with.

Who the hell did the guy think he was to question him? "No."

"What of the other matter?" the deep voice asked again.

He had no clue and he wasn't stupid enough to say that. "It's being handled."

"You better make damn certain of that. Do whatever you must to clean things up. I'm not going down because of a mess you dragged me into."

With that the line went dead.

Lawyers were always a pain in the ass, weren't they? Lawyers could always be replaced, and if the bastard became too much of a pain, they'd just find another one.

A knock at the door startled him. He opened it to Kevin dressed in green scrubs.

"You wanted me?"

He turned back to the gurney. She was still hooked up to the respirator, but he saw there was no need of that. She'd bled out. Her heart rate was too low. He sighed, walked over, covered her with a sheet and motioned to the body bag on the floor. "Get that and help me put her in it."

The babe still squalled over in the heated bassinet.

He had to get rid of the woman. She'd known too much, asked too many questions when she should have just ignored things, gone along with it all. He'd still have her baby in the end no matter what she wanted, but she'd have been alive.

He unhooked the IVs, the breathing tube, and waited while Kevin wrapped the woman's lower body. They lifted the bloody mess and awkwardly placed her in the black body bag.

The babe continued to cry.

He had another buyer.

And more waiting for precious little bundles.

• • •

Washington, D.C., October, the present

Where the hell was his wife?

He was married. Still.

Quinlan Kinncaid looked up at the ceiling in his darkened living room. The streetlights didn't glare into the window of his penthouse suite above the family hotel. He sighed and raked his hands through his hair.

What the hell was he doing? He'd left the rest of the family earlier. They'd all taken Mom out for her birthday, so hopefully the surprise party he and his siblings had planned for tomorrow night might actually work. Probably not. Mom knew everything.

Well, just about everything. Hell, his entire, interfering family knew just about all there was to know about the others—but that was the way it had always been in his family. Now, though, now he had a secret that none of them knew and he wasn't about to tell them.

Not that he didn't want to. He just didn't know how.

Two words, dumb ass. I'm married.

And chaos would undoubtedly ensue.

His phone rang, jerking him from his thoughts of his missing and estranged wife.

It rang for a third time before he finally wrestled it from his pocket, automatically sliding his thumb across the screen to answer the call before it went to voice mail. Figuring it was one of his brothers about last-minute details, he didn't bother looking at the caller ID before he answered.

"Hello."

Silence. He rubbed a hand over his face. He really didn't have time for this.

"Hello?"

A throat cleared. "Quinlan?"

He sat up, barely wincing at the pain in his thigh. "Ella?"

"Oh thank God. Thank God I got you. I know you probably don't want to hear from me and I'm sure you've already moved on and that's fine. Really." She paused in her rush of words. "But I've got to talk to you. I don't know who else to trust, who else to—"

"Ella?"

"Yes, it's me. I know, I know I walked away and I've never been sorrier for anything I've ever done, Quin. I'm sorry." Her voice stumbled. "I'd say I'm sorry a thousand times and I know you probably don't want to help me, but I don't know who else to trust, who else to—"

"Ella." He stood from his leather couch and walked to the window, looking over the D.C. night winking and spread out before him. "Calm down, take a deep breath."

She was always so . . . calm. Spirited, yes. Funny and quirky, smart-ass even, but always a level of calm. Nothing much rattled her. But this?

He'd never heard her this way. "You're not making a lot of sense."

"I'm scared, Quin." Her voice trembled over the phone. "I don't know what to do. I don't even know what's real anymore. I can't see past . . . I don't know. I just . . ." Her voice skipped for a moment.

"Ella, I can't hear you very well. Calm down, babe. Tell me what I can do to help."

For a moment there was silence on the phone. Then he heard her take a deep breath in and blow it out.

"I don't know how to tell you this. I called weeks ago and — never mind, that doesn't matter. Did you get my letters?"

He shook his head, then realized she couldn't see him. What the hell was she talking about?

"Letters?" he asked. "What letters? I haven't received any letters from you. Hell, I haven't received anything at all from you. Not even a text."

She made some sound, part groan, part laugh? "Oh God, that's just . . . perfect. Of course you don't know what letters. That doesn't matter, or it does. It really does, but not now." Again she was quiet. Again he waited, so glad to hear her voice, that smooth Southern drawl, even if he had no freaking clue what the hell she was talking about.

Ella cleared her throat. "Look, there's something you need to know. I just don't know . . . I don't know . . . Hell, I don't know how to tell you but I'm scared. I can't eat, I can't sleep and it's too late for me to fly out to you. I could take a bus or — "

"Why are you scared, Ella?" He fisted his hand on his hip, worried because he could hear the fear in her voice.

"God, Quin, where do I even start?" She laughed but it held no amusement to him. "They won't let me go. I know they won't. I thought I could help. Thought I was doing good. I bought into it all and that was so stupid. God, I was so stupid and naïve and . . . They want her, Quin, and I'm afraid, I'm so scared they're going to just take her and I won't be able to stop them. I won't be able to stop them. Can you come out here please? I know I don't have a right to ask you. I know I don't, not after throwing it all away and—"

He closed his eyes and pinched the bridge of his nose between his thumb and forefinger. "Honey. Stop. Just stop."

She did.

"Deep breath. Come on, I can hear you."

He heard her inhale, then exhale.

"Now, who is scaring you?"

For several seconds there wasn't anything other than her sniffle.

"Did someone hurt you?" he asked, straightening, anger flashing through him. "Ella?" he snapped.

"No. No, I don't think so. I can't remember," she said, her voice almost a whisper at the end.

He started to ask what she couldn't remember, but then shook it off and headed back to his bedroom.

"Okay, we'll talk about that later. Who's scaring you, baby? Tell me." And he'd damned well take care of them. In his room, he strode to the closet, grabbed a duffle and tossed it on the bed, along with a couple of pairs of jeans and shirts. "Where are you?"

"T-Taos. Taos, New Mexico. I'm still here."

"Okay, and what's your number?" He grabbed a pen off his nightstand and the pad beside it.

"Five seven five—" She cut out again.

"Ella. Ella, I can't hear you."

"Hang on. I need to plug in." He heard her rummaging on the other end of the phone.

"What's the number again?" This time he wrote down the entire number and read it back to her to make sure it was correct. "Is that right?"

"Yes."

Taking a deep breath, he asked, "What's your address?" When she told him, he wrote that down as well, then ripped the paper off and shoved it in his pocket. "So if I call you back in a bit, you'll answer?"

"Yes. God, Quin, I'm so stupid. Do you have any idea—" Her voice broke again before she continued, "how good it is just to hear your voice, Quinlan?"

At least she could call him; he hadn't had a number to reach her, but he didn't see the point in saying that. "Same goes. You're okay now?" he couldn't help asking. "Are you safe right now?"

She didn't answer him for a moment.

"Ella."

"I think so. I don't know."

"I'm coming out there," he said as he shoved his stuff into the bag and grabbed his small overnight off the counter in the bathroom.

"I could come to you. I can drive partway tonight and —"

"I'll be there in a matter of hours, Ella." He zipped the bag shut and hurried to the safe hidden in his office down the hallway. Punching in the combination, he quickly grabbed the papers he wanted, some cash, and shut it. "Now, who are you scared of?"

Taos. He was heading to Taos. He'd need a damned jacket. He grabbed his Marmot jacket and shoved it into the bag, then jerked on his black wool coat. As an afterthought, he grabbed his briefcase and hefted it over his shoulder as well. Bags, coat, cash. His cane. Glancing around, he saw it leaning against the side table in the living room where he'd been sitting when she called.

"Ella?" She still hadn't answered him.

Cane . . . anything else? He scanned the area. No. He was good.

"Ella, answer me."

"I don't—I don't know who it is exactly. I just know they want her, Quin. They want her! And I know, I *know* they'll take her from me, no matter what I've told them. I *know* it!"

He pulled his door shut and hurried to the elevators. "Who? Who will they take?" She wasn't making any sense and that worried him almost as much as the stark fear in her words, in her hurried speech.

Her quick breaths panted through the phone.

"Okay, someone, you're not sure who is going to take someone else? Who are they going to take?"

Again her phone cut out for a minute.

"Ella! Hello?" The elevator dinged but he didn't get in just yet. He held the private elevator with his hand. He'd lose the signal inside it.

"Who are they going to take?"

He heard her inhale. Exhale.

"The baby," she said quietly.

He froze.

"Whose baby?" he asked very carefully.

For a long moment there was nothing, just silence. He thought he'd lost her or she'd hung up, or her battery finally died. But then he heard her sniffle and inhale again.

"I'm sorry, Quinlan. I'm *so* sorry and I know I can never make it up to you. I *know* that."

Oh God, she *wouldn't* . . .

"Ella," he said, whether in plea or command he wasn't sure.

"She's yours, Quinlan. Ours."

He couldn't say anything . . . His? His baby? Their baby? *His?*

Shock. Then anger burst and flared. He opened his mouth. Bit down. Opened it again.

"How . . . When . . . How could you . . ." he managed past the tightness in his throat. Very softly. Very quietly.

"I'm *sorry*. God, I'm sorry. I was helping them, or thought I was. They asked me to help and they wouldn't let me tell you, said it could compromise things. But it's all lies. Women are missing, Quin. Dead. I know they killed her. They wanted her baby. And they just took it. I know they'll take mine too! I don't know any more who to trust. Except you. I'm not supposed to be calling you, but I don't care what I screw up for them anymore. Please, Quin. Help me."

He couldn't say anything. Hell, he couldn't see. He rubbed his eyes and blinked, but that didn't really help. Squeezing his eyes tight, he tried to understand, tried to make sense of the whole damned conversation.

But he couldn't.

All he heard was *baby. Yours.*

Her voice echoed through the pulse thundering against his ears. ". . . be mad at me. Hell, yell at me, be pissed at me, I wouldn't blame you."

"Well, that's great of you, Ella," he said.

"Look, hate me even. God knows I hate myself just knowing how this hurts you, how I've already hurt you. But please, *please*, Quinlan, I *need* you. *We* need you. If you can't come out here, I'm leaving. I have to get out of here—"

Her words tripped and rattled in his mind, broke his heart and made him wonder what the hell he'd been waiting for for the last few months. Did he even know this person? Nothing made sense.

"When . . ." He took another deep breath.

"Please," she begged. "Please, help me. You'll keep her safe."

His daughter? Hell yes he would.

He opened his mouth, pissed, confused, and knew the words hot on his tongue were probably not the ones he needed to say. Instead he closed his eyes, took another deep breath and another and counted very slowly to ten. A hundred would probably be better but he didn't have the patience for a hundred.

"Ella. Are you at home?"

"What? What has that—"

"Yes or no. That's really all I can handle right now."

A beat of silence. "Yes. I'm at home."

"Good, stay there and don't move until I get there." He took another deep breath as he bit down. "Then you and I, dear wife, are going to have one long conversation about many things."

"You're coming?" she asked quietly. "You're really coming?" Again her voice broke on the end and he heard her swallow.

"God, what kind of—" She was pregnant. Pregnant. The word kept rattling in his brain. Pregnant. He probably shouldn't yell at her. Probably, but damn it.

Very carefully he said, "Ella, I'm heading to the airport now." He checked his watch, calculated the time difference. "I'll be there in about five hours, probably less. I need to call the airport and have them fuel up the jet. I'll be landing in Taos and I'll call you."

"I can come pick you up."

He nodded. "Okay. Now, is there anyone you can call to stay with you until I get there?" She was scared. Terrified, to be honest, he could tell that much. He raked a trembling hand through his hair.

He heard something in the background.

"Someone's here," she told him suddenly.

He frowned.

He heard her sigh. "Oh, it's just a friend. I'll see if she can stay. Or I'll go stay with my neighbors the Richardsons after she leaves. Then you'll be here and it'll be okay."

A friend. He set his briefcase in the elevator and then tossed his duffle bag inside. He bit down. "Mrs. Kinncaid . . ." He shook his head. They'd get into that all later after he made certain she was safe. "Stay put. I'll be there soon."

• • •

New Mexico, October, the present

Can't die . . . can't die . . .

The lights. Too bright. Too dim. Everything in contrast. Where was she? She blinked and tried to focus.

The street blurred before her. She saw the dark river of asphalt. The tall, wavering streetlights. Flickers of lights zoomed to and fro farther down the way.

Where was she?

She stopped, the road cold beneath her bare feet. Her foot hurt. Her ankle hurt.

She raised her hands and saw there was blood on them. Blood and scabs on her mangled wrists. Her shoulders hurt. Her head throbbed. Hell, her whole body seemed to pulse with pain, almost distant and dull, but not quite enough.

The cold wind blew against her legs and she looked down. Something shimmered, dark and glossy, along the bottoms of her legs. Why couldn't she think?

Something important.

She put her hands on her stomach.

Important . . .

And remembered.

Her stomach.

The baby. The baby . . . *Her* baby.

The bump was different. Smaller, softer. She pressed her abdomen with her bloody hand splayed on her stomach.

No. No. No.

Images, disjointed and fractured, jumped in her brain.

A baby crying.

Red hair.

A room. A room where she'd been tied down.

They'd taken her baby. Taken it. Taken her sweet little girl.

No. No. No.

She stood there, shaking from cold, from shock. Ice in her veins.

"Ma'am?"

Bright. Too bright. Bright, bright lights.

"Ma'am?"

Slowly, she turned and blinked.

"Baby. My baby," she whispered.

Someone walked toward her, the image dark against the bright lights. A hand reached for her. "Ma'am . . . I'm . . . help . . ."

A man's voice, faded and loud, then silent against her eardrums.

"No, please," she whimpered.

"You're safe now. You're safe." The world tilted and she tried to make sense, but nothing did. Nothing solidified in her mind. Nothing congealed to a whole complete thought. Cold. So, so cold. Why was she so cold?

Quinlan. She wanted Quinlan. She'd called him. He was coming to help. Help her. Help them.

"Ma'am. Stay with me . . . stay . . ." A static of radio voices tunneled to her, swirling and merging, fading . . .

"Stay with me. Help is on the way," shouted down at her. ". . . name?"

The sky was dark, then bright. Red. Blue. Red. Blue. Dark. The darkness grew . . .

She tried to pull away. Tried to go. *Have to find her. Have to find her.*

"Ma'am, what's your name? Your name?"

A dog barked somewhere and kept barking, jerking her back to here, to now, away from the darkness for a moment. She could feel the darkness getting closer though, whispering to her. Sirens screamed louder and louder.

"Ma'am, calm down. Calm down." Hands held her and she blinked, finally focusing. A policeman. A cop.

She licked her lips. "Cop. Help. Please."

"What's your name?" he asked. Dark hair, dark eyes.

"Ella. Ella." She grabbed his shirt. "Help me. They took . . ." She tried to take a deep breath, but her chest felt funny, tired. So damned tired. "Baby. They took my baby. My . . . my . . . Please, I need him. Please. They took her."

"Him? . . . Ella! Stay with me! What's his name? Stay with me!"

"Quin." She licked her dry, cracked lips. Dry. So tired. *Have to find her. Have to find her baby . . .*

"Ella! What's his name?"

"Quinlan Kinncaid . . . D.C. . . . The baby. Took her. They took her. Please . . ." She wanted Quin. "He's my . . . my . . ." She tried to swallow; the world unfocused again in bright blues and reds as sirens screamed in her ear. "Husband."

She saw his lips move, knew he leaned over her, but the darkness grew, a terrible monster, and swallowed her whole.

Part I: Beginnings

Chapter 1

February, earlier that year

"Where the hell are we going?"

His brothers looked at him and no one answered.

Quinlan Kinncaid took another deep breath of recirculated air and stared out the jet's window. Wherever they were headed, it was south of the Washington, D.C., area. He shifted in the leather seat of the Gulfstream V and figured this was just another WTF moment in a long line of similar situations over the last few months.

He'd chosen not to say anything. It was pointless, he'd learned that years ago as the youngest of five boys. No one ever listened to him anyway. And the last few months of his recovery? Well, his older brothers did what they did best, bullied the hell out of him when he wasn't doing what he was supposed to. He'd heard too many times that he needed to take it easy and rest more, take a breather, don't push so hard. Or to get off his ass, get out more, do this, do that. The lists were endless.

He was tired of them all, it just took too damned much energy to fight off four older siblings than it did to go along and bide his time.

However, he couldn't really blame them. Hell, he'd be the same way if the roles were reversed.

Kinncaids protected. Kinncaids stuck together. Kinncaids kicked anyone's ass who messed with one of their own. And if one of the asses happened to be a Kinncaid's, so be it.

His brothers were worried. They had given him a choice. Not only were they worried about him, they were worried about his parents, who were also worrying about him. Guilt trips worked. So it was either go along willingly or Ian, the meanest of them all, would *knock his ass out and he'd wake up where they wanted him to.*

Sibling love at its finest.

"You know, you could say this is an intervention," Gavin said, shifting in his seat and motioning with his tumbler of whiskey.

"An intervention?" Quinlan just looked at them all. An intervention of what? He didn't drink anymore, half the time didn't take the pain pills he was supposed to take, and God knew his leg hurt like a freaking bitch half the time. He didn't gamble. The last time he'd gotten laid had almost killed him, so sex had been a no go for some time as well. He didn't do much of anything. Hell, he'd even cut back on his hours at the family hotel in D.C.

Gavin, one of his twin brothers, nodded. "Yeah, an intervention, and I have to say I think it's a freaking great idea. I was really needing to get away."

Brayden, the other twin, sighed. "You might have been, but I wasn't. I didn't want to leave Christian for this long."

The two were identical, built like linebackers and with the inherited Kinncaid dark hair and cobalt eyes. Gavin had always been the jokester, Brayden the more serious.

Gavin waved his hand. "All the women are staying at the hotel doing the spa thing with Mom, and Dad's got Ryan to keep him busy with golf. Grandkids, grandparents and women. She'll be fine. Trust me, I'm a doctor, I know what I'm talking about."

"You're not my wife's doctor," Brayden said, taking a sip of his own drink. Vodka, if he went with habit.

"Well, no, that would just be weird, Bray. I deliver babies, and if I had to I'd deliver my niece or nephew, but I'd rather enjoy familial births rather than be the one delivering them if it's all the same to you. Your doc is Strong, right? Good ob-gyn."

Quinlan rolled his eyes and let the two talk babies and wives and birthing plans—whatever the hell those were. All his brothers were married. All had kids. All were living that *happy family picket fence Little League* bullshit.

Okay, maybe his brothers' lives weren't exactly bullshit. They were happy and he was happy for them and he loved all his nieces and nephews. Really, he did. But he'd always figured that life wasn't for him. He'd never actually thought it was for him, even if his mother was forever complaining that she just might not live to see the day he married, let alone gave her a grandbaby.

Now, even if he did think the picket fence, big diamond ring, home every night was for him, who would he trust with that? That thought was too damned deep for now and he was more concerned with what his brothers had planned than whether he might get married. Ever.

"Dad will probably write us all out of his will for leaving him with them all," Aiden, the oldest, volunteered as he sprawled in his chair, tucking his cell phone back into his pocket.

"Nah, he'll love every minute of it," Gavin added.

"So again, why are we all on the plane heading south?" Quinlan asked.

Ian, the second oldest and often most silent of the family, tossed him a water bottle. "We are all here because I told them we were going. I didn't take no from them any more than I took it from you."

"You mean I'm not the only one lucky enough to be threatened to come along?"

"Threaten is such a dirty word," Ian said, grinning and leaning back. "I prefer persuaded."

Quinlan looked at each of his older brothers. "Waterboarding is frowned upon, you know."

"Personally," Ian continued, "I found it generally got me the results I wanted, if the time allowed."

"You know, we could just be happy we're taking a small break. Away from the kids, the women and the grandparents—Lord love them all," Gavin muttered.

"You're the one that moved closer to home," Ian told his brother.

Gavin shrugged. "And you didn't?"

"Not that close." Ian shifted and sighed. "Besides, how long has it been since we've done this?"

No one said anything for a long time.

"Never," Quinlan said, looking at each of his brothers. He chuckled. "I was still in school when you went AWOL."

"I didn't go AWOL. I was exploring my options." Ian frowned at him.

"Yeah. You keep telling yourself that." He leaned over and punched Ian in the arm. "So thanks."

Aiden grinned. "Bet that hurt."

"Not as much as I thought it might. So again," he said, "where are we going for our overly extended time of brotherly bonding?"

No one said anything for a moment. Then Brayden looked at him. "You know, I don't remember you being such a smart-ass before."

"Side effect of the meds I take."

Several of his brothers laughed. He only smiled.

"Well, I for one am damned glad," Brody Kinncaid said.

They had a few cousins. Brody and Conner were the only two they'd claim. Brody came, but Conner was in Taiwan.

"Were you also threatened?"

"Hell, no," Brody said, plopping down beside him. "I figured it would be like those summer trips we were forced to take as kids when our parents met at the Vineyard." He sighed. "Miss those times, truth be told. Now we work all the time."

"If you didn't defend scumbags, you might enjoy life better," Ian told him, grinning.

"Yes, but since I've gotten so much practice, cousin, you'll know I can adequately represent you if any of your sins ever come to light."

Ian snorted and took a drink. "Johnno said he'd try to make it and Gabe is flying down tomorrow."

John Brasher, Ian's business partner, and Gabe Morris, one of D.C.'s finest brothers in blue.

"Fun time had by all."

"And if we get arrested in New Orleans, then our dear cousin will be able to get us out."

Brody flipped Ian off and settled back against his seat.

New Orleans? Huh. Quin wouldn't have guessed Ian would pick New Orleans for a trip, but Quin had always loved the city.

"New Orleans?" he asked his brother.

Ian shrugged. "If you don't like the destination, too damned bad. You pick the location and plan the trip next year."

Next year. Another trip with his brothers . . . He grinned.

Quin looked around at them all. Yeah, this trip should prove interesting. He'd just go with the flow. He was good at that, after all. He tended to forget things more now than he had before, he knew that—more from people's expressions than having to look at a schedule or something and see that he'd missed something else. He couldn't run anymore and damned if he didn't miss his morning runs. Or skiing. He really missed skiing this winter with Aiden and his gang. For the last couple of years they would invite him to go out to Colorado and hit the slopes with them. He loved to ski and he damned well missed it.

So he'd go along with whatever his brothers had lined up, at least as long as it suited him. Going along with it, just taking what came his way. It was about all he was good at anymore.

• • •

New Orleans

The boys were all settling into their rental. Someone, probably Aiden, had rented a house in the Quarter with plenty of rooms and enough genuine antiques to make Brayden see dollar signs. The rest were well on their way to enjoying the day in an inebriated state.

He took a deep breath and sighed as he walked down the sidewalk.

He'd always enjoyed the French Quarter here in New Orleans. It was almost like a work of art in and of itself. Music wafted on the air, several different pieces. Someone was practicing a violin, a guitar also rode through a window.

The houses here had ahold of him, always had. He'd thought about purchasing one once upon a time, but then . . .

Hell, why hadn't he? 'Course, if he had, it now would not be worth what he would have paid for it after the housing market crashed. Still, though, he'd have his own place.

Now?

Now he was the only sibling that still lived in the hotel. Aiden had, once upon a time, and even Brayden and Gav had spent their time in their own suites on the upper floor of the family hotel in D.C.

But now they all had their own homes, their own families to fill them.

And he had what?

A limp?

A job he didn't enjoy anymore?

An empty bed that he honestly had no desire to fill—last time had almost killed him.

He had his shrink appointments, which were supposed to be helping him deal with things. Maybe Dr. Garner was helping, he wasn't pissed off anymore. Wasn't suicidal or anything—homicidal maybe, suicidal no.

But he also wasn't . . . wasn't . . . *him.*

Something was missing. The excitement. The fun. The fear. Something. Anything. Because frankly, he felt nothing. Nothing other than fear or panic in the dead of night after a nightmare. Other than that?

Nope.

And that worried him. He was learning to deal with the fact his body and mind would never be the same as they had been before Elianya Hellinski. Small things became large. Insomnia some months, too much sleep others, constant pain. Then there was the fact his mind wasn't as sharp. It often took him twice as long to complete tasks—and that was on a good day. Appointments and people often slipped his mind. That pissed him off more than the physical changes. Being around people got on his nerves—which in turn made the rest of the clan fret and worry. He'd wanted to know the whys of his limitations and no one could tell him for sure—lack of oxygen when he coded several times, the chemicals from the drugged cocktails Hellinski had poured down him—who knew? In the end, the reason didn't matter, he'd learned. What mattered was simply dealing, and where he'd have once thought that would be easy, he'd learned it sure as hell wasn't. Especially when he remembered what he—and his life—used to be like.

The worst, though, was the worry on his mother's face, his brothers' hovering, the scrutiny of every little damned thing until many days he just sat in his office, working but not wheeling and dealing like he had before. Family interactions—hell, *any* interactions, he kept to a bare minimum. He'd changed his apartments at the penthouse from the traditional antiqued look that graced all the rooms to a modern black leather, chrome, and glass look. You'd have thought the family found him hoarding sleeping pills or something.

Maybe he would buy a house down here and set out on his own . . . Why not?

He frowned as he waited for a family to cross the street in front of him. He didn't want to go to Bourbon Street. Instead he turned back and went over a block.

The houses lining the streets were a multitude of colors. Some were set off the sidewalk, looking like mini-plantation homes behind half walls and iron fences. Others hid behind tall walls with broken colored glass along the top. Still others were stucco, locked up tight unless you were allowed into the courtyard and inner sanctums.

Be fun to buy one of these old homes and fix it up, see what he could make of it—himself.

Not with the help of his brothers or his loving, well-meaning parents.

If he bought a house here and moved . . . then they'd all leave him the hell alone.

He looked up and saw the corner market. Matassa's. He could run in and grab some bottled water and something to eat, see what the little market had.

The interior was tight, a little cluttered for his peace of mind, but it was clean and seemed pretty well stocked with whatever anyone might want. He went to the produce section, his mind still on the idea of moving here.

His family would worry he had lost his mind.

He, who had previously been the workaholic, always flying from one hotel to the next to check on things, always working the next deal, making certain every minute thing was working smoothly, even knowing their managers were competent or they wouldn't have been hired. That man had faded into the background, if he even existed anymore.

He picked an apple out of several and then another.

For Quinlan Kinncaid to buy a house in the French Quarter and then move? Yeah, his family would freak.

He chuckled to himself and turned and knocked into someone. He dropped his cane and reached out to steady them . . . her.

Chapter 2

Her.

Her hair was . . . was it blue? Cotton-candy blue with pale pink ends that curled softly above her shoulders.

Quinlan blinked and realized how small she was. The woman only hit him mid-chest. Her eyes, big, round and blue with little brown and gold flecks in them, stared at him in surprise.

"Sorry. I'm so sorry, I wasn't paying attention," she muttered. "I'm never paying attention." She tried to put an orange back and several rolled off.

She wiggled a bit and grinned up at him. Dimples. Deep dimples made her seem more impish, more human because her skin was flawless. Other than a faint scar he could barely see along the top of one eyebrow.

He realized he still held her upper arms, very in-shape upper arms, and slowly let her go.

"Your hair's blue," he blurted.

Her brows rose.

"I mean . . . You okay? I'm sorry, my mind was elsewhere and I wasn't paying attention either. You're all right?" He never took his gaze off her.

Emotions and expressions flittered across her face, so easy to read she'd be horrible in negotiations.

"*Cher*, I'm always all right, better than all right. I'm just sort of klutzy sometimes." From his eyes, her gaze slowly lowered and took him all in and then meandered back to his eyes. Her dimples winked at him again as she grinned. "And you look like you're more than okay too." Quickly she bent down and he got a lovely view of her ass covered in black and gray tie-dyed yoga pants. Her arms were muscular and toned as she rose and handed his cane to him. "Again, sorry about that."

"Hey, Ella!" someone called from behind the register.

"Hey, Tiny. You get any decent strawberries yet? 'Cause you promised you'd order me some, hon. And I don't see any pretty red organic strawberries. You making me wait till next week?" She propped a hand on her hip, clearly waiting for the man's reply.

Hell, Quin would go to the French Market and find her some fresh strawberries.

He shook his head. What the hell?

She looked back at him and winked, and those damned dimples woke up his libido. Or it might have been the tight yoga pants, weird as they were. Or the tie-dyed pink tank top that made his suddenly awoken libido think of all sorts of things he'd like to do with her.

Shaking his head at his derailed thoughts, he cleared his throat. "Thanks."

"Ella, darlin', you shoulda come in this morning, like you said you was going to. Then you'd have gotten your fresh strawberries. However, me being such a wise and kind soul," the older man behind the counter said, "I saved you two pints. Here ya go."

She grinned again and Quinlan almost groaned. What the hell was the matter with him? "Aw, bless your heart! I knew I could count on you, Tiny. Lisha have her baby yet?"

The older man shook his head and set two containers of strawberries on the counter. "Nope. Swear woman's going to give me gray hair."

The woman . . . Ella . . . looked back at him and grinned. "Tiny always complains about his wife giving him gray hair."

"How do you think I got all this gray anyway?" he said, chuckling and bagging the bright red strawberries.

Ella turned to him then. "Sorry, man, for knocking into you. You sure you're okay?"

He bent a little closer to her, glad when she didn't back away. "I'm *always* better than okay, hon. Name's Quinlan."

She threw back her head and laughed. Bright, clear laughter that curled inside of him and beckoned . . . She wagged her finger at him. "That's not a N'Awlins accent, *cher*. You here for business or pleasure?"

"More like a kidnapping, though my brothers claim it's an intervention."

"Of?"

"Making me have fun again?"

Fun? He didn't know how to have fun?

"Oh, honey, if fun's what you're after, you're definitely in the right city for it." Ella Ferguson studied the tall man in front of her. His refined handsome features weren't as rugged as she usually went for, but he was damned attractive. Or maybe it was the way he'd blurted out that her hair was blue and the grin that tipped up the right edge of his mouth, allowing a single dimple to peek out at her. Green eyes, the color of the ivy that covered her courtyard wall. Thin but wide lips, the bottom fuller than the top, arched russet brows. Freckles. Just a few, but they speckled across the narrow bridge of his straight nose.

Well mannered, and well dressed in an *I don't care what I look like* kind of way. His jeans were well worn, and was that paint on the edge of one of the pockets? His leather shoes were pricy, she knew because she used to have a thing for shoes—okay, she still did, but that was beside the point. A dusty aqua button-down shirt over a dark gray T-shirt. His shadow was several days past five o'clock—then again, he wasn't wearing a watch, she noticed. No ring either. His shadow was darker than the burnished hair that looked like it needed a cut. Either he didn't care or was just too busy to worry about haircuts.

Maybe he was a . . . a . . . a what?

The game she used to play as a kid always snuck up on her at the most inopportune of times. Find a person, look at their clothes, the way they wore them, their appearance, their walk, talk and interactions with others and guess what they do—where they come from. Why they might be here.

Though he'd answered the last question. She realized she was staring at him.

And that barely-there grin said he noticed her staring.

"Your hair's not blue," she stated.

It was his turn to laugh and his chuckle was almost rusty, as though he wasn't used to laughing.

"You should do that more, honey."

"What?" he asked, his brow furrowing. He laid a twenty on the counter along with two apples. "And her strawberries."

"No, that's okay."

"It's a beautiful day, in a beautiful city, and buying a lovely woman strawberries doesn't seem like too high a price for that."

True. "But they're my strawberries," she argued.

"You can buy the next batch." He nodded to Tiny, who was grinning, his white teeth flashing bright in his dark face.

"She buys batches every week. Dependable and loyal is our Ella."

"You know how to charm the girls, Tiny," she told him, taking the bag of berries the man—Quinlan handed to her. "You got my other stuff?"

"This one knows how to charm as well, I'm thinking. And I've always got your supplies." He then hefted up a box filled with food staples, apples and oranges. A box of cookies.

"Cookies?"

"For the little ones."

"You are a softy, you know that?"

"I am blessed is what I am, I can afford to help others. Now you get going or you'll be walking home in the dark and that's not good, no ma'am, not good at all."

"Yes, sir." She hopped up so her feet weren't touching the floor, leaned over the worn Formica counter and kissed Tiny's cheek. "You take care of Lisha and that baby."

"Always do."

"I know." Ella hopped down and grabbed the box, pulling it toward her and dropping the bag of strawberries on the top. "Gotta go. I'm already running late. Classes ran a bit long."

"Here, let me help," his starchy Yankee voice said.

She grinned. "I've got it."

"Undoubtedly. But my mother would be appalled if I let you carry that wherever you're heading."

"About two blocks from here actually."

"Well then, I'll carry it for you."

She didn't want to seem rude. Men were so touchy about pride.

He hooked his cane over his forearm and took the box from her, tucking it under his other arm and then sliding the cane down to grip it in his left hand. He raised his brows. "After you."

"You know, I shouldn't let you carry that. You might be some sort of criminal or something."

Again he chuckled. "Or something. Not a criminal." Then his brows furrowed. "Though that's a good point."

"I know your name is Quinlan and you're here with brothers, and find blue hair shocking. You're visiting our fair city. Other than that, sugar, I don't know a thing about you."

"True. So you should get to know me. I'm Quinlan Kinncaid,

never been arrested or accused of any crime. I'm the youngest of five boys, my parents are still married after all these years. I'm the only sibling not married, so Mom's busy trying to set me up with people and friend's daughters, nieces, granddaughters, whatever. I used to be a workaholic and now I'm just here to enjoy the company of a beautiful lady." He stood still, her box still under one arm, his other hand gripping his cane.

She glanced at Tiny, who shrugged but said, "Got good eyes."

At this the man in front of her frowned. "Good eyes?"

"Never mind." She wasn't about to explain Tiny's devout Catholicism and yet his equally devout superstitions that came from who knew where. "You try anything and I warn you, I'll kick your bad leg out from under you and leave you lying in the street. And in the Quarter, who knows what is on the street, sugar."

"Fair warning." He waited until she preceded him.

He followed her out the door and into the early evening. Not too late, but the day was getting away. The sun would set soon and she still had to get ready and go out with the girls. She sighed — normally, she'd hurry, but this time? Now she had to wait on Quinlan.

"Interesting name you have."

"What?" he asked, limping beside her. She opened her mouth to ask for the box back, but one look at his arched brow and she figured that wouldn't go over well.

Men and their pride. She knew men were stupid about it for some damned reason. She'd learned that years ago as a kid, and she'd learned it even more since then.

"So what are you really doing here and why aren't you still a workaholic, Quinlan?" She led them across the street.

"Well, there was . . . an incident and when I woke up . . ." He stopped and shifted the box a bit. "When I woke up things were just . . . different, you know? Got to learn to live with limitations now, even if I don't like it."

"Limitations?" she asked, baffled for a second. "You mean your cane? Are you serious?"

They walked on toward her goal. Limitations.

"Yes, my cane. Things are just different now."

"Different, so what? Different is just different, doesn't change who you are."

"I'm not a workaholic, that's changed," he reminded her, shifting the box again. "Some things take longer. I don't remember stuff as easily as I used to. Simple things like carrying a box are not as easy as they used to be."

Again she started to ask for it but kept the words behind her teeth. They were almost there anyway.

"Well, it's midweek. You've got expensive shoes and you're up and about fine, so I'm betting your life is still blessed. Most can't get away in the middle of the week with their brothers because of jobs. So whatever it is, I'd say, probably rudely, get over it." She turned a corner and waited. When he didn't appear she sighed and then stuck her head around the corner. "You coming or not? I haven't got all day. I can take the box in if you're busy and need to get back."

He gave his head one shake and then walked toward her, or thumped his way toward her. Made him mad, had she? "You're like a butterfly that suddenly bites."

"What?"

"Nothing. You think I'm whining."

She shook her head. "You said it, not me, so you must agree."

His eyes narrowed.

"Look, I deal with people with real problems, and I'm sorry if I sounded insensitive. That's not nice. I'm sorry that life is not what you planned it, but so what? Life isn't about plans, you know. Life's about doing, helping, being more. Ya know? Because no matter how far down you are, or think you are, there are still people with a lot worse problems. People that need help."

She stopped in front of the door. "By the way, you married, ever been married — no, you said your mom was trying to set you up," she answered her own question. "Bad breakup?"

Normally, the only people who visited the shelter were workers, cops, lawyers, and sometimes doctors. Generally, none of them just brought someone. At the same time, all help was appreciated. Making people aware was one way to achieve that, she knew.

Were there any women from up north inside? Any with Yankee ex-husbands or boyfriends? She ran through the list of women in her head. No, all were local girls. Longest-distance one was from Shreveport. So they were probably okay.

"Come on." She opened the door with a security code and led

him inside. Crazy? Yes, but he'd offered, so she'd take him up on it. Besides, maybe he'd become a donor. They needed all the help they could get here. "Don't take it personally if no one wants anything to do with you, you're a guy."

Before he could say anything to that, she shut the door behind them and started to take the box. But he shifted it away from her.

"Miss Ella!" a young voice cried. "You came!" Railey Anne came dashing down the stairs into the foyer. "Who's that?"

The little girl with braids on both sides of her hair grinned up at them, even as she stopped at the bottom of the stairs.

"That is a new friend who offered to carry my box. His name is Quinlan."

"Like the fruit?" the little girl asked.

Ella snorted. "No, Railey Anne, that would be kiwi, his name is Quinlan."

"Oh. Okay. What did you bring?"

And then more voices floated in. She turned and took the box from him and talked to several of the ladies who came in to say hello. The kids all gathered around and she handed the box off to one of the women, saying, "Tiny sent cookies for the kids."

Mora shook her head. "He always does. Nice man, Tiny." Mora darted a quick look at the new arrival and dashed back to the kitchen.

"Hey, Railey Anne, where's your mom?"

"She's trying to help Trevor with his homework, but they're arguing. He doesn't want to stay here anymore." The little girl shrugged her shoulders. "I told him we were safe here, but he says he hates it here." She squeaked the toe of her sneaker across the hardwood floor. "Are you really Ella's friend, Mr. Q?"

"If she'll let me," his deep voice said from behind her.

Ella glanced back over her shoulder, then continued to talk to the women and the director, Hannah James. Ella could see bringing Quin had made them nervous, and all those here knew how dangerous men could be. She hoped one day they would also remember and know soul deep that not all men were like that. She'd helped here and at other shelters long enough to know that particular journey was a solo voyage each woman had to take herself.

Shaking off the thoughts, she called out, "Okay, I better run."

She'd planned to stay longer, help the younger kids with their homework or read with them, but Quinlan had scattered the residents to the four winds. Time to get him out of here.

"Oh, and Hannah, could you give Ilene the berries on the top?"

Hannah laughed. "I don't know if she'll still be craving them. She got really sick the other evening and said strawberries were the berries of Satan. Thanks, though, Ella. You're a godsend."

Ella shook her head. "Nah, but I'll let you think it, and the berries aren't from me, they're from Quinlan. Quinlan . . . ?"

"Kinncaid," he supplied. "Maybe the kids will enjoy the strawberries then."

"Without a doubt," Hannah told them. Her look told Ella that she wanted to know who Quinlan was.

"Later, Hannah."

"Oh, definitely, El."

They hadn't spent an hour inside, more like half. Now it seemed she'd have plenty of time to get ready for this evening.

Quinlan was quiet as they walked down the sidewalk.

Finally she cleared her throat. "So, you staying around here?"

"A few blocks up. Off Burgundy."

"Not a hotel on Bourbon?"

He shook his head. "Not a chance. You?"

"What makes you think I'd tell you where I live?"

"So I could walk you home?"

She laughed and he grinned. "Keep dreamin', sugar."

"Oh, I will, honey." He drew the last out, so that it wasn't in his northern syllables. For a few minutes they walked on in silence.

"So, the shelter, you work there?"

She shook her head. "No, but I help out as much as I can."

He nodded. "How many are there?"

"Why do you want to know?"

He stopped and held his hand up. "Nothing nefarious, I assure you. Just curious. Doesn't look that big from the outside. Wondered where they all slept, what the kids did after homework."

She sighed. "Well, there are several families. Six kids. A few more women that bunk together in the attic."

"How old is the little girl? Railey, wasn't it?" he asked.

He'd paid attention. She wasn't sure if that was a good thing or bad thing. "Five, almost six."

"Almost six, and her birthday will be in a shelter."

"Hey, don't judge. Her birthday in a shelter will be safer than any of her previous birthdays. It took her father breaking her arm before her mom finally found the guts to leave. Do not—"

"I'm *not*," he interrupted. "I'm just thinking out loud. It just makes me mad there have to be shelters at all. Kids should be safe. Women should be safe. You find the person you want to marry, are brave enough to go for it, no one should have to live in hell for that. And definitely not kids an—"

His eyes narrowed and flashed, not at her, but at the situation.

"Yeah, well, nothing's perfect and marriage is overrated."

He took a deep breath. "Cynical, huh?"

"Realist, thanks."

He stopped and she said, "I gotta get going. Thanks for your help, and the strawberries."

He waved a hand as if swatting her words away. "You're welcome. If I wanted to send something to the kids, can I just drop it off there? Or do I have to give it to you?"

She thought about that for a minute. "Well, you could drop it off, but I'm not sure if anyone would open the door to you."

He nodded, opened his mouth and then shut it. Then opened it again, scratching one side with his forefinger. "I know you need to get going, but I was wondering if you'd like to do something later."

She grinned. Man had that aura about him that he normally got what he wanted, but now he seemed . . . nervous. His other fingers drummed along the top of his cane.

"Something? What sort of something did you have in mind, sugar?"

He grinned again, his single dimple charming. "Dinner? Or if not, drinks, breakfast? Midnight beignets and coffee?"

"No, I'm busy this evening, drinks maybe after, midnight beignets don't really taste that good, but it's the very best time to get them. And breakfast?" She laughed and winked at him, patting his arm. "Sugar, breakfast with me . . . well, that you'll have to work for."

He chuckled and said, "Let me see your phone."

"Why?"

"So I can put my number in it."

"Honey, Southern women *never* call a man. Didn't your mama teach you anything? You want to contact me, you're gonna have to contact me." She motioned for him to hand his over.

"So you'll put your number in my phone?"

"It's been awhile for you, hasn't it?"

He handed the phone over and she caught his scent again, light, springy and citrus. Something by Armani, she thought.

Ella quickly entered her info into his contacts. He took the phone back and quickly tapped the screen of his smart phone. Hers soon buzzed in her pocket.

He smiled. "Just making sure it works."

She cocked a brow. "Wow, if you don't know, it has been awhile."

His gaze narrowed, though his dimple remained. "You're a handful, aren't you?"

Ella glanced over her shoulder and walked backward up the street. "Only the brave venture forth."

Quinlan watched her until she turned another corner down the block. Her house? He didn't know, didn't care right then.

He glanced again at the screen on this phone. *L Blue.*

. . . it has been awhile . . .

She had no idea. No idea. No one did. His therapist knew he'd worried about his sex drive, or lack thereof. Stress and fear.

Stress he got.

Fear? Who feared sex, he'd wanted to know. What guy feared sex?

Dr. Garner had said it hadn't been sex that he was scared of but the memories of before and what it all led to.

Whatever.

The fact he could have happily seduced Ms. Ella . . . Ella . . . what had she said her last name was? He couldn't remember. But he'd go for Blue for now. Blue, like her hair.

Who had blue hair? Other than little old ladies? It wasn't bright electric blue, but soft, cotton-candy blue. And the pink tips?

She'd had a tattoo on her left wrist. He hadn't gotten a good enough look at it to see exactly what it said. Light cursive writing made up the letters. He'd have to study it later. During midnight beignets.

Grinning, he found his way back and into the house. Just as he opened the door, Brody said, "What the hell? You just left me here to fend for myself with the old dogs?"

"We old dogs can still bite, kid," Ian said, stepping into the entry with a tumbler of scotch.

His older brother's eyes studied him. "We're supposed to head out tonight for lots of fun at some club, live music or some such that Joshua owns."

Joshua was Brayden's brother-in-law.

"Whatever." He started to go around them.

"What are you so happy about?" Ian asked.

"Blue hair," he said and made for the stairs, hurrying up them as much as his leg would allow. Damned if he'd take the lower bedroom.

In his room, he stared at the phone for a moment and thought of what to say in a text. *You get home all right?* He typed before he thought better of it. Or was that stupid? Of course it was stupid, he should have said something else. Like *great to meet you*, or maybe *thanks for the afternoon*. Something. Now he'd sound like some sort of stalker or mother hen or . . .

His phone dinged.

Of course. Did you?

He smiled. *Yes.*

While he thought about what else to say, she typed back.

Thanks for going with me, and if you honestly want to donate something or whatever to that shelter, I'm sorry I gave you a hard time. Still want beignets?

He smiled again and realized he hadn't smiled this much in a long damned time.

Midnight. Café Du Monde. Will that work?

She sent him back a wink. A wink? Was that a yes or no? He wasn't about to ask.

He'd just have to wait and see. His window looked out over a courtyard. A fountain trickled in the center of the red-bricked haven. What was it about this city that made him do impulsive things? He'd rarely been impulsive in his entire life. When he was a kid and almost died in the icy river and lost his best friend, impulsiveness had a cost, he'd realized.

So he'd just done what he was supposed to and then aimed for better no matter what it was. School, sports, college, work. And that had gotten him where he was on top of it all, or so it seemed. Women he'd carefully selected through the years to date.

Until her.

Was this a mistake? He looked down at the phone.

What did he know of her?

She made him laugh.

Her hair was blue. He grinned at the thought. She helped others. Took them groceries and supplies and bought strawberries for someone down on their luck.

He took a deep breath.

. . . only the brave venture forth . . .

Well, no one ever said the Kinncaids lacked bravery.

Chapter 3

New Mexico, October, the present

The man's phone rang. Cursing inwardly, he pulled it from his pocket and glanced at the caller ID. Figured. God only knew what it was this time, but after the incident at the Retreat, he should probably take it.

He smiled at his wife and their dinner guests, excusing himself. The Taos restaurant was busy and noisy.

"Hello?"

"Where are you?" the voice asked.

He weaved his way through the noisy diners, wincing as someone dropped a glass on the tiled floor. The air was filled with chatter, laughter, flatware striking the plates as people consumed the various Mexican foods they'd all ordered.

The outside air brushed a chill across his face as he stepped out onto the sidewalk. "I'm in the middle of dinner."

"Well, there's a problem."

He sighed. When wasn't there a problem lately? Knowing his partner would get to it sooner or later, he waited.

"There are police all around the house in Albuquerque."

He stilled. "Which house?"

"Labor and delivery, or that's what we've mostly used it for lately."

"What the fuck are you doing there? What the hell have you done now?" he whispered into his phone, walking farther away from the crowds and leaning against the wall of the parking lot.

Silence answered him.

"Explain."

"I was trying to stop a major loss. Ella's baby was sold and—"

"You did what?" he hissed. He'd already decided that no matter the money, he was going to let this one pass. Not the deal, but this particular baby. Something had told him a few weeks ago, she was just too much trouble. If the baby was already sold, they'd just give the winning parents another baby—who would know? There were too many questions already surrounding this woman. She'd blatantly said she wasn't interested in adoption. Granted, he'd thought about it. Had even started an auction for her baby.

"You heard me. The perfect kid. And she was bolting. Or would have been. Her husband was coming. Just what do you think would have happened to our little commodity then?"

"What the hell did you do?"

"Took her. Drugged her tea, put her in my car, and drove to the house. Induced labor and everything went fine, for the most part."

"For the most part?"

"Well, her placenta didn't detach properly. Figured she'd bleed out and no problem."

No problem. No problem? There were probably ways around it all, but Ella, he had learned, was rather connected.

Connected in a big way to people who might not let a sleeping bastard lie.

"And?"

"And apparently she got away or something. I don't see any ambulances, but there are cops everywhere on the street and in the house."

The house. Damn it all to hell.

"Idiot," he hissed. "Why did you use the fucking house? There's no way to keep it contained there. No way for—"

"We've used it before. If she'd woken up at the Retreat, we'd have had to get rid of a body more than likely or forge a death certificate for the baby."

Yes, and clearly that had never been done before.

"Get your ass back to the Retreat and make sure there is nothing left of her ideas or worries at her place. Is she alive?"

"I don't see how."

He sighed. "If we're lucky, she died. You have the baby?"

"I left her with Kevin."

Great, got better and better. At least, though, there was the auction and he had a buyer on the line. Even if he upped the price just a bit. Price was stupidly high. Already it was at almost a quarter of a million. Most babies didn't go for a fraction of that.

But then most babies weren't as high end as this one. Perfect baby for perfect parents. It was what he did.

"Get your ass back here. Now."

He tucked his phone back into his pocket and sighed, looking around. Should have just killed the bitch when he had the chance. If he was lucky, Ella Ferguson Kinncaid was in the morgue and not the hospital.

Chapter 4

New Orleans, February, earlier that year

Quinlan looked out over the crowd at the Café Du Monde and wondered if he should get a table or not. He glanced back and saw that there were plenty, so no, he'd just wait.

What if she didn't show?

He'd ditched his brothers back at some bar on Bourbon Street, which was fine with him. They'd asked him where he was headed and he'd only flipped them off.

Of course, knowing Ian, he probably had some sort of tracking device on his ass so his brother could keep tabs on him. And everyone worried about him? Ian would do well with a dose of Paxil.

He glanced over to the cathedral lit up bright tonight, probably every night.

One more had joined their party earlier. Brayden's brother-in-law, Joshua Montreaux. Joshua was Christian's biological brother and a darlin' of N'Awlins. Bachelor that he was, and his family owning banks all over the South with the headquarters in New Orleans, made the man every Southern mama's dream son-in-law. The siblings, however, shared very few characteristics other than those wickedly pale eyes they both had inherited from a grandmother or something. Brayden's brother-in-law was a diverse man of business.

The man had showed up with a limo and had taken them out to dinner. Then he said he knew a great place he wanted to take them. That was after most of Quin's siblings had consumed various amounts of alcohol during the afternoon and well into the evening.

Avante Garde was a club Joshua owned.

Wonder-fucking-ful. In the heart of jazz and they'd listened to karaoke . . . in costume. Not Quin's thing, but from the way the place was packed, a long wait line to get in, and the amount of booze and food flooding the time-warped venue, Joshua had apparently clicked on something.

Whatever. Quin was just glad to have left.

The boys had all protested when he'd risen and said he was leaving. His brothers wanted to have fun. Wanted him to have fun. His family needed to know that he was capable of having fun. Otherwise, he might what? Swallow pills? No.

He'd counted down the minutes until he could leave and get here. As his brothers were only a couple of blocks over, it had been within easy walking distance. Now he stood here on Decatur waiting, watching and wondering if she'd actually show up.

Part of him figured she would, she was daring—and quirky. Part of him figured she wouldn't because she didn't know him from Adam or Jack the Ripper. Then again, maybe she figured with his gimpy leg, he wasn't that big of a worry. Hadn't she heard of Bundy? He walked a few paces one way, then the other, scanning the crowd and listening to the street musicians around Jackson Square.

He saw her first, walking down the sidewalk toward him with a group of friends.

He smiled. She came and daring won.

Her pale blue hair seemed almost white under the streetlights and he almost laughed outright as she wobbled on impossibly high shoes.

She was dressed in some sort of short, flowy, dark sundress, and he figured she was cold. But it wasn't that cold, just sort of chilly. The shoes though . . .

He laughed, it was a wonder she didn't break her neck. They were tall platforms with straw or cork or something. He knew women called them something specific but he couldn't remember. He just liked the way the dark ribbons from the shoes laced and wound around her ankles and up her calves. Toned calves.

She broke away from the pack and came toward him, smiling, her dimples winking at him.

"My friends wanted to make sure I got here safely," she told him as she stopped in front of him.

He nodded to them and the girls hooted and hollered, encouraging her, and waved at him.

"They look like my brothers."

She glanced over. "Your brothers enjoy going drag?" She cocked an eyebrow at him.

He laughed. "God no. I meant they looked like they're having a good time."

"They always have a good time. The one on the left with all the dark hair is Marie and the redhead is Shalon, then there's Jif and Leigh with all the scarves."

He thought she muttered something about damned shoes.

"So, sugar, you'll have to bear with me, or rather with them."

When she turned he noticed the skin under her left arm and saw there was a hint of ink next to her breast.

Now he was fascinated. What was it?

The speakers hidden in the striped green awnings played the opening chords to "I Dream of You . . ."

She hummed a few bars. "They worry."

"It's good to have friends who worry about you," he told her and nodded to her friends again.

"And brothers?"

He chuckled. "Upon rare occasion."

Hurrying footsteps made him turn so he stood in front of her. "Speaking of."

There were two of his brothers now. Aiden and Ian, and dancing — weaving — in front of them was Brody, who was trying to hurry to — him?

"There he is!" Brody hollered from only feet away.

"And there is my entourage worried about me."

She giggled and slid her hand into his, shocking him for a moment. But he grasped her cool hand and smiled down at her. "We are blessed, sugar." She pointed over to the darkened corners across the street. "Some aren't nearly as lucky."

Homeless souls sat huddled against closed storefronts.

"See, told you he was fine." Brody came up to his other side and slung an arm around his shoulders, almost throwing him off balance. Quin stepped to the side, careful to make certain he didn't knock over Ella. "And lookie, guyzzzz, he's wish a pretty girl." Brody blinked. "I'm drunk, I'm really drunk." He leaned over Quin and blinked at her. "Is your hair blue?" He turned to Quin. "Dude, I think her hair's blue."

Aiden snickered and pulled Brody off.

Ian held his hand out. "Sorry, I'm Ian, Quinlan's older brother."

Brody snorted. "One of 'em. Older broshers, that is. Got a bunch. Pain the ashes. Asbes. Asses." He shook his head.

"That's our cousin Brody," he said to Ella and then nodded to

Aiden. "And that's Aiden."

"How many are there?"

"Two more who are twins and God knows where, though Mom's practically adopted two others that are with us, somewhere. Or will be. Never mind. There are a lot of us."

Ella stuck her hand out. "I'm Ella Ferguson, nice to meet you guys."

Aiden and Ian nodded. They were buzzing, as Ian never got more than that, if he was even that far in the inebriation realm. Man had control issues.

"You did good, man!" Brody said, swaying.

"Now that we know you're alive and well," Ian said, slipping an arm around Brody, "we will leave you in peace. Have fun."

He took a deep breath and Ian shook his head. "Not babysitting. He took off after you and refused to go back in. Thus we're wandering around the Quarter. You're on your own."

"He's so gonna get some," Brody mumbled.

Quinlan slid his eyes closed.

"We are leaving now." Aiden took Brody's other arm.

"Hey, you guysh. Think she has a pink-haired friend? I like pink," Brody mumbled. "With a fluffy." He waved his arms around his neck.

"Fluffy?" Ella asked, laughter in her voice.

"Boas," Aiden told her, turning. "He was last accosting a bachelorette party at the Cat something or other. The women were all wearing pink boas."

She laughed. "Fluffies."

Ian nodded to him. "Come on, Casanova, let's find a cab and get you home because I'm not hauling your ass there if you pass out."

"No, Junior, we'll leave you in the gutter," Aiden said as they walked away.

"Fuck off, I'm not jchunior. Broooody. That'sh my name."

They stood there watching for a moment.

"Wow," Ella muttered. "You guys are all handsome and he's going to feel like . . . well . . . horrible tomorrow."

"Oh well." He turned and led her into Café Du Monde with his hand at the small of her back, the material of her dress silky beneath his touch. He felt a shiver dance down her spine. "Sorry about that."

She laughed. "As I said, people who care. At least your brothers left you in peace." She motioned over to her friends, who had grabbed a table and were already eating fluffy powdered-sugar fried dough.

Then she opened her mouth and sang a few bars of the song blaring from the speakers.

They turned and made their way to a table, grabbing beignets and coffees. They settled at a little iron table.

". . . dream a little dream of me . . ." Her voice was husky and alluring as she sang the last few bars and settled across from him.

Just like that afternoon, interest stirred from just listening to her, watching her . . . enjoying her.

"I've always liked that song," she said, grinning. "Sorry, sometimes . . . okay, lots of times I just sort of sing along with whatever song I hear."

He smiled. Desire swirled and gripped him.

He sighed and sat back, glad that something still worked, because frankly, he was starting to worry that he'd have to get a script for Cialis or the little blue pill. When a guy didn't find women interesting or get a hard-on when there were plenty of beauties who were interested, he worried.

Even if he hadn't admitted that to himself before now.

But that was one worry he obviously didn't have to keep.

She had a sexy voice, of course, he just wanted . . . to listen to her talk.

Okay, and he wanted her.

Was her skin as soft as it looked under those lights?

He wanted her.

He smiled.

Ella opened her eyes and waved to her friends across the way. His brothers were nowhere to be seen. Thankfully. Guys out on the town. But these were of a different variety. Not frat boys, not businessmen out after meetings. They were older. Clean-cut and . . . men. Two of the ones she'd met—Aiden and Ian?—had worn rings. The drunk had not. And they were all so damned good-looking.

Quinlan though, he'd looked good this afternoon. Now? Now he looked really damned good.

Dressed in slacks and a dark green button-down, the sleeves

rolled up to his elbows. One hand rested on the table, the other tapped on the top of a cane. She picked up a beignet and bit into the sugary dough. She could feel his gaze on her. Feel it even as she watched his gaze quickly skim over her and then more slowly from head to toe. Not in a bad way; she had enough experience with that. No, this guy was just interested, which she already knew, or she wouldn't be here.

Fine with her because she was interested in him. She'd thought about him all damned evening. So they'd play the interest game, because it wasn't like it would be more than that.

If she was lucky, they'd have fun for the night. Maybe the rest of the weekend.

After that?

Well, from his watch and the shoes and the cut of his clothes, the man had money, and if Ella knew one thing, it was that men couldn't be counted on and rich men were the worst. Not that she needed to count on them. No, indeed. If she did anything *on* him, it wouldn't be counting. Unless it was how many times . . .

She shook her head. Good Lord.

The man oozed confidence and charm and money.

And enough sex appeal she noticed other women noticing him.

Though there was something in his eyes, something that said maybe he wasn't as confident as he wanted to be.

Damn.

She was always a sucker for the wounded.

He'd mentioned an incident earlier today and she'd wondered what incident could shake such a clearly confident man to question himself and his purpose.

"Ella!" Shalon hollered across the way.

She looked over to them, grinned and waved. Her girlfriends shouted and high-fived each other. "Have fun! Call us tomorrow!" they shouted over each other. "Deets for dinner!"

She nodded to them.

Crossing her legs, she almost groaned at the ache in her feet. She was lucky she hadn't fallen crossing the street to meet Quinlan. With her luck, and a great-looking guy, she'd splat in these stupid weird-ass shoes Shalon had gotten for her. They looked hot, she knew, but they were evil, wicked torture devices.

When they'd stood side by side, she realized he stood much taller than her—but then most did. She was a short woman at five-three and a half, and as a short woman she had curves she wished were less pronounced.

Up close he was even more handsome than she'd remembered, if that were possible.

This morning she thought she was stressed about everyday stresses, but hey, if he wanted a good time, she was all for that. Man looked like he knew how to make a girl's world go round. He looked like he could use some de-stressing as well.

Bad. Very, very bad. She sighed.

"You came," he said.

Oh God. She could only stare at him and arch a brow.

He arched a brow as well and a slow smile lifted the corner of his mouth.

Ella shifted in the chair and cleared her throat. "Were you worried?"

His grin turned into a smile. "About many, many things."

She glanced to the side to see her friends. Shal was giving her a thumbs-up and Marie was nodding as they made their way down the street.

"Sorry about my cousin earlier. And thanks for coming to meet me. I wondered if you actually would, to be honest. You don't know me or anything. Though I promise I only had beignets and coffee in mind."

Yeah, like she hadn't heard that before. "You should get some original lines."

"Well, I don't normally pick girls up in the café or market or wherever."

She ran her gaze over him. Handsome, intense, with a hint of vulnerability, and he was funny in a not-sure kind of way. Laugh lines that seemed unused, and honestly, he wasn't trying to overly charm her, well . . . it seemed . . . normal. In this not-so-normal place.

She noticed again his fingers were long, elegant, but there were nicks on them, and a few scars. From what? Did he play the piano? Was he an artist? She still wondered.

Who knew?

Who cared?

Up close, she noticed his eyes were the color of lush green grass. Straight-on green, not hazel, not aqua. Just green. She thought she'd imagined that this afternoon. He had a few freckles dusting across his face and along the backs of his hands and wrists. She hadn't noticed that before.

The café was quieter than usual. She leaned toward him just as he did her.

"Quinlan."

"Ella." They both spoke across the other and grinned.

His single dimple only showed up in his laugh lines. Hell, she had dimples, and she knew damn well that hers didn't look half as good on her as his did on him.

"It is good to see you again," he told her.

She watched as he slowly shifted in the chair, not managing to hide the slight wince.

"Knee or something else?"

"Knee and femur."

She waited but he didn't say anything else.

Silence lengthened and stretched. Finally, she cleared her throat and took a sip of chicory coffee, raising her brow at him. His eyes were intense on her. Maybe he just didn't talk too much, and as handsome as he was, he seemed . . . almost out of practice at this or something.

"So what do you do, other than help those less fortunate?"

She licked the powdered sugar off her thumb and saw his eyes darken, narrow. She shook her head. "I'm a yoga instructor and I play with any medium of art and I love music."

He grinned. "Yoga instructor. Do you enjoy it?"

She should probably clarify. "Well, it wasn't what I thought I'd be doing or went to school for—though I did go to school and am a certified instructor. Yes. I do enjoy it and my other odd jobs I do."

"What did you go to school for, if I may ask?" He bit into a beignet and the sugar dusted his dark shirt. She watched as he chewed and the muscles rippled in his throat as he swallowed.

"Um. I've a marketing degree . . . ." She shrugged and sipped her drink. "I'm not really the suit, five days a week type, I discovered."

He grinned. "A free spirit stuck in the business world. How long did that last?"

44

"Something like that. And not long."

"Sounds like there might be a story."

"We all have one." She leaned up on her elbows and tucked a strand of hair behind her ear. "So, you and your boys here for pleasure? You never actually said, though you mentioned them kidnapping you for a good time."

He twisted his mouth and glanced in the direction his brothers had gone. "They'd say that, I'm sure."

"They were married or had on rings. Though not the last one."

"Brody. No, he's single and will undoubtedly stay that way as long as possible."

He looked at her, his brows drawn. The wind blew through the courtyard and his scent carried to her. Something rainy, but spicy and wonderful, and she wondered what it was.

"Well, this is the place for fun," she said, not hiding her skepticism.

"No, nothing like that. Those men love their wives." He shifted in his chair and rubbed his thigh. "They actually came down here to remind me what a good time was."

"You don't know how to have one? A good time?" she asked, cocking a brow and taking another drink. "Sugar, I find that hard to believe. Everyone knows how to have a good time."

"Not so much anymore I don't, no." He shrugged. "Once upon a time . . . yeah." He sipped his coffee and winced.

She laughed. "Chicory, not for everyone."

He shook his head. "Apparently not."

"Questioning how to have fun," she murmured. "Sounds like woman trouble."

He snorted and took a drink of his water. "Oh, you've no idea."

Be a shame if he were married. She did not do married men in any form or fashion.

"So, you married? Still? Like in the middle of the separation and that's why your mom is trying to set you up with friends' daughters?"

He stared at her for a long moment. "If I was married, even if separated, I wouldn't have asked you to join me here or anywhere else, Ella."

"Men are men."

"And they say I've become cynical."

She grinned. "I'm not cynical."

He studied her for a moment, his head tilted to the side. "Maybe not."

"Fine, then, a bad divorce? No, if that was the case, you'd be going for overtime with the ladies." She wiggled in her seat.

"Really? And you know this because . . . ?"

"Observation, darlin'."

He rubbed his leg again. "No, no divorce or bad breakup. Life, for lack of a better explanation. Look, I don't really know how to do this anymore." He rubbed the corner of his mouth with a finger. "Truth be told, I used to be smooth and would have tried to talk you into bed by the end of the night." He kept his gaze on her.

Had he just . . . She frowned.

He blushed, or at least it appeared that his cheekbones flushed a bit.

"Well, that's straightforward enough, sugar. So you won't try to sweet-talk me into bed by the end of the night?" She gave him a playful pout. "What a shame."

He only grinned and shook his head. "You are a handful, aren't you?"

She laughed and leaned up, touching his arm. "Care to find out?"

His gaze dropped to her lips. "What do you think?"

"But what if I'm not interested?"

"Then you're a really good actress." He covered her hand on his arm with his other one. "If you weren't interested, I'd simply say good night, Ella. And then I'd go back to the house we're renting and listen to my brothers give me hell on my lack of charm with a beautiful woman who has an endearing way of saying sugah." He brought her hand to his lips and kissed her knuckles. "And I'd have to wonder if you weren't lying."

She smiled. "Oh, I don't know if you lack charm per se. I think you've just forgotten how to use it. Or rather you use it in a different way than most men. Though you are doing pretty damned good, if you ask me."

He opened his mouth, ran his tongue around his teeth, then shook his head. A witty comeback?

Again silence settled between them. From here, she could see the sinewy muscles of his forearms and knew from the way his shirt fit him that his shoulders would be muscled as well.

"So what exactly do you do, Mr. Not-sure-you-want-to-charm-me-into-bed Quinlan?"

"This and that. Not as much as I used to. And, honey, I never said I didn't *want* to charm you into bed."

She smiled and leaned closer to him. "Ah, see, you do remember charm."

"Is that what that is?" he asked quietly.

She sighed and said, "Thanks for tonight, by the way."

"Would you like something else? Go somewhere else?" His fingers tapped on the edge of his water glass, even as he continued to caress her knuckles with his other hand. "Or something?"

"Go somewhere else? Like one of the bars? Plying a lady with alcohol is frowned upon."

"Honey, I've never had to ply a woman with alcohol."

Witty comebacks indeed.

She raked her gaze over him again and licked her lips. "No, I don't image you would have to, Quinlan." She laughed. "See, there's that charm again and the straightforward talk. You're supposed to toss a few innuendos in there."

"Really? Like what?"

"Oh, I don't know, like . . ." She stopped. His green eyes were locked on her and she lost her train of thought. "Um . . ." She licked her lips.

"Like?"

"What?"

He laughed, again a rusted sound as if he didn't laugh much.

"Look, frankly, I don't have a lot of experience at this sort of thing."

"What sort of thing?" he asked, smiling, lines bracketing his mouth.

"How about we get out of here and go get to know each other," she said, taking a deep breath. "Or something . . ."

His gaze narrowed on her for a minute. "Or something . . ."

They pushed their chairs back and he offered her his arm. Did he always do that? For a minute, she just stared at it again.

"What?" he asked, tilting his head.

"It's been awhile since a guy offered me his arm . . . That's not true," she added as she remembered. "Someone did."

Ella frowned at the memory and shook it off with a smile.

"And he did not leave a good impression. I'll have to change that. I'd offer you my hand but something tells me that wouldn't go over any better. Between my arm and my hand, I have to offer you one or you're likely to break something in those lovely shoes."

She chuckled and they made their way out onto the street, which was less crowded than normal but still busy. A sax melted and stepped along the air with the blasts of a trumpet from up the street. A sitar player leaned against the iron fence of the square and strummed some sort of depressing tune.

Looking up the way she saw the glass and water musician was set up on the corner. Stepping on an uneven brick, she wobbled and he gripped her hand and arm.

"Steady. And you were worried about my knee?"

"Says who?"

"You, you kept looking at my cane and leg. I promise neither bites."

She grinned up at him. "Maybe I do though."

He paused for barely a second. "I can but hope."

She laughed. "It's these shoes. My friend got them for me. Said they were a sure deal."

"Sure deal? Of what? A broken appendage?"

She laughed again. "Come on, Quinlan. Let's walk on a lovely night, holding each other up so neither of us lands on the street." She shivered. "We can talk about things."

"Like what?"

"Whatever you want to talk about."

Chapter 5

They walked for over an hour, passing galleries he made a note to visit later. There was an old bookstore on Pirate's Alley she swore was a favorite place. They talked and laughed and watched as tourists snapped photos, stumbled along, or kissed in the bright streetlights or darkened alcoves. They discussed music and art, things they liked, things they didn't. He was smart, knowledgeable, and he listened.

He walked her back to her place holding her hand. Was she being stupid? Probably.

"I don't normally do this sort of thing, you know."

"I got that impression. And neither do I." At her stoop, he stopped her and pulled her around to face him. "You were right about a couple of things earlier. It's been awhile for me."

"Really? 'Cause I have to say, sugar, you don't look like the type of guy that it'd be awhile for."

He grinned down at her. This was stupid on so many levels. So he was visiting from out of town. So she didn't really, really know him, but damn it. She missed the feel of a man's hands on her. The way a man's hands could heat her skin with a single barely-there touch. Quin's hands were calloused, long-fingered, and reminded her of an artist's hands. Or maybe it was that stupid paint she'd seen on his jeans when they met.

Quinlan was frowning. She reached up and rubbed the crease between his brows.

"I have a confession to make," she told him.

"Really? What? You live with your mother? You've changed your mind? Please tell me you're not really a man or something, because then I might just have to cry myself to sleep tonight if that were the case." He brushed a strand of her hair away from her face, but kept it between his fingers. "I love your hair, weird as that sounds. Blue hair should not be sexy."

She shrugged. "I like my hair too. Next I think I'll go purple."

He chuckled. "You'll make purple sexy as hell, I'm sure. So confession?"

"No, I'm not a guy, no pickle surprises for you."

He laughed outright and tugged her closer. "That's a relief."

"And if you suddenly didn't want to come in, I'd understand. Though I too might cry myself to sleep." It had been *way* too damned long for her as well. She never did one-night stands . . . or rather she had never. Not before now.

"Confession?" he asked, leaning a little closer to her.

She stepped backward up her front step so that she was closer to his height. "Well, see, the thing is, it's been awhile for me as well and the thing is . . . I'm serious about not doing this."

"Not doing this?" He frowned, then nodded. "That's fine."

"What? No, I mean, this, yes, but this, this . . ." She huffed out a sigh. "I mean . . ." She motioned between them, then behind her. "Asking guys over. Or only after just meeting them. Or well, the rest . . . something . . . and see, I don't want you to think—"

He moved quickly, his lips on hers before she had time to think about it. To plan to ask him. To tell him . . .

His lips pressed softly at first, then more demandingly. The . . . whatever was between them sparked, flared and engulfed.

His hand moved from her hair to cup her jaw, his fingers caressing softly on the back of her neck, giving her chills, even as he pulled her closer toward him.

He tasted like powdered sugar and coffee from their midnight snack, he smelled like the promise of sin with a hint of redemption.

To hell with it.

Ella leaned into the kiss, giving him as much as he was giving her. She kissed him back, sliding her tongue along the seam of his lips, teasing, tempting, asking . . . She moved her hands from between them, rubbing her fingers under his jacket, up his crisp dress shirt, soft beneath her fingers. She could feel his muscles beneath his shirt.

"Confession," he asked against her mouth, licking her lips.

"Um . . ." She kept kissing him as he nibbled on her lips, his other hand moving softly on her arm, one thumb caressing the vein in her neck.

"Your confession . . ." He kissed her again, moving from her mouth to her jawline, kissing softly along her jaw.

"Oh, um . . ." He kissed wonderfully. She'd been kissed before, quite a bit actually. But Quinlan, he was good. No, he was great. She reached up, cupped his jaw and turned his mouth back to hers, where she sealed his mouth with hers and devoured.

He pulled back, his cheeks flushed, his eyes intense. "We should probably get inside if this is going to continue. Not that I'm pressing or . . ." He took a deep breath and raked a hand through his hair. His cane was tucked up under his arm.

"Quinlan, shut up." Normally, she went in through her courtyard and the door that led to her kitchen. Her front door led directly into her bedroom. She dug a key out of a loose brick and opened the door.

Thank God she'd picked up yesterday and did her laundry. At least things were put away and lingerie wasn't hanging haphazardly out of a drawer. The mosquito netting hanging from the ceiling around her queen-sized bed fluttered in the slight breeze that blew in when she opened the door.

Quinlan waited on the threshold, a grin tilting the edge of his mouth up on one side. "Well, that's convenient."

She jerked him in. "Yeah, sugar, tonight it most definitely is *very* convenient because I don't wanna wait anymore."

Ella shut the old double doors behind them and then leaned back. Streetlight flooded into the room from the side windows. The ceiling fan made a slight whirring sound in the quiet. Too quiet.

For a moment, they merely stood there, her against the door, him standing close, almost too close. Breathing, just breathing — barely.

Quinlan stood silent and still for a beat longer. Tension stretched between them, coiled, tightened the air and her skin. Then he stepped toward her. "You sure about this?"

"No. Yes. I'm sure I don't want you to leave."

He smiled and nodded. "Okay, then."

She laid her hand on his chest and he leaned in and caged her with his arms on the doors behind her. His eyes, bright and wicked green, met hers as he slowly lowered his head.

"So it's been a bit for the both of us?"

"Uh-huh," she whispered, still meeting his gaze before dropping her own.

"Well, they say it's like riding a bike," he whispered before his lips sealed hers. The man could kiss, his lips warm and soft, yet firm and demanding. His hands were everywhere, caressing, pressing, rubbing. The silky material of her dress rubbed against her sensitive skin.

Ella wanted to feel him against her, not the dress. She stumbled over the buttons of his shirt until he finally helped her. She shoved the sides of his dress shirt aside, running her hands over the tight, rock-hard muscles.

"Oh my," she whispered. Man was ripped.

Her dress was a little navy number, with halter straps. The material slid against her as he teased her slowly, caressing her through the dress. He grinned a sensual one-sided grin and said, "The top or the bottom? So many choices with a sexy little dress."

His fingers played with the clasp before she felt it give, and shivered as his fingers tickled the nape of her neck. The straps gave way and the dress slid to her waist before he quickly shoved it down her legs. She stepped out of it, glad she'd worn the stupidly high wedge shoes.

Yoga kept her in shape, she knew, but she also knew with her short stature she was curvy at best, a bit top heavy thanks to a full C cup and a narrow waist that made her hips look wider no matter how many goddess poses she did. Men didn't always prefer the curvaceous, she'd learned, and . . .

"What have we here?" he asked, his gaze skimming down her. "My God, you're perfect," he whispered, his hands clasping her waist, flaring out over her hips. "A dragonfly?" He traced the wings below her hipbone.

"I like dragonflies," she muttered.

Her bra and matching panties were like many things she owned. Multicolored. This set was swirls of blues, greens and purples.

He leaned to the side and raised her left arm, and traced the symbols just to the outside of her breast. "And what does this say?"

She looked at him from under her lashes. "Beauty."

A muscle bunched in his jaw. "So many lovely surprises you offer, honey."

His fingers trailed along the edge of her bra before dipping inside and deftly unclasping the front clasp.

"You are beautiful," he whispered, kissing her jaw again and moving down her neck, even as his fingers played with her breasts, cupping, weighing. "Absolutely beautiful."

The man might walk with a limp, but damned if he wasn't a girl's fantasy. She shoved his shirt off his shoulders and he shrugged out of it completely. He was tall, and well-defined, broad shoulders tapered down to a narrow six-pack and trim hips. Man worked out.

He was simply . . . simply . . . "Lickilicious," she muttered.

"What was that?"

She shook her head as his hands trailed lower. "Nothing."

He danced them back to the bed. His kisses robbed her brain of all thought, of anything. They shed the rest of their clothing before she could think, before she could breathe. Then they were pressing skin to skin, body to body on her sheets.

Before they got too carried away, she said, "Bedside drawer, here, let me." She rolled over and found protection. "Unless you carry your own in your wallet?" she asked him as they settled back together.

Quinlan shook his head. "Nope, been awhile, as I said."

"You can tell me why later, if you want to. Right now, I just . . ." She leaned up and kissed him, nibbling on his jaw. His aftershave tasted so good, citrus and not, something dark and promising burst onto her senses. She kept kissing, kept licking even as she worked to get the stupid wrapper open.

"You just what?" He licked her neck, kissed and laved her collarbone.

"Want you. I just want you." Her skin felt tight, tingly, on fire, her blood hot and fast in her veins.

His hand moved slowly over her. "I want to savor though."

She hooked her leg over his hip. "We can savor later, unless you only plan to do this once?"

His laughter against her rubbed his chest against her breasts and she sighed. His hand moved along her arm, down her ribs to her belly.

"Please, Quin." She'd never wanted this so badly before.

He found her with his fingers, playing her through her silky panties. She felt a tug, heard a rip, and then his cool, long fingers were on her, sliding along her, slipping into her until she was moaning and gasping and only one thought echoed in her brain. Want.

She ripped the condom wrapper open with her teeth. Her hands trembled as she slid it on him, gripping his thick hot length. "I'll have to get some more of these," she muttered.

"Hopeful, are you?"

"You've no idea," she told him, biting his chin.

A muscle bunched in his jaw. "Good. Because I won't last long the first time, and after that I'm going to make you beg," he told her, licking her neck, biting her earlobe, jerking another shudder from her.

Quinlan rolled them and pressed her to the mattress and she thought something flashed in his eyes before he settled between her legs. She opened, welcoming him.

His thumb still played her, circling that one spot that shivered currents through her even as his fingers thrust into her, deep and deeper, bringing her closer and closer.

"Now, Quin. Damn it. I don't want to go without you." He twisted his wrist and she groaned. "Oh God."

He chuckled again and then gripped himself, playing along her slick opening. "You don't have a lot of patience, do you?"

"No."

As soon as he moved his hand, she surged up to meet his thrust, her moan melding with his, "Oh, yeah!" as he slid in long, hard, and deep.

"Yes!"

They moved together, awkwardly for a moment, then settled into perfect rhythm. He wrapped his arms under her, arching her back as he leaned down and pulled her nipple into his mouth, sucking hard, biting down gently.

She mewled as her blood turned to molten lava in her, moving faster and faster.

His hips pumped into her and she met him thrust for thrust until a light sheen of sweat covered their skin. "God, you're sweet," he told her, his lips moving against hers before he kissed her.

He kept moving, kept stroking.

She ripped her mouth away from his, trying to draw a breath. Trying to . . .

"Oh God. Oh God. Yes. Yes."

The fire caught, burned bright and exploded through every nerve in her entire system. She screamed as every muscle in her body contracted and tightened, freezing the breath in her lungs.

Her eyes flew open.

Quinlan threw his head back and yelled, "Thank God! Yes!" He stilled and pulsed inside her, sending her into another shivering orgasm.

He opened his eyes and met her gaze and for a moment the world froze. Then air exploded from their lungs, mixing and melding as his mouth met hers and he slumped to the side, pulling her with him.

"Sorry," he panted. "A bit quick."

"Not sorry," she panted back, licking his chest. "I wanna do it again. And again."

He laughed against her and kissed the top of her head. "You, Ella, are one of a kind."

"Well, I should hope so."

His laughter rumbled up his chest, even as his hands continued to move on her, caressing, calming now.

Ella blew out a breath and took another deep one, the scent of her lotions laced with the scent of Quinlan and their lovemaking.

She wasn't going to worry about tomorrow or the next day, only right now and the time she had with Quinlan. And if the remaining time was anything like the time they'd already shared . . . it would be amazing.

"So, sugar," she said, turning her head and kissing his biceps. "Was it as good for you as it was for me?"

His eyes were closed, but he grinned and chuckled. "Honey, it was better, in case your bed moving across the floor escaped your notice."

Her laughter mixed with his.

• • •

Quinlan glanced at the woman sprawled across him. The sheets were tangled around them. The quilt was somewhere on the floor.

Her lashes were a — light brown, pale amber? He still didn't know. An earlier shower had taken care of the mascara and any other makeup. Freckles dusted across the bridge of her nose, and across her shoulders he'd noticed. Her face begged to be drawn. His fingers twitched with the need to sketch her, but he was happy where he was.

He pulled her closer and stared at the ceiling.

His phone vibrated again, for the umpteenth time. Of all the times for his battery to decide it wanted a longer life. They could just leave him the hell alone.

He wasn't going to text or call anyone. He was a grown man, for the love of God. They wanted him to get on with life and that was what he was doing, and doing it pretty damned well if he said so himself.

The ceiling fan whirred, a bit off balance, in the quiet early morning.

He took a deep breath and for the first time in a long time he realized he was relaxed, honest to God relaxed—and it wasn't just from great sex either. He knew the difference. There was something in the air here.

All too soon, he'd probably be on the plane home with his brothers. There was lots to do this next week. Meetings he was slated for.

He didn't care. He hadn't cared in a long time. He'd tried going back to work for the last year, but everything was wrong. He wasn't the person he had been and something was missing. Some piece of him.

And as of yesterday in a hole-in-the-wall market in the Quarter, he'd thought he just might find himself again. Either that or the blue-haired witch had completely enchanted him.

"You gonna call them back?" Ella asked him quietly.

He glanced around her pale green walls, the white furniture, and could hear the sounds of traffic on the street. He saw pictures of Ella and her friends framed on her dresser.

The place was not nearly as neat as he normally liked his space, but then, honestly, Ella's place reflected her. Artsy came to mind. Explosions of color in artwork and throws, pillows with splashes of colors like faded rainbows. Even her potted plants and ivies were in tie-dyed pots.

She shifted and the sheet between them caressed over skin, teasing, but not nearly as much as her smooth pale skin.

"Someone's awake," she said, moving more onto him. She stacked her hands under her chin on his chest, her blue hair tussled. He ran his hands through it, still surprised at how silky and soft the strands were.

"So."

He grinned. "So."

"Lots of party plans today?" She wiggled and the sheet rubbed against the hard-on he'd had since he'd woken up with her in his arms.

"Don't know yet. I doubt it. Have no idea what the boys are doing." He leaned up and kissed her gently. "Don't really care what they're doing." He knew what he planned to do and that was spend more time with the woman lying on him. "What are your plans for the day?"

"Well, rich boy, I gotta go to work."

Of course she did. Most people did. He'd had meetings slated for this week himself until he'd been ambushed by his brothers.

"Not just yet, you don't. We still have time." He trailed his fingers along her spine, her skin smooth beneath his hands. He caressed her back, cupped her ass and pulled her harder against him as he continued to kiss her, sliding his lips over hers. He'd learned the taste of her, the feel of her skin under his hands, under his lips, against his skin. He knew the way she shivered if he kissed her just there behind her ear.

She shivered now as he ran his tongue up her neck.

"I'll be late," she whispered on a moan.

"I'll hurry," he told her, breathing deep the scent on her skin— flowers and herbs.

"That's what you said last time," she moaned as he jerked the sheet from between them and her skin met his, her supple breasts smashing against his chest, her nipples berry hard and begging for attention.

"Last time I lied." He cupped one perfect breast and circled her nipple with his thumb. He'd learned through the night things she liked, things she didn't, what brought her closer to the edge. "I can do quick."

"Oh, sugar, you can definitely handle quick, and slow and anything else you please so well—" She broke off on a moan as he licked her breast before pulling the center into his mouth.

"Glad you noticed," he said against her. "This time, I don't want you to be late."

Their bodies moved in the early morning light. She was sensuous, sexy, and so alive. So damned real his breath caught. He slid a hand down between them, found her slick and ready with desire, just as he had every time they'd come together.

Her eyes met his just as he slid into her hot, wet sheath.

Looking down on him. For a moment, a memory, jagged and from *before*, sliced into his brain, freezing him.

She stilled and leaned over, curling into his chest, kissing him softly as her small hands cupped his face. "What's wrong?"

He opened his mouth and shook his head, closing his eyes, concentrating on Ella. On her blue hair, which surprisingly pulled a grin from him. The way she smelled, the way she felt, the way she fit against him, on him, with him . . .

It was different.

She was different, this was all different.

He opened his eyes and stared directly into hers. Quinlan started to roll her under him. Instead he rolled so that they lay staring at each other.

Her hands still held his face. "It's okay, whatever it is."

His eyes slid closed as he thrust up into her, glad the earlier memory hadn't shriveled his cock.

"It's you and it's more than okay," he said against her lips. "You, Ella, are amazing." He hiked her leg up over his hip and thrust into her harder, loving that little mewl right there, that sound in her throat when he hit that spot just right inside her tight sweet body.

Her tongue teased his lips. "Look at me, Quin. See me."

He opened his eyes again and saw her watching him, her eyes more blue with green striations leading to the amber flecks near the center. He loved the way the colors shifted in her eyes as they made love. "I do."

She moved her hand and he caught her left wrist, tracing the letters of *love* that scrolled up her inner wrist with his tongue. He loved her tattoos.

Her shiver danced through him. For long moments their bodies undulated in a slow buildup. But he knew it wouldn't last. She was like fire in his hands, uncontrollable and unpredictable.

She arched and pulled him even deeper.

"God, Ella," he groaned. "Have I mentioned how much I like waking up with you?"

Chapter 6

New Orleans, four days later

Aiden looked again at his phone. "He hasn't answered a single damned call from any of us in about two days. None of us have seen or heard from him since we all ate at the Magnolia Grill Friday evening."

"He's fine. The boy is getting laid and God knows he needed it," Ian told him.

Gavin and Bray snorted and closed their menus. They were all at the Magnolia Grill again on Decatur. Their last night. One night more than they had originally planned. All thanks to their little brother.

"So we just leave him here?" Brody asked, sipping his drink. "Should of left his ass this morning. As it is, we'll be a day later getting back." He looked over the menu. "Wish I'd met a little blue-haired devil to keep me busy."

They'd all met the woman Quin was apparently spending time with a couple of nights ago. Here at the Magnolia Grill actually, but no one had seen either of them since. Brody had spent most of the meal apologizing to her for their previous meeting.

Ian slapped Aiden on his shoulder. "Brother dear, you are the oldest, but we are all old enough to make our own choices. Stop being the mother hen. We brought him here to have a good time. Quinlan isn't seven and drowning in the frozen river anymore."

"Feels like it," Aiden muttered, shoving his phone into his pocket. "He could at least text for us to go on. How do we know the woman didn't steal every cent in his wallet and leave him for dead in an alley in the Quarter or in some bayou?"

"Because she has no criminal record, they've been holed up in her place for the last two days, and his credit cards haven't been used," Ian told him.

Aiden just stared at him. Okay, so he didn't know all of that. He did know the woman Quinlan was spending time with had no criminal record, the rest was a total lie. He knew the two were actually in Vegas because that's what the credit cards said. They were currently holed up in the Bellagio. However, he was not about to share that info unless it was absolutely necessary. As yet, none of his brothers had figured out the plane wasn't even here in New Orleans, but in Nevada.

"I'm not the only mother hen, it seems," Aiden said.

Ian's grin faded. "I didn't pay attention before, and if I had, Quinlan wouldn't have been hurt in the first damned place." He swallowed all of his water and wished it were something stronger, but hell, he'd been doing stronger all weekend. "I won't make the same mistake again."

"Fine," Aiden said.

They all ordered and then Ian waited. Aiden didn't disappoint. "As long as Quin seems to be having a great time, I won't worry about him."

Gavin snorted. "Yeah, right, that's all we've done for the last year." Gavin took a long swallow of beer.

"So it seems like," Brayden said.

It was just them this evening. Gabe and Johnno were back at the house, nursing hangovers and just chillin', they'd said. Fine. Christian's brother had not been seen since that first night when he took them all out to his club, but then he was generally as busy as the rest of them, so that wasn't a surprise.

What was a surprise, at least to Ian, was not only the youngest of them getting over whatever the hell kept him celibate for the last year—which Ian knew was mainly one Hellinski bitch—but the rest of his brothers and their amount of worry for one grown man.

Himself and his own worries he understood and owned. He shook his head.

Brody leaned up and added, "You guys smother him. The tighter you do it, the more he figures to hell with you and closes up."

Ian smiled, and then there was Brody—Junior.

"We're his brothers," the twins both said before giving each other irritated looks.

"So?" Brody said. "We're the same age. I daresay, other than Aiden, through the years I've spent the most time with him." He leaned back and laughed. "And some damned fine times those were too. He'll be fine. Man always had a woman. Last year or so has just been unnatural."

"Yeah, well, regardless how well you know him, Junior, we'll still make sure some slag doesn't take advantage," Ian said.

Brody glared at the nickname. "Fine, don't listen to me." Then he frowned. "Slag? What the hell's a slag?"

"Ian here is picking up lovely euphemisms from his wife," Aiden said.

Their food arrived and their conversation moved onto other topics, but Ian's mind kept along the track he'd told the others to get off of.

First Quin almost died, then he just wasn't himself. Ian knew Aiden missed their brother the way Quinlan used to be. The workaholic. Charming and social. A mind so sharp he never made notes. Now he worked, but it wasn't with any sort of passion that he'd had for it before. He often forgot things that he never would have forgotten before. Now the charm was more rote and he'd only do social on a dire threat or when there was no other option. Maybe, whoever this woman was, she would help bring their brother back.

Or at least one that cared about something. Because Quinlan Kinncaid didn't care about anything anymore.

Ian knew that feeling well. The nothing was not a place he wanted his brother to be.

• • •

The next morning

"Why isn't he back yet?" Ian asked yet again.

Aiden tilted his head and looked at him. "You said we were worrying too damned much," he told him, zipping up his own bag.

Ian just shot him a look that hopefully said without words what he thought of that. "I am merely cautious and it's served me very well."

"Cautious, paranoid," Gavin muttered. "They're like twins."

"So which are you?" Brayden asked. "And please, can't you all just shut the hell up?"

"Silence would be fantastic," Brody added, easing into a chair.

"Headache still?" Aiden asked.

Most were stumbling around, or more accurately, easing around. The stumbling had been most of the week. Now it was time to pay the price. After their days in New Orleans, they all wore shades. Aiden rubbed his brow. Surprising to Ian's way of thinking, because normally their perfect eldest brother was a control freak enough that he wasn't about to get drunk multiple nights in a row—or stay that way throughout their entire trip. Like Brody, their cousin.

"Fuck off," Brody said.

Ian continued to pace. His brother's phone was turned off. Maybe the battery was out, because he couldn't locate the damned thing anymore.

"You could just GPS track his ass," Gavin said. "Mr. I-am-all-seeing-and-all-knowing and—"

"I already did that."

"I was joking. Damn, Ian. Chill. This is not exactly healthy behavior."

"Healthy behavior does not always keep people alive."

Aiden grunted. "There are so many inconsistencies in that comment alone."

"If he's on the plane then he'll be here," someone said.

"He better damn well be," Brody muttered. "I missed two meetings this morning alone and I don't remember what I had on the schedule this afternoon."

"Junior," Gavin started.

Brody threw a stuffed pillow at him. "Everyone, please, I beg you, just shut the fuck up or I'll find a way to kill you all."

Ian walked to the side of the courtyard and dialed Roger—the longtime Kinncaid pilot.

The courtyard was quiet, the voices of his brothers and cousin rumbling out to clash with the soothing sounds of the fountain and birds, the muffled traffic from beyond the old thick, brick, ivy-covered walls.

"Yes? Mr. Ian?" Roger answered.

"Everything all right?" he asked. "And how long until you get here?"

"About an hour."

Ian grunted. "Please tell me you have more of my brother than just his cell phone sitting on his chair." Ian knew that much because the phone had been moving for a couple of hours now, or it had been until the battery died.

Roger was quiet for a moment. Then he muttered something and said, "Indeed. I thought he was asleep, but the kid hasn't slept since he got on. Looks like shit and was using his cane, limping bad."

Worry tightened his nerves and he frowned at the ivy. "He's okay though?" So Ian had told his brothers to knock off the mother-hen worrywart shit. Didn't mean he had to. He was paid to worry about people. Maybe he was the workaholic in the family now.

"Reeks like a brewery and she wasn't with him. Didn't ask—"

"Ella?"

"Yeah, pretty thing he took with him. Blue hair. Strange that."

Definitely Ella.

Fine. He started to grill Roger about his brother. But damn it, he supposed since Quin was safe and on his way, it didn't matter. After the last year though, and almost losing one of their own, it was harder than he would have thought to back off.

He rubbed his fingers over his lips. "Never mind. You're heading back here and that's all that matters. The wolves are getting restless."

"Well, I can't very well be in two places at once, boss. He tried to get me to go back to New Orleans when we landed in Vegas yesterday, or whenever the hell it was, day before. I figured I'd just stay there. Either he'd be ready to go or you and the boys would call me back."

Ian grunted again. "See you soon." He turned to see his brothers sprawled in the iron chairs around the courtyard. "And Roger? Thanks."

Aiden merely raised a brow at him. "Worrying needlessly, am I? A mother hen, I believe you called me last night."

"This morning."

"When the hell ever."

Gabe and Johnno rambled out of the house, showered and dressed if not in completely top form. John had a beer.

Ian saw Aiden shudder as John set the beer on the table between them and sat down.

"Want one?" John asked Aiden.

"No, thanks. I've had enough for a good long while. I am getting too old for this shit—fun as it was." He looked up at Ian. "Just tell me he's okay," Aiden said.

Ian held his brother's cobalt stare—so like his own—and nodded.

"Roger said he'd be here soon."

"Where was he again?" someone asked.

Ian shrugged, dodging the question, not sure he should tell them.

"You don't know?" Aiden asked him, standing to pull his own phone from his jeans pocket before he ducked beneath the red umbrella and sat again at the little iron table. He needed food.

"Didn't we go through this last night?" Brayden asked.

"None of you are his mother," Brody said. "Maybe he has a girlfriend now, though hopefully not the blue-haired chick. She wasn't his normal type. Another one that'll get his ass back on track."

"A girlfriend? From a weekend fling? Or practically a week fling by the time we finally get home?" Gavin snorted. "I thought you, of us all, would know that is not how the game is played."

"He hasn't had one since her," Aiden said.

"She wasn't his damned girlfriend, Aiden," Ian muttered.

"You know what I meant. He hasn't had or been with or . . . At least Ella made him smile. She's different, though."

"At least the kid got laid." Ian thought of Ella and her blue hair and quirky attitude and couldn't hold in the grin.

"Point is, it was only this morning that I started to . . ."

"Fret?" Aiden asked.

Ian flipped him off.

"I will as soon as I see my lovely wife. Thanks for your concern."

Ian grunted.

"So where was he?" Gavin asked.

"Who the hell cares?" Brody said, leaning back and taking a long drink of his beer. "As long as he had fun, got laid and comes back smiling. Fine. Maybe then he'll toss that damned chip off his fucking shoulder."

Aiden sighed. "Look, Ian, no one holds you responsible for what happened to Quinlan or any of the rest of it. Certainly not Quin."

Aiden took a drink of coffee and grimaced.

"And that's why I went with the hair of the dog this morning, cousin." Brody motioned to Ian with his beer bottle. "Ian apparently likes his coffee strong and black—practically thick. Nasty stuff. Apparently this morning none of us beat him to the coffee pot."

"We should just head to the hotel, eat a bite, then head to the airport," Aiden said.

lan shook his head. "If you travel—for pleasure—to a city where the Kinncaids have a place, do you *always* head there sooner or later?"

Aiden arched a brow. "Does that question actually need answering?"

"It's Pavlovian."

"And everyone loves the profits."

"That we do," Gavin said. "I take it from the fact Ian's no longer pacing and wearing us all out with his mother-hen routine this lovely morn that we know where the lost and wayward is? Because I might just deck the little shit for leaving us stranded for another day."

"Yep. Heading back as we speak," Ian told him.

"'Bout damn time. I'm ready to go home. Though I'm starving."

"Your brother thinks we should hit the hotel," Brody said.

Gavin shook his head. "No. I want the Clover Grill. I will eat there before we leave and that will be this morning. I want the whole cardiological nightmare. Over easy, I think."

Aiden raised his hands. "Fine. Clover Grill. I've already checked the hotel anyway, so we're good."

"A guys' extended weekend, a vacation," Gavin told Aiden. "Or did you miss that point?"

"I'm not the one that missed it," Aiden muttered and picked up his coffee cup and immediately set it back down, frowning at the sludge. "I'd really just like to know where the hell our little brother decided to spend his weekend."

"Well, wherever he went, I would bet he took the interesting Ella with him," Brayden said from his spot on the lounger.

Ian cleared his throat. "Vegas. They went to Vegas."

A moment of silence before several curses filled the air.

"And he left us here?" from Brody.

Chapter 7

Quinlan waited at the airport.

Where the hell was she?

He shoved his hands into the pockets of his woolen coat and scanned the horizon again. From the small regional airport, he could see the highway and headlights from cars and trucks zooming either way.

Finally, someone turned in. He reached down and grabbed his bag, and pulled his phone out again. Battery was almost dead.

Local time it was after ten. His body told him it was after midnight, but he wasn't tired.

The car pulled into the lot. Not hers, he saw, or not what he remembered her driving from New Orleans. Not to say she hadn't gotten a new vehicle.

A man climbed out.

Quin walked back to the desk and asked the woman behind it, "Are there any cabs I can call?"

She grinned. "Might be awhile. Cabs aren't needed around here much, ya know?" She jerked her head to the highway. "There's an airport vehicle we rent out when needed. Nothing fancy, but it's currently free if you need it."

"Is there a rental place near here?"

"Not far but it's closed. You'll have to take the beat-up SUV. Gotta get your info before you can take it, though."

He sighed. "Fine, whatever." He quickly signed what was needed, passed over his info and credit card.

Then he was in the car, thankful he hadn't unpacked the little charger that could either be plugged into the wall or into a car. He plugged his phone in and tapped in Ella's address. No reason to worry. None. So she'd been scared. Her words all jumbled and tripping over each other.

Maybe her phone died.

Maybe she had to go somewhere.

She was pregnant. He did the math. If she'd gotten pregnant

early in their relationship, she was almost due. Maybe she was in the hospital.

Maybe her friend took her out to eat and they'd lost track of time.

Maybe . . .

Maybe . . .

Maybe whomever she was scared of had her.

He shook his head. "Don't go there." He pulled out onto the highway and followed the voice app on his GPS to the address she'd provided him.

Fifteen minutes later, he pulled into a nice house off of Blueberry Hill. Stucco walls and a little yard. There were vines along the arched stucco gate, probably pretty when it wasn't so cold. And it was cold. He shivered and hurried up the drive, looking both ways.

The house was dark.

Her car, the little Kia Soul that got excellent fuel mileage, sat in the driveway.

A dog barked next door and he took a deep breath.

If she was pregnant, maybe she was just tired and didn't hear the phone.

Or maybe she'd fallen.

He pressed the glowing button for the bell. And waited. And waited some more. "Ella!" He knocked on the door.

Nothing. He didn't hear anything.

He looked into the window of the door and then to the side window, but nothing. It was dark inside the house. Dark.

Ella wasn't scared of the dark, but she'd never left anything in pitch black either. Very little light shone from the street.

She also always left her porch light on. Or she had in New Orleans. A habit, and habits were not generally given up.

He waited a minute more then banged on the door again. "Ella! It's me, Quinlan! Ella!" He banged harder.

The dog across the street kept barking, sounding closer.

Quin beat on the door with the side of his fist, but he already knew . . . feared no one was home.

He sighed and walked around the side of the house, wishing he'd brought his phone from the rental so he could have some damned light. He tripped over something but managed to catch himself.

All the windows were dark.

"You're trespassing," a voice said from the gate.

He whirled around and walked back around to the front of the house. From the streetlight he could see it was an older gentleman.

"I'm looking for Ella. She gave me this address," Quin told the man, who stood there staring at him.

"Ella?"

"Yes, she's my . . ." Quin stopped. What had she told these people? He actually didn't care. "Ella's my wife. She called me earlier today, about four hours ago, actually, and knew I was coming. She was supposed to meet me at the airport to pick me up. But I can't get her on the phone."

The man stood there for a minute.

"Wife? You're her husband?"

Quinlan nodded and stepped closer, holding his hand out. "Yes, Quinlan Kinncaid."

The man humphed. "Quinlan Kinncaid, is it? Finally remember you have a wife? And a pregnant one at that?"

Quin took a deep breath. "It's complicated."

The man finally shook his hand. "Marriage really isn't that complicated, son. I'm Herb Richardson. My wife and I rented this place to Ella. Watched over her for the last few months. We were out earlier today. She's not here? Her car's here."

Quinlan turned. "I know. She called and had to get off the phone, low battery and her friend was at the door. I haven't been able to reach her since."

"Did you get the right number?"

"I got her voice mail plenty of times."

Again the man humphed. "Well, son, at least you're finally here."

He frowned. "You know who I am?"

"I've a feeling I know a lot more than you do, Mr. Kinncaid. Come on over to the house, I'll grab the key. Wouldn't normally use it, but told the girl at dinner a couple of nights ago that if she didn't keep in contact with us, I got to go over and check on her. No family, in her condition, it's just not safe to be alone."

Quin didn't need to hear the censure in the words to know what the man thought.

He took a deep breath. "What's been going on?"

He walked beside Mr. Richardson, a man as tall as himself,

straight shoulders, straight back. Retired military, Quin would bet. White hair, grandfatherly, in a healthy way.

Across the street, he followed him into a much larger house through the side door. "Carmine, we've guests."

"What? At this time of night? Is it Ella? I haven't been able to get that girl all evening." She came into the kitchen from the side, carrying a basket of laundry. "Well, guess it's not Ella, but her man, then, isn't it?"

Quin held the woman's stare and held his hand out. "Yes, ma'am. She called me earlier, not making a lot of sense."

"But you came. And she called?"

He glanced at the clock. "Yeah, surprised me too." He couldn't help but smile. "I heard her voice and . . ." Then he shook his head. "She was scared, worried about someone taking her baby . . . our baby."

He realized with a jolt that was the first time he'd said that to anyone.

"Our baby," he said softly.

"Oh, it's your baby. She's told us all about you." The woman was small, probably didn't come to her husband's chest, and her hair was cut in a fluffed bob. She set the basket on the kitchen table. He glanced around. Bright yellow kitchen, dark cabinets, red countertops.

"Girl is head over heels in love with you, you know. 'Bout time you tracked her down."

"Carmine."

"Well, or time she called him. And look, he flew right out here." She arched a brow at her husband.

Mr. Richardson shook his head and took a key off the hook by the door with a bright pink ribbon on it. "I never said the man wouldn't come if she ever called him. I just wondered why he let her get away to begin with."

Quinlan didn't take offense. "I've been asking myself that very question for months."

"So you're not stupid, just slow. At least you're here. Come on. Let's go check."

Mrs. Richardson grabbed a jacket off the hook behind the door and slid into it. "We should have already gone over there."

"Maybe she's just out with friends," Mr. Richardson said.

"She doesn't go out with friends, not after . . ." she trailed off.

"After what?" Quin asked.

"I don't know. She stayed up at that place she worked a few days and then came back. Girl was different, scared of her own shadow. I asked her to stay here, but she just shook her head and said not to worry." She leveled a narrow-eyed look at him. "I know what she told me. I know she missed you and—"

"Carmine," her husband said as they walked up the little path of Ella's bungalow.

"Well, they should be together. I just know she's crazy about him, wishing they were still together, not enjoying the whole experience like she should. It would help settle her if you two would get back together."

He couldn't help but grin. These two reminded him of his parents. "Thank you, Mrs. Richardson. If I couldn't be here, I'm just glad she had you and your husband."

They reached the house.

"Odd. She always has the porch light on," Mrs. Richardson said.

Mr. Richardson unlocked the door and stepped inside, flipping the light.

Quin blinked. "Ella! Ella!" The layout was simple. The door opened into the living room, a half wall separated it from the kitchen. She wasn't in either. A hallway to the side led to a bathroom and darkened bedroom. No one was here.

Chills danced over his skin and panic slithered through him.

No. She'd be fine. She was just . . . was . . .

He stood in her bedroom and . . . could smell her.

God.

Goose bumps peppered his skin. He could smell her: citrus, herbal, light flowers, and he could almost swear vanilla. The scent brought tears to his eyes. God, he'd missed the hell out of her.

He scanned the room. Bed was made. Nothing was on the dresser. In fact, nothing was in the closet. Not really. A couple of boxes. He walked back down the hallway and into the kitchen.

A bag sat beside the door, another zipped black overnight bag near the door. He reached into his pocket to call her again and remembered his phone was charging in the rental.

A blinking light in the dim kitchen caught his eye. He flipped on the light.

Her phone sat on the counter, the cord snaking into the outlet.

She didn't have her phone.

He took a breath and had to take another.

"Where is she?" Carmine asked.

He could only stand there and shake his head. Then shake it again. No. She'd called him. She'd called . . .

His gut twisted.

"Call the police," he said, or thought he did. He cleared his throat. "Call the police. We should call the police."

Chapter 8

Quinlan Kinncaid closed his eyes and sat back in the seat.

He tried to shut his mind up. It wasn't working.

They'd already refueled and the gang would be on here shortly. Probably with a hard time and tons of questions, none of which he would answer.

As if he could.

Damn. Today was Monday. He realized that when he was checking out earlier. Where the hell did Sunday go? He didn't have a single clue. Or rather he did, but he did *not* want to think about what happened on Sunday evening. Sunday night? He hadn't read the papers that closely.

He rarely drank. Not after everything that had happened before. He'd learned the hard way drugs didn't have a taste in alcoholic drinks, at least not the ones the bitch had poured into him before she'd tried to kill him and everyone else in his family a year ago. After she failed to kill him, he learned the docs didn't approve of vodka painkiller cocktails. They were frowned upon for one's recovery.

He wondered if he should be worried.

Fuck yes!

He remembered some things over the last couple of days. Okay, the beginning was bright and shiny. His brothers ambushing him for a mini-vacation of fun in New Orleans. A men's getaway or whatever. Aiden had been thinking classy fun. Hell, most of them were. But Bourbon Street was Bourbon Street and sooner or later all tourists ended up there and classy ended up bead-covered and vomiting in the gutters. Eight males away from home and wives? Pack mentality. Nothing classy about it.

Ella.

He remembered her tie-dyed pink shirt and blue hair. He remembered running into her, literally, while grabbing a few things at the grocery store on Ursuline.

Not that any of them did anything shocking, at least that he knew of. The first night he didn't have more than a glass of wine, watched as his various brothers, cousins, and friends achieved several levels of inebriation and then the bead tossing commenced.

Probably a video on YouTube somewhere.

Fine with him. Then was the club Christian's brother had taken them too. Cheesy when explained but fun nonetheless, and brilliant if risky from a marketing standpoint. He remembered having a business discussion with the man on the fact he didn't foresee the club lasting forever, but it was fun for now and had already paid for itself.

Profit was profit. Great.

Café Du Monde.

And then her house.

Yeah, he remembered that.

He was clear on walking her home after they'd talked and laughed, walked the streets of the Quarter. He remembered heading back to her place and all the worries that he would never again be able to slide hard and thick into a soft, slick woman—well, she'd shown him how stupid that fear had been. But it was a big damned fear, one he'd only shared with his therapist at some point and didn't mention again.

With her, though . . . with her, there was no need to worry. He gotten hard just thinking about her.

They'd talked.

A lot.

He'd laughed and felt free for the first time in too damned long.

Spending the next couple of days looking for art supplies for the shelter, meeting up with her for dinner with his brothers, where they'd all drank. He and Ella had walked the streets until almost dawn just talking, listening to others play music, laughing, talking more. Then drinking some fruity concoctions out of slushy machines. Her place, where they made love just after dawn. Champagne for breakfast, on the plane . . .

He didn't remember which one of them mentioned Vegas, but one of them had. He remembered the fun ride to Vegas, the fact that they'd made love most of the way there while drinking champagne off of each other, giggling and laughing.

Apparently, he'd had *copious* amounts of bubbly for the last couple of days. He winced behind his shades.

Vegas was bright, so bright and fun. He remembered laughing.

Remembered getting a room — or suite, rather — at the Bellagio.

Gambling. Something he was good at, he knew, but rarely did at the tables. He enjoyed the everyday gamble of business. However, he was almost two hundred grand richer on this return trip. A definite plus there. He apparently played at some point. He didn't remember actually playing, though there was a vague memory of cards, and that left a slick fear in his gut. The fact the concierge asked him if he wanted to cash out this morning when checking out confirmed he hadn't completely lost it and robbed a bank or what the hell ever.

The rest was rather blank. Sort of. Mostly. Sort of.

He remembered the scent of her skin, the taste of her, the silky glide of her beneath him, over him, around him. He knew how husky desire tinged her voice. The way her eyes glinted with passion as he thrust into her. The way she chuckled against him. The tattoo low on her hip with one word, *Trust*, below a dragonfly. *Love* was stenciled in flowing letters along her inner left wrist. *Beauty* scrolled along the side of her left breast in Hindu. He'd traced every letter with his tongue. He damned well remembered that. Her strange and quirky hair reminding him of pale blue cotton candy, though the silky strands had slid through his fingers.

And.

And.

Elvis.

He remembered a flash of Elvis and this morning he'd had a ring — not cheap either, as both his and hers had been billed to his room — on his fucking finger.

A. Ring.

Holy fuck.

He thumped his head back. Then bit back another curse as his head pounded. He honestly hadn't felt this hungover since before the Hellinski bitch. She'd given him a couple of hangovers he'd never forget.

This hangover, though, just might beat hers, and he had no one to blame but himself. Or the champagne. Bubbly was bad. All the effing bubbly's fault.

He'd sworn he'd *never* get married — more than once. God knows he'd said it plenty to everyone in his family.

Yet?

Yet.

Elvis.

The. Rings.

And . . .

The note.

The. *License.*

He shied away from the last. The former though . . .

. . . I'm sorry. I know it's rude to run out, more than rude. But we didn't . . . we shouldn't have . . . I have to go. Thanks for the great weekend and don't worry. Call your lawyers and get an annulment or whatever and get back to me. Neither of us wants to be married. I don't want anything except the wonderful memories. Best to you, my darlin' Quin. ~ Ella

She'd left a five-carat diamond ring on the note for him to find. The platinum band his account said he'd also gotten her was *not* there.

She left the more valuable ring and kept the simple band. Why?

God almighty.

He leaned forward and gripped his head just as Roger, their pilot, said, "Boys'll be on in a bit, Mr. Q. You need anything?"

When they were younger, the pilot and driver and whoever else had started referring to them as Mr. First Initial. Kept things easy, he supposed. Too many Mr. K's in this family.

He almost shook his head. Instead he just waved his hand and mumbled, "Nothing. Thanks, Roger."

The door gave a hiss as Roger opened it. Several minutes passed before the herd stampeded in.

This should be good.

Elvis? For some reason, Elvis in his mind was in drag, which made no sense whatsoever.

His family would kill him if he didn't do himself in.

Last time he was this impulsive and stupid with a woman it liked to have killed him and his whole family — or part of them.

This time?

He'd only gotten married. God.

Who knew? He didn't remember signing a prenup.

Prenup. Or was that lost? He'd have to talk to Brody — at some point. Clearly, he hadn't called his lawyer, or said cousin and the rest of the family would have undoubtedly tried to stop the damned wedding.

Oh my God.

She could . . . Hell, he'd have to check with Brody. Though not now.

What did he really know about her?

. . . I don't want anything . . .

Ella . . .

He saw her blue-green eyes with amber flecks in them, weird hair and pale skin. He knew so much about her, but so little. She volunteered at shelters and gave her afternoons to the elderly and taught yoga. He'd enjoyed her yoga, in more ways than one, which was totally beside the effing point.

What the hell did he do?

Ian slapped the back of his chair and slid into one across from him.

"Vegas?"

"Hey, little bro. Got tired of our party and went and made your own, huh?" Gavin muttered as he sat beside him. Someone else sat down, but Quinlan didn't open his eyes, move, or remove his shades to see who it was. Didn't care.

"So who was the chick? The cotton-candy-haired one? Eliza or Ellen or whatever?" Aiden asked, also across from him. The others piled in quickly. Clearly they were ready to go home as well. And why the hell wouldn't they be? They'd *planned* to go home *yesterday*.

Home.

How the hell would she get home?

He'd left a message with the front desk in case she returned, along with an envelope of money—more than enough to see her safely back to New Orleans.

However, *she* left *him*, hadn't she?

Whether that was a good thing or a bad thing he still hadn't decided. *Bad* echoed through his brain. Knee-jerk, probably, but he did have his pride, stupid as it was.

"Hello?"

Seat belts clicked into place throughout the cabin as the jet fired up and everyone was ready for takeoff.

Quinlan ignored them all until he felt someone take his wrist. He jerked then and glared at Gavin. "Leave me the fuck alone."

Gavin held his hand out. "Just making sure you were okay, 'cause you look like hammered shit. Worse than Bray, and he's pretty bad."

No one said anything for a long while as the plane took off and cabin pressure built. By the time his ears popped, the boys had gotten waters and drinks, whatever they wanted.

He wanted nothing.

Gavin handed him water anyway. "So, spill before one of them beats it out of you and then I'd have to play doctor and patch you up. After I help them, of course."

He only flipped them all off.

"I already said I was fine, didn't I?" he snapped.

Aiden just stared at him, as did Ian. Why did those two have to be sitting across from him. Those two could pull off the worried, nearly pissed-off father routine way too well. He could hear Brody and Gabe arguing about God only knew what. Bray was nowhere to be seen. Sorry bastard was probably sleeping. Would be nice. Apparently no one was going to let him get away with that. Couldn't really blame them though, as he had left them stranded.

"So," Ian finally said, sitting back, opening his own water. "Vegas."

Quinlan tried to ignore him.

"At least you didn't come home with some gold-digging wife," Aiden muttered.

"Nope, I left her in Vegas," he told them.

"Speaking of, what happened to what's her name you ditched us for?" Ian asked, his gaze sharp. "Heard she went with you, or did you take someone else?"

Gold-digging wife? If only. No, she wasn't even that—which, all things considered, he should be thankful for. But—okay, he was—but damn it. She'd slipped out like a thief in the night. After everything they'd shared.

Connected.

He'd felt connected to the woman like he never had before.

How the hell was she going to get home and—

Gavin shoved his shoulder.

He shoved him back.

"Maybe I did get married."

Gavin scoffed. "You?" He laughed and then laughed some more.

"So it's true, then," Bray grumbled from somewhere behind them all. "Satan's building a ski run in hell?"

Quinlan took a deep breath.

"And if you did," Ian started, his gaze still searching, and seeing too damned much, "where is the illustrious Mrs. Quinlan Kinncaid?"

He shifted and shrugged. "No idea."

"See, he's not married." Gavin chuckled. "He'd have to be drugged again and out of his mind."

That was just a little too close to the truth. He shifted again in his seat.

Ian's eyes narrowed and now Aiden was leaning forward. "Or just seriously drunk."

Bray leaned over the top of the seat. "If it's Ella, at least she's pretty, even if she's a bit weird."

Brody joined the group. Ever the lawyer. "Please tell me there was no marriage, and if so, you have a prenup somewhere, somehow."

Quinlan shut his eyes and leaned back, ignoring them all. Their joking was too damned close to the truth and he didn't want to deal with any of it just now.

"So are you or aren't you?" Aiden asked.

As both rings were sitting in his pocket along with her damned note, that was an easy answer, though he wasn't about to admit that. "Apparently not. She's left me the ring and a sweet note and I've no idea where she is."

"Do you have any idea *who* she is?" Gabe asked, joining the conversation. "It is Ella, isn't it? Or did you elope with some Vegas showgirl?"

Several mutters and curses filled the air.

"I only ask 'cause I married this really sweet Vegas showgirl once. God, she had a pair on her, and legs that went on for fucking ever. And," he continued, holding a hand up as questions were lobbed at him, "I didn't remember her. I remember getting hitched. Remember the weird preacher dude and—"

"Can they be preachers in Vegas? Isn't that like a priest in Sodom and Gomorrah?" Bray asked.

"Anyway, he wore this weird lime green suit, which is how I found him, and he said we never signed the license, which is how I slicked by. Don't even remember her name. But she had the best ass I've ever seen and a dimple just . . ."

Great. Why didn't he just shrug them all off.

"You should all see your faces, shocked to amused to completely pissed," Quinlan said, forcing a laugh.

They all sat back and huffed.

Aiden pointed to him. "I knew *you* couldn't be that stupid. Gabe, well, he's a different story. I write it off to him being a cop and too many close encounters with death."

"Hey!" the cop said. That rankled. "Why? Because I'm too stiff? Too predictable? Too set in my ways to find a great girl for a weekend fling and then marry her?"

"Yeah, we all foresaw your trip to Sin City," Gavin said and sighed back himself. "This was, overall, a fun weekend. We should do it again. This time *all* of us, and not just some of us while others go seek diversion elsewhere."

Ian was the only one who continued to watch him. Great. Just great.

Let him wonder, let him look. Let him search. Maybe then Quinlan would know where she was, because he had a marriage certificate for Clark County, Nevada, and it was notarized and had both legible sigs on the bottom of it.

He. Was. Married.

How the hell did that happen?

Married?

Insanity. Ella. Laughter?

Laughter. It had been so long since he'd really laughed and with her it had been . . . so easy. So . . . right. He'd even told her about the hell last year of being drugged and almost killed. How he got his permanent limp. Yeah, everything had been perfectly right.

Stupid too, apparently.

And champagne. *Lots* of champagne he'd licked off her heated skin, her chilled skin . . . off the dragonfly tattoo low on her hipbone. He remembered running his tongue along the Hindu symbols along the side of her left breast, tracing them with his finger. The way the lights played in her hair. A memory pierced his brain of him running her hair through his fingers while she said she wanted to change the color.

"To what? I thought you were going purple next time," he'd said.

"I'm thinking pale, probably white if I can find someone to get it that color with a dark purple stripe in it." She'd wrapped her arms around his neck and pulled him down for a kiss . . .

Champagne. The bill showed seven bottles charged last night. And absinthe. Wicked evil brew that. What the hell had possessed him to order the green liquid, he had no idea.

Alcohol and impulsiveness. Dangerous partnership.

And a taunt. He remembered that. She teasing him that he never was spontaneous.

The memory slipped away.

He closed his eyes and decided he'd worry about it later. He caught Brody's eye and his cousin lifted his thumb and pinky to his jaw in the classic *call me* sign.

He might just have to.

Chapter 9

Las Vegas

Ella Ferguson sat in the airport waiting on her flight. She had watched earlier, hiding in a coffee shop at the hotel, when Quinlan had climbed into a limo and headed — she presumed — to the airport.

God her head hurt. But then it had since sometime this morning, early. The walls and sidewalks had finally stopped spinning a couple of hours ago. She knew she'd been stupid. Beyond stupid, really. She was rarely this idiotically stupid. She'd always, always done what she was supposed to.

What was expected of her — well, most of the time. Yes, she had a few tattoos. Three, so what? And yes, her hair was whatever color she felt like dying it. So what? That did not make her an irresponsible person normally.

She remembered making love early this morning. How she remembered as gone as they both had still been, she wasn't sure, but they had. He'd made the comment that his family would love her.

She had met his brothers back in New Orleans. They'd all headed to Magnolia Grill.

Group like that . . .

Family like that? Love her? Yeah, right.

And the panic had slammed into her and swallowed her up.

She was married.

Again.

To another fast-playing rich boy.

What the hell was the matter with her? What had she been thinking? She hadn't been thinking, that was clear enough. Drinking and thinking were not synonymous or even symbiotic — no, more like polar opposites.

She twirled the platinum band between her thumb and forefinger.

What had she done as soon as she'd realized the folly of her grand weekend? She'd lain there, looking at that beautiful ring she couldn't really remember picking out. Where had they gotten the rings?

Married.

She *liked* Quinlan, he was funny and quirky and hid it all under that solid seriousness. But they'd gotten past somber Quinlan sometime down in New Orleans. They'd talked, cooked, laughed and dreamed.

Connected.

She'd jokingly told him he was wasting time feeling sorry for himself.

Too wrapped up in what he could no longer do, in what had almost happened rather than what didn't happen, or what he could still accomplish with his life. The fact he was in a position to help others had honestly seemed lost on him. She'd told him he should help others in worse situations than he'd been in, put things in perspective. So he limped, had a cane, couldn't run a marathon or 10K anymore. So what?

Yeah, they'd connected. Stranger things happened, she supposed.

Married. The thought kept screaming in her head.

And his family?

Old money, the Kinncaids. Old traditions, she would bet.

Something to do with hotels.

She didn't care.

She'd been down that road before. Married a rich boy from the Garden District in college and then he'd chosen his family over her when it came to that. She got a nice settlement and heartbreak. She no longer trusted men—especially not trust-fund boys.

Yet, Quinlan didn't exactly seem that way. Not really.

What the hell did she do now?

See her lawyer when she got home?

Or maybe she could just file an annulment?

She'd have to look into it. Or maybe just leave it be. She'd left the papers with Quinlan, let him take care of it. When he sobered up . . . it wouldn't be like he'd really *want* to introduce her to his family, at least not as his *wife*.

Right now, her head freaking hurt way too damned much to figure out any of it. The kid screaming and running between his mother and other waiting passengers was driving spikes into her brain.

Really, couldn't the woman control her kid?

Kids.

Her birth control pills were at home, they had to be because they were not in her purse, or the bag she didn't remember packing. Not really. She remembered making love on the plane. That was about it. God, had they been smart or stupid? Probably stupid, it wasn't like *any* of this could be termed in any way or fashion smart.

She put her hands over her stomach for just a second. Nah. Wouldn't happen. Instead, she rubbed the side of her head.

Just move on and forget him. That's all she needed to do. Just move on, and in time she wouldn't remember the way his chuckle sounded deep in his chest as she lay her head down, or the way his heartbeat lulled her to sleep. The way her mouth watered at the very scent of whatever cologne or aftershave he wore. The way his fingers raked through her hair, or softly grazed her skin. Maybe it was a good thing she didn't know more about him.

And now what?

Go back, what else was there? She had a life in New Orleans, and a job. This was just a great and fabulous weekend to write down and remember. To forget if she could for now. It wasn't like she had never had a one-night stand before. Granted, it had been years, and okay, yes—*years*. Since college and her divorce from Lance—that she hadn't wanted, but had too much pride to beg when a man didn't want her. And the guy her friend Marie had set her up with.

Twice. She'd done the one-night never-look-back twice.

And both of those times? No backward glances.

You weren't married to either one of them. And she'd spent the weekend with Quin. The weekend.

God. She was *M.A.R.R.I.E.D.*

Maybe she should have waited for him to wake up and they could have discussed it all. But really, what was she going to do? Wait for him to sober up and look at her with the *what the fuck did we do?* look she saw in her own eyes every time she looked in the mirror?

No.

Coward, maybe she was. Okay, that was a given, and that was fine. Her heart would survive for another day. Sooner or later she'd forget him. And he'd forget her.

She'd gone back to the hotel after he'd left and asked the concierge if there was a message for her. There had been. His phone number and a *Call me ~Quin*. She'd stood there looking at the message and didn't realize he'd left something else until the man handed her an envelope with money and another note. *You didn't have to run, you could have ridden home with me. We could have talked about this, which we will have to do. I've got to get the plane back and get my brothers. Here's some money to see you back to New Orleans.* Something was scribbled out. Then again, *Please call me. Yours, Quin.*

Yours.

She was not going to read more into that word than he'd meant. What else would he sign? Love? She had folded it up and put it in her purse and made her way to the airport.

Now here she sat wondering how she could be so . . . reckless? Irresponsible?

It was his eyes, those damned haunted green intense eyes. And that smile. His laughter. His voice and . . .

The announcement for the flight pulled her attention back. They started boarding the plane and she waited. She had enough she could have gotten a first-class ticket, but she'd save the money. She always saved money. It was the only smart thing to do. Call him? Maybe. Maybe not.

Who knew what the future held?

• • •

Washington, D.C., two weeks later

Quinlan stood staring out the windows of his penthouse suite. The brothers were all at home, with their wives and kids. Families.

He was staring out a dark window.

Family.

He'd never wanted one of his own before. Not like his brothers had. Things, apparently, change. When death sat and whispered in your ear, it made you sit the hell up and ask what was important.

Family was damned important.

It was the *all*, he had realized at some point. When? Had he already realized it and that's why he didn't remember halting any of the crazy things he'd done two weekends ago?

Maybe, or maybe it was just that Ella solidified it all for him.

You could do so much more than feel sorry for yourself, Quinlan.

Family . . .

It was what he wanted, deep down inside.

The more he thought of family, the more he thought of her.

Ella.

Of her note . . .

"*. . . move on and find someone else . . .*"

Anger licked through him all over again. Fact was? He wasn't sure he wanted anyone else.

The question was *why*.

Did he want her simply because she didn't want him?

He raked a hand through his wet hair and rubbed his thigh, which was hurting like a bitch.

The lights of D.C. twinkled and spread out before him. From here he could see the Mall, the white hallowed walls of the Capitol. He wanted answers and of course there were none.

He sighed and walked to his black leather couch and all but fell on it.

He reached for the remote and clicked on the TV. He didn't want to watch anything. He wanted to . . . to . . . *do* something. What, he had no idea.

Twitchy.

He was damned twitchy and couldn't sit still.

Maybe he'd go to the gym. He reached for his damn cane and cursed as pain radiated through his leg as he stood. Maybe not the gym. Where did that leave him then? Pacing, apparently. Or limping.

The wedding bands sat on his black granite countertop mocking him. The lights glinted off the platinum of his and winked off the perfect diamond of hers.

An image of her hand flashed through his mind.

She'd reached up to him, the diamond ring sparkling brilliantly as he slid hotly into her and kissed her palm.

Mine.

But she didn't want to be his.

After he'd dropped his brothers off upon arriving back from their mini-vacation, he'd had Roger fly him back to Vegas. He'd looked for her, asked around, then flown to New Orleans, but she hadn't been home either. Not knowing what else to do, he'd simply come home and waited.

He sighed and continued to pace. Maybe he'd go down to the office. He couldn't sleep. He'd already tried that and here he was at three a.m. pacing. The bright lights of D.C. mocked him from beyond the windows.

He needed to do something.

Something.

Anything.

He'd head down and work for a while . . . Maybe then he would be able to forget.

• • •

"Sally said you were in early, like before she arrived there at seven," Aiden said without preamble when Quin answered the phone.

He glanced at the clock. It was nine. He needed to get in touch with Uncle Broderick's law firm before noon. That was a call he really didn't want to make. He'd already dodged Brody's call. Father or son? His uncle would be like telling his dad. Brody, on the other hand, was like his brothers — plus a lawyer. Brody. Yeah, he'd be giving his cousin a call and not his uncle. Though his uncle would probably learn. God, he hoped not.

He just needed to see what he needed to do, what papers he might draw up to protect his family from . . .

He shook his head.

Ella wouldn't come after his family. Or him. She wasn't that way.

But you could be wrong; you were before.

True. So just to be safe, he'd talk to them and see what he needed to do. Be safe, even if it was a bit late.

Quinlan sighed and leaned back. "You know, I'm beginning to think I'm damned if I do or damned if I don't, brother."

Aiden was quiet.

"It's not that, Quin. It's just been a hard year and — "

"You think I don't *know* that? It's me that still has to do physical therapy sessions and is stuck with this damned cane and — "

"Then you should also know that no matter what, we will all worry about you."

"Well, you all need a damned hobby then." He closed his eyes.

"What's the problem, A? I came to work early? So what? A few weeks ago you were wishing I was here more like before. Missed me being here. Now you don't want me here? Don't want me to—"

"Shut up. You know that's not what I meant." Aiden muttered something. "You were there before five this morning."

How the hell did he know that? He glanced to his door and knew that Aiden knew everything that went on in this place. "So?"

"Look," Aiden said, sighing. "Just don't . . . don't overdo. Mom will have my ass."

He rubbed his hand over his face. "Did everyone just forget I'm an adult and have been for some time. And anyway, how would my 'overdoing' be your fault?"

"Because I'm the older brother, dumb ass."

Quinlan smiled. "I'm not a dumb ass, numb nuts."

Aiden chuckled. "I'll be in later."

"Checking up on me?"

"No, I just call to annoy. Ian's the one that checks up and keeps us all appraised. Which reminds me, what did you do? He was on his PC most of the flight, and just after we dropped you off and he was almost home, I heard him on the phone to John."

Quinlan closed his eyes and thumped his head on the desk. "And?"

"I heard your name and he snarled *what*? Boy was pissed."

Great. How did he think he'd keep this a secret?

Well, he *had* already told them the truth, and if they didn't believe him that was their problem. But Ian would be calling or . . .

No, Ian would wait. He was a damned sneaky bastard.

Quinlan looked at the framed photo of him with his brothers last Christmas. He was pale and in a wheelchair, but they all stood before the decorated tree. The other photos were of his nieces and nephews and his parents. One of him and Aiden on a business trip in the Bahamas.

Yeah, family was everything. Because no matter what . . . they were there—at least his was. Sometimes more than he'd like.

"Hello?" Aiden said.

Quinlan shook his head. "What?"

"I said, whatever he found out he was pissed. What did you do?"

"Nothing you don't already know."

Aiden scoffed. "Well, whatever problems arise, we've got your back. You know that, right?"

Quin nodded. "Yeah, I think I remember that after you guys kicked the Traynworthy boys' asses."

Aiden chuckled. "I'd forgotten about that. They deserved it." A woman's voice floated through the phone and two high squeals and laughter.

"Gotta go, Quin. I'll see you in a bit."

Chapter 10

Taos, October

Quin stared at the ceiling in the Richardsons' spare bedroom. He could have stayed over at the house, but the Richardsons had nixed that idea. They wanted to be sure this was what Ella wanted—him being here. His first reaction was to tell them to fuck off.

Then reason settled.

He knew they cared for her. They'd watched out for her when he hadn't been here. So he agreed and thanked them for their hospitality.

The cops didn't do a damn thing, at least not in his opinion. They'd asked a few questions, made some notes and said they'd be in touch tomorrow—today as it were—if she hadn't turned up.

The Richardsons vouched for him. He provided his name for the police, his number, and then nothing.

She was an adult. Thankfully, there wasn't a waiting period to look for a missing person.

But she was still missing.

Missing and scared. He'd told them about the phone call. The Richardsons had said she was scared of something or someone. And again they'd actually vouched for him saying no, she hadn't been scared of Quinlan.

He should probably call Brody. Just in case.

He might be stupid when it came to women—seemed a given at this point. But he knew enough to know that the police always looked to relatives when someone went missing. Hell, he was the perfect suspect. Wife gone and hiding, no contact with her husband for months, then he finds out about a baby and she goes missing?

Luckily he could prove he didn't know, that he had no clue and that he'd been in the air on his way here when she went missing. He had the time stamp for the rental on the receipt and Mr. Richardson could corroborate when he'd arrived, as the barking dog—a husky—was theirs.

Where the hell was she? He glanced at the clock on his phone. Three a.m. Christ, he hadn't slept. Couldn't sleep.

He kept hearing her voice. Her voice and the fear and . . .

Screw it.

He slid his thumb across his phone and pulled up Brody's contact info. Maybe he'd send the man a text. Text. He didn't want to talk to anyone just yet. They'd have questions and he didn't have any answers.

Might need you. Like really need you. Just an FYI.

He grinned. His cousin would love that.

Then he thought about another text . . . Or not . . .

Ian. It was five a.m. on the East Coast.

Hell. The man probably knew he was married, not that Ian had ever flat out said as much, but Quin knew his brother knew.

Might need that help you offered me once. Will call later. He left it at that.

He tossed his phone onto the bed beside him and then got up, wincing at the ache in his leg. He reached over for his cane and pulled on his jeans. Cold here. Damn. Mountains. He hadn't packed a pair of sweats. But that was the least of his worries.

Pacing one way then the other, he wondered what he could do tomorrow . . . The cops weren't going to look for her, unless he pushed like hell for it. Then again, they probably would, he just wanted them looking now. He wanted to be looking now, he just had no idea where to start.

So he'd damned well push if she wasn't over there come morning.

As of now, the lights were still off in the whole damned house. He could see it from here.

Maybe he could go to where she worked. If she stayed out there before, maybe she stayed there again . . .

Could be. He'd ask Mrs. Richardson in the morning where exactly Ella had worked. From the way they had talked earlier she didn't teach yoga anymore at the studio but at some retreat place or something. And she volunteered at nursing homes. If he had a name, he could simply drive wherever-the-hell it is and see if they'd seen her.

Something was wrong. He'd felt little things being off for months and hadn't damned well paid attention to them, too wrapped up in self-pity again. Life hadn't been the way he'd wanted it. So the hell what. So she hadn't been right there with him, he could have damned well kept in contact.

Hindsight was an evil damned bitch.

God, please . . . he prayed, stopping in the middle of the room.

He couldn't lose her now that he'd found her again.

• • •

The following day

Quinlan stood in the office of the police chief in Taos. Ella still wasn't here. She hadn't showed up during the night, not early this morning either. He'd dodged his brother's and cousin's phone calls that morning. Spoke to the Richardsons and found out what he could about what his wife had been doing.

He'd called and spoken to the chief a couple of times. He had the feeling no one was taking this seriously. Not as seriously as he wanted them to be taking it.

It was already stretching into the twenty-four-hour mark. He rolled his head around on his neck, trying to get the tightness out.

Where the hell was she? He'd been up to the Retreat and found nothing. Weird place for pregnant women. Out in the middle of nowhere, a big sprawling adobe complex that billed itself as a sanctuary from the busy demands of the world. It had taken him almost an hour to drive up there. Now he knew it had been a wasted trip.

"Look, it's not just me. Her neighbors, like grandparents, or parents or whatever, know as well. This isn't like her."

"She's stayed at the place she works, the Retreat, they said before. The Richardsons. The Retreat person we contacted agreed with them."

"Yes, and I just came from there. No one has seen her in two days. She didn't come into work yesterday. Called in and said she wasn't feeling well. She called me, scared and worried. I've told you this. My wife, my pregnant wife is God knows where and . . ."

"And?" the chief asked. He shifted and stood. "Look, Mr. Kinncaid, I looked you up. I know you're used to getting your way, and though I appreciate you wanting to help, perhaps you could let us do our jobs."

"Then do your damned job and find her." His phone vibrated again in his pocket.

"I'm also concerned that you show up and she's missing."

"Really? Really? I get here and realized she's missing. We've been over this. You do the timeline. My whereabouts are tight until we called the cops." Who had done too little. "You know what. Never mind. I'll make a few calls until someone does something."

His phone buzzed again. He looked again. Not her number. He'd put it into his phone. Ian. Again.

Aiden had already buzzed him countless times. It was Saturday afternoon.

Saturday afternoon.

"Mr. Kinncaid, maybe she knew you were coming and just took off instead of wanting to work things out."

Ran from him, the man meant.

"You have no reason to trust me, I get that," he told the man, taking a deep breath. "But my wife is missing and I'm about to rain holy hell down on your entire career and this police department if you don't start looking for her. She's pregnant. Scared someone is going to take the baby. What part of this picture do you not get? She wouldn't have just left. She was waiting on me, she wouldn't worry her neighbors like this either. She's just not like that."

Again the phone buzzed. He glanced at it. Ian. Fuck it.

"What?" he snarled into the damned thing.

"Hello to you to. Where the hell are you? It's Mom's party and—"

He closed his eyes. "Ian, tell her I'm sorry. But I don't have time right now. I need you to find out who the hell will help me here in New Mexico. Because the local cops sure as hell won't."

A beat of silence.

"Where are you?"

He jerked the door open and said over his shoulder, "Never mind. I'll call the feds, maybe they'll be more interested in helping me."

"Mr. Kinncaid, wait."

He walked out and into the hallway.

"Kid?" his older brother asked.

"I need a federal contact out here. Can you get it for me?"

"Depends on where you are, more specifically what the hell are you in the middle of?"

"Mr. Kinncaid. Please, come back and let's talk a bit more."

He gripped the edge of his cane and saw the Richardsons talking to another cop.

"Ian, I'll have to call you back. Tell Brody I'll need him too."

Carmine turned to him. "Oh, thank God you're here. They won't listen to us. Her car. Did you look in her car?"

He nodded. "This morning before I drove over up to the retreat place. It was full of stuff, luggage, boxes. Full."

"She wouldn't have left all that in the car. Why won't they listen?" Her voice trembled. Mr. Richardson pulled her into the circle of his arms. "We'll find her." But his dark brown eyes bore into Quin.

The chief of police motioned them all into a side room. They all filed in along with another cop.

"Okay, we'll go through this again from the beginning. And we'll need a photo."

Which the man, or his patrolmen, should have asked for yesterday — earlier this morning? Whenever.

Quinlan pulled her photo up on his phone. "I have one from about six, seven months ago."

"Oh, there's one here. I was always taking photos of her," Carmine said, and pulled her own phone out. She scrolled through a bit and showed it to the chief.

He nodded and smiled. "Pretty. Can you send it to me?" He gave her his email and watched as she typed it in and sent it to him.

Quinlan started to ask, but waited as the chief sat back down.

Carmine handed the phone to Quinlan. "I took it of her a few weeks ago when we were at the farmers' market."

The breath caught in his chest.

"God, she's beautiful," he whispered. Ella stood in the sun, her hair pulled back from her face in a knot. She was holding an apple. He chuckled. "An apple. We met over apples."

"I know," Carmine said and patted his knee.

So damned beautiful his chest hurt. She was in a pair of yoga pants, black, but a purple tie-dyed shirt stretched over a very pregnant belly. She was holding the apple in one hand while the other cradled her stomach, and she was smiling at the camera. Pregnant. She was carrying his baby.

His wife, his baby.

"God, I missed her," he said softly. "She was always beautiful, but now . . . she's just . . ." Pregnant and smiling. "Wow."

"I can send that one to you and the others I took," Carmine said.

He gripped the head of his cane and realized his hands shook, nodded and just stared at that smiling face he'd fallen in love with. He zoomed her face closer and traced the dimples. Swallowing, he handed the phone back and looked to the chief. "You have to find her. Please," he said.

The chief was studying him. "Holy hell?"

Quin held his stare. "And then some."

"We've already written the report up, I'll get it pushed through and sent out everywhere. We'll get her photo circulating as well. Might want to send it to your friends, email, online social medias, that sort of thing."

Yeah, like he had a Twitter account?

"We'll want to talk to you more."

He nodded. "Fine. I'm not going anywhere. I'll help however I can."

His phone buzzed again but he didn't answer it.

• • •

Washington, D.C., later that day

Ian Kinncaid sighed as his mother wiped her nose on Jock's white handkerchief. She was decked out in some sort of silky dress that reminded him of a peacock with the blues and greens melding together.

"Have any of you heard from him? Seen him today?" she asked.

No one asked to whom she was referring. He checked his phone again; still not so much as a text after that last short burst that had told him nothing other than his brother was in New Mexico and not here in D.C. to make their mother's party. They were all waiting, planning a family meal here at the hotel before the party.

What the hell was going on with their younger brother now?

Aiden said, "Mom, don't worry. I'm sure he'll be here later making a grand entrance."

Gavin shook his head. "I'm sure he's fine. You know Quin. He

94

doesn't do crowds too much anymore. Maybe he just had a bad night and needed some quiet time."

Aiden made a noise in his throat.

Jock merely looked from Aiden to Ian and back to his wife. "Kaitie lass, don't worry. He'll be here. You know he will."

Ian checked his watch again and stepped away.

Aiden stepped up beside him and pulled at the collar of his tux. They'd gone all out on planning Mom's party.

"Have you heard from him?"

Ian shook his head. "Not since he called earlier. And that's not a convo you want to hear about just yet."

"Kid's been weird the last few months. Where the hell is he? Mom's crying for God's sake, she's so worried. He better have a damned good explanation for this."

Ian agreed, but he also knew there was only one thing—one someone that could possibly pull Quin away from them all without the kid saying a word.

He pulled his phone out and noticed that none of the calls he'd made previously to Quinlan had been returned.

He pressed his brother's number again—simply by hitting redial.

Kid wasn't going to answer any more this time than he had the other times Ian had tried to call him. Or Aiden or whoever else in the family had tried.

He waited for the voice mail to click on.

"Hello?"

Ian glanced to their parents and then stepped away. "Where are you and what the fuck is going on?"

For a minute there was only silence.

"Quinlan?"

"She's not here. No one knows where she is, Ian."

Ian frowned. "Who's not there?"

"Ella. She's not here. You said—you said if I ever needed anything . . ."

Quinlan didn't sound right. Normally short, his voice had held a slight irritated edge of late. But now, now he just sounded . . . flat, controlled. Too damned controlled.

"Ella's not there?"

"She called me last night, worried and scared. I flew out here. She was scared, Ian. Scared someone would . . . fuck." Quinlan blew out a breath. "Jesus Christ, I want to hit something."

Ian looked up as Rori stepped up beside him and rested her hand on his shoulder. Aiden was watching him.

"What's going on?"

"She wasn't here. Didn't pick me up like she was going to. We can't find her. The police are finally looking. Got here and she wasn't . . . *We can't find her.*"

He heard the fear in his brother's voice.

"Where are you?" he asked again.

"There's more," his brother said.

Ian listened, but Quin didn't continue.

"Where is he?" Aiden asked quietly.

Ian shook his head.

"Ian . . ." Quin took a deep breath.

"Are you in New Orleans?" he asked his brother, wishing now he'd just kept tabs on Ella, boundaries be damned anyway. This wasn't going to be good.

"No. No, I'm not. She was so scared when she called. Terrified."

"Of what?"

"So I flew out here and she's missing. The police are at least looking into it now. They didn't last night when we called them. Or maybe they did and I just didn't see it."

Ian had no idea who the "we" was, as all of the people Quin might have with him were standing in this room.

"Okay. Okay, I'll see what I can find out on this end and—"

"Ian. She's pregnant. Due in a few weeks."

"Fuck." Ian strode to the windows overlooking the Potomac and ran a hand over his face. "Yours?"

"Yeah."

Ian shook his head. "Did you know?"

"Oh yeah, I left my pregnant wife to fend for herself. I'm just that great a guy."

"I just—"

"Until last night, I didn't know a damned thing. She was scared they were going to take the baby. Our baby. A girl from what she said. She was rambling and not making a lot of sense, honestly. And now she's missing."

"Right when you show up. Where are you, Quinlan?"

"At the police station in Taos."

"Taos? New Mexico?"

"Yeah."

Then he shook his head and snapped his fingers at Brody. "We'll head out there, Quinlan. Don't talk to the cops. They'll just focus on you and —"

"I already know that, but I'm talking to them anyway. Filed a missing persons report because I pushed like hell with the chief of police here and —"

"And I'll bring Brody, just in case."

For a minute there was only silence again. Then Quinlan cleared his throat. "Tell Mom I'm sorry I missed the party."

"A few others of us will apparently be missing it as well." He glanced over at the people now standing there watching him. The rest of the family. Great. "What do you want me to tell them?"

"I don't know. The truth?"

Ian laughed. "And that would be what?"

"She's my wife, Ian. Ella's my wife."

Ian sighed and ran his hand over his head again. "I know, Quin. I've known. Leave me the fun stuff. Ass. Keep your phone on you. I'll call you back."

Ian hung up and shared a look with Rori. Then he turned to his parents. "Quin won't be making it. And Rori, Brody and I need to leave."

"Is he okay?" their mother asked. Jock put his hands on her shoulders.

"He's not in the hospital with a bullet wound or —"

"Not funny," Rori muttered.

Both his parents narrowed their eyes at him. Ian held up his hands. "Sorry. He's . . . Look, he . . . he . . . ."

Brody cleared his throat and raised a dark brow.

"He went to get your birthday present," he said finally. "And . . ."

"And?" Aiden asked. "This birthday present was in Taos, New Mexico?"

"Yes. Um . . . well . . . he wanted to introduce you." That sounded good. He looked to Rori, who smirked.

"Please, keep going, love. Can't wait to see how you'll do this," Rori said softly beside him.

"Introduce? You mean a girlfriend?" his mother asked, smiling. "And he wants to introduce her? To us? Like bring her home? Oh thank God, I've been so worried about him."

No one said anything for a bit. The last woman Quinlan had brought home almost killed a good portion of them.

"Sort of," Ian hedged.

"A . . . boyfriend?" his mother ventured. Then she said in a rush, "Because if he's gay, that's okay. We'll welcome whomever he loves."

Brayden chuckled. "This is going down in the family books."

Ian could have fun with his little brother, but sadly this wasn't the time. "Mom, Quin's not gay."

"Well, he hasn't dated anyone."

"Might be a reason for that," Brody finally ventured.

"For God's sake, I heard you say Ella," Aiden said. "What has she got to do with Quinlan not being here?"

Ian looked at his older brother. "Ella's missing."

"Who's Ella?" their father asked.

Yeah, how to explain that one?

Taking a deep breath, Ian stretched his neck. "Ella's Quin's . . . wife." What the hell. "His missing pregnant wife."

Chapter 11

New Orleans, late February

Quinlan grabbed enough food at the market to feed both him and her for a couple of days. He'd taken the afternoon off of work, flown down out of Dulles, and here he was.

Why the hell not?

How many years had he put in? He owned the business, or part of it. They had a board, plenty of managers. He could take a few afternoons off, a few days, and the Kinncaid empire would not fall down around their ears.

He checked his watch again. He hoped she was okay with him just showing up.

Quinlan sat on her stoop with the bags and opened a bottle of water. The light was fading quickly. He hoped to hell she didn't walk home in the dark.

He also wondered if the shelter had gotten his gift. He'd called last week and made sure a local art store had delivered the supplies he'd wanted the kids there to have. He hoped the kids enjoyed it. Granted, his family had always helped others, but after Ella two weeks ago, he'd looked into local shelters in the D.C. area. Especially women's shelters. He knew that many of them left with their kids, had no place to go. Kids like to draw and art was a great way to deal with issues you couldn't let out any other way. He'd drawn enough in the last year, and even more in the last couple of weeks. In the last week, he'd painted again. So he also researched art therapy in theory and then talked to Dr. Garner about starting art therapy projects in a couple of the shelters, maybe even some of the after-school programs. He'd gotten the balls rolling and, actually, he enjoyed it. Enjoyed knowing he might be able to help someone, or at least give a kid a reason to believe, to just be able to breathe. Art had done that for him, though very few knew that.

Hell, it had helped him deal with the mess in the last couple of weeks—lovely mess that she was. Drawn, sketched, painted.

Painted her. Painted New Orleans. Painted colors. Bright vibrant colors. He'd forgotten how much he loved art.

Until color had come dancing into his life.

He'd thought about asking his brothers to donate as well, but then didn't. He wanted this for his own—his own secret, for some reason.

But he did want to share it with someone.

"Well, there's a sight I didn't expect to see, sugar," she drawled, pulling him from his musings.

And there she was . . . dancing color.

He tilted his head and studied her, noticing her hair first and the fact she was dressed in more tie-dyed yoga clothes. The clothing melded orange and purple together in a bright burst that worked and matched her hair. "Purple this week, huh?"

"The blue was too . . ." she started, coming closer. "Blue."

Quinlan grinned and nodded. "Purple is a bit different, but you are as well." It didn't bring out the blue of her eyes as much as the blue had. Now her eyes looked darker, more greenish, the amber flecks near the center more prominent.

She just looked at him until he pulled himself up to his feet and held the market bags out. "I come bearing gifts."

She stopped at the bottom of the stoop. He watched her take a deep breath. What if she wanted him to go? If she did, he'd probably go. After he tried to talk sense into her. They were married . . . as stupid and impulsive as that had been, they were married.

Brody would have lots to say when he learned about this trip, but Quin didn't care. He'd called his cousin a couple of days ago and fessed up, sent him copies of the marriage certificate, listened as Brody had yelled and ranted at him for thinking with his dick and not with his brain.

Personally, he was so damned happy his cock worked—and very well at that—that he didn't care what he'd been thinking with.

He hadn't planned this, but as she'd told him the day he met her, plans often went awry, so what were they going to do about it?

"Bless your heart, thanks. Now I don't have to go shopping. What did you bring? Come on." She motioned to him and he followed her around the corner of her house and into the courtyard. They used the kitchen entrance and she held the door open for him as he carried in the bags. He had a backpack slung over his shoulder with extra jeans and a couple of shirts. "So?"

"So," he said, setting the groceries on her wooden countertops. He turned and looked at her.

Her grin tugged at him and he stepped closer, leaning his cane to the side. She didn't move back.

That's one thing he liked about her. She went toe to toe with him, or at least he remembered her doing that.

"I missed you," he whispered as he leaned down and kissed her.

Her sigh wafted across his mouth. "I missed you too, even though I knew it was stupid. And I tried like hell not to."

"Maybe not stupid."

"Oh, sugar, stupid on so many levels."

He kissed her, kissed her again, so happy to have her in his arms. "Maybe I like being stupid, consider it living a little," he told her, remembering something she'd told him in Vegas.

"Why are you here? Didn't you get my note?" She pulled back. "Oh my God, you didn't get my note, did you?" She shook her head.

"Yes, I got that lovely bit. Which reminds me, how did you get home? Did you get the money? Did it cover your ticket? You could have ridden home with me, Ella. I was worried and didn't know if you got home okay."

"I'm here, aren't I? Yes, I received your note and the money, which I didn't need."

At his narrowed look, she added, "But thank you."

He tugged her closer. "I have a confession to make."

"What? We're not really, legally married?" she asked, her eyes hopeful.

Well then. He could only laugh, though what was funny, he wasn't sure. Maybe the fact he'd spent years loudly proclaiming his aversion to the matrimonial state and here he was married to someone who clearly would be happy to not be married to him. The irony wasn't lost.

"Oh, honey, we are very," he said, leaning down and kissing her, "very much married. Really, really married." He nibbled on her lip. "And I'm told very, very much legally."

She sighed into him. "This'll never work. I'm here, you're . . . wherever you're from." She kissed his jaw even as her fingers went to work on his shirt, her fingers cool as she slipped them beneath his T-shirt.

"D.C. Washington, D.C."

"I'm not the politician type of wife."

He picked her up and walked to the bedroom kissing her all the while, all but ripping her shirt off of her. "Great thing I'm not a politician then. I've thought about you all damned week. And the week before that. About this. About us." He slid a hand beneath the waistband of her yoga pants and grinned as he kissed his way down her body, tasting, savoring, enjoying. He stopped at the dragonfly tattoo and kissed the winged creature no bigger than an inch in fading shades of green, blue and purple. *Trust.* He traced the letters with his tongue.

Her hands tugged him up and back to her mouth. "Now. You can play later."

"I want to play now, honey."

She hooked her ankles in the small of his back. "Later. I want you now. You're not the only one who missed this, missed us, thought about it all this week." She arched up, trying to come into contact with him. "And all last week."

He grinned down at her. "Nice to know you missed me. I'll make sure you always do."

He took them up quickly, the fire between them already out of control and burning them both before he'd known what had happened.

They lay there shuddering after, the room cool without the heater on. He huffed out a breath and fell to the side of her, pulling her closer to him.

He still had his jeans on. Damn. And they hadn't used anything. Hell.

"Ummm. Condom. I'm sorry, I wasn't thinking and —"

She shook her head. "The pill, we're good."

He sighed and pulled her to him, kissing her forehead. "Next time we're going slow and easy . . ."

"Who the hell wants slow and easy when our way is so much more fun?" she quipped.

He laughed and kissed her long and deep.

• • •

One month later

"What are you doing?" she asked herself in the mirror. She had to tell him. She just hadn't worked up to it yet. About the time she thought she wouldn't have to, he'd surprised her for dinner one evening, having flown in for the weekend. What the hell did she say to that? He came every weekend for the last three weeks. This was the fourth weekend.

Not that she wanted to say much of anything. She liked spending time with Quin. It was great. They'd talked and laughed, spent time at the shelter. She'd watched as he'd sketched the kids in caricature, bringing smiles where before there had only been wariness.

They talked of expanding homes, of music, of their work.

Work.

"Tell him," she told herself in the mirror before tugging the towel tight and opening the door.

Taking a deep breath, she said, "You know we really need to figure out what we are actually doing," she muttered as she hurriedly dressed. Steam wafted out of the bathroom from their hot shower, where he'd already left her.

He laughed as he buttoned his shirt. "Babe, if you need to figure out what we were actually doing, I'll be more than happy to—"

She threw a pillow at him and he batted it away.

"That is not what I mean and you know it."

"I think going along as we are is working just fine."

She sighed and fiddled with her T-shirt before pulling it on.

"What?" he asked. "What are you going to say this time?"

"What I've said before. This isn't going to last, Quin. Not you and me. We're from different worlds."

Who could just fly into New Orleans for a lunch or dinner? Just because? The weekend she could understand, but every weekend since the first time he'd shown up on her stoop with food, not so much.

How did she . . .

"Look," he told her. "I don't want to end this."

"Ending 'it'—this—whatever it is between us or isn't—"

"*Is*," he said, staring at her with a look she already knew as stubborn. Quinlan was incredibly laid-back and pretty easygoing, but on some things he was as hardheaded as they came.

"It's the smart thing to do. Ending it, that is. Come on, be honest, have you even told your family yet?" She stopped breathing, and for one stupid second hoped.

"Not yet, no." He raked a hand through his hair.

She waved her hand and swallowed the surprising sting of disappointment. "See, that's my point. We both know this isn't . . . meant to be or whatever. We're a fun time to each other. The smart thing to do is to get this annulled or whatever we need to do." She already knew that his eyes tightened whenever she brought up divorce. Why, she had no idea. It wasn't like they had a real marriage.

He nodded and zipped his carry-on. "Maybe it is the smart thing." He turned to her then. "Honestly, though, I'm kind of tired of always doing the smart thing. It's what I've done all my life, Ella. I want . . . I want . . ."

She cocked a brow. "Your leg back. I know, I've heard of all the things you can't do. Ski. Run. Marathons. Tennis. Poor you. Get over it. You are beyond blessed, stop worrying about what you see as limits and see what you can accomplish."

He narrowed his gaze at her. "That's not what . . ." He raked a hand through his hair. "I can be pissed at my limitations, they're mine," he snapped. Then he shook his head. "Look, my leg is beside the point, we have something between us. Something special, and I want to see where it goes."

"Yes, it's called lust, Quin." She hurried around her room, grabbing up stuff and hurrying into the hallway. He had to leave this alone.

"Why do all your yoga pants hug your ass? Not that I don't enjoy the view in tie-dyed black, but I don't like that everyone else gets to see it. Can't you change at the studio?"

Really? That was a concern? "Sugar, I've dressed like this for years and haven't been accosted once."

Okay, that wasn't exactly true, there was that one time, but she sure as hell wasn't going to mention that now.

"You take cabs to the studio? Or gym or whatever?" he asked as she walked past him and into the kitchen.

She muttered to herself as she jerked open the fridge in the small kitchen and filled up her pink water bottle.

"What?" she asked at his mumble.

"Do you take a cab to your yoga thing?"

"Thing? You mean my job? For most of us, jobs are not 'things' but necessary parts of life."

He took another breath and held up his hands. "Fine. Do you take a cab to work?" he asked precisely.

Her head tilted and she just looked at him. "Protective much? Quin, I survived just fine before you. I'm fine."

"You know when you get all snappy it turns me on."

"Everything turns you on."

"I'm a guy, where you're concerned that's the truth. So that's a no, you don't take cabs?"

"Not always, why?"

He opened his mouth, thought better of it and shut it. She just stared at him.

"Fine. I don't like it," he blurted.

"Excuse me? Don't like what? The fact I work?"

"You want to pick a fight, don't you?" he asked, shaking his head. "No, I'm fine with you working. I don't like the idea of you walking the Quarter by yourself. Please take a cab."

"Honey, you worry way too much." She shoved the water bottle in a multicolored bag she always carried. "No one will hurt me. Everyone walks here."

He walked over to her and put his hands on her shoulders. "I know you are independent and used to being on your own. And though we don't know where we or us will be tomorrow . . . for now, you are *mine*."

His?

Her eyes flashed, but she didn't say anything.

"I protect what's mine." He leaned down and kissed her softly, just a press of lips against hers. "Always."

She stared at him for a moment and he wondered what she would say.

Finally, her breath huffed out. "Fine, if it'll keep your sensibilities aligned I'll take a cab."

He didn't smile.

"This time," she had to add. "It's amazing I managed in life until you ran into me."

He smiled behind her as she went back to the bedroom.

"Are you staying another day or not?" she hollered from the room.

He was already packed, and honestly, he probably should get back to D.C. But he didn't really want to.

"Tomorrow. Don't worry, I have things to check on at the hotel here." She came back into the living room, her bag slung over her shoulder.

"You can stay there with me tonight if you want."

She shook her head. "I like my own space. Hotels are so . . ." She scrunched up her nose. "Sterile."

They gathered their stuff and she grabbed her keys. He waited while she locked up and looked up and down the street. Granted, there were not many people out now. Too early in the morning, but still . . .

He caught the glance from the corner of her eyes. "Look, why don't we compromise. You can walk me to the studio, call a cab and go to the hotel?"

He supposed that was as good as it would get. "Yes, I'll beat any would-be muggers off with my cane."

"Oh, I know you would. And I could"—she skipped ahead of him and whirled her bag around—"beat them with my bag."

He smiled, innocence flashing briefly in the midst of this place.

She waited for him. "You know, it's Monday. You could go with me tonight to the shelter."

"Sure. Railey Anne's mom find a job yet?"

"No, not yet." She released a breath he hadn't realized she'd been holding. "Okay? Just like that?"

"Yeah, why not?"

Her eyes ran over him from the top of his head to his shoes. Businessman that he was, he knew he also fit in here, morning or night, on these streets.

"I still get surprised to see you helping out at the shelter, I don't know why. Stupid, I know, but you don't exactly look like the shelter type."

So he hadn't been in a while, that was true. "It's not like I haven't ever been to shelters or helped out. Mom used to take us over our holiday breaks."

"Really?"

He nodded. "I hear the snobbery in that one word."

She shrugged. "Sorry."

"It's okay. Mom gave medical care where she could. Kids need care and they don't always go to the clinics near the shelters, even if they are free. Mom has a way with people, they just sort of trust her."

She chuckled and he laced their hands together. He didn't think about the fact she didn't pull away. He was just glad of it.

"So what did you do there while she did her nurse thing?"

He didn't correct her assumption that his mom was a nurse, as he hadn't told her his mother used to be a pediatric surgeon. She already shied and dropped hints about the differences in their economic brackets. Stupid as hell is what it was.

Intelligent was intelligent. Beauty was beauty and chemistry was chemistry.

Married was married.

"Drew. Colored. Painted," he admitted. It was the only time he did any of those things after Susy died when they were seven. "Whatever. I usually drew with the kids. Brought some paints a few times. Easier though to just do stuff with markers and pencils and whatnot."

She tilted her head again, the sun glinting off the purple strands. He sort of missed the blue. Cotton candy, Aiden called her.

He smiled.

"I have yoga at the senior center late this afternoon."

"I know, I remember. And tomorrow morning at the nursing home."

She pulled on their joined hands until he leaned down.

"You are really short," he muttered.

She kissed his cheek. "You are just used to a family of giants."

"Fe fie fo fum . . ." He waggled his brows. "And you make a pretty princess."

She shoved him. "Hurry up. I'm going to be late."

"My fondest wish . . ." She glared at him.

• • •

The night grew quiet around them as they sat on the couch. Dinner was done and the kitchen straightened up. His flight was in the morning.

She shifted again beside him.

"What aren't you telling me?" he finally asked. She'd acted off this morning, but he just wrote that off as her running late. Lately though, she was quieter, and that just wasn't like her; he'd come to realize she shared her thoughts, opinions, hopes, dreams, whatever was on her mind. This weekend, though, she'd been too quiet.

Finally she turned to him and took a deep breath and then another.

His stomach tightened. He reached over and picked up her hand. "Just tell me."

"Before I met you, I applied for a job." She shrugged. "I've been thinking of moving for some time and well . . ." She blew out a breath. "Confession. I got the job and accepted it."

He sat there for a minute and then another. Finally, he stood up. "Okay. Where's the job?"

For one stupid moment, he wondered if she'd say in the D.C. area. Of course not.

"New Mexico. Taos, actually."

He strode to the window. "New Mexico. What kind of job?"

"Well, a yoga instructor like I am here."

"What's wrong with here?"

He heard her sigh, but he didn't turn around. "Nothing, but I've never been one to plan my choices around a man. I did that once and it ended badly."

He turned and looked at her. "When? What happened?" Then he shook his head. "Never mind, I guess it's none of my business." She'd never mentioned a job or a possible move, but then why would she? She'd been adamant from the beginning about what she thought of them together, of their marriage.

"Quinlan, I've tried the rich boy marriage before, and trust me when I say it would not work. Not for the long haul."

He shook his head. Married. She'd been married before. "You never said you'd been married before."

"Like that would have made a difference. We went to Vegas, we got drunk as college co-eds and visited a twenty-four-hour marriage chapel, for God's sake!" She stood up and started to pace. "Can we just leave it at the fact that Lance and I did not work? He chose his very important family, very prominent family."

"Over you? Man was an idiot."

She raked a hand through her hair. "He knew we were from different worlds before I did."

"Different worlds? Hell, Ella, this is the twenty-first century! No one cares about that crap. We're married."

She held up her hand. "I don't want to be, Quin. I'm a free spirit, you even said."

"You're *my* free spirit. Do I . . ." He bit down. "Damn it, Ella. We're married! Why won't you give us a chance?"

"You're a great guy. An amazing guy."

He simply looked at her. "If this is where you say something stupid like 'it's not you, it's me,' I'd advise you to keep those words to yourself."

"Okay, then." She paced away and then back.

He had no idea what to say. "Why? Is it because of this other guy?" A dark feeling crept into him. "Did he hurt you?"

She shook her head. "Not in the way you mean. No. It's just . . . He came from a family like yours and . . ." She swallowed. "I'm not going into it all. It just didn't work, Quinlan."

"So what? A marriage when you were younger didn't work out," he tried. "That's not to say ours wouldn't. It was a while ago, when you were younger?"

She merely looked at him. "Yes. Years ago, actually."

"Okay then. I still don't see the problem, Ella. We're adults. I want this. I want you. I want—"

"Fine. You want this? You want me? If this marriage is so damned real, so important to you, then why haven't you told your family about me?" she said on a rush, and he saw it then, a flash of hurt in her aquamarine eyes before they flashed angry. "Why haven't you told them about us? About the marriage at all? It's been over six weeks, Quin, since we did the deed. Two weeks apart and every weekend since. Why in all that time haven't you told me what they thought of our little surprise?"

He could only stare at her.

And she only stared at him. "See. I was stupid to think . . ." She sighed. "Again. I don't blame you, I don't, not really or maybe I do. I don't know. I just know I'm not the type of woman a man like you takes home to his mother. I was taught that the hard way once. Guess I needed another reminder."

He slashed his hand through the air. "Stop it. Stop talking about yourself that way."

"Evidence speaks, Quin."

He'd fucked up. He hadn't known what he'd wanted, he'd wallowed in self-pity and wondering what to do and now here he stood.

"I'll tell them. We can call them now."

She swallowed, then met his eyes, her chin jutting up. "Now?" She shook her head. "I took the job, I've already got a place to live. I'm going to New Mexico and I don't want you to follow me."

Quinlan could only stand there. He blinked then blinked again.

"This isn't it. We are *not* over."

She swallowed and her eyes, always so bright with life and laughter, dulled. "I get you were probably confused and I know you were working through what happened to you and what that woman did to you."

He'd told her of Elianya one night.

"What does that have to do with us?"

"Quinlan, there's not really an us. We were . . . we were a good time for each other. We were . . . we were sort of a weekend fling that went a little longer than either one of us anticipated."

"A weekend fling?" He wanted this to work for them. "I was looking for houses back home for us, guess that was a mistake too."

She blinked but didn't say another word.

"I was thinking and planning on a future for us and you were already moving on," he said softly. He walked back to the bedroom and grabbed his bag. "All you had to say was no, Ella. That one word and I would have respected it and left."

He grabbed his jacket and walked to the door.

"And yet, you never once told anyone about us, did you? For someone planning for us to be a permanent us, that seems odd."

He was pissed, angry at her for not seeing them as he did, and at himself for exactly what she was accusing him of.

"You can't have it both ways, Quinlan."

He turned back and looked at her standing there in leggings and one of his damned T-shirts that swallowed her.

"Did you tell anyone about us?"

She nodded. "Yeah, I told Shalon and Marie, who told me to go for it. Who wouldn't want a handsome rich husband? I only said I didn't need a rich husband, handsome was negotiable. I didn't tell them that you had yet to tell your family about me."

He swallowed and nodded. "We can make this work."

"Maybe, maybe not," she said, waving her hands as she started to pace. "But I want time to think, to follow through with my own plans without you there telling me what we need or don't need to be."

There might still be a chance.

She held up her hand. "I leave at the end of the week and I already talked to a realtor."

"Realtor?" The ground that had been so solid and real for the last month had shifted, quick as hot sand, and he couldn't find even ground. Realtor?

"I need some time to think." She leaned up slowly, her small hand on his shoulder, and kissed him when he leaned down. "I'm sorry."

He only looked at her. "I am too, Ella. I believe in us, as stupid as that clearly is. I'm not filing. If you want free of us so damned badly, you file. Brody Kinncaid is my lawyer. He's in New York, have yours contact him." He opened the door, still angry, still . . . damn it.

"You didn't have to run, Ella. You love it here. If I bother you that much—"

"It's not all about you, Quinlan. I applied for this job and thought of moving before I met you. And then you showed up and things changed, and after you . . ."

"You mean after us?" Us, not us, who the hell knew?

"Quinlan, sometimes you don't listen or you only hear what you want to. This won't work, not in the long run, why won't you see that?"

"Or maybe I'm the only one who actually hears. I always thought of you as courageous, Ella. At least be honest with yourself. You're the one running. You're the one that doesn't really want this. I don't blame you for being pissed at me for not telling my family. I should have dragged you to meet them the first week. I messed up." He stepped toward her, but then shook his head. Damned if he'd beg for something she didn't want. This time, she could damned well come to him. He reached again for the door, and without turning back to her, he said, "If you need anything, you know my number."

With that, he walked out, having forgotten his stupid cane. He wasn't going back for it.

At the hotel, no one asked what he was doing there. The next morning, he flew home and tried to forget her.

Chapter 12

Albuquerque, October

Noises mumbled down a long tunnel.

Wake up. Have to wake up! There was something she needed to do. Something.

Her eyes wouldn't stay open, it was so hard to focus. So hard. She quit fighting it and finally let her eyes shut. Sounds rocketed through her eardrums but didn't make any sense. In and out, loud then nothing.

"Ella!"

She opened her eyes to bright lights shining.

Panic iced through her. They were back, back, and they'd take her baby.

She jerked.

"Whoa. Whoa. Settle down. You're in the hospital. Ella, can you understand? You need surgery."

She blinked up at the man above her. Doctor.

Doctor.

Couldn't trust the doctors. Couldn't trust them at all.

She tried again to twist away. "My baby. I want my baby. Where's my baby?" she tried to ask, not sure if she did, if they heard her. She screamed the words again, and yet barely a sound came out. Her hands shook as she tried to lift them, tried to . . . to . . .

"Ella. You need surgery. The police want to talk to you, can you do that?"

She barely heard as someone mentioned something about a few minutes, but that was all.

"Ella. Ella, I'm Detective Hudson. We need your help to find your baby."

Baby. Baby. Her baby girl. "She has red hair," she whispered.

"Who has red hair?"

"Baby," she whispered, trying to keep her eyes open. Chills danced over her skin, again and again. "Like her father. Red."

"Okay. Ella, do you know who took your baby? And it was a girl? Did you have a girl?"

The question echoed to her. She nodded.

She tried to swallow and realized her throat hurt. She blinked up at the policeman. Brillo pad, rusted Brillo pad flashed through her brain. The man's fuzzy hair stood up. She focused on his face and realized he was older; his dark flat eyes bore into her.

"Who took your baby, Ella? Do you know?"

She nodded. "They did. The Nursery. Just like the others."

He frowned and she shut her eyes. "I don't want to be here." Doctors couldn't be trusted, nor the nurses. They lied. They all lied.

Tears welled up and she tried to sit up, but the cop's hand on her shoulder held her down. "Be still, Mrs. Kinncaid. It is Kinncaid, isn't it?"

She nodded. Too tired to explain it all. Did Quinlan know? "Please, please, tell my husband."

Her voice was barely more than a whisper. Not that it mattered. She tried to sit up again, tried to roll to the side so she could sit up, but again the policeman held her down.

"The officer said your husband is Quinton? Kinncaid from D.C.?" the cop asked.

She shook her head. "No, Quinlan. Please tell him."

So stupid, how could she be so damned stupid? She'd trusted the wrong people, believed the lies. She whispered Quinlan's name again.

"He's on his way. Someone's already contacted him. He reported you missing earlier today. Can you tell me, Mrs. Kinncaid, who took your baby? Do you know?"

She tried to focus on his words, the question, her answer. Did she know?

"I want my baby. I want my daughter," she tried again. There was too much to explain. She had to go. Had to leave. Had to get out and find her daughter.

"Please. Please help me," she begged him. "Please. Help me. I have to find her. Lisa took her."

His eyes, something in the dark depths shifted. "I'll help you, Mrs. Kinncaid. You have to help me though. Who did this?"

"Help me get out of here. Please," she whispered brokenly, feeling her eyes tear up. "Please . . . have to stop them."

"You need help too. Let us look," the cop told her. "That's what we do."

She tried to get up, tried to push his hands away.

"Lisa?"

"Hammerstein," she mumbled. "My baby. Please . . . I have . . . to . . ."

More voices asked her to calm down.

The doctor was back. She shook her head. "No. No. Please. Let me go. Let me go," she yelled, or tried to. Only broken fragments of her words whispered out.

Tears slid down her cheeks. "I have to find her. I have to find her." Tears choked her, her chest tightened. Her daughter could be anywhere. They would lie. Lie and keep her daughter from her. She had to . . .

She saw the syringe. She knocked it out of the nurse's hand. "No. No, I have to leave. I have to find her." Again she tried to sit up, gripping the cop's jacket in her fist, straining to sit up.

Someone knocked him aside and stood in front of her. She realized they were moving her, the lights along the ceiling blinking, flashing. Bright. Dark. Bright. Dark.

Still she tried to get away. Crying and begging in broken whispers that no one heard, she reached over and jerked out the IV she felt in the back of her hand.

"Damn it."

The lights grew blurrier.

"We need to get her into surgery," a voice said.

She tried to tell them no, tell them to wait. A face floated above hers. "You are safe, Mrs. Kinncaid. We're going to help you."

Quinlan, she needed Quinlan. He'd find their baby.

Their baby.

A jagged memory of holding the small body against her knifed through her just before everything went dark.

• • •

En route to Albuquerque, October

Quinlan tapped his fingers on the armrest of the unmarked police car. Some detective with the state police — Quin didn't remember his name — was driving with his partner.

They'd found her. The call had come in just a few minutes after he and the Richardsons had left. Mr. and Mrs. Richardson had decided to stop off at the store, but he headed back to their place. No idea what to do.

He should call his brother. Ian had called him earlier letting him know that they were on their way. Ian, Rori, Brody and Aiden.

Whatever.

He didn't care.

"Do we not know anything else?" he asked them yet again. "You know, we could have just flown out there in half the time." The jet was still at the airport, but the cops who delivered the news offered to take him. He'd tried to talk them into letting him fly out there, but they argued. He hadn't had time to argue. Should have just ditched their asses and flown out to Albuquerque anyway.

The driver looked in the rearview mirror and met Quin's eyes. "Only what we told you, Mr. Kinncaid. We'll be there soon."

Soon.

Not fucking soon enough. He hadn't been fucking soon enough.

They'd found her in Albuquerque, traumatized and bleeding.

No baby.

No one knew where the baby was. An Amber Alert had been released for his infant daughter.

What the hell had happened?

"You have someone you want us to call for you, Mr. Kinncaid?" the other detective asked from the front seat.

He shook his head, and held out his phone. "I'll call them. They're on their way to Taos anyway."

Quinlan had called the Albuquerque police department and had spoken briefly to a Detective Hudson, who hadn't really told him a damned thing.

All he knew was that his wife was now in surgery. Still, no one knew who had the baby, who took the baby. At least he knew it was a girl. A baby girl.

He swallowed and sighed, rubbing his hands over his face. "How much longer?" It felt like they had been on the road for hours. He couldn't get there fast enough.

"About an hour. Perhaps you'd like to call whomever you mentioned before?"

Part II: Decisions

Chapter 13

Taos, early March

He filed the paper away and leaned back. Great job done. The transfer went wonderfully smooth, but then they generally did.

Only a few times had any issues arisen, and when issues arose they were handled quickly and efficiently.

Transfers were a way of life. A service provided, a needed product supplied.

That's what he did. That's what he'd built. The fact his products were squalling bundles of joy to those who could not have them, well, so be it.

He wouldn't be where he was today if he had let emotion rule all along. Emotion often drove, but should never, ever rule. Logic and sense should rule—and his did.

He turned to his partner.

"How many do we have lined up?"

"Two more, due later this summer and fall. Why?"

He turned his plush leather chair around to stare out the window overlooking the courtyard and the mountains beyond. "I want another bigger incentive. Something . . . special. Something a bit different from our norm."

His partner stared at him for a moment with one brow arched. "Different how? It's not like the buyers know anything other than what we tell them."

True. New parents, once faced with that perfect newborn, did not ask questions. They never wondered if the papers, the information given on the child's birth parents' medical history, was fact or fiction. Assumptions were easier to believe when given a dream come true.

He did that, he provided dreams to those who'd forgotten how to believe, for whatever reasons—emotional, psychological, biological. He gave couples the presents of all presents.

That is what he wanted.

"Yes, I know, but I want an angel that has it all, looks, history, a well-placed family, intelligence, the promised perfect child." He turned back and leveled a look at her, this woman who went along with whatever he wanted, with whatever he asked.

She walked around the corner of his desk, rested her hips against the edge and leaned back, smiling at him. He knew that smile, she wanted him.

"There's only one small problem with that, dear." She slowly untied the side of her scrub.

He rather liked these knew wraparound scrubs. Looked great on her and they were even easier to get her out of than the traditional ones. He should know, God knows he'd taken enough scrubs, and everything else, off the woman.

"If such a perfect woman is in a situation to provide us with a little bundle, she probably won't want to give it up."

He shifted in his chair, resting one elbow on the arm and rubbing his lips with his finger as he watched her.

"And that is a problem why? We'll work on her, talk her into our philosophy of helping others, recommend what would be best for the baby."

She snorted. "Yeah, and if she still doesn't want to give up a baby?"

"Well, then we do what we always do and simply take it."

She grinned and laughed. "And you always say I'm greedy."

He gripped her hips and tugged her closer to him, kissing her now bare, smooth stomach.

"Can you imagine what such a perfect bundle of joy would go for? The buzz of that auction alone?" he asked her, looking up and seeing the greed in her own eyes.

Her fingers slid through his hair. "A boy or a girl?"

He shrugged. "With the right prospective parents, the right spin, it won't matter. The history, the blood is all that would matter."

She chuckled. "The blood and the money."

Now all they had to do was find her. Surely, somewhere there would be a perfect supplier. They'd just have to look.

• • •

Taos, April

Ella told herself she loved it here. She did. A week into a new job was nothing to judge it all on. So things were different here. There was still snow on the ground, for God's sake. She wasn't used to snow, but apparently it was the end of ski season.

Focus!

"And now, everyone's favorite. Breath into child's pose." They had finished an hour of beginner to intermediate yoga class this evening and had moved fluidly through all the stretches.

"Breathe in," she said softly. "And out." She glanced up to see and check postures, to make sure everyone was okay.

A class this new, she still was working on getting to know everyone's names. She had two older people, one of whom was a diabetic. She wanted to keep an eye on her.

"Expel any negative thoughts and energies through your breathing." She waited a moment. "Focus on all the positives in life."

She gave them a few more moments and then class was over.

"Namaste."

The class went from still and tranquil to bustling, with people talking and laughing. She watched them, happy with the middle-aged couple that decided to try something new together. The single moms, the young gallery owner . . . all of them. They were strangers to her.

Usually she connected to people, but as yet there wasn't anyone other than her landlords, the Richardsons, whom she'd had any contact with.

"Excuse me," a woman's voice pulled her attention back to the here and now.

Single woman . . . mother? No, the nurse.

"I'm Lisa and I wanted to say I love your class. Usually, I don't want to stay after the first week. Some of these are like gurus of health and what all nots. I feel like a fake taking the class when all I want is a workout, ya know?" Lisa asked, opening a bottle of water and taking a drink.

"Ummm. Yeah, I guess so. I figure I'm more like an intro into yoga, get people into fitness and healthier choices. If you want the cheesecake for dessert, that's your choice."

Lisa laughed. "You get it."

Ella shrugged. "I don't know if I get it exactly, but I'd rather turn people on with a lighter version of yoga than turn them off with an intense version of it." She nodded over to another instructor coming in. "If intense is what you want, Mark's your man."

Lisa snorted. "He's not really my type. I'm more into the scruffier look."

Ella laughed. "What did you say your name was again?"

"Lisa. I'm Lisa Hammerstein."

"Ella Ferguson, but then I guess you already know that as you've been in my class three times this week." She grinned and grabbed up her stuff, telling others bye and wondering what else she needed. She had a class at the assisted living home tomorrow before she came here. Talk about light yoga.

Lisa was leaning beside the door tapping on the screen of her phone.

"So you teach here three times a week?"

"A few more classes," she told the other woman. "And I give a few sessions out at the retirement homes a few times a week."

Lisa nodded. "Cool. How is that working out?"

She grinned. "Well, you have to be really careful with elderly, they have lots of pride, so it's a matter of making sure they don't hurt themselves, ya know? Mostly, though, it looks like it'll be a great fun group."

Lisa tilted her head. "Look, this might sound weird, but I'm an RN for this group and we're looking for someone to implement an exercise program for a group or groups of pregnant women."

Bundling up, Ella wrapped her multicolored scarf around her neck. "I only teach yoga."

"Yes, but have you taught it to pregnant women before?"

She nodded. "Yes. It's perfectly safe. There are a few moves they shouldn't do, but otherwise it's mostly stretching, balance and, really, focus." Another class? Did she want to teach another class or two? She didn't need the money, but it wasn't like she was doing anything else with her spare time. "Honestly, I don't know. I'm new here. I just moved here a little over a week ago and started work."

Lisa opened the door for them. "Tell ya what, I'm thirsty, and there's a great place around the corner. If you're not busy, we could grab a drink, I'll tell you about the Nursery of Dreams and you can decide."

What the hell.

Ella followed Lisa a couple of blocks down and across the main road to a little organic food store the other instructors had talked about. You could get some great smoothies and juices from here, or so she'd heard.

"I recommend the super green with a shot of energy," Lisa told her.

Instead Ella went with the berry and they settled at an indoor table with a chess board for the top.

Quinlan had mentioned he'd liked chess. She'd never played. She ran her finger over one square. God, she missed him.

Taking a deep breath, she said, "Okay, tell me why I should teach yoga to a bunch of pregnant women."

Lisa smiled and laughed and launched into her pitch.

The next day Ella parked her car in the gravel parking lot. It had taken almost forty-five minutes to drive up here from Taos. In the mountains, though not near the ski runs, the Nursery of Dreams, or the Retreat, as Lisa called it, sat nestled back in a meadow of pines. Well, there were pines on one side, scrub brush opening up to the plains on the other side to the valley below. A sprawling one-story adobe structure sat against the pines. There was even a stucco wall around part of the structure. Probably making a nice courtyard.

She climbed out and breathed deep. One thing about this place, the air was so clean up here. Not like back in New Orleans, where the air was thick with the slow-churning Mississippi and the ever-present Gulf of Mexico. The air in New Orleans was . . . sluggish, slow. Here, though, it was bright, crisp, full of pine, and tickled her nose.

Grinning, she grabbed her yoga mat and walked up the stone-paved walk, the gardens a mixture of stone, cacti, sculpture and some sort of plants, their brittle shoots stunted in the still snow-splotched ground.

She saw pregnant women everywhere she looked. Most were young, her age or younger. Some teens. A couple older. Several asked her where she was heading, what she needed, how they could help her.

Nice place. The inside was like most places in Taos. Clean, almost bare, woven rugs, big windows to enjoy the views, *latilla* ceilings, kiva fireplaces in the corners. There was one great room, she noticed, where a couple of people, very pregnant from the looks of it, were sprawled reading. One was knitting.

Knitting?

She'd strangle herself. Though she'd always wanted to learn, there was something about those long needles that just confused the hell out of her.

"You made it!" Lisa said, coming from a hallway that led off the central desk. Sort of like spokes on a wheel, she thought.

"I did."

"Any trouble?" Lisa asked her, shaking her hand and motioning her to follow.

"No. Drove slow enough a couple of locals in their trucks blew by me and yelled, I'm sure."

Lisa laughed. "Locals drive like bats outta hell around here. And if you don't know the road, go slow."

"I figure I was helping them work on their daily dose of patience."

"Most aren't so bad. We're sort of laid-back around here, unless it's right before the first snowfall or hard freeze, and then everyone everywhere is scrambling it seems like."

She followed Lisa down the hallway, past several rooms, two courtyards, other hallways that branched off.

"What exactly is this place?" she finally asked.

"The Retreat. It's sort of like a weekend spa for expectant mothers. That's our main source of income, frankly, but we're also a live-in community for other expectant mothers that want, or in some cases need, a slower, more unplugged way of life."

"Unplugged?"

Lisa nodded as they walked down the hallway, sun bathing the tiled floors and walls in warmth that she felt every time she walked through a patch of sunlight.

"Yes. We encourage limited use of computers, cell phones, television. Organic foods you take the time to cook, or learn to cook in some cases." Lisa grinned. "I know, it would drive me bonkers as well, but it works. Some that come in with blood pressure issues relax enough that it's not so much of an issue. Still needs monitoring but not, usually, a trip to the hospital."

Unplugging. "And they live here? Sort of like assisted living but for the pregnant woman, not the geriatric."

"Yep. Not all of them, though most you see today are here for the long haul, at least until they deliver."

She looked around and wondered what the cost was to stay in a facility like this.

It wouldn't be cheap, she knew.

"So who am I meeting again?"

Lisa stopped in front of a door. "A couple of our doctors, Dr. Radcliffe and Dr. Merchant."

Ella took a deep breath and followed her new friend into the room. Dr. Radcliffe was older, and reminded her of an older Mister Rogers for some reason. Or Ichabod Crane in a cartoon she'd seen once when she was little. He was nice enough, polite and jovial, but something about him just sat wrong with her. Dr. Merchant, on the other hand, offered her water or coffee or tea. He was a bit younger than the other doctor. Handsome with salt-and-pepper hair. She wasn't sure if he was in his late forties or early sixties—one of those guys who could be any age and you couldn't really pin it down.

The interview consisted of mostly questions about her classes, her form, her yoga practice and her experience.

"Are you married, Ms. Ferguson?"

She lifted the cup of coffee and blew on it. "Umm . . ." Taking a deep breath, she finally said, "No. We're separated."

"Ah. Then if we wanted you to teach a sunrise yoga class, you could possibly stay the evening before, or if a session ran late you could stay overnight?" Dr. Merchant asked, making notes on a pad.

She just looked at him.

"We ask because for those that have families at home, we like to make sure schedules allow them the most time with their families except in extreme cases. If you have a family, spouse, children, whatever, we like to work with our employees to ensure a good work fit with their home life," he told her over the top of his black-rimmed glasses.

Dr. Radcliffe leaned up and laced his fingers together. "We don't believe in jobs creating more strife in lives any more than they normally would." He raised his hands, motioning around him. "Family is the bedrock of our practice. And happy families make happy people and happy people create wonderful successful work environments."

She could only blink. Were they for real? Who spouted that? For a girl who'd cut her teeth in the Quarter of New Orleans, waiting tables, dodging grab-happy co-eds and would-be drunkards, she knew how to work for a paycheck.

"Umm. No, no children."

He nodded and went back to scribbling.

The interview didn't take long, not even half an hour. She wondered about some of their questions. But they always explained their reasons behind them.

The pay was great, and if she got hired on later for more classes, they could discuss benefits.

Before she really thought it through—though what was there really to consider?—she'd agreed to teach a practice session in about an hour to those here to see how it went.

The session went really well.

For the first time since moving, she'd had fun. Really had fun and had laughed. The women were open and loved the yoga session, begging her to come again tomorrow. By the time she'd climbed back in her car, she was scheduled to teach two sunrise classes a week, two evening classes and both every other weekend.

On the way back down to Taos Valley, she cranked the radio and sang along, happier than she'd been in a long time.

The move was the right thing to do.

And if she sang loud enough, believed hard enough, it would be true.

• • •

Six weeks later

New Mexico is wonderful! Land of enchantment! Love it!

Ella stood in the pharmacy section of the local store. Holy hell.

She'd called Quin the night she moved here, letting him know she'd arrived safely. She'd even drafted several emails but never sent them.

He hadn't called her back. Before, when she'd been in New Orleans, he'd call just to call. Send her a text just to say he missed her. Email her stupid funny jokes or cartoons.

Nothing. She changed her phone to a carrier that got better service up here in the mountains. She could send him her number. Or was that just a pathetic, *please call me*? Then again, maybe she should send him something. What? Text him a photo of the mountains?

No, they were over. She'd wanted it over, or she'd thought she had. Would he really want her back? She'd ended it, and if she missed them, then . . . then what?

Work it out?

No, they were over. He hadn't even mentioned to anyone in his family about their marriage. Did she need more proof than that?

But he'd come to her, how many times? Had tried to talk her into coming to D.C. a couple of times, but so what?

No, they were over. She'd made that decision. As her mother used to say, she'd made her bed, so she had to lie in it.

God, it hurt more than she thought it would. But it was for the best, wasn't it? She'd been down that road and there was no way she was going to go down it again, wanting a man, a life, while he hid that life they were building from a prominent family.

Her sessions at the Retreat were working out great. Weather was perfect. Her new house was just her size, her landlords were wonderful.

And her realtor from New Orleans had called to tell her someone wanted her house for the asking price.

She'd be dumb not to take it, so she'd told the man to sell it and gave him her lawyer's contact information to finish the sale. She didn't want to mess with any of it.

One more stress to worry about.

One more.

The house.

Her failed marriage — again.

And now?

Now she'd passed out during the evening session of yoga. One of the girls had hurried to get a nurse — Lisa.

Lisa's questions had tumbled over each other as she'd helped Ella to a chair. The women had all been worried. Ella had a time of it convincing them she was okay. They'd all wanted her to stay tonight.

But one question Lisa had asked her rolled in her brain, over and over.

"Are you pregnant?"

"Of course not!" she'd told Lisa.

"Dr. Radcliffe can run a blood test tomorrow if you want."

She'd shaken her head. "My eating habits have been off. Stress." She'd waved them all off and apologized for having to cut the class short. Laughing, she'd told them, "And that's why it's very, very important that your head is the last thing to come up. If you stand too quickly from a couple of the poses, you could end up sprawled on the ground like me."

Several of the women laughed. Lisa merely leveled a look at her and walked her to her car.

"I'm staying out here tonight. Call me if you need anything. And I'm telling the docs on you."

"I'm fine."

"We take care of our own. We all like you, Ella. Call me when you get home."

Just as she'd climbed into her car, Lisa added, "Go buy a pregnancy test. If you've had sex in the last couple of months you could be pregnant. Nothing is one hundred percent, you know, says so on all the damned boxes."

She'd rolled her eyes.

She wasn't rolling them now.

Now she was standing in the aisle of the local Albertsons Market in Taos wondering what to do.

Could she be?

No.

They'd used protection just about every time they'd made love — well, there were those totally blank hours of Vegas.

Just about were probably the operative words here.

Her appetite had been all over the board, hungry and starving or just flat-out sick to her stomach. But mostly, she was hungry. She turned down another aisle. Feminine products lined the shelves. Ella jerked. When was the last time . . . ?

She hadn't felt very good for weeks but figured it was stress. It *had* to be stress. Just stress. Stress of her and Quinlan, not sleeping well, being tired anyway, moving, a new job, selling the house . . .

But then last week she started to get her appetite back without the nausea so much, which made no sense, but she felt like she was eating all the time. At least when she wasn't working. She made a tub of trail mix earlier in the week and it was almost gone. She normally only had to make it a couple of times a month.

When was the last time . . .

Really? Before Vegas . . . Before Quin. And her doctor had started her on those new pills, which she hadn't refilled right away. So her periods were a bit stretched and off, so what? That was nothing new and the whole reason she'd gotten on the things to begin with years ago.

She wasn't . . .

She couldn't be . . .

Stress. It was just stress. Her hands shook.

She stood there staring at tampons and pads, her heart thundering in her ears. Slowly, she pushed the cart farther down the aisle. Condoms.

Yeah, hadn't used those a couple of times.

Oh no, her pills would be fine.

She should have started soon after Vegas like the next week or so. She had spotted, she remembered that, but nothing major, and she wrote it off as the new pills. The doctor had even warned her that the switch in pills could lead to irregular periods the first few months. She'd started the new pack the next month. God knew her and Quin did it enough when he came to see her. And she didn't remember what all they did in Vegas. That weekend was still a blur.

Oh God.

And then she'd taken this job and moved and . . .

And . . .

There wasn't anything else.

Oh God.

Pregnancy tests seemed to wave at her from the shelf.

No.

No.

No.

But she took a deep breath and reached a trembling hand out and picked one up.

Which one? The blue one? The pink one? The cheap one?

Ella just grabbed one and then reached back and grabbed another. And then two others.

She didn't remember finishing her shopping or how exactly she got home. Thank God she didn't have to teach any other classes tonight.

She was late.

She couldn't be late. She was never late. You couldn't technically be late if your hormones were so screwed up that you weren't even regular on the damned pill.

Oh God.

Somehow she made it into the house. She left the groceries on the counter and dug out the bag with the tests.

Taking a deep breath, she simply stared at them.

Her phone rang. She started to let it go to voice mail but then noticed it was her elderly landlords across the street.

"Hello?"

"Hi, dear, it's Carmine. Herb and I wanted to see if you'd eaten, and if not, we have plenty. Come on over."

Ella smiled. "I'd love to, Mrs. Richardson, but I'm really wiped tonight. I think I'm just going to take a bath and then hit the bed. I have a sunup class out at the Nursery tomorrow morning."

"Oh, I forget you got that other job too. Honey, you need a man, not another job."

"Mrs. Richardson, in my experience, men are basically three other jobs." And the root of much stress.

They hung up laughing.

Reality crashed back down.

"Can't hide from the truth." She took the boxes and went back to her bathroom.

Now what that truth would be . . . well, she was about to find out.

Chapter 14

Taos, May

Pregnant. She was pregnant.

Two pink lines. Actually eight, as there were two little sticks in each box and she took them all, stretched out over one weekend. Sure that the one before had to be wrong. Positive that there must be a mistake and the next morning or evening the new one would give her a different answer.

Nope. No such luck.

Dr. Radcliffe had confirmed it. They were currently waiting on blood work to make sure that everything was fine. She had been terrified that her taking her pills would have an adverse effect on the baby.

The doctor assured her that her low dose of estrogen would not harm the baby.

Maybe he just told her that.

Almost three months along.

She'd heard her baby's heartbeat.

Oh God. That fast little swish-wish sound echoed in her soul. She'd been terrified, shocked and . . . and . . . thrilled. Utterly thrilled.

"You had no idea?" Dr. Radcliffe had asked with raised bushy gray brows and a grin.

She'd shaken her head, looking again at the monitor to the little blob on there. "No. None. I'm not the most regular person. I spotted and thought it was just a short period. The new pills I started late and with everything, the move and what all not, I just . . . No." Wow.

"Well, from measurements and your best guess, I'd say you're about three months along." His eyes leveled at her. "You need to eat more and we'll get you started on prenatal vitamins."

She could only shake her head and reach for Lisa's hand. Lisa squeezed it. "Congratulations, Mom."

Then Ella frowned at the screen and said softly, "I had a miscarriage before. Years ago."

The doctor put the little sonogram wand away and wiped the clear gel off her lower abdomen. "How many years ago and how far along were you?"

She thought back. "Oh, back when I was in college, about seven years ago, and I wasn't this far along."

He lifted one big shoulder. "These things happen. There's nothing I can see that you should be worried about."

They'd talked more, he'd answered the questions she'd had that day, Lisa had answered others, and Dr. Merchant had answered yet more when he'd told her congratulations a few days later.

A few days ago, when yet another issue arose in her life before she'd figured out what the hell to do about her current mess.

So here she sat in the courtyard of this coffee shop. Waiting.

Ella sat back, hoping she appeared more relaxed than she felt. Her legs were crossed and she couldn't stop her right foot from swinging. A habit her mother had tried to break her of, telling her ladies sat still.

Whatever.

Like she could sit still. A local FBI agent had contacted her and wanted to meet with her.

Ella waited and thought, *As if I don't have enough problems right now?*

The FBI? Why did they want to talk to her? What had she done? Sure she'd downloaded a couple of songs from that one website and then her freaking computer died. She figured that was karma for her. Her mother taught her not to steal, and the one time she had, though everyone probably did it at least once, her computer died. No more after that. A song cost less than a dollar—a new laptop, considerably more. Hell, even trying to get the thing fixed cost more than the stupid songs would have.

So what did the feds want with her?

She hadn't done anything, at least nothing that she knew of.

The smells of coffee wafted from inside the coffee shop out into the little courtyard.

The man who'd spoken to her yesterday knew she liked to come here and wanted to meet her here to discuss something.

Considering it was a public place, and the fact he was a federal agent, she supposed she should.

Her hands trembled. Did everyone always feel this nervous around cops? Were FBI agents technically cops? Law enforcement, so yeah, they probably were cops. Super cops! God, her mind could not stay on track these days.

She put her hands over her thickening stomach. How could she not know she was pregnant? Granted, she'd heard of women going into labor and claiming not to have known they were pregnant. She'd always known they were nut jobs. But for her?

She thought she knew her body pretty damned well.

Apparently not.

So here she sat. In a new place, with her new job, about to talk to the feds about God only knew what, and she was pregnant.

She closed her eyes and took a deep breath. Time to focus on what was around her before she stressed herself out to the point she puked.

Taos was slushy today. Cars splashed by on the street. There had been a late snow. Who would have thought? Wrapped in her jacket and scarf she was fine. The locals — one of which she was not yet, or didn't consider herself — sat in shorts, hiking shoes, and a fleece jacket. She'd be frozen. Her body was still used to New Orleans weather and mild winters. This was cold by any of her standards. The day was still overcast and it had been drizzly this morning.

Checking her watch, she bounced her foot. When was he going to get here? Agent Jareaux. Like off that crime show she'd seen a couple of times until she had nightmares. Bad things in the brain left bad nights for her. So she tended to steer clear of things that would bother her.

Like commitment? Marriage? Calling the father of her baby and letting him know?

A foot scuffed along the flagstone and she turned.

There he stood, had to be. He was serious, and his eyes scanned the entire place.

Dark hair, not too tall, not too short. Just normal. Well, normal with the exception that even though he had on jeans he still had a button-down on with a jacket. But she supposed he couldn't just walk around with a gun strapped on. This was New Mexico, but it wasn't the old west. She took a sip of her chai. Then again, she knew ranchers around here had rifles in their trucks and plenty of people had their concealed licenses. Hell, they ran ads for the latter in the paper. She shook her head.

Very persistent man. He'd come by the studio twice and left his name and number. He'd called her phone three times and she'd finally agreed to meet with him after he'd told her who he was and that it was imperative that they speak.

So, what the hell did he want with her?

Or rather, what did the feds want that it was imperative that they speak with *her*?

He walked to her, his own cup steaming, and stood for a moment. Then he held out his hand. "Hello, again, Ms. Ferguson."

She sighed and decided to come clean. "I go by another name."

"Really?" He motioned to the chair. "May I?"

She shrugged. "Well, as you are the one who wanted to speak with me, I suppose you should, unless you want to just stand there."

He chuckled and sat across from her. He was handsome in a classic popular-guy jock type way. Strong jaw, straight nose. Though there was a bit of a hump to it. He'd probably broken it at some point, and with his job she figured that was likely. The color of his eyes was a piercing gray, which might be pretty if not for the fact they were . . . flat. Like he'd seen too much or something. Reminded her of the cops she knew from New Orleans, or worse, the guys on the street. Not the ones too high or drunk to worry about life, but those that were beaten down by life, by what they'd seen, or been part of. Guys with eyes like that, in the shelter, were often struggling to get back to where there was level ground.

And this guy? What all had he seen and been a part of to have that absence in his eyes?

He looked at her and smiled. All happy charm, except for his eyes. She didn't trust that fake charm.

"You look like you're wondering what you're doing here and what I could possibly want with you." He took a drink of his coffee and winced. "I told you before we are not trying to scare you. We need your help."

Well, it was steaming. What did he expect?

He tilted his head and studied her. "So how far along are you?"

She jerked. "H-how did you know?"

One side of his mouth kicked up, but it wasn't a smile. "We know quite a bit about you, Ms. Ferguson. And we'd like your help."

She just looked at him.

"Look, here's my card."

"Yes, I have several others that you left for me." She'd even called the local FBI office to verify he was who he claimed to be before meeting with the man. He was a special agent with the FBI. She still had no idea why he'd contacted her, what exactly he wanted.

He shrugged. "You are a smart woman, a strong one from what we know of you. You're a straight shooter who likes to help people. The elderly that you teach yoga to three times a week. The shelters where you help teen mothers and expectant mothers. You are a person who doesn't like to see the less advantaged taken advantage of."

She held his flat stare. "Okay, and . . . ?"

"And as such a person, we'd like to talk to you about helping us."

She shook her head. "Help you? You've mentioned that. I'm just me, how in the world would I help you? And with what—exactly?"

He took a deep breath. "I can't tell you everything, yet. Only once you agree."

Uh-huh. "And I'm supposed to agree now because?" She waved her hand for him to continue.

He smiled at her. "You are a wary woman. I can deal with wariness. Look." He leaned up on his elbows. The wind blew from behind him and she caught a whiff of his cologne. A little more light and flirty than she would have imagined a serious guy like him wearing. Made her think of Quin and his cologne. Woodsy, spring rains, and just Quin . . .

She sighed and leaned back as Jareaux continued.

"We've been waiting for a while to find someone. And then you just sort of happened along. You are pregnant, which is what we were really waiting for." He frowned. "You are, aren't you?"

She couldn't help it, she laughed. "Whether or not I am will wait." Ella shook her head. "That's your criteria for me helping you? Are you nuts? You have any idea how many pregnant women there are out there?"

He didn't smile. "Lots, and few are in a position such as you."

"And I still don't know what that position is." Until she did, she wouldn't be helping him—them.

He sighed and looked around. "Are you working for the Nursery?"

"You mean the Nursery of Dreams? Well, not really. I mean maybe."

"Maybe? Aren't you a yoga instructor out at their retreat place?"

Now it was her turn to frown, and she rubbed her arms from the chills that danced along her skin. "How do you know all of that? Are you people watching me?" She put her hands on her stomach again so he wouldn't see them tremble.

Ella Ferguson was skittish. Great.

Jareaux held up his hands, hoping to put her at ease. He would put her at ease. She was going to help him crack this case and it would be big. He knew it. He'd been waiting for someone like her to come along and help him out. "Look, I'm not going to hurt you or your baby." He had to put her at ease. He sighed and raked a hand though his hair. "I—We'd like someone to sort of keep an eye on things there. Let us know if there is anything odd going on out there."

"Odd, how? Place seems great to me. Pregnancy abounds and the atmosphere's just happy. The women take classes, on all sorts of things," she said.

"Yes, we know. The ages of those at the Nursery's retreat are all over the place. The ages range from young teens to the mid-twenties for the most part. There are also a couple of thirty-something surrogate mothers."

She just looked at him with those big blue eyes.

Woman was pretty in a weird way. He'd use weirdness, hell, he'd use Satan's girlfriend if it helped him get out of this damned place. Why they were all out at the Retreat, as those out there called the place, he wasn't exactly sure. But they were and everyone seemed to love it. Yoga, diet classes, meditation, even some business classes for those who wanted it. No cell phones. No laptops or iPads. Technology was pretty much left at the door.

"Don't you find it odd the lack of technology or whatever they allow?" he asked her. "Who doesn't have a cell phone or access to one in this day and age? I would think it would be dangerous for a pregnant woman *not* to have one."

She shrugged. "Many believe our electronics are in direct correlation to the increase in cancer. But whatever. I don't really care what their rules are. I was hired to teach a couple of yoga classes up there. By a twist of fate actually. A woman in my class who's a nurse told me they were looking for someone to teach yoga to a bunch of pregnant women. I took it. Good thing too. I'm pregnant," she said, as if she still didn't believe it.

He could use that.

"Kind of a drive though, isn't it?" he asked, knowing the drive up to the Retreat was over half an hour away. "Guess you love your work."

She just looked at him. "I don't know that I'd call it working exactly. I teach yoga a couple of times a week up there. Though another one of the doctors asked me if I'd consider more classes."

More classes up there would be great, would give her great access, might get this rolling a lot quicker.

"And you're pregnant."

She took a deep breath. "Honestly, I haven't told many people yet. It's still . . . so damned new. And so freaking scary," she muttered to herself.

"Why? I thought . . . well, most women . . ."

She just raised a brow. "I'm not exactly scared about the pregnancy or being a mom. I'm kind of worried about a phone call I need to make."

"To?"

"Quinlan."

"Ah." Probably the father. Woman with the strange hair and perky disposition bothered him for some reason. He just wanted someone he could use to break this case, make his name and get the hell out of this backwoods position.

But to do that, he'd have to gain her trust.

"What's 'ah' about it?"

"Nothing." He shifted and studied her. Confident woman. She didn't cower, didn't hunker in her chair, met all his stares dead-on. "So you interested in helping us?"

"Because I'm pregnant?"

"And you're single."

She jerked. "No, I'm not actually."

She said it as if she wasn't exactly sure. "You sound like you might doubt that statement."

Her eyebrows lowered. "I, well, I don't think I'm single."

He quirked a brow. "You're not? So the father . . ."

"Doesn't know yet. But he will and then he'll be hounding me for everything again."

"Everything?"

She waved her hand. "Oh, yeah, everything. Once he finds out about the baby, he'll fight me on the marriage with a vengeance. Granted, if I go to him now, then he'll think the only reason I want him back is because of the baby, and I knew when I left New Orleans and . . ."

He tuned her out. Woman was flightier than he'd thought originally, but he could still work with her. Then what she said clicked.

"Wait, you're married?"

She grinned. "You mean the FBI doesn't know everything? Really? And here I thought so highly of the sainted bureau. I mean, the stories you hear . . ."

He held up his hand. "Please explain."

Where to begin. "I'm married, actually. Or I think I am."

"You think? Isn't being married sort of like being pregnant? Either you are or you're not?" Lines furrowed across his forehead.

"You'd think, huh? Enter Vegas, Elvis—I think—and a man who claimed he wanted to stay married even though he hadn't told anyone about our marriage, other than a lawyer. I decided I didn't want to be married then."

"And you do now?"

She thought about that and shrugged. "I realized I probably did before I ran. I mean moved. But things were said, or not, as the case was, and well . . . here I am."

"Ahh." He sipped his coffee again. "One of those."

She quirked a brow at him. "One of those?"

"Commitment-phobes. Had one myself. I chased her down, turned out to be a waste of time on my part."

She only shrugged and looked out over the courtyard.

He cleared his throat. "So, Vegas . . . sounds . . . rushed, so I guess that makes sense. Mistake and all. So why haven't you annulled it?"

Ella just looked at him. There was a question. A mistake.

Except it didn't actually feel like a mistake, did it? It had, or seemed like it should, but . . . not really. Not when they were talking and laughing and planning things . . . Not that she wanted to admit that. It never really had, even as she'd tried to convince herself that it was a mistake of gargantuan proportions. But when they were together, it was almost . . . too easy . . . too perfect.

That scared her.

Had scared her.

So they fought. Stupidly, and she'd . . . she'd . . . fucked it all to hell and back. So what if he hadn't told his family yet? As he'd kept pointing out, they were married.

And now what?

"So the father, will he be a part of the baby's life?" the man across from her asked, jerking her back to the here and now.

"Quinlan? Oh, hell yes. Soon as he knows, I'd imagine."

"You haven't told him" He *tsked* and there was slightly less professionalism in his voice, not as clipped and calm as before.

"See, you're a guy."

"So?"

"So the way you just said that tells me I've waited too long already in telling him, but how could I tell him when I just figured it out myself a couple of weeks ago?"

"You haven't told him in two weeks?"

"Not quite two weeks, more like one and a half and how do I tell him? By what? Calling him? *Hey, it's me, remember, your wife? Yeah, so apparently at some point we weren't careful enough and surprise, I'm pregnant!*"

He just looked at her.

"I'm still trying to get my brain around the idea of having a baby and how I missed it up to this point and how was I to know that I ran from a totally perfect and wonderful guy because I was scared, which will just make him right and now if I say I want it all too, he'll just think I only want to because of the baby and then—"

"Breathe." He held both hands up. "Please, don't pass out or anything."

She took a deep breath and a drink of her chai.

"Look, Ms. Ferguson."

"Kinncaid, actually. Or it was. Not sure if it still is. How do I find out?" How did she find out without calling Quin. She *needed* to call him. "Maybe I'll ask him to come out here and then I can tell him." She nodded. That was a better idea. "I could tell him we need to talk to work things out whichever way they go and I have something really important to talk to him about." She frowned. "He'd come. Probably." He'd been really pissed before. "Maybe." Then again, maybe he'd expect her to come to him, and could she? The doctors told her to be careful with her previous history. No, if she told him it was serious, that she couldn't come to him but she wanted and needed him to fly out here, he'd be here. She knew that—or hoped she did.

The man across from her took a long drink of his coffee and didn't take his eyes off of her. Black from what she could see in his mug. Probably didn't put any sweetener in it either.

Finally, he sighed and said, "Why don't you wait on that phone call." He shifted. "Look, both of us have things to do and somehow this whole conversation is not going the way I thought it would go." Then he looked at her, his eyes narrowed on her. "Your hair had pink and blue streaks in it last time I saw you."

Now the stripes were purple. She'd changed it to pink and blue when she moved here because purple reminded her of the last time she'd seen Quinlan, and then she realized she needed something new and the pink and blue bothered her so she changed it to varying shades of purple.

"I bet you made special agent really quickly, didn't you?"

He shook his head. "Whatever. Look, the thing is, we need a . . . contact on the inside."

"Contact? You mean a mole? Why? What for? What are you looking for? Or investigating?"

He rubbed his hand over his face and tapped the card. "Think about it and then let us know, please. There are girls and babies going missing. Now, maybe that place has nothing to do with any of it. But if it does, we want to know."

She thought about that for a minute, thought of the young girls out there, the lonely women. Some of them had no one. Others had lots of people and lots of money. Missing babies?

"Missing mothers and babies? Since when? Why don't you send someone else in? Someone trained or something?"

He took a deep breath and opened his mouth.

"Oh, I get it. The economy. Budget cuts. What are the chances of having a handy pregnant agent? You can't fake pregnancy in a place that deals with that very thing or they'd find out. Plus, let's face it. Me, you don't have to pay, do you? I must be a . . . what's it called . . ." She tapped the tabletop, her mind not latching on to the damned word.

"Possible pain in my ass, it's looking like."

She chuckled. "Agent Jareaux, that's no way to sweet-talk me into being your . . . what's the damned word? I swear pregnancy hormones are depleting my brain cells."

"Informant?"

She snapped her fingers. "Your informant. That's it exactly. So tell me why would I possibly want to be your informant? I have enough stress in my life right now, thank you very much." She took a deep breath and smelled . . . roasted green chilies. She could swear the spicy scent was laughing at her. "God, I'm hungry."

"Are you always like this?" he asked, leaning up on his elbows, his eyes studying her and fingers beneath his chin, a small smile tilting the edges of his mouth upward.

"Like what?"

He licked his lips.

"Like what? Go ahead. I've been called flighty, driven, a total bitch, eccentric and weird. Take your pick. My fave is gold-digging trash. So which would you choose?"

He frowned. "None of those. Who called you trash? Your husband?"

"Quinlan?" She laughed and laughed some more. "No, Quin didn't call me that. He'd kick anyone's ass who did . . . well, possibly. He would have before and . . . Never mind. Though if you want to be technical about it . . ." She took another deep breath and smelled something . . .

"I have *got* to get some of that food I'm smelling. So if you want to finish this, and by the way, you really need to work on your sales pitch, we better go find out what smells so good, because otherwise my brain is only thinking of food and you only sound like *blah-blah-blah*. Maybe I want green chili enchiladas. With eggs. Huevos rancheros. Is it ranchero if it is not red sauce?" She stood up and grabbed her hobo woven bag that was also her purse. She glanced back to make sure he was coming. He stood there with a confused look on his face.

"Look, you have some explaining to do. I won't agree to help you unless I know more details. You are right. I like to help people." Missing girls and missing babies. She put her hand over her stomach. "And you've caught my interest, though I can't think right now because I'm suddenly starving and I want whatever smells so damned good." She motioned to the inside. "I'll ask the coffee shop dude. He's a local so he'll know where the smell is coming from. You coming?"

He shook his head and followed her, opening the door. "Pain in my ass it will be, weird one though you are. But that's okay, I can work with weird."

She laughed. "You might think so, but I usually either drive people crazy or they become overly protective. I don't get it, but whatever."

She heard him sigh and mutter, "I do."

Ella smiled and led the way to food, knowing she might help the man after she learned more. Probably.

Chapter 15

Taos, July

Ella finished up her evening session and looked around. One of the girls was missing. She'd been about six months along when Ella was hired on here.

"Hey, Sally," she asked the nurse who was helping with their class that evening. "Where is Nadia?" Nadia was pale, pale hair, pale eyes, and a slight Russian accent. She'd been in every class Ella had taught.

Sally paused for just a second while rolling her mat up before she brushed it off and finished sliding it into its case. "She left. Went home," she said.

Ella frowned, sliding her own mat into its case and gathering up her towel and water bottle. "Really? That's great! Where'd she go to? And did she have the baby yet?"

Ella hadn't worked this past weekend. She'd had the weekend off, and with her extra classes she'd picked up here at the Retreat, they'd offered her full benefits if she'd help out in other areas as needed. So far that had only consisted of helping out in the juice and organic shop two weekends ago and leading a handful of approved hikes through the woods on marked paths.

"Who are you guys talking about?" another young woman asked. Fran, with her wild red curls and freckles and bright personality, was a favorite of everyone. She was always trying to help others. "Nadia?"

Sally didn't say anything.

"Nadia, yes. When did she go home?" Ella asked Fran.

Fran shrugged. "No idea. She was in class Thursday evening, but . . ." Fran frowned. "I don't know. She wasn't at breakfast Friday morning, I don't think, but I was working the kitchen that day, so I might have missed her."

"Well, she changed her mind, I heard, and went home." Sally slung the mat over her arm and waved at them. "I've got to go, ladies. Ella, you heading home or staying tonight?"

"Oh, I'm heading home," she said.

They waited while Sally left and others filed out.

"You know what's weird?" Fran asked her. Fran often wanted to talk to her and Ella didn't mind.

There were questions about pregnancy, but life too. Business and school. She liked the girl, who wasn't much further along than she was. She'd graduated in May and was working her way through some online college courses. The Retreat was even helping her because she just wanted to get her degree in sonography for right now and was working her way through her general requirements to apply for the program. Ella knew she was a hard worker from a broken family and on her own. Maybe she just reminded her of herself.

"So what's weird?" she asked Fran.

She looked around her. "Well, I was on cleaning duty as well, ya know? And in Dr. Merchant's office there was something on his laptop, just before the screen saver came on. And it was the form."

"Form?"

"Yeah, one of the forms we fill out if we're blessing our kids to someone else." The way she said it . . .

"You know, you don't have to give up your baby if you don't want to."

Fran sighed and rubbed her growing belly. "Oh, I know that, you know that, but they're all for it. And I know it would be better for the little guy, but still . . ." She shrugged. "I'll admit, I'm sort of rethinking things, but then . . ." She shook her head. "See, the form was on his PC Friday evening before he came in from the other office, through the doors, ya know? The conference room thing?"

She nodded. The conference room could be reached through doors on both ends from both Dr. Merchant's and Dr. Radcliffe's offices. And from the middle door that opened to everyone else.

"So if she went home, why was the form on his computer? Why was space for adoptive parents filled in?" she asked softly, leaning in.

Ella blinked. So far, she hadn't seen or heard anything really to validate her working with the FBI. Jareaux called her once a week to check in or they met at the coffee shop or someplace to eat.

If anyone asked, she was supposed to tell them that they were just friends, a guy that wanted to see her, but she wasn't ready.

She still wasn't sure how she felt about that, but she hadn't argued. She still thought he was nuts. Place was a great place.

Already, she'd seen several families leave with new bundles, crying and taking pictures of their new babies. Not all the adoptions came from the girls that lived here. They had other patients that lived and worked outside of the Retreat.

"Really? Where's Nadia from?" she asked.

"No idea. Nadia was really quiet, ya know? She didn't say much, didn't share much. Once I asked her if the father would want the baby and she only said that the father would kill her if he knew she was here. I have no idea what that meant, but she wasn't joking, or didn't seem to be."

She nodded and walked to the door with Fran, flipping off the light at the door. The wall of windows was dark and let no light in, but then it was cloudy so why would it?

"Sometimes this place is creepy," Fran told her. "I remember this one night, when I first came here, I could have sworn I heard someone screaming and crying." She shuddered. "They said it was the coyotes."

"You didn't believe them?"

"Well, I guess you could write it off to some ghost of a mother who died or something, didn't sound like coyotes to me. And I know what they sound like. Sometimes, I wish I could leave here and just go somewhere else. Somewhere that seems real, ya know?" the girl asked her.

She smiled. "I know. Maybe they'll let you come stay with me a few nights if we ask them tomorrow."

Fran's smile lit up her entire face, her eyes twinkling. "You think they'd let us? Oh, that would be awesome! Will you ask the doctors?"

She laughed. "I can ask, Fran. That doesn't mean they'll agree, though."

"Yeah, you're probably right. Thanks, though, in advance." Fran waved and walked off down the hallway. Ella watched her for a minute before heading out the doors into the chilly air and climbing into her Kia Soul and heading down the mountain.

• • •

He watched her from the window in the courtyard. The night was still and sound carried.

The little curvaceous yoga instructor was a pleasure to watch. There was something about her that drew people to her. He should know. She'd drawn his attention enough since they'd hired her.

And she was pregnant.

It was almost too damned perfect.

Perfect.

Pregnant.

Alone.

He wanted to know more about her. About her past. Her interests. She was creative, artsy, intelligent.

Pretty.

And the father?

He'd find out and then he'd make plans. Tugging his scarf tighter around his neck, he let the night settle around him. They'd get rain tomorrow. The pine-scented air felt damp to him.

Her headlights cut across the stucco as she backed up and headed down the gravel drive to the highway.

If the baby were a candidate for adoption . . . a quiet adoption . . . and the father turned out to be of merit . . .

Maybe millions. Definitely he could get a couple of hundred grand for the right baby from the right parents—for the right parents.

He'd have to look into her a bit more and start planting seeds. She was already fragile, he knew.

Vulnerable. Questioning and worrying.

It was almost too easy, how simple it was to tell them something. And the right ones, they always believed him. Always. Few had ever questioned.

Nodding, he headed inside to pull up her file and make a phone call. She just might be their new ticket.

• • •

"Jareaux."

"This is Ella."

He sighed. "How can I help you today?"

She frowned and leaned back into her couch. How could he help her? Was he serious?

"Did you get my message?"

Again he sighed. "I think so."

He thought so? She'd learned after "working" with the man for the last couple of months, that she really didn't actually like him. He always acted like she was wasting his time. She opened her mouth, shut it then opened it again. "You think so?"

She heard him inhale. "Look, Ella, the thing is, we need more than your worries or suppositions."

She blinked. "You didn't get my message, did you?"

If he had, surely he wouldn't be blowing her off.

"The one with a girl who went missing? Yes, I did. But as I've stated before, we need hard evidence. This girl, I ran her name, Natasha—"

"Nadia."

"Yes, Nadia, and she's basically a transient. She's got a rap sheet and has been all over the place. There's no way to know for certain that she's actually missing."

"Except that she's no longer at the Retreat."

She heard him shuffling papers on the other end.

"Did you see someone accost her? Did you see or did anyone see what happened to her?" he asked, all calm and reason.

She shook her head and thrummed her fingers on her growing belly. "A young woman is missing."

"So you think."

Pissed, she hung up the phone. So far there wasn't anything concrete to pass on. She'd looked. It wasn't like she could crack the computer files. She didn't know the passwords and it wasn't like she would be in the offices anyway.

Her phone rang.

Jareaux showed up on her screen. Screw him. He wouldn't listen. He never listened. She'd talked to girls, to Fran, to Nadia, to others. There was a pattern. Women, usually young girls that had no one, went missing.

How to prove that? She had no idea.

Chapter 16

Taos, September

"No. No. No. You can't have her. You can't have her. She's mine. She's my daughter," she said. Dark legs loomed out of the fog in front of her, and she scooted back, even as a hand reached for her.

"Nooooo!"

Ella jerked awake, a scream still caught in her throat. Her heart thundered against her ribs and in her ears. She took a deep breath and tried to calm down. She shivered and shook, her large T-shirt stuck to her back, her chest.

A sob caught in her throat. Stupid. Stupid. Just a damned dream, but she was having them more often. Nightmares where someone was taking her baby away.

She raked her trembling hands through her hair and rested her elbows on her up-drawn knees.

She wished there was someone to talk to. So many things, so many worries, so much . . . She'd talked to Lisa, brought a few things up to Jareaux, but she wanted a best friend she could tell anything to. Her friends from before, back in New Orleans, seemed a world and lifetime away.

And nothing to do about it. She'd chosen this lonely, stupid, self-righteous road, hadn't she?

"Chin up and keep going," she told herself.

No more naps for her. The early evening crept shadows across her room. Still shivering, she reached over and flipped on the lamp. Light flooded the room. She'd left the walls the soft taupe color but colors splashed everywhere else. Orange pillows, deep wine and red blankets and throws. Bronze lamps. She went for chic SoHo, or shabby chic. Or something.

No one stood in the corner holding a knife or a gun or scalpel or syringe. There. She was losing her mind. Like someone would be standing in the corner of her room in the shadows?

If they wanted to . . .

"Get a grip." Taking a deep breath, trying to still her nerves, she climbed out of bed. These days her center of gravity was off. Way off.

Two and a half more months, or thereabouts. Nine weeks. Nine more Mondays.

She rubbed her stomach as the baby shifted and twirled inside. "Ballerina, are you? Thanks for waking me up." She patted her stomach.

Her bedroom door was open, and from the doorway she could see most of the house, as it was small. But it suited her fine. Rent was cheap even though it was in a nice neighborhood, and it was quiet. The landlords across the street lived in a larger bungalow-meets-pueblo-style ranch.

The Richardsons were nice people. Mrs. Richardson had already knitted a baby blanket for her. They often invited her over for dinner. And she'd finally broken down and told them who she was, not that they didn't have her legal name—her maiden one anyway. But none of her legal documentation had been changed, so it wasn't a lie or a problem. For a couple that had been together over fifty years, they kept after her to call Quin. Email him or even text the man.

Calling . . . she should. She wanted to. Emailing seemed cowardly and texting cruel. *Hi! Remember me? We're married and I'm pregnant! It's yours. Call me.*

Yeah, right. Besides, she'd written the man and she hadn't heard from him. Granted, she hadn't actually mailed the letters. She'd given them to Jareaux to mail because he said they had to make sure she wouldn't give anything away with the investigation and they'd let him know she was perfectly safe.

Still . . . Maybe he hadn't gotten them, or maybe he was so pissed at her he didn't want anything to do with her. Maybe he'd moved on.

Calling was the way to go at this point. If she could. She could. She'd just ignore what the feds said or advised.

Call him.

Her reasons for not doing so seemed . . .

Childish now.

Stupid.

So what if he hadn't answered her letters, or called her on her new number, so what? That didn't mean anything. Or maybe she should contact her lawyer to contact his? That seemed cold.

If they could just talk this out, maybe . . . maybe . . .

And what if . . . what if he hadn't gotten her letters yet? Maybe he was traveling overseas or something. She'd only sent the three, and after that, after he hadn't answered her, she quit. Probably should have just emailed him. But that seemed so . . . so . . . impersonal. He had emailed her once not long after she moved, and then she found out and she just couldn't email him back because what would she say . . . Rather, how would she say it?

On the one hand, he might have gotten the letters and then no longer wanted her, didn't want his kid.

That didn't seem like the man she knew, the man she'd fallen in love with.

On the other hand, if he didn't know, which seemed more likely for whatever reason, regardless of the letters she'd written and given to Jareaux, then . . . then he didn't know about the baby and now if he found out, who knew what he'd do.

. . . *how would you fight a man like that?* . . . The counselor's voice from her therapy sessions shivered through her.

Ella knew Quinlan well enough, he might not ever forgive her for this.

Hefting herself up off the couch, she walked—or waddled—to the kitchen. God, her hipbones hurt. She rubbed the crease between her thigh and torso. Perfectly normal, the doctor told her. There were lots of *normal* things about pregnancy that really didn't seem normal at all if anyone asked her.

At the sink, she filled a glass with cool water and gulped it down. What did she do?

Agent Jareaux was right. Something was so wrong at the Nursery. She knew it, sensed it, but had no proof. Yet. She'd get it. The girls from her dreams? What did that mean other than her hormones were wacked and giving her nightmares—again normal, or so she had read. Her nightmares, though, didn't seem normal. Was she terrified of something happening to her baby? Yes, that was a given. The rest though?

The missing girls?

There were so many questions and no answers. Her fears grew by the day of someone taking her baby. The Nursery had started to pressure her to think about adoption. Not that they'd said that so bluntly, but she wasn't stupid. A hint here, a dropped comment there.

Hell no. Over her dead body.

So many worries, so many questions, so many things she didn't understand.

Who did she ask? The lights across the street lit the dining room window of the Richardsons'. She knew she could go over for dinner, but honestly, she just wasn't hungry. She could go over and just listen to them, but she wasn't in the mood.

She wished . . .

She wished Quinlan were here. Wished she hadn't panicked and bolted. They could be together now. It was easy to fantasize about them together in New Orleans, decorating the nursery for their daughter. She wished she hadn't waited so damned long. So what if he thought she decided to stay married because of the baby? Did it really matter? Really? It seemed to before in the beginning and maybe it still would if she wasn't in this situation where it felt like a giant clock were ticking off her time. Her reasoning was before. Before. Before there were bigger worries than herself or what someone might think of her or the lack in her.

Now? Now she was just ashamed of herself for her stupidity.

Now she was scared.

Did Quin know or did he not?

Did she take the chance and contact him even though they'd told her not to?

The glass clattered as she set it on the counter and realized her hands were still shaking. Her phone taunted her from where she had it charging on the counter.

Sighing, wishing she weren't so nervous, she snatched it up and went to the living room. The cool breeze wafted through the house from the open windows. She wished she didn't have to leave the windows open, but there was no air conditioner in this place. Mostly she didn't need it, but lately she was hot all the damned time.

She leaned her head against the back of her deep forest green couch. She loved this one. She'd seen it in the store and bought it that day. Still chilled, she pulled on the large soft cardigan she left on the back of the couch.

Her doctor had advised her to take it easier, as her blood pressure was up. So she'd canceled the classes she was supposed to teach tonight. She had her volunteer classes tomorrow at two separate nursing homes. But she enjoyed those. Did she want to stick to the same regimen or switch it up a bit? Not that it mattered.

She tapped her phone on her thigh.

Stalling.

Coward.

She was a coward.

Quinlan.

He was nothing like Lance, so why had she pushed him away? Really. She'd been happy with him. They'd been happy together. She was her own worst enemy. She had been scared, yes. But still. He'd come to New Orleans *every* week to try and get her to make a go of it. Not in a needy way either.

There was nothing needy about Quinlan.

Quinlan was confident, had been coming to terms with doing more with his life. He'd claimed he'd wanted her.

And she'd fallen so hard for him, he'd have shattered her if he'd left her. If he'd turned from her the way Lance had.

Too many similarities in the situations—the counselor would tell her to make a list or something.

She sniffled and realized that she was crying. Oh God. She'd *really, really* messed up this time. She wiped her face on the sleeve of her sweater.

Damned hormones.

God, he hadn't wanted to walk away from her before, but she'd been stupid and pushed him away and then she ran.

Ran, because she had a new job with a new place to live, then she'd learned she was pregnant and didn't let him know.

But he could have found out. Could have . . . Might . . .

Even if he had shown up at her door when she first moved, she'd still have been stupid. After she learned she was pregnant? Who knew?

Quinlan was proud and she had hurt him, she knew that now. But it hurt too that he never told his family about her, about them, about their marriage.

So you walked out on him before he could walk out on you. Really brave.

Pride. She had hers, God knew. And he did as well. Why would he keep running after her if she kept shutting him down?

"We're married, damn it. Why won't you give us a shot?" he'd all but yelled at her.

She'd been too proud to say what she really felt: *I'm too scared. I love you and you could hurt me.*

And she hadn't wanted to admit that either. So she ran, learned she was pregnant and didn't let him know he was going to be a father. She'd had three weeks or thereabouts to let him know before she'd agreed to Jareaux's plan. Then a few weeks later she'd written the first letter, and soon after two more.

Not that the letters really mattered.

Now? Now though?

"They'll take your baby too. They always do." The voice from the dream floated through her mind and sent shivers down her spine. She should have let Quinlan know immediately when she knew.

Should've. Could've. Would've . . .

It wasn't going to get any easier. She unlocked her phone and the screen image popped up. Hers and Quinlan's cheeks smashed together, both laughing as they'd taken a self-portrait.

What if he'd moved on? What if he'd found someone else. Granted, no one had contacted her with divorce papers of any kind. Or an annulment. But then did he have to? Who knew?

The baby kicked again.

She sighed and patted her stomach. "I know. I know. I love you and your daddy will love you too. I'm sorry for keeping you from him." She sighed and dialed. "He'll probably kill me if he doesn't strangle me first. But I'm pretty sure he'll love you regardless." Pretty sure.

That made no sense, but then her mind was messed up these days.

The phone on the other end rang. And rang again.

Chapter 17

"What about Mom and Dad's anniversary? What are we going to do?" Brayden asked from behind his paper. He was probably looking up obits and estimating possible estate sales for his antique shop.

Ian looked over and saw Christian giving Quinlan a hard time. Quin ignored her and set his phone on the side table, plugging it in. Ian thought his brother really needed to lighten up some, but then since New Orleans, nothing about the kid was light. New Orleans? Yeah, Quinlan had been getting better before then and for about two months after that. Then after one of his trips down to see the lovely and slightly eccentric Ella, the kid had all but clammed up and hit the gym all hours of the day and night again.

He'd fallen hard for that girl.

As much as Ian wheedled and gave Quinlan hell, his brother wouldn't break. Only dug deeper and stubbornly refused to discuss Ella. No one else knew. Though maybe Aiden did, or at least the fact he was head over heels in love with that woman. Kid was getting great at evasive answers.

Then there was Brody. Yeah, Ian would bet their cousin knew something. He and Quinlan had seen a lot of each other during the New Orleans and Ella time, and even after. Then again, those two had always been close.

Granted, he could just run a few searches and learn a bit more, but that seemed . . . dishonest toward his little brother. He'd already run a few searches back when he and the girl first met and the kid was missing for two days in fucking Vegas. Not that Ian wouldn't do whatever he had to at some point if he felt he really needed to, but as it was now, he'd leave it be.

He rubbed his thumb over his lips. Quinlan *was* an adult, God knew, and the kid was tired as hell of them all . . . hovering.

Ian understood that feeling, and he had a feeling if everyone kept smothering Quin with worries under the guise of help, he'd leave.

Then again, maybe it was time the kid moved away from home. When he was younger, Ian always thought of Quin being some sort of artist or something. At least until that fateful winter morning when Quin and little Susy Cooley had fallen through the ice on the river. Ian still remembered how blue his little seven-year-old brother had been. Dead. He'd had no pulse and hadn't been breathing. He and Aiden had performed CPR on that little body and by the grace of God had gotten their brother back. Little Susy had not been so lucky. It had taken a couple of hours to find her and they never got her back. That day had changed Quinlan. He'd become quiet and focused, his art set aside. He and Aiden had been in high school, the twins in middle school. Shaking off the thought, he focused back to the here and now.

Quinlan lightly shoved Christian away and stood up. "I don't want to meet one of your friends, sis. Thank you anyway."

"How about one of mine?" Rori asked.

Quinlan just looked at Rori, who had plopped down on the couch when Christian and Quinlan stood up.

"Some of your friends will likely kill me," Quinlan said. Then added, "Again. No, thanks."

"That woman was not a friend," Rori said.

"You haven't dated in far too long. You know," Christian said, grinning, "they make little blue pills that—"

Quinlan threw a pillow at her. "I don't need to know about my brother's ED issues."

"There are no ED issues," Brayden said from behind his paper.

"I'm going to get something to drink." Quin started for the door. "Anyone want anything?"

"Check on the kids," Ian told him. "Please."

Quinlan walked from the room and it seemed as if everyone sighed.

"I can't bloody well believe he thinks my friends would kill him," Rori muttered. "I'll have to think of a way to get him back for that one."

Quinlan's phone rang. Then rang again, buzzing along the table-top.

"Leave the boy alone," Ian said from his chair. "And he's not wrong. Most of your friends would kill him."

"Just because they *could* doesn't mean they *would*. And besides, my friends are your friends and most of them family and his friends, so that hardly makes a bit of sense," she muttered.

"Yes, dear," he said with a grin.

She narrowed her gaze at him.

Quinlan's phone rang again, shrilling out an annoying ring tone.

"He needs a date," Christian said. "How long has it been? He always dated, more than any of the rest of you. I used to call him hound dog. I mean, really."

Ian grinned. "Maybe he's become more selective."

Of one particular light blue-haired woman. Quinlan had always gone for the sleek, suave women. Long-legged model types. The kind that graced magazine covers or did lingerie shoots. Which had made him such an easy mark for Hellinski before.

Ella Ferguson was none of those things. She was short, almost as short as Aiden's wife. Big eyes, and artsy. She was so not Quin's normal type that when Ian had learned what he had on the plane, he hadn't really worried.

Now though? Ian bit down. "Maybe he has someone he doesn't want any of us to know about," he said. Then added, "Yet."

Brayden just snorted behind his paper. "I have other things to worry about besides Quinlan's love life."

"We are worried about the lack of it, keep up," Christian told him. "And if he has met someone, why hasn't he introduced her to the rest of us?"

Brayden flipped the edge of the paper down and gave her a look over the corner before flipping it back up and continuing to read it.

Ian checked the time and wondered when his other two brothers would get here. Gavin might not be able to, but that was always the way it was with him. They were trying to plan something grand for Mom and Pop, so they'd all agreed to dinner here.

"Mom did ask me if I thought Quin could be gay," Brayden said from behind the paper.

Christian rolled her eyes and snorted. "We could only be so lucky. If he'd been born a couple hundred years ago, he'd be a rake of the first order." She frowned. "Come to think of it, you all probably would have been."

"I think he met someone and fell for her hard," Rori muttered, even as Ian leaned in and kissed her neck. "My friends would kill him . . ." She frowned.

"They would."

"Bugger off," she said to him.

"Later, darling, and only with you."

Quinlan's phone rang for a third time. Who in the world was calling?

"Could he have picked a more annoying ring tone?" Rori muttered.

More quips and curious statements swam around on Quinlan's lack of dating, and on what his deal was lately. For the last three or four months or so anyway.

His phone rang again. And then again.

"Who the bloody hell? Leave a voice message," Rori said. Then she grinned. "Then again, paybacks and all that."

"You shouldn't." Ian leaned over and kissed her neck. She was wearing that perfume that just . . .

He growled.

"Hello, Quin's phone."

He could hear a female's voice as he nuzzled his wife's neck.

"Yes, this is Quin's phone."

"Hang up," he told her, nibbling up her neck.

She giggled. God, he loved that he could make this hard-ass woman giggle. "Will you stop, I'm trying to talk and can't concentrate when you . . ." He took her earlobe into his mouth. She tried to swallow a moan, shook her head and tried to push him away.

"Who is this?"

The female answered and he stilled just as Rori did at the answer, which he heard.

"Try again, luv, I don't bloody think so." She looked at the phone. "Yeah, right. Who is this?"

No answer.

"Well, bye to you as well," Rori muttered, frowning.

Quinlan walked back into the room and tossed a Coke to him. Ian snatched it out of the air. He watched his brother. "Your wife called."

Quin froze. "What?"

Brayden's paper rattled and Ian didn't take his eyes off his brother.

"Some chickie called," Rori said. "Asked for you and claimed to be your wife."

Quin's face set, he walked to them and snatched the phone out of her hand. "Thanks so much for answering my phone."

"Wife?" Christian asked.

"Wife?" Brayden asked.

"If I had a real wife, she'd be here with me, don't you think?" Quinlan said, scrolling through the phone.

"What's the number?" Ian asked, noting that Quin's statement could be construed in several ways.

A muscle bunched in Quin's jaw. "Out of Area." He shook the phone as if it would suddenly give another number like the fortune-telling eight ball. "I hate when they say that."

"Maybe she left a voice message?" Christian said. "And why would someone claim to be your wife?"

"Maybe she's delusional," Brayden said.

"Well, perhaps she wants money," Rori said. At everyone's silence, she said, "What? Just because you don't think he dates doesn't mean tweed boy here didn't get it on and bang the bloody hell out of some playboy-groupy who's trying to get something out of him."

"Your view of me is so encouraging," Quin said and walked from the room. "I need to get going, let me know what you guys decide."

Ian pushed up from the couch and followed his brother out. "Where are you going?"

Quinlan stopped in the middle of the hallway. "Not now, Ian."

Ian stepped up beside him. "Yes, now. What the hell is with you? Is this about Ella? You haven't been yourself since that first New Orleans trip. And now this phone call?"

Quin's head snapped up, his gaze narrowing. "What do you know of Ella?"

Ian looked at him. "I know you fell for her hard. I know she went with you to Vegas but you left her there as she wasn't on the plane with you when you got back." Ian started to add what else he knew, but didn't. "I know that you flew down to New Orleans every week for almost two months and then you suddenly stopped. Kid, you were happy." He put his hand on his brother's shoulder. "What you do with your life is none of my business, I know. I'll help you any way I can, Quin. You only need to ask. You know that."

The muscle jumped in Quin's jaw. Finally he took a deep breath. "Not yet."

"She worth it?"

Quinlan opened the front door. "Is Rori?"

Ian arched a brow.

"I thought she was," Quin said.

Quinlan kept walking down the steps and sidestepped Aiden, who was walking up the drive.

"Hey!" Aiden said, taking all three front steps at once. "Sorry I'm late. What did I miss?"

"Quinlan's wife," Ian said, watching his brother climb into his silver Mercedes.

Chapter 18

"And lean into the stretch, opening up the chest, breathe through it . . ." she told her class of pregnant women. There were new additions and some who had left; some had their babies and moved on. Others had simply been weekend warriors.

This evening her class consisted of the regulars — there were only five of them — and a few others.

She hadn't eaten today, but then she hadn't really eaten anything since the night she'd tried to call Quin, and that was about three weeks ago. Her doctor had already noticed her weight loss, but she just really wasn't hungry.

The idea that Quinlan had moved on had been a punch in the gut, in the face, in the heart.

Her eyes stung yet again and she had to focus on moving everyone into the next move. "Remember to press against the inside of your thighs with your elbows to gently coax the muscles into the stretch." She checked to make sure everyone was squatting correctly.

So what if he was with another woman, some perfectly pedigreed woman with a snitty British accent?

She honestly didn't remember the rest of the session; it was an easier one and she went through the moves, or assumed she did. No one said anything else to the contrary, bless their hearts.

The others quickly filed out, though a few gave her strange looks. So maybe she threw in a new stretch or something.

"Hey, you feeling okay?" Fran asked her, coming up.

"Sure, why?" she asked, straightening too quickly. She slammed a hand out as the room spun.

"Oh, I don't know," Fran said, deadpan, putting a hand under Ella's elbow. "Might have something to do with the fact you're very pale, weren't with us at all in class, kept tearing up, and you are dizzy. I think we should go see Dr. Merchant."

They both preferred Dr. Merchant's easy personality to Dr. Radcliffe's more somber one, or one of the other part-time doctors.

Sally came over. "Ella, are you all right?"

"I know you kept going and coming, Sal," Fran said, "but she's been off the entire session. Look how pale she is."

"Hello, right here," she told them both. "I'll just take some juice and then we can head off. No reason to call the doc."

"Oh, he's still here," Sally told them.

"No—"

"She'll see him," Fran said.

In the hallway, they passed Lisa, who hurried to them. "What's wrong?"

"Ella's not feeling well."

She had noticed her fingers were more swollen in the last couple of days, but then she'd felt like crap anyway.

"Juice and home. I just need some rest."

"Uh-huh," Lisa told her. "Come on, Ella."

"Really, guys, I just want to go home. That's all."

She wasn't about to tell any of them what was really wrong. They walked down the hallway of the exam rooms and Fran waited with her while the other two went to get the doctor.

"I wanted to head home. Eat a bite of soup maybe. And some bread. I'm tired," she said, sitting on the stupid table.

Fran sighed and looked at the closed door and then back to her, and Ella really saw her friend, who looked large enough to pop.

"You okay?" she asked her.

Fran shrugged. "I saw something I wanted to talk to you about tonight. Remember Nadia? Well, when I was cleaning the offices last week, I checked the files."

"What? Why?" Damn it.

"You and I both know things here are just weird. And Nadia still bothers me and now there are no files on Nadia. I looked."

"You did what?" she asked her. "Are you mad?"

Others had suddenly left, or something had gone wrong with their deliveries. Not many, but enough that she wondered.

She hadn't thought that others might wonder as well.

"No, I want to know what happened to her. I feel like I owe it to her or something, ya know?"

"Fran, leave it alone." She scooted off the table and grabbed the young lady's arms. "I'm serious. Don't go borrowing trouble."

"Like you're not? I'm not stupid, Ella. I heard you on the phone to Jareaux. I know you're supposed to—"

The door opened. "Evening, ladies. I was about to go home and the nurses tagged me." Dr. Merchant strode in, dressed today in jeans and a polo, and she saw Dr. Radcliffe out in the hallway.

"You all right, Ella?" the older doctor asked.

"I'm fine," she told them.

"Yes, well, let's just see about that, okay?" Dr. Merchant told her.

They checked her heart rate, her blood pressure, which was up, and her blood sugar, which was low.

"Ella," Dr. Merchant chided. "You need to take care of yourself and the baby. You've lost another couple of pounds."

Sally shook her head and the outside world flashed with lightning, thunder shook the windows. "Storm's hit earlier than expected."

Great, now she'd be stuck driving in that mess.

"When's the last night you had a good night's sleep?"

She shrugged. "I don't know." Not in the last few days for certain.

"Why, still experiencing the nightmares?" he asked her. "Your file says you're still seeing the therapist. Have you discussed this with her?"

She sighed. "Yes, Dr. Merchant. I've discussed my fears and the fact my nightmares stem from my fears and where she believes my fears stem from."

He leveled a look at her over his glasses. "I see."

"I'm just tired, I didn't sleep well, so I was running late and simply didn't take the time to eat properly today."

"All day?" he asked her.

She rolled her eyes. "Not as often as I should have, not what I should have. I know that."

"Headache?" he asked her.

She sighed. "Yes, can I go, please? I just want to go home and rest."

He narrowed his eyes as he studied the chart. "Ella, the weather is turning nasty out, and we'd all feel better if you stayed here tonight, rather than if you drove out in this."

At that moment the storm hit, wind howling and ripping through the pines and across the plains. A bolt of lightning streaked across the sky.

"Um . . . Well, I hadn't planned on staying, but honestly, I don't want to drive in this."

"And with your dizziness, I'd feel much better with you staying here this evening. Plus," he added, scribbling on the notepad, "we can monitor your blood pressure. It's higher than I want to see, and in your condition, Ella, it's nothing to ignore. You need to rest."

Anxiety skittered through her. "I know I need to rest." And she didn't want to drive home in this. "I'm going home in the morning though."

He shared a smile with Sally. "We'll see how things are in the morning, shall we?"

"Fabulous." They listened to the baby's heartbeat and thankfully everything was fine.

Once she was in an assigned room at the opposite end of the hallway from Fran's room, she breathed deeply. The storm was still raging and supposedly there was a whole line of storms moving through.

She ate dinner, low-sodium soup, with the rest of the live-ins, or some of it. Tasted a bit bitter to her and she still just wasn't hungry. The herbal tea also tasted off, so she stuck with the water, even though she was told the tea would help with her blood pressure. Some of the women wanted to play a game or two of cards or something. Others went to the main room to watch a movie. Most of them, though, at least in their hallway, were tired and headed to bed.

Ella just wanted peace and quiet. She and Fran made their way back to their rooms talking about her classes and what they wanted to do after.

After their babies were born.

Fran knew about Quinlan, apparently knew more about Jareaux than Ella had thought before. They didn't say another word about Nadia or their shared worries; they both knew this wasn't the place to discuss it—later at her house, they would.

Yawning, she hugged her friend good night. "I don't know about you, but I'm off to bed."

Fran nodded. "I think I'm going to work on the baby quilt I started."

"Did you finally choose the last color patch?"

Fran laughed. "Yes, I just chose another blue. I started to choose a yellow and then a green and finally a white, and that was just too many choices. So I went with another blue." She grabbed a bag out of the corner and opened it. "See, what do you think?" Fran pulled out a piece of folded fabric.

The blues were different shades and prints. Ella knew nothing about quilting, but Mrs. Richardson had bought her a set of idiot-proof knitting looms. She'd already made several baby hats and was working her way through pink blocks. She only needed two more large blocks and then Mrs. Richardson was going to show her how to stitch them together to create one large baby blanket.

Thankfully, she'd brought her knitting bag. Lisa had gotten it from her car earlier and it was in her room. So was a set of scrubs and some PJs. She had no idea whose PJs, nor did she care.

Settled in bed, her mind again on Quinlan and what she'd thrown away, she knew she wouldn't sleep. But in minutes, her thoughts drifted and she was out.

• • •

Ella jerked awake and lay there, her heart racing, her breathing ragged, sweat drenching the T-shirt she wore.

Another nightmare. She tried to remember, but God, her head was killing her.

She sat up, breathing out and trying to calm her racing heart. Her head hadn't hurt this badly in a long time. She could practically feel her pulse against the inside of her skull.

God.

Where was she?

Oh, yeah, the Retreat.

Thunder ripped so loudly through the air the windows shook and she jerked.

Lord, she'd never calm down at this rate. Climbing from the bed, she shuffled to the bathroom and got a drink of water, washing her face with cool water. Her head freaking hurt.

Maybe, with the storm, Fran was still awake. What time was it anyway? She walked back to her bedside and picked up her phone. After three in the morning. She could try to just go back to sleep, but her head hurt so badly. Could probably just press the intercom button, but she'd check on Fran first.

The lights were all low in the hallways, the lightning outside flashing, stabbing against her eyeballs. She winced and raised her hand, the other trailing along the wall.

She'd stayed before when the weather turned bad, but there was usually someone around. Was the power out?

No, the lights were just low. Her head hurt so badly that things seemed to have a sort of aura around them. She made her way slowly down the hallway but noises bounced off her eardrums. Thunder. Something else high-pitched. A beep, dull. Rhythmic.

She followed it, trailing her hand down the wall, her other hand on her stomach.

What was that noise?

Beep. Beep. Beep.

Someone's voice floated through a door, or was it? Thunder shuddered the building.

A scream built and built. She stopped, pressing against the wall as the scream ripped through the air. Panic bloomed and streaked through her veins.

Oh God.

She tried to hurry toward the sound. Toward . . .

Fran's room.

She reached the door, and pain pulsed again in her head. She stopped and reached for the latch but the door was already cracked. She pushed it open and saw . . .

Saw . . .

Red. So much red in such a pale room. Red splashed across the bed, the wall, pooled on the floor.

She gasped and masked figures turned to her. Fran's face was pale, her eyes staring at the door, at her.

Ella opened her mouth to scream as pain ripped through her head and the world went black.

Chapter 19

Two weeks later

Ella sighed and waited, pacing in the small living room. Her bags were packed, her car was packed. She'd probably get Jareaux's damned voice mail like she had the last several times she'd called. Next she was calling his office if he—

"What do you need, Ella?" he said in lieu of hello.

"Excuse me?" she asked him. "I was helping you. Why haven't you called me back? I've left several messages. I even left messages at the office number."

"Yes, I'm aware," was all he said.

"Jareaux, you're the one that approached me for help. I've done my bit."

"Really? And where's the evidence I've told you I needed from the beginning? You being worried or scared does not make a case," he said.

Ella closed her eyes. "I'm done. I'm calling my husband. You don't really care about any of the women up there. You don't care about helping them or anything. Nadia went missing and what did you do? Nothing."

"There was no proof—"

"You and your damned proof."

"That damned proof makes a case, Ella. The case has completely stalled due to the fact you couldn't deliver any evidence. I don't have time to babysit you or hold your hand. I have other cases as well. Please don't call me again."

Fury slid through her. "You bastard."

"Good-bye."

Ella sat on the sofa and stared at the wall.

What was she going to do? He'd been right, why wasn't he listening to her? The Nursery was not what it seemed. Nadia and Fran, their babies . . .

Screw him.

She should just leave. Go. Drive to D.C. to Quinlan, just get the hell out of here.

Running never helps anything, Ella.

She shoved the voice away. But sometimes running saved lives, and right now she knew she had to leave, knew she needed to get out of here. No matter what they tried to convince her of, she knew Fran's death wasn't just one of those things that happened, a statistic. She knew what she'd seen. After that night, she'd been groggy for another whole day, almost two. They'd told her her blood pressure was too high and they needed to keep her to monitor her, to give her meds.

Of course she was upset, they assured her. Apparently Fran had gone into labor, placenta abruption. She'd found her and pressed the intercom button, they'd told her. But her own blood pressure had spiked and she'd passed out from all the excitement.

She didn't believe them. For the four days they'd kept her at the Retreat, it was a blur, a blur except for the panic. Images danced in her brain — real or not, she wasn't sure. They'd all tried to talk to her in quiet, calm voices. Sally and Lisa patting her hand. Dr. Merchant trying to get her to talk. The psychologist had even sat beside her bed. The only one she'd spoken to had been Dr. Radcliffe. She'd turned her head, looked at him and said, "I want to go home now."

He'd narrowed his eyes at her, nodded and scribbled something on a paper on her chart. He was the only one who didn't try to tell her what she'd seen.

She remembered the scream. Remembered the voices and the masked figures beside the bed. And there was a vague memory of a baby's cry.

They'd finally let her go when she convinced them she needed to grieve at home, away from the place where her friend died.

Ella knew she had to get out of there. Had to, but still the last few days she hadn't felt well.

She knew they wanted her baby. No one had ever come out and actually said that, and when she'd admitted her fear to Lisa, the doctors had talked her into speaking to the psychologist that came once a week to speak to the girls giving up their children.

She hadn't liked that doctor and she didn't want to talk about the benefits of offering her child for adoption. Her fears, she'd been told, simply stemmed from her estrangement from her husband, from worrying that a man from a wealthy powerful family could sue in the courts for custody.

She'd transferred her fear.

Yeah, well, maybe that was a buried fear. But she'd learned, growing up where she had, that it was better to listen to that quiet voice inside. If Quinlan wanted to sue for custody then she'd cross that bridge, but right now she was more worried about the Nursery taking her child. The girls up there were so isolated, so alone, and the feds had dropped the ball.

She'd left five voice messages on Jareaux's phone after Fran had died, and he'd never called her back. She'd called him a lot to tell him of her worries. Mostly, he listened to her and told her not to worry, that they were building a case, it just wasn't there yet. Then he just started to blow her off because she wasn't getting him proof. He needed hard facts and evidence. But she hadn't been able to give him that, not really. It was just little things that weren't adding up.

Proof. Always needed proof. She didn't have any . . .

Muscles tightened across her stomach and she winced. "Okay, okay, don't worry, little one. Momma will figure something out."

Suddenly, tired and just wanting it all over, wanting justice for Fran as well, she realized Jareaux had never asked to meet her at his office. Always it was away from the office, some restaurant, some coffee shop, some park or museum. Never his office. He'd asked her early on to contact him on his cell.

Granted, she hadn't thought anything of contacting someone on their cell phone; after all, everyone had them, everyone carried them. A person was more likely to answer a cell phone.

But now?

Now she didn't know who to trust. Who not to trust.

She'd trusted him to help her. That had been a huge mistake, clearly.

She grabbed Jareaux's original card beside the charging station for her phone. Taking a deep breath, she called the office number where she'd left a call-back message before.

"Hello? Hello?" someone said on the other end, and she realized she was lost in thought again.

"Yes, hello, my name is Ella Ferguson Kinncaid. I was wondering if I could speak to someone in charge? I had been working with

Agent Jareaux on the Nursery case and I would like to speak to someone else about it."

"I'm sorry, what case?" the other person asked.

"The Nursery case. Missing babies, adoptions." She sighed and rubbed the base of her spine. Maybe she shouldn't be calling the office, but damn it, the man dragged her into this. Someone was going to help fix this.

There was a pause, silence, and then, "Who did you say you were again?"

"Ella Ferguson Kinncaid. I've called before and left messages for him to return my calls but he's apparently a very busy man."

Again a pause, and then the woman said, "Would you hold please? For just a second?"

Ella didn't even get a chance to say yes or no before the elevator music came on.

She listened to . . . jazz . . . made her homesick. God, she missed New Orleans, the heavy air, the scents, the music, the vibe.

The vibe here was different. It seemed fun and fresh in the beginning, but now it just suffocated.

Finally the line clicked. "Hello, this is Special Agent Sabino, can I help you, Ms. Kinncaid, is it?"

She rubbed her forehead. "Maybe. I'm just tired of getting brushed off by Agent Jareaux after he roped me into this mess."

The woman cleared her throat. "Jareaux? Which case was it again?"

"God, don't you people talk? The Nursery case, the missing babies. I told him, I tried and he doesn't listen anymore because I couldn't get him any hard evidence."

"Okay, calm down."

"Calm down? He asked for my help and then brushed me off when I didn't help him quickly enough or some crap. A girl, a young woman is dead, I don't care what they say. You can figure it out. They keep the babies, and I think they killed her."

"Ma'am? Slow down."

But she didn't want to slow down. She just wanted to leave. "I'm leaving. He can find his own damned evidence."

"Ma'am. Ma'am, I understand you're upset, perhaps you could explain this case to me?"

The words gave her pause. Maybe it was the emphasis on *this case*, the slight rise of tone at the words, as though they were more of a question themselves rather than part of the question as a whole.

"Agent Sabino, was it?"

"Yes, ma'am."

"I'm tired. I'm tired, I'm pregnant, and I know they are going to take my baby, just like they did Fran's, just like they probably did the others. The Nursery may honestly help people, but they hurt others."

"You fear for yourself right now? Has someone threatened you?"

She shook her head. "Not in those words, no, but . . . but . . . I know. I know they're lying."

She remembered the blood . . .

And why did Sabino sound as if . . . "You don't know about the case, do you?" she asked softly. Then anger licked hot and fast through her. "Was there ever a case on the Nursery of Dreams? Was Agent Jareaux ever—"

"Don't worry about Agent Jareaux. Why don't you come—"

"Forget it. Forget all of you. Clean up your own messes. I'm out of here."

With that she disconnected, even as Agent Sabino's "Mrs. Kinn-caid, wait!" echoed.

Her hands shook. So damned stupid. So stupid. Stupid. Stupid.

Oh God, what the hell did she do?

Her hands trembled. She just wanted Quinlan. She wanted him.

From memory she tapped in his number and waited . . .

"Hello?" his voice answered.

She just stood there beside her bag . . . She licked her lips, cleared her throat. "Quinlan?"

"Ella?"

Tears filled her eyes and trickled down. How was she ever going to make this right? His voice, his calm deep voice anchored her. How could she be so damned stupid?

"Oh, thank God . . ."

• • •

She hung up the phone. He was coming. He was coming out here.

170

She smiled, wiped a tear as his last words echoed in her very being, ". . . I'll be there soon."

He was pissed. She heard it in his voice, so tight, so controlled. So much to tell him. But he was coming. He was flying out now. She'd do whatever it took to make this right.

Lisa knocked on the door again. "Hey! Open up, El."

Patting her belly, she said, "Just a bit longer, darlin'. Hang on just a bit longer. Then you can come and meet your daddy. He's coming to help us."

Smiling, she opened the door. "Hey! Guess what?"

"I don't know." Lisa glanced around, saw the bags and asked, "Where are you off to?" She motioned to the bags sitting in the entryway.

For a moment, she kept the words behind her teeth, but then, "I'm done. I'm going to D.C. or will be. I was, but Quinlan's coming out here. I just got off the phone with him."

For a moment, her friend, her only friend here, just looked at her. Then Lisa blinked her big blue eyes and smiled. "Really? And what brought this on? I thought you guys weren't speaking."

Ella shrugged. "You know me. Impulsive."

Lisa stepped in and said, "So he's coming? Now? This elusive husband of yours?"

Ella couldn't hold in the smile or the laughter. "Oh yes. He's most definitely coming. He'll be here in a few hours."

"Well, either way, this is a reason to celebrate. Let's have a cup of tea. It's important for you to stay hydrated, you know. When did all this happen?" Her friend moved into the kitchen and grabbed two mugs, two herbal tea bags from the white cabinets above the sink. "And have you been using the tea I gave you this week?"

"Um . . . actually, no. I mean . . . I haven't . . . the tea. Yes, I've taken the tea twice a day, Nurse Bossy."

Her friend just leveled a look at her. "I'm glad he's coming out here. He should be a part of all this, Ella. After your episode, you know you need to take it easy. High blood pressure during pregnancy is not to be taken lightly. Maybe he can make you slow down." She popped the mugs in the microwave.

Ella twisted her fingers and tried to relax. "We'll see. I doubt he'll be easy about this all but he is coming. I'm happy and yes, I'm watching my blood pressure and it's up a little, but nothing like it was."

"As long as he knows you don't need any added stress, Ella. The doc's really concerned about your blood pressure."

"I'll tell him."

Her friend arched a brow and only hummed.

Why wasn't Lisa more excited for her?

"Look, Lisa, it's not really any of your business, you know. It's my marriage."

Lisa held up her hand. "Honey, I'm your friend. I just don't want to see you get hurt. He never wrote you back, he didn't tell his family for almost two months, and I just think . . ."

For some reason, she lied. "Well, he's excited about the baby, thrilled and he's flying out here tonight. Right now, as a matter of fact. Should be here in four or five hours."

The microwave dinged and Lisa took the mugs out, then she turned to the sink and added cold water to one of them. Her friend did know her because Ella hated hot tea.

Ella sat down on the couch. "Please be happy for me. We're going to be a family. He's so excited."

"And why didn't he come after you wrote the letters? Or answer them? You said he had your email? Even if you changed your phone number, he still could've gotten in touch with you."

Ella rubbed her stretched stomach and felt an answering elbow or knee press across her palm. "We both made mistakes, Lisa. We want to work it out. We're excited. He's excited."

Again, a lie, and though she trusted Lisa, Lisa still had ties to the Nursery. Maybe it would get back to whomever to just leave her alone.

"Of course he is." Lisa handed her the warm mug. "Now, drink your tea and I'll go. Or rather, I'll help you get anything here ready because you just don't know how to take it easy, Ella."

She just wanted Lisa to leave. Sipping her tea, she wished Lisa hadn't stopped by. Her phone trilled out its notes and buzzed from the countertop where she'd plugged it in while talking to Quinlan. It was probably him calling back. He'd worry if she didn't answer soon.

Ella shook her head and took a big drink of tea. "Don't worry so much. I'm good. I'll rest until he calls for me to pick him up at the airport." She licked her lips. "Though maybe I should run to the store."

They chatted while they drank but something . . .

Her phone rang again. "I need to get that, thanks for checking on me. It's probably Quinlan." Ella shook her head, suddenly dizzy.

"Something's wrong," she muttered. Or thought she did. Her tongue felt funny. She tried to stand up, but weaved and fell back onto the couch.

"Oh, dear. That was quick. Don't move just yet, honey," Lisa's voice floated along her eardrums . . .

"No . . ." She shook her head. Felt someone take her arm. "No . . ."

They'd take her baby.

She blinked and tried to focus and saw Lisa's clear blue eyes narrowed down at her.

"No, please . . ."

"Won't be long," she thought she heard.

"Quinlan . . ."

Lisa's laughter floated on the air, mixing with the ringing phone, and then was swallowed.

• • •

The pain woke her.

She gasped and tried to wrap her arms around her stomach, trying to hide, trying to protect . . .

Her arms didn't move. Wouldn't move. Why couldn't she . . .

She blinked and tried to focus as images wavered and blurred before her. God, her head hurt.

"There you are. I was worried I'd given you too much," the voice said, floating down a tunnel to her ears.

Things were fuzzy . . . so fuzzy . . . but the pain.

Oh *God*.

Talons bit into the base of her spine, wrapped around her abdomen and squeezed. She cried out.

"You always, always know when the Pitocin kicks in, don't you?" Lisa's voice warbled and it took Ella a moment to understand the words.

Her hands. She jerked but they didn't move. She twisted and pulled.

"Now, be still." Lisa's voice floated somewhere from above her. Somewhere far above and yet right beside her. The light pierced her eyes and stabbed against the pain in her head. So bright.

"I don't want the IV coming out again."

The voice sounded so normal, but none of this was normal.

Was she in the hospital? What happened? Why couldn't she remember?

"Have to . . ." She licked her chapped lips. ". . . to . . . leave . . ."

She needed to leave. She'd *tried* to leave. She remembered packing . . .

Where was she? She couldn't really see beyond the lights.

Pain built again, tightening not just her abdomen but also across her thighs. It wasn't time.

Wasn't time yet.

She wasn't due for another month almost.

Oh God.

Humming, someone was humming Handel. Lisa.

The room swam in and out of focus. She screamed as another contraction ripped through her.

"I know it's intense, but you're ready. You're already dilated and have been for the last week and effaced. I don't think we'll have any problems."

There was a slight swish and whoosh . . . like water. Swish. Whoosh. She'd heard it before. It was like . . . like the . . .

Baby's heartbeat.

"Please," she said again.

"Please what?" Lisa asked. "I have to go see about a few things, but don't worry, I'll be back. We'll see then how far along you are."

The woman she thought was her friend, dressed in bright stupid cheery scrubs, walked out the door, closing it behind her with a quiet snick.

Ella jerked and jerked again. Her hands and feet were bound. She couldn't move.

No. No. No. This was not happening, this couldn't be happening. No. This wasn't how it was supposed to be. Things were going to be different. Quinlan was coming. He'd been calling her phone. He was flying out here to Taos. To her. To them. He'd been upset, of course, she'd heard that in his voice. But he'd called her wife. Called her Mrs. Kinncaid. He'd told her not to worry, that he'd be there, that he'd help.

He'd help her. Help her keep their daughter safe.

Pain pulsed through her wrists but she kept working at them. Gritting her teeth, she raised her head and looked down at her right wrist. An eyebolt, about waist level, was sticking out of the light wooden bed frame. A zip tie was threaded through and secured her wrist.

No. No.

She shook her head back and forth. Oh God, what did she do? What did she do?

Think. She had to think. No, this wasn't happening.

She strained and pulled, jerked and twisted her arms and hands. The ties burned, her muscles trembled, and still she couldn't get free.

Leaning her head back, she screamed and screamed and screamed until her throat hurt.

"Help! Please God, someone help! Help me, please!" she begged. And still she yelled and screamed more, hoping someone would hear her, help her. Help them.

She'd waited too long. Too long to get away . . .

Jareaux's voice swam through her mind . . . *Help us find the evidence* . . . Evidence of what they were doing.

Evidence of the births with no records, evidence of adoptions not meant to be, of the wrongness of it all.

She wasn't stupid. She'd never really been stupid about anything other than Quinlan.

Quinlan.

No. No! She had been so close to being safe, to seeing Quin and telling him everything, of begging for his forgiveness . . . So close, so damned close.

Another pain started to build.

"Please!" she screamed. "Somebody help me! Please, help me!" Again, she screamed and screamed until her throat was dry and her neck hurt. Still she couldn't move, couldn't get the zip ties to loosen no matter how damned hard she strained and pulled.

They, the Nursery, were *not* going to do this to her. To her baby, her family.

This was an adoption agency. She knew what they would do. What they'd done before.

If the children were already slated for adoption? The money already taken from prospective families and then the mother changed her mind?

Hundreds of thousands.

She'd bet more. Jareaux never actually told her, but it had to be.

That was a lot of reasons to want her out of the way.

There was a clinic here in Taos. Is that where she was? Jareaux knew of the clinic. Maybe . . . maybe . . .

She narrowed her gaze and tried to focus. The wall swam from blurry to vivid. A regular wall with an older door, like a closet? Looking up, she realized the ceilings were higher than normal. Where was she? This wasn't a clinic. She took a deep breath, trying to calm down. The medicinal scents she was used to were the first she picked up, but she also smelled dust and . . . and . . . mildew?

A window to her right showed the afternoon sun through the cracks.

She screamed again and again. And kept screaming, jerking at her bindings, wishing there was a way, any way out. Maybe someone would hear her.

Please, hear her.

"Please, God," she moaned. She blinked and looked up. Noticed the bags hanging from the IV stand. Saline. A bottle hung up there as well. She followed the line and noticed it wasn't hooked up yet. What was it?

She blinked as things still focused and swam. She couldn't make it out but doubted it was good.

Her baby.

She opened her mouth and screamed again.

"Help! Help!" She screamed and screamed, but no one ever came.

Another pain ripped through her abdomen. Claws tightened along her spine and quickly gripped around her hips, her stomach, even her thighs.

"Oh God." She whimpered and tried to curl up on her bed.

She knew what she was supposed to do. She was supposed to be breathing and . . .

Her baby . . .

They were going to take her baby . . .

"Please, no, please, please . . . *Please!*"

Her hands shook and not from pain, she wasn't really feeling the pain in her wrists anymore. She had to get out of here. Had to.

She jerked on her bindings, working them back and forth against the bolts. Blood slicked her wrists, ran down her palms, twirled around her fingers to drip onto the floor. Her hands were bleeding. She'd broken the skin, she didn't care. She had no idea how she'd get her legs free if she ever managed to get her arms free.

Something beeped on the small monitor set on the bedside table.

What were the heartbeats supposed to be?

She had no idea. She couldn't really remember.

The door opened.

"Let's see how we are progressing, shall we?" Lisa asked, sipping from a Sonic cup before she set it aside, and said something softly to someone else.

Who?

"Go to hell," she snarled, her voice already raspy.

Lisa only smiled and walked closer. Lisa pulled a syringe out and put it into the back of the IV inserted halfway up Ella's arm.

"Please," she said, but it sounded like a whisper.

Lisa merely smiled. "Don't worry, this will make it all easier . . ."

"Why?" she mumbled. Her vision took a nosedive and the swishing sound grew louder. She blinked.

"I love how quickly the meds work on you," Lisa said and chuckled. "As to your question . . . Why? My dear, you and your baby were just too good to pass up."

Ella tried to stay focused, conscious, but things swam in and out, away and close.

She heard someone screaming at some point and realized it was her. Bright flashes of clarity. Dull, cloudy waves rolled over her.

The pain. She focused on the pain . . .

Her baby. She had to stay with it for the baby . . .

But it was so hard . . .

Time passed but it meant nothing, nothing. How much time, she had no idea. The pain crashed into her like the rising tide, relentless. Wave after wave. Taller waves, bigger waves, until she was drowning under the onslaught of pain.

Someone was talking to her.

She couldn't make out the words.

A sharp sting on her cheek. "Listen to me! Grab your legs and push!"

It was then she realized her hands were no longer bound. She tried, but her arms felt funny, rubbery. Her hands slipped off her legs and someone cursed.

Something wiped at her palms, fingers.

"Now! Grab and push!"

Ella hissed, feeling the tightening muscles across her stomach, back, everywhere, and gripped. The wave of pain rose, bearing her with it, and she pushed. Listened to the voice and screamed.

Pushed and screamed.

How much longer? How long had it been already?

Hours. It had to be hours.

Cloudy . . .

Flash.

Lisa was pacing, running her hands through her hair. "You can do this. You can do this."

Who was she talking to?

The wave was coming again, coming hard and fast and higher than the others. They all felt higher than the others.

Ella took a deep breath and realized there was an oxygen mask on her nose and mouth.

Ella wanted it over. Just over.

Images flashed again, almost popping in her mind . . .

The pain built, grew to a monster and burned through her. There was no way she would survive this. It wasn't time. The baby was too early.

"Too early," she muttered behind the mask.

"What?" Lisa's voice floated to her. "It's fine. All the tests show she's fine. Now push. Push. I see the head."

Ella bore down. Pain unlike any she'd known before grew and swallowed her, burned through her. And then she heard the baby cry.

A weight on her stomach.

Ella blinked. Blinked again and looked down, saw the bright red hair, the scrunched-up pink face, and cried again. So beautiful. She shoved the oxygen mask down.

Her daughter. Her baby. "Hi," she whispered brokenly. Her hands shook, her fingers numb as she gently touched her daughter. So soft. She leaned and kissed her daughter on her head. "You are . . ."

Perfect. She was perfect. Little fists pumped jerkily in the air. Pale skin; a blotch marred the inside of her right arm. A birthmark.

Just like her own.

She grinned, even as Lisa massaged her stomach and said, "Come on. Come on. Push!"

She delivered the placenta even as pain ripped inside. She winced and moaned.

"Oh well," Lisa muttered. At least she thought she did, but she didn't ask, focused as she was on her daughter

Perfect. "You're so perfect. You're just—"

"Not yours," Lisa's voice cut through.

"No," she whispered, shaking her head. "No. She's mine."

She tightened her hold on the bare skin of her little girl.

Lisa shook her head and reached for the baby, jerking her from Ella's grasp.

The baby cried and squirmed as Lisa held her and put her on a scale across the room.

Ella shook her head. "Mine," she tried to say, but it came out more as a broken whisper. "Mine." So weak. So . . .

She couldn't focus again, couldn't see . . .

Had to get up. Had to . . .

Lisa turned and there was another syringe in her hand.

"No. No. Please no. My baby. My baby. You can't have her. She's mine!"

"For a quarter of a million, she's not yours. Bidders win, they get her."

She tried to bat the needle away, but her hands shook so badly, her whole body shook so badly.

The baby's mewls and cries pierced straight into her.

Lisa just said, "Shhh. Shhh . . ." Cool fingers brushed across her forehead. "It'll all be over soon. If you're still here when I get back, I promise to make it quick. Your placenta didn't detach properly, so I doubt it'll take long. But I do promise to make it quick if you're still here later. A large dose of heparin because, sweetie, you're already bleeding, and you'll just go to sleep, so I doubt I'll have to."

She blinked and kept whispering pleas as Lisa stood there fussing with the IVs.

What did she mean? The words jumbled around in her brain, falling like puzzle pieces.

"No . . . No . . ."

Lisa walked over and picked up her baby.

"Please, please. She's mine. She's mine." Her voice was hardly more than a whisper. "You can't take her. She's mine."

The bright scrubs disappeared through the door.

"Noooo! She's mine! She's mine!" she tried to yell, though it was little more than a rasp. She tried to get up but couldn't.

The door shut.

Wake up. Wake up. Wake up! But she didn't wake up any more this time than she did the last time. She shook her head, back and forth, back and forth. No. No. No. Her damp hair was sticking to her damp face.

Lying there, she sobbed. Sobbed and sobbed. "No. No. No . . ."

Her eyes fluttered open and she looked up. Up at the IV lines that she followed like clear snakes to the bottles hanging above.

Heparin.

What was that? She looked at the IV catheter where Lisa had plunged the syringe of heparin . . . heparin . . .

What did that do?

And then she knew.

Oh God. She'd bleed to death.

Bleed to death . . . something important Lisa had said . . . something . . . bleeding . . .

The walls faded before they focused sharply.

No one would ever look for her daughter. No one knew.

Quinlan would never know. He'd never know she loved him and wanted the family. Never would know his daughter. He wouldn't even know to look for their daughter.

Taking a deep breath, she tried to sit up. Her muscles didn't want to work. Instead she rolled over and pushed herself up with her arms until she swayed, sitting on the side of the bed. The room spun.

She could feel the hot blood draining away, running out of her.

Her wrists were bloody. Not old blood, but new warm blood. She watched as if it were someone else and pulled the IV from her arm with bloody fingers. Liquids went everywhere.

Strong. *Have to be strong.* Chin up, keep going, as her mother always said.

She had to be strong. Had to get out of here. Had to or all would be lost. No one would find her daughter if she didn't.

Another sob caught in her throat. She stumbled to the door and pressed against the wall.

The wall was soft . . . squishy.

She blinked.

Soundproof.

She stumbled and fell into the hallway. Slowly, putting her hands on the wall, she stood.

When would they be back? They? She? Her thoughts jumped and swirled.

The hallway wasn't too long, but took forever. Lights came through three small windows at the top of the front door.

Just had to get to the front door.

Door. For several minutes she fumbled with the knob and the lock. Finally she pulled it open and cold wind blew on her face. Had to get out. Just get out . . .

She stumbled down the stairs and kept going until she fell and the world went quiet . . .

• • •

Ella moaned and opened her eyes . . . Where was she? Dark. It was dark.

She slowly stood and moaned, the world around her tilted and swam . . .

Grass. Grass? Why was she lying on grass?

Where was she? A house or building was in front of her.

Away. Have to run . . .

Run . . . Get away . . .

She stumbled out into the light. Where was she?

Can't die . . . can't die . . .

The lights. Too bright. Too dim. Everything in contrast. Where was she? She blinked and tried to focus.

The street blurred before her. She saw the dark river of asphalt. The tall, wavering streetlights. Flickers of lights zoomed to and fro farther down the way.

Where was she?

She stopped, the road cold beneath her bare feet. Her foot hurt. Her ankle hurt.

She raised her hands and saw there was blood on them. Blood and scabs on her mangled wrists. Her shoulders hurt. Her head throbbed. Hell, her whole body seemed to pulse with pain, almost distant and dull, but not quite enough.

The cold wind blew against her legs and she looked down. Something shimmered, dark and glossy, along the bottoms of her legs. Why couldn't she think?

Something important.

She put her hands on her stomach.

Important . . .

And remembered.

Her stomach.

The baby. The baby . . . *Her* baby.

The bump was different. Smaller, softer. She pressed her abdomen with her bloody hand splayed on her stomach.

No. No. No.

Images, disjointed and fractured, jumped in her brain.

A baby crying.

Red hair.

A room. A room where she'd been tied down.

They'd taken her baby. Taken it. Taken her sweet little girl.

No. No. No.

She stood there, shaking from cold, from shock. Ice in her veins.

"Ma'am?"

Bright. Too bright. Bright, bright lights.

"Ma'am?"

Slowly, she turned and blinked.

"Baby. My baby," she whispered.

Someone walked toward her, the image dark against the bright lights. A hand reached for her. "Ma'am . . . I'm . . . help . . ."

A man's voice, faded and loud, then silent against her eardrums.

"No, please," she whimpered.

"You're safe now. You're safe." The world tilted and she tried to make sense, but nothing did. Cold. So, so cold. Why was she so cold?

Quinlan. She wanted Quinlan. She'd called him. He was coming to help. Help them. Help her.

"Ma'am. Stay with me . . . stay . . ." A static of radio voices tunneled to her, swirling and merging, fading . . .

"Stay with me. Help is on the way," shouted down at her.

The sky was dark, then bright. Red. Blue. Red. Blue. Dark. The darkness grew . . .

She tried to pull away. Tried to go. *Have to find her. Have to find her.*

"Ma'am, what's your name? Your name?"

A dog barked somewhere and kept barking, jerking her back to here, to now, away from the darkness for a moment. She could feel the darkness getting closer though, whispering to her. Sirens screamed louder and louder.

"Ma'am, calm down. Calm down." Hands held her and she blinked, finally focusing. A policeman. A cop.

She licked her lips. "Cop. Help. Please."

"What's your name?" he asked. Dark hair, dark eyes.

"Ella. Ella." She grabbed his shirt. "Help me. They took . . ." She tried to take a deep breath, but her chest felt funny, tired. So damned tired. "Baby. They took my baby. My . . . my . . . Please, I need him. Please. They took her."

"Him? . . . Ella! Stay with me! What's his name?"

"Quin." She licked her dry, cracked lips. Dry. So tired. *Have to find her. Have to find her baby . . .*

"Ella! What's his name?"

"Quinlan Kinncaid . . . D.C. . . . The baby. Took her. They took her. Please . . ." She wanted Quin. "He's my . . . my . . ." She tried to swallow; the world unfocused again in bright blues and reds as sirens screamed in her ear. "Husband."

She saw his lips move, knew he leaned over her, but the darkness grew, a terrible monster, and swallowed her whole.

• • •

183

Albuquerque, New Mexico, October

Jareaux stacked the files on the side of his desk and glanced toward the window. Late afternoon sun slashed through the panes.

He really hated this damned place. Glancing at his watch, he wondered what he'd do the rest of his Saturday. He'd just wrapped up a major case and already was getting recommendations for it—or so he'd heard.

Thank God, maybe he'd finally get the hell out of this shithole. He hated this assignment. He wanted a coastal town, not a desert-landlocked backward place. Could have been in worse places, he supposed.

The case he'd closed with the crate of kids, that just might get him out of here.

A knock on the edge of his desk drew his attention from the window to the woman leaning against his desk.

"Did you hear, Jareaux?"

Agent Sabino. Smart woman, independent as hell and probably ate nails for breakfast. He found her to be a bitch. She never helped him.

"Hear what?" he asked.

She tilted her head. "Remember that woman that called yesterday, or was it the day before? The one called looking for you? The pregnant one? Something about helping you with a case that doesn't exist? Missing babies and missing mothers."

He paused in stacking the folders just so and gave her his full attention.

"What are you talking about?"

She smiled. "Ella Ferguson Kinncaid. Just reported missing, came across the fax a minute ago." She studied him. "Thought you might want to know. Her family is rather connected it seems. Inez will be all over this, I imagine."

"Why?"

"Because most in the office know Mrs. Kinncaid has called here several times this last week to speak to you. And in case you haven't figured it out yet, Inez runs a tight ship. Woman claims to be working with you and her story never changed, Inez is going to find out what the hell's going on. Especially when that woman is a missing pregnant woman whose in-laws go to senators' Christmas parties and probably share the same country clubs or something." She smiled again, but it held no humor. "Thought I'd let you know."

He watched her turn away and walk out the doors. He sighed and raked a hand through his hair.

Fuck.

This was all he needed.

Ella was missing. Woman had been nothing but trouble since he met her. He was not going to let her ruin his career.

Chapter 20

Quinlan didn't know what the hell to think or do. He'd talked to the police, spoken face-to-face to Detective Hudson and a special agent with the feds. The doctors, the nurse — some forensic nurse. He didn't remember. Ian had plenty of questions as well, but then he was Ian, didn't he always have questions?

Hell, Quinlan had plenty of questions as well, and no damned answers.

He sat alone in the waiting room for now. Where the rest were, he didn't know. Ian, Rori, Aiden, and Brody had descended less than an hour ago. He wondered when the rest of his family would descend. He was under no illusions that they would not. Didn't matter if he'd rather they stayed away for a bit until he at least knew what the hell was going on.

No. Kinncaids stuck together.

The Richardsons had called him. He'd let them know when she was found, but asked them to stay in Taos until he knew something for sure. Now he was glad they weren't here yet. They were older, they didn't need to be pacing hospital waiting rooms or corridors at all hours of the night. He still didn't have any news for them.

Mr. Richardson had told him they'd be over tomorrow.

Brody strolled into the waiting room and muttered something about western cops wanting easy fixes.

Whatever.

Quin just wanted to see her. He hadn't really seen her yet. Not yet, not really. He'd seen her through the window, but then the feds had shown up and wanted to talk to him.

Someone sat down beside him in the chair in the stupid waiting room. He knew these walls intimately, had counted the number of scuffs and scratches in the pale yellow paint.

Why couldn't he see her yet?

"Mr. Kinncaid?" the person said.

He jerked and turned to the man beside him, dressed in a white lab coat.

"I'm Dr. Forrester," he said, holding out his hand. "You want the good news or the bad news?"

Seriously? Quin only raised a brow and shook the man's hand. "Right now, I just want to see her. I've been here for over an hour and I still haven't gotten to see her."

His nerves were frayed and he'd snapped at everyone who called to the point that he'd finally just handed his phone to Ian, asking his brother to tell everyone to just leave him the hell alone for a while.

The police believed she'd had a baby. Which means the doctors must believe it as well.

So where the hell was the baby?

"Quinlan?" Brody shook him by his shoulder.

Finally, he looked from Brody to the doctor. "Whichever. Just tell me something and let me see my wife."

The doctor nodded. "Right now, she's in PACU — post anesthesia care — and being monitored. We've managed to stop the bleeding, given her a couple of bags of blood and fluids. Her hormone levels are still high enough she couldn't have had the baby more than a day ago." The doctor sighed and raked a hand over his bald head. "Her tox screens are off. I've given those reports to the authorities."

"What does that mean?"

"We want copies as well," Brody interrupted.

"Her blood levels show depressants, how long, I'm not sure. Other things usually found in post-op patients. So we're wondering about that as it's not available to just anyone." He took a deep breath. "Her INR levels are insane. She was already bleeding, and frankly, I'm surprised she's not dead."

"INR levels?"

"That means that whoever delivered the baby did not do so in a hospital, which was evident in how she was found. She should never have been given a blood thinner, which is what the INR basically measures. Looks like someone gave her a large dose of heparin, with the torn placenta and the fact she was probably hemorrhaging already. Had the police not found her when they did, she'd have bled out, and then I wouldn't be talking to you, you'd be talking to the medical examiner. The torn placenta would have bled her out eventually anyway, and the blood thinners sped that process along."

Well, that was blunt.

He took a deep breath. And another, past the tight bands squeezing his chest.

Who the hell would . . .

"Bastards," Brody mumbled, pacing away from them and then back.

Quinlan couldn't think. None of this made any sense.

Brody's phone rang and Quinlan watched as he glanced at the caller ID and then walked away, answering whoever it was on the other end.

"Does anyone know where the baby is?" he asked the doctor, looking into the man's tired eyes. It was after midnight. He knew the man had probably had a long night already, but then so had he.

"You probably know more about that than I do. I only know she had one, and I know the police are looking."

"I wish they'd look more. We told them last night she was missing. Why are so many of them here?" He shifted and rubbed his thigh. "Shouldn't they be doing something . . . anything to catch the sorry bastards who did this. *Who* would do this to anyone?"

The doctor cleared his throat. "There is another possibility the police asked me about." He took a deep breath. "There's no way to tell if the baby was born alive or not. From her hormone levels and her mutters from earlier, I'd assume it was. However, things can often go wrong, I won't lie about that. If it wasn't for the irregularities in her tox screens, I'd say it was perfectly normal if the baby had been stillborn, and if she lost it, for her to be in denial that she did something with the baby's remains."

Quinlan pierced the man with a glare, as any words he wanted to say wouldn't help the situation.

The doctor slapped him on the shoulder. "I just wanted you to know the possibilities that the police are questioning. I, however, don't even consider that one on the map, and that's without even factoring in the ligature marks. I guess they need to cover all their bases though. However, whoever took the baby wasn't concerned for her welfare, clearly, other than the fact she was pregnant. They couldn't have cared less about her, and as that factors in, it is possible something went wrong with this forced delivery and I have no way of guaranteeing the baby was born healthy or not."

Quinlan tried to picture that. What if something had gone wrong?

What if she'd lost the baby or something and . . . She loved kids, loved helping people, and she clearly wanted the baby or she wouldn't have been having it.

The baby . . .

"No. No. One of the policemen told me she was adamant the baby was alive and that someone took it. And why would anyone give a pregnant woman blood thinners?" Then something else the doctor said jarred him. "Ligature marks? What did you mean?"

The doctor sighed. "As for the ligature, well, you'll see as soon as you see her, she was clearly bound. Ankles are a bit bruised, which tells me her ankles weren't restrained for long. Her wrists, though, are traumatized, she'll need physical therapy." He looked straight at Quin. "As for the blood thinners, there could be a couple of reasons, but neither of them is relevant in her case." The doctor stood and offered his hand again. "You should be able to see her soon. We're just watching her vitals for now. The bleeding, which, luckily, we stopped. And we didn't have to perform a hysterectomy. Anyway, I just wanted to let you know what all we were, or might be, dealing with. She'll be sedated for a while."

"For how long? Can't she help us if she's awake? Answer questions for the police or —"

"Mr. Kinncaid, your wife almost died. We tried bringing her out of it post op, but frankly, I didn't like her stats. She's lucky to be alive and is my first priority."

He stood, shoving his cane into the utilitarian multicolored tiles and shook the doctor's hand. "Of course, of course. Thank you, Dr. Forrester."

"No problem. I'll be around. I want to keep an eye on her. You'll see her soon."

Brody stood against one wall.

Raking a hand through his hair, he all but snarled. "I don't know what the hell to think at this point." He huffed out a breath and looked up to where Brody stood.

"Ian called, he's around in some corner somewhere with better wi-fi reception. Anyway, he's been looking into her, and there's something you should probably know."

"What?"

"Well, she was currently employed and volunteered at a couple of places. One was at a resort — the Nursery. Or actually, the Nursery of Dreams."

"I know, he mentioned it earlier, and . . . ?"

Brody took a deep breath. "It's a high-end adoption agency, Quin."

No. No, she would not have given his child away. No. She'd have . . .

"Brody, she wouldn't do that. In fact, she was scared of someone taking the baby."

Brody didn't say anything at all. Another family came into the waiting room and a toddler was crying for M&Ms from the vending machine.

"Don't look at me like that," he told his cousin. "I know things between us are messed up. I know she didn't tell me until two days ago. Hell, no . . . I don't know what the fuck to think right now, but I *know*. I've told you what she said, I've told the cops, the feds." No, she'd wanted help. Knew he'd help *them*. The idea she'd give up the baby was idiotic.

"Maybe she changed her mind," Brody said.

He shook his head and took another deep breath. He *hated* not knowing everything. Rage beat against his chest.

"Either way, it wouldn't matter, as you are the father and did not give consent to the adoption. I've already started to draft—"

He held up his hand. "Just please be quiet, Broderick."

"Look, none of the family knows anything about her. About the two of you. Though Ian does, as he's been looking into her for the last five, six hours or so. Either way, Rori and Ian are talking about heading out to Taos to see what they can find out."

"And?"

"And your parents are coming—"

He shook his head. "Get Aiden. Tell him to call our parents because I just can't right now. Mom and Pops right now, no. I'm sorry. I love them, but I can't deal with them just yet." He was tired. He'd have to talk to them eventually, but now was not that time.

He sat in the chair and dropped his head into his hands.

"Ian said he was checking the local hospitals for babies and births and someone matching Ella's description. I even mentioned to the locals in charge that you had hired your brother's security firm and that we wanted everyone to work together. Not sure how well that will work in reality," Brody muttered.

The carpet patterns bothered him. They were off a bit, or he hadn't figured the pattern out yet. And carpet patterns didn't matter, even if he'd stared at the damned things for hours.

"Gavin called and said to tell the cops or whoever to check local midwives as well since more and more women are starting to have their children at home."

He looked up. "What?"

"Gavin says birthing clinics and home births are becoming the option for many women. We need to see if that Nursery thing has a clinic or midwives on staff."

"Are midwives the only ones that can deliver babies?" Quin asked. "Besides doctors?"

"How the fuck should I know that?" Brody snapped. "I'll find out. Not that it would really matter. Honestly, Quin, any person could deliver a kid if they wanted it badly enough. The human race thrived for eons before med schools. Just be glad they didn't simply gut her, take the kid and leave Ella dead."

Nausea greased his stomach. "You can stop talking now," he said, not even looking at his cousin.

Quinlan hadn't thought of that. He'd just wondered where . . . who had taken . . .

Oh God, his baby could be anywhere . . .

Brody was doing something, fielding calls. Ian and Rori were checking and researching. Aiden was probably somewhere doing something. He wanted to *do* something. But he didn't want to leave her alone.

She'd been alone. And scared. He'd replayed their conversation a dozen times since they'd found her.

And where had he been?

Maybe he'd had it right the first time. What the hell did he know about being a husband, let alone a good one like his own father and his brothers. He'd already completely fucked it up and now his wife lay somewhere in this hospital and their child . . .

His baby . . .

No, Quinlan wasn't going to leave her.

But . . .

Doubt slithered in. She hadn't contacted him in almost half a year. What if she'd . . . She hadn't wanted to be married to him. He'd tried. Time and again he'd gone to her, and just when he thought she'd come with him . . . she ran away.

Had she known she was pregnant then?

Why hadn't she told him?

If she'd ever tried to give his child away . . .

Rage roared through him, hot and heavy. His hand trembled and he gripped his cane until the knob bit into his palm. No. No, she would not do that. He bit the fury back until the bitter taste was all that was left.

Chapter 21

"You can see her now," a nurse said. "We've moved her into a regular ICU room. She probably won't be there too long. But while she is, only two at a time, okay?"

Quin just stood there. He could see her now?

What the hell would he say to her?

"I didn't know, Brody. How could she not tell me?" he asked his cousin for the umpteenth time.

Brody's hard blue eyes held no mercy. "I don't know. I can't imagine what you're going through," he said, slapping him on the shoulder. "But we're all behind you, you know that, right?"

"Someone hurt her, though. They hurt her. I'm so . . . so . . . fucking pissed and I can't . . . I don't . . ." He took a deep breath.

Brody cleared his throat. "I get that, I do. But as you said, she called you and tried to explain. She did tell you, late, but she did. She was scared. They just got her before . . ."

"Before I could," he finished.

"So she doesn't need an angry husband right now. Though, granted, you've every right to be. She's alone, she's scared, she's confused, and no, she's terrified. Worst case, the baby died, Quinlan. Best case, someone took the baby from her. Whether she told you earlier or not, should have let you know as soon as she knew or not, is irrelevant right now. Since we've been here, we've learned that she was perfect for whomever did this. Alone and without a family to help her. They targeted her, preyed on her, terrorized her, if the snippets of cop talk I heard are true. And stole her child—"

"*Our* child." He glared at his cousin he loved like a brother. "*Our* child. Everyone's said 'baby,' I don't know if she had a name picked out for our daughter."

Brody was quiet for a moment and then said, "Just . . . keep a cool head. She's in a fragile place, Quin. Just be careful with her."

"Christ, what do you think I'm going to do to her, Brody?" With that he stalked off and left Brody standing outside the doors of the hallway. The nurse stood waiting patiently for him.

Scared. She had been so scared on the phone.

Ligature marks.

". . . you'd be talking to the medical examiner . . ."
Bastards.

He knew she'd been scared. And preyed on and targeted.

What he was pissed about was that she didn't *have* to be. She— and their child, their baby girl—could have been safely at home.

Why? Why? *Why* the hell hadn't she just *told* him sooner?

He was pissed he'd missed out on everything.

Enraged he didn't get to hear the damned heartbeat or feel a kick.

But was that really important right now?

He took another deep breath and tried to calm down, tried to focus.

No. No, it wasn't.

So he'd swallow his damned anger and make sure Ella was okay.

And they'd damned well find their baby and the bastards that had done all this.

After that?

He wasn't going to worry about that just yet. There was too much to worry about before then.

Carefully, he pushed the curtains aside. The ICU rooms were on the ground floor.

"She's resting. If all goes well today, we'll move her later to her own room."

He nodded and stepped into the dimly lit room.

She lay on the bed.

His first thought was that her hair wasn't right. Absurd though it was, he noticed, and that bothered him. Her hair was dark, with a touch of red in it. Brown? Dark red? Some brunette color. Where was the purple? Or blue? Or purple streaks? Or even pink?

And she was too pale. Deathly pale. Her freckles stood out on her face, and dark circles bruised the skin beneath her eyes. He slowly walked to the side of the bed. She was hooked up to wires and tubes. He followed the clear and dark tubes to the bags hanging from the IV stand. Saline. And blood.

He set his cane aside and picked up her hand. Her fingers were so cold. He bit down on the insane urge to wake her up. To see her eyes flutter open, to know that she was just cold and not dead.

He looked at the monitor and followed her heart rate, her blood pressure, until he'd pushed back the panic.

Her wrists were bandaged and wrapped in white gauze. Physical therapy because some monster had bound her.

He closed his eyes.

"I'm sorry. I'm sorry I wasn't there for you, you stupid, stupid proud woman." He leaned over and breathed deep, kissed her forehead. "Don't you know what a phone is? Or rather a calendar?"

She didn't answer him. He didn't expect her to. Taking another deep breath, he sat in the chair beside the bed and waited.

"This I'll defend," he muttered. Some damned job he did, and how was he supposed to defend someone who didn't even want his defense?

God help them both.

• • •

Albuquerque, early Sunday morning

"Have you found her yet?"

He waited, but no answer was forthcoming. Finally, he looked up from the papers he was working on.

She stood at the window, looking out over the dark mountains. "We know where she is."

"Really? And where might that be? You told me you had it taken care of, but it seems to me that perhaps you do not."

She didn't move. He watched her.

She would not be the first to fuck up. To betray him.

No one, no one betrayed him.

Not if it compromised the business. He ran a damned successful business and he would continue to do so. If someone or something got in the way, he took care of it.

"She ran, or was going to. In fact, if I had been two minutes later, we'd have lost her. We worried she was too—"

"And now, do you have any idea of the heat you've brought down on us? The scrutiny? It would have been better to just let her go."

"How was I to know she had scared herself into running to the one place we thought she was scared of. Between the meds we were giving her and the session with our lovely shrink, we were sure she was scared the father would take the baby away."

Neither of them said anything for a moment. Finally, he took a deep breath and asked, "How did she get out?"

He watched her swallow and shift. Worried, was she? Stupid bitch had better be worried. He'd disposed of those who had irritated him less than she did.

"She was unconscious. We'd unbound her during delivery. She was bleeding too much from the placenta, which ripped when she expelled it. We had unbound her so it would be easier to move her later and dispose of her." She shrugged. "I was only gone for a bit. Kevin and I took the baby away to the motel room for now. When I came back, there were police all over the damned street. Somehow she got out. And got help." She turned to him then. "She's in the hospital."

He merely looked at her and continued to look at her even as she shifted.

So damned stupid.

"If you cost us anything . . . time, trouble . . . Damn it." He tapped his pen on the blotter. "It'll only be a matter of time before they come here searching for answers."

"It won't be a problem. What is she going to remember anyway? We'll claim she ran from us because she was delusional and afraid we'd take the baby. We were more worried with her peace of mind and the health of the child with her spiraling into paranoid delusions. We've no idea what happened to her or the baby."

He sighed. She only saw the dollar signs. Why was that? He really needed people to see the larger picture. So few did see the larger picture, could see the various layers and all the ripples one little pebble could cause.

He frowned and leaned back in his chair. "You should have made certain she would not be a potential problem or just have left her alone."

"We'd already sold the baby, what did you expect would happen?" she snapped. "For a quarter of a million, I have a feeling the new parents would be rather disappointed and might, just might cause problems of their own."

"How? By going to the cops? Who the hell is going to admit to *buying* a baby? Besides, it was a girl." He stopped and stood, turning to his own window. "Girls outnumber boys, plain and simple. Another girl would have come along in a day, a week, whenever. You could have given the couple that one."

"And done what with her? She was too curious, and I think she knew far, far more than she was letting on. I still think she's working for someone. The feds, the cops, another family, I don't know. She just asked too many pointed questions, her and Fran both. After the Fran incident, she just clammed up, which isn't like her. Acting up and then just running, leaving? She was packed."

He sighed and studied her. She'd been with him for a while, saw this as a business as much as he did, and yet she could be so very squeamish when it came to some of the darker aspects of things. And so bloody cold when it came to others.

"This wasn't my mess. You tried to talk her into things she didn't want. She was never into any of it. From the beginning and the papers. Who signed them? If you were just going to make her a donor, you should have waited for me and we could have done it together, efficiently and cleanly. Like we have so many other times before. This . . . this mess you've created . . ."

She looked at him.

"Is there a father that will make an issue of things?"

"Not since everyone who would be of concern will think the baby is dead."

"You hope," he muttered. Then he shook his head. "You should have called me instead of trying to take care of the situation yourself."

"It all went well."

One of her quirks. She could take babies, talk women out of their children, lie to them, but she had a problem with killing them.

"We should have left her alone."

"The couple wanted a girl, from a more affluent line, a child with brains and beauty. Did you look at the parents? Child is perfect. Parents paid the money and we're happy."

"She's not."

"If we're lucky, she'll be dead soon," she muttered. "I gave her a large dose of heparin."

"So? With the blood she was losing, I'm sure they immediately started her on a coagulant. She's in the hospital, they'll notice in her tox screens. And she's clearly talking to the police, and if that's the case, I'm sure the father won't be far behind. When you push someone far enough into the corner, they only come out biting you in the ass."

She shrugged. "Fine, we tell them the baby died."

He fisted his hands. "We can't do that, they know where she was, or did you forget? You're the one who called me upset because the cops were all over the house here in Albuquerque. Remember? Didn't you say the street was crawling with cops. If she was hemorrhaging, then all they have to do is follow a damned blood trail to whatever door or window she crawled out of. You. Fucked. Up."

For a moment, she said nothing, only sighed. Then, "Fine, we'll say we don't know what happened, that she was anxious and paranoid someone was going to steal her baby. That we wrote it off, but maybe someone here was watching her and did try to steal her baby."

He thought about that. Hmmmm. "Maybe. Guess I could use you."

"You could, but then I'd take you down with me," she told him sweetly. "And you worry too much. If it does lead to us, then what? We have the papers where she signed the child over for adoption, but as she left, we have no idea where the baby is, who she might have given it to or trusted in her deluded state. Besides, who will they believe? A flighty yoga instructor with a penchant for weird hair, estranged from a seemingly wonderful man, or a respected and decorated physician?"

"Will she remember anything?"

"No. Might claim to have heard the baby cry, but that's normal, isn't it? Denial of the truth? How many times, when we told a mother that something went wrong, did they say the same thing? 'But I heard my baby cry'?"

Yes, but most of them had.

"Well, we can do nothing but wait and see, can we?" She paced one way then the other. "We've been in worse situations before. We'll get through this one. So we won't borrow trouble for now."

He hoped not. He needed a plan in place if things went south. A lot of money was at stake with each transaction, he knew that. She knew that.

But other things were at stake as well. He supplied others with merchandise when they asked because his operation was discreet and those bigger fish were not ones that he would want to piss off. So not only was a small fortune on the line but his life. And if his life were on the line, then by God, he'd make certain hers was as well.

He sighed and paced away from her. "Did she keep any records of anything?"

The woman shook her head. "I don't think so. While she was at the Nursery the other night, I checked her house. Place was clean. Her laptop was locked but what would she have on it? DVD of the sonogram. Baby books, the normal crap." She walked to him. "I checked everywhere, worried she'd taken files or something with as much as she was here and there . . . all the girls she talked to. The suspicions she raised, but her place was clean."

That didn't mean there wasn't anything. Didn't she know that?

She shook her head. "You worry too much. Her place was clean. I searched places a meth addict would have been proud of."

"So where is she?"

She waved a hand. "University Medical."

"Who was the father again?"

"Um. Some rich boy. And you know how those types are. They don't want scandals and secrets to mess up their perfect lives. We've done them a favor."

"Yes, but did she ever give you his name?"

"Kinncaid, I think. Kilarney? Kirkpatrick?" She took a deep breath and shrugged. "She only ever called him Quinlan or Quin."

He'd look in the file. He hated surprises and he didn't like leaving things up to chance. He'd have to make a few calls.

"No more on-your-own shit. We clear?"

"But you profit as well."

"We both profit as long as we don't get greedy. Get greedy and the whole damned thing could come crashing down. How do you think this operation has lasted this long?"

She pouted. "You're just pissed you were left out of it."

In more ways than one.

For a minute he only stared at her. Then he sat again behind his mahogany desk and shuffled files around.

"Will I see you later?"

Jaycee Clark

He shook his head. "No, I'm meeting with the buyers. Here as a matter of fact. And I've a family engagement tonight."

He heard her sigh, heard the whisper of scrubs as she walked to him and turned his chair to face her. She shimmied out of her pants and straddled his lap, her legs going over the arms of his chair.

"Then we wouldn't want to waste any more time, would we?" She leaned in and kissed him. Lust hit him hard as her heat burned him through his slacks. She deftly unbuckled his belt, unbuttoned and unzipped him. By the time she had her hand on him, he was hard enough he simply gripped her and thrust into her hot, always welcoming warmth.

"One day," she whispered in his ear, "you'll realize I'm better than she is."

He doubted it. She started to ride him.

He'd never leave his wife for this woman.

But damned if she didn't have her uses.

After she left, he cleaned up in his bathroom, washed and dried his face on one of the perfectly white towels folded to the side of the mirror. He walked out and stood again at the window, watched as she climbed into her car and drove away.

That woman was trouble. He knew it, but he needed her for now. Later? Well, she wouldn't be the first one he'd have to get rid of, would she?

He sat behind his desk and pulled up Ella's file.

Ella, he actually liked the woman and respected her, but that wouldn't stop him. He read through her file quickly.

The father wasn't listed in the first few pages, only later in notes that his lovely assistant had added. A Kinncaid from the D.C. area. Rich and dangerous. Which was why Ella had asked to be paid in cash. She was scared of the guy, or so she'd first claimed after the initial interview.

Later she mentioned they were just estranged.

Either way, a man like that? If it were the former . . . well, a man who controlled his woman generally didn't like it if the woman gave the man's baby away.

Not that she'd wanted to give her child up at all. He knew that, he'd spoken to her about it himself.

He saw "hotels?" written in the margin.

A quick search brought him what he needed and didn't want to know.

Damn it.

Prominent family, his ass.

These people were *all* about family, and they were not only affluent but powerful as well. They adopted kids, or one of them did, based on a write-up in a hotel magazine. There was not a complete family photo. He'd like one so he'd know who he had to watch for.

Shit. Why hadn't he vetted this one more closely?

He tapped his fingers on his desk.

Then again, maybe it was a different Kinncaid?

He looked at what he knew to be forged adoption documents.

Mother's signature.

He squinted. Surely his assistant could have done better than that.

And the father?

Quinlan.

Quinlan Kincaid. The signature was missing an *n*. He drew a deep breath. He just might have to kill that stupid, albeit sexy, bitch yet, or rather sooner than he wanted to. Kinncaid had two *n*s.

He did a search.

Yes. Same family.

He sat back again. Maybe the rich guy was an ass, which was irrelevant. If Ella made it to the man, or if he found out, he could cause problems. Because though they could claim Ella had signed the document, Mr. Kinncaid would undoubtedly state he'd never signed the damned thing.

This was a clusterfuck waiting to happen.

He jerked out his desk drawer, rummaging until he found the plain black-and-white card he'd used several years ago. He'd saved it because one never knew when he'd need certain services.

He stared at it for several minutes. Probably have to use the guy again later if things kept on as they were, and wouldn't that be a pinch in the damned checkbook?

He dialed and waited. Three rings later a Southern voice drawled, "Hello, Doctor, to what do I owe the pleasure?"

"I have a job for you."

"One would assume. And?"

"And I'll make it worth your while if you hurry. Like yesterday."

He waited and looked out the large picture window of his office, the predawn sky slowly fading black to blue. Taking a deep breath, he started the story and told the man all the particulars.

"And when I find her?"

"She's become a problem I need . . . taken care of."

Silence. "Well, I assumed. People don't call me to discuss the weather. How quickly do you want this finished?"

"The sooner the better. Today."

"Give me her name."

"Ella. Ella Ferguson. Or Kinncaid. And she's involved with a Quinlan Kinncaid of the D.C. area. Family owns hotels or some such. She's currently in University Medical in Albuquerque."

"That ought to be easy enough. I'll call you."

"Soon," he blurted. "The sooner the better."

"As soon as I know something." The phone clicked in his ear.

He blew out a breath and leaned back, her image filling his computer screen. If they were lucky, all would be over soon.

Pity though.

She was a beautiful woman. Pregnant or not, he'd rather liked watching her give her yoga classes. He looked to the door. It was time to make a few adjustments to things before the cops showed up and shut them down completely, because that was coming as soon as the next sunrise. He was surprised they hadn't already tried to shut the whole operation down, but it was coming. Then again, he hadn't been answering his phone. Perhaps he should get rid of it in the next day or so.

He rubbed a hand over his face. Had it all just happened yesterday? This had been a long damned weekend. At least the timing was working to their advantage, gave him a bit of time to get things in order.

He had the buyer already, had the baby, who seemed healthy enough, and now . . .

Now he had loose ends to snip.

Part III: Reckoning

Chapter 22

University Medical Hospital, Sunday morning

Quinlan stood outside her room on the third floor. Everyone else was scattered about the waiting room down the hallway. Ian and Rori were arguing when he'd left. John Brasher, who'd showed up at some point with Aiden, was somewhere, and there was the Jareaux guy from the FBI who wanted to talk to him, or to Ella. He'd told him what he could, which was damned little. Why didn't the feds talk? He'd already talked to an Agent Sabino, who had only left sometime earlier saying she'd be back. He was okay with Sabino, she seemed to get it all. She questioned, pushed a bit, but seemed to get he didn't know much.

Jareaux though. That man was pushy with his questions and just annoyed him. The man had kept staring at him—why, Quin had yet to figure out—until he needed air, and he didn't like to leave Ella for more than a few minutes.

Aiden stood beside him. His other brothers, Gavin and Brayden, had stayed home—thank God. He just couldn't deal with *all* of them right now, well-meaning though they were.

"You okay?" Aiden asked.

Everyone had been asking that and honestly he had no answers. His brothers wanted to know where she'd been and why he hadn't known about the baby, and his sisters, or sisters-in-law, simply told him to be there for her. His mother was pissed she hadn't known he was even married; Pops hadn't said a word other than, "You'll know what to do."

Really? Because he really didn't think he would, and yet it was the sanest advice he'd been given.

Below, the hospital was a bustle of activity. Carts wheeled, speaker announcements bulleted out, shoes squeaked across the easily mopped floors of the lower-level ER and ICU. But not here. Here women rested in hushed halls. A baby cried behind a door and laughter floated from another.

They'd moved her earlier today even though she still hadn't really woken up in the ICU. She'd moved a bit, and he thought she'd tried to say something behind her mask, but other than that, nothing.

He hadn't been into this new room yet. They'd just moved her and then the cops and his brothers had shown up.

The door before him was bare of any blue or pink bows or ribbons. No one laughed within.

"Hey," Aiden said, grabbing his shoulder. "You're not alone, you know. This isn't the crap from the last year or so—where we just give you lots of space. We're all here for you and whether you want us or not, you damned well need us right now. This isn't just you, Quin."

"I know. I know that. I do. But I really don't think I can take one more piece of advice, one more well-meaning comment. One more . . ." He stopped and bit down. "Aiden. . ." He raked a hand through his hair. "Where the hell is the baby? Where's my daughter?"

He knew it was a girl, she'd told him as much on the phone Friday night. The paramedics said it was a girl, and her medical records, though not actually released to him, had shown she'd been pregnant with a baby girl. And it wasn't due for over three weeks.

Aiden tilted his head. "Are you sure it would be yours?"

Quinlan ignored him and walked into the room, almost glad of the quiet hush of the room.

Was it his?

His gut and knee-jerk reaction was *hell yes*. But what did he honestly know of Ella? The timing was right and the Ella he'd known in New Orleans, or thought he'd known, had not been sleeping with someone else.

She still lay hooked to IVs.

He limped over to the bed, easing down into the chair beside her.

The heart monitor didn't beep, but as he'd learned down in ICU earlier in the day, he was calmed by watching the small square mounted to the IV stand. Slow and steady, then erratic, then steady again. The clear oxygen tube was still under her nose and there were still bags of clear fluids and blood on the metal curled hooks.

He'd passed other rooms. He didn't remember looking into them. But he'd been in labor and delivery rooms last year when Brayden and Christian's baby was born, when Gavin and Taylor had a kid. Christian's room and Taylor's had been bursting with gifts, and flowers, and stuffed animals. Balloons.

None of that was here.

But then, there was no baby, was there? He should get her some flowers anyway. Just because. Or would that look like a sympathy gift? And why the hell did he give a shit about flowers just now? He huffed out a breath and raked his fingers through is hair.

Where the hell was his child?

He leaned over and took her hand in his. The long pale fingers lay lax in his. At least they were no longer cold, and her cheeks didn't look as pale to him. He didn't know where she'd been.

What she'd been doing or who she'd been doing it with.

The police were looking through her life here, and the FBI. He'd talked to a couple of them, but he'd been useless in helping them. The cops acted as if they didn't believe he hadn't known about the baby prior to Friday. The feds, though, had stood up for Quinlan just as Brody had jumped in. Apparently the FBI did not believe he had anything to do with the disappearance of his daughter or with his wife's abduction.

So many thoughts swirled in him. He couldn't ask her just yet, she was still out.

But they needed to know so much.

He rubbed his fingers over the back of her knuckles. He remembered kissing them before. Remembered the sound of her laughter.

The way her coaxing voice could almost chide. A cutting glance from her eyes. Her lips could tilt just so at one corner, making him want to kiss her. Then make love to her. But then again, he had. They had. More times than he could count, and in some cases remember.

And that was what ate at him the most.

This was why he hated to give up control. Shit always happened when he relaxed and gave up control. Give up control and he almost gets killed, give up control and he ends up married. Give up control and let her have her space . . . and she calls months later claiming to need his help. Because she was pregnant with his baby and didn't tell him sooner. And now?

Kinncaids and defending.

He put his head on the bed and stared at the floor.

He knew without talking to the man just what his father thought about it all — other than he'd know what to do.

It wouldn't matter, not really, and it didn't, that she hadn't wanted to be married to him. Not if she was pregnant. He should have swallowed his pride and . . .

Kinncaids accepted responsibilities. Period. And it wasn't even about accepting responsibilities but doing what was right simply because it was right.

How did he not know about the baby?

Why the hell had she not told him about the baby?

Because she didn't want the marriage. Didn't want you. Didn't want the whole package deal.

And he had?

Since when?

Hell, his whole family was shocked as hell and he had no one to blame but himself.

He looked at her pale face, freckles standing out across her nose and cheekbones. Her lashes were still long and curled against her cheeks.

Other than her hair, she didn't look any different. Shouldn't she look different to him after so much time, after having a child?

Women were supposed to gain weight, weren't they? Why then did she look like she'd lost weight. Her wrist bones were even more prominent and fragile than he remembered, even with the bandages. Her arms smaller, her cheekbones more bladed. Her eyes sunken with darker circles, the only real color on her almost chalklike complexion.

Blood loss.

"Please wake up. Please open your eyes."

He wanted her to open her eyes. Wanted to see them flash at him again, wanted to see her cheeks blush as he knew they could. See her dimpled smile.

She had called, begged for his help. He'd tried, but it hadn't been enough. Better late than never, he guessed, sighing. None of it mattered right now. Now, he just wanted her to wake up so they could . . . he could . . .

Could what?

Ask her. Ask her . . . talk to her . . . yell at her? And what kind of man did that make him? Hell if he knew, though he figured not a very good one. He laid his forehead on the edge of the bed.

"Please wake up. We need you so you can tell us what happened, so we can find our baby. Please wake up, Ella. Come back to me. Please."

The minutes ticked by and he paced to the window, staring out at nothing. He was so damned tired he could barely think. Ella moaned.

He whirled around and saw her frowning. Quin hurried back to the bed.

"She's mine! She's mine! Noooooo!" Ella mumbled.

Quinlan stood beside her bed. "Ella. Ella, wake up. Ella. You're safe now. Come on, you're safe."

She gasped and opened her eyes. Those eyes. He'd remembered those eyes. Thought about, dreamed about and missed those eyes. Those beautiful blue-green eyes, and yet now they were different. The sparkle was gone. The innocence he'd always seen in them.

For a second, a fleeting second, the fear vanished as she looked at him.

Ella. His Ella looked back.

Blink.

Fear, shock and confusion slid back into her, the blue shifting more to green.

He ran a hand over her hair, wrong hair on her. The lackluster brunette, with a bit of red, was plain and dull against the white pillow. He was used to seeing it shimmer in whatever color she had chosen. Now it was longer and touching her shoulders. He'd noticed the roots looked red to him, as burnished as his own. Why did she cover up such a beautiful color?

He had never thought of her having normal hair. Or he had, in a vague, *I wonder what she would look like normal . . .* thought. Stupid thought. She looked wrong.

Wrong and lovely.

And still his, by some twist of fate or God's grace, she was his—at least legally.

But her eyes weren't bright and full of laughter like he remembered. Her hair—he missed the blue color. Blue or purple or whatever color.

"Hey," he said, brushing a strand of hair from her forehead.

She shivered and he realized her head was damp. Sweat. Cold sweat.

"Bad dream. That's all it was." He kept his voice calm, noting how her eyes darted around the room. How she searched, looked with fear fighting hope.

"You're safe now, Ella."

A breath shuddered out and she closed her eyes.

Quinlan kept running the tips of his fingers over the edge of her ear as he brushed her hair back. And again.

Her hand moved, and without opening her eyes, she stopped his hand. Her fingers trembled and then she clasped his hand, her fingers tightening.

"Quinlan?" her voice trembled and then she opened her eyes and focused on him. "Quinlan? Is it really you?" she barely whispered. More like a fractured whisper.

"Yes, baby, I'm here."

Her eyes held his and filled. "How? When? I made it? You made it?"

She tried to swallow, licked her lips.

He sighed and reached over, pouring her some water. He opened the straw, pulled it free and set it in the water, all the while wondering how to . . .

He stared at her for a moment as she took a tentative drink and he wondered what to tell her. What to keep from her. The cops didn't tell him, the doctor didn't say anything other than to keep her calm. How the hell did he do that?

How could she not tell him?

Did he even really know her?

Yes. You know her.

"What do you remember?" he asked, setting the cup on the bedside table. He let go for a moment to lower the rail on the side of her bed before sitting beside her. He reached for her hand again, careful of the bandages around her wrists, and she clasped it. Her brows furrowed and she looked at him, as if trying to remember.

"I called you. I called and we talked."

Several months too damned late, but he didn't say that. Instead, he nodded. "You did. You did, surprised the hell out of me. I'd all but given up and . . . Never mind." He looked down and then met her gaze again. "You're alive and safe, the other. . ." He shook his head. "Doesn't matter."

He tried to understand. Tried to . . .

Her breath came faster, her fingers tightened on his. "Should have told you sooner. So much sooner. But I was scared and stupid. So stupid. But I knew time was running out. They were going to take it. Take it anyway. I told them no. Time and again. No. No. I wanted the baby. I told him they were watching me, but I didn't have proof. He always wanted proof and I think . . . I think he lied too, but . . ."

Now she was breathing like she'd run a mile and the machine was beeping.

"Calm down. Deep breath . . . Ella. Ella." Her eyes looked past him. "Ella, look at me. Right here. Look at me."

He took a deep breath himself, hoping she'd follow. The scents of disinfectant, bleach, and old food hit him. Hospitals. They all smelled the same. He should know, having practically spent half of his childhood in one. "Right here. Eyes on mine. Remember?"

Why he'd said that he had no idea. A memory flashed in his mind, they'd stood in front of Elvis and she'd been nervous. He'd said that then. Her aquamarine eyes had locked onto his. The image burned its way into his brain. Her hair was cotton-candy blue then with pink tips. And then she'd smiled at him, a bright wonderful smile, her eyes flashing with nerves and humor.

There were no nerves now. No humor.

Only confusion. Only weariness and panic.

Panic.

He'd kill someone for putting that look of terrified helplessness in her eyes alone.

Forget whatever else the bastards had done, and they'd sure as hell done plenty.

"Oh, God, Quin. Where is she? She's so tiny! Where . . ." Her voice was so broken and raspy.

"Ella—"

She interrupted him. "Lisa. I thought she was my friend," she whispered to him, twisting on the bed, as if to sit up. He held her down, felt her trembling. "I remember. I packed my bag. Was ready to leave to go see you. The car was packed. I didn't even tell him I was leaving. I didn't care anymore about helping them, I just had to leave. I called, spoke to another agent, and she acted like she didn't know what I was talking about. What if he works with them? I had to get to you. I was scared they'd stop me some way. Scared that I couldn't save her." Her words tumbled and tripped over each other. Her voice sounded scratchy and hoarse. Like a really bad case of laryngitis.

"Who? Who did you trust?" he asked, hearing people out in the hallway.

"Baby. Our baby, Quin." Tears filled her eyes, trembled onto the edge before trickling over to slide down her pale cheeks. "They took her. I know it. They took her. She took her. I couldn't get away! I couldn't get away! My baby!" she tried to scream, but it came out as a high-pitched wheeze.

"Who, Ella? Who did this to you?" He rubbed her arms, trying to calm her down, seeing her stats skyrocket.

"Lisa. The tea. Drugged the tea at my house, I think. The tea on the couch. Lisa." She started to strain, her hands shaking in his.

The door opened and a nurse came in, the federal agent behind the nurse.

"Lisa who?"

"Hammerstein. Lisa . . . The—the bed. I couldn't move. I couldn't move!"

"Shhh. Enough. Enough, Ella." He picked up her trembling fingers, touched her bandaged wrists.

The nurse was checking the stats on the monitor and shaking her head as alarms began to sound.

"Ella, Ella, look at me," the agent said from beside the bed.

She never looked away from his own eyes, never glancing to see the agent.

"My baby. I want . . . Couldn't get away. Tied down. The baby was coming. I screamed and screamed and screamed and no one came." Her voice raked his nerves raw even before the words tumbled and righted into place. "Why didn't anyone help me? What . . ." Tears streamed down her face and her breaths came in gasps. "Where is she? What did they do to her? A baby. Our baby girl. Red hair. She has red hair. Oh God . . . Oh God, Quin . . . Quin . . ." Her face crumpled and she tried to scream again, arching and twisting to sit up. Her broken voice made his chest tight. Her words . . . "I want my baby! I want . . ." Her broken voice.

He pulled her to him and wrapped his arms around her. "I know . . . I know . . ." Tears filled his eyes.

The agent said something else, and he felt Ella tense at the man's voice.

"I need to sedate her," the nurse said.

"Not yet," the agent snapped.

"I have my own orders, sir, and you shouldn't even be in here," the nurse shot back.

"Ella," the man said.

He watched the nurse put the syringe into the IV and depress it. Ella sobbed and screamed broken wheezing screams against his chest.

"I want my baby. I want my baby . . ."

"It'll be okay, love." How, he had no idea. He was so confused and worried and scared and *pissed*. But none of that helped them now.

"We'll find her," he whispered into her hair, gently rocking her. "We'll find her. I swear it."

He felt her relax against him, the tension easing out of her.

"I *needed* to talk to her!" the agent said, leaning into the nurse.

She propped her hands on her hips. "I get that, but I'm *not* going to compromise her health and the doctor does not want her more stressed. Her blood pressure is still too high."

The doctor had walked in at some point and checked the chart, the monitor, his eyes meeting Quin's as the agent and nurse argued. The nurse stood there with the doctor. "She's to be kept calm."

Quin nodded, rubbing his hand up and down her back. "She had a nightmare and woke up. She doesn't remember much but . . ."

"Clearly knows they took her baby. Poor thing," the nurse said as she helped ease Ella back down.

Quinlan didn't want to let her go.

He sat back in the chair for a moment while the doctor checked her vitals and whispered in the medical jargon that was familiar to him, yet still meaningless.

The doctor gave him another look and then the room was quiet again.

He grabbed a tissue and gently wiped her cheeks, her eyes.

The agent rattled the change in his pocket. "Damn it," he muttered. "What exactly did she say?"

"She didn't say much, but she said she, referred to a woman she trusted . . . Lisa, I think. Sounded like maybe Lisa drugged her tea. Something about tea on the couch and being packed to go . . . Lisa Hammerstein." He stopped.

"Okay, good. Packed to go where?"

He looked up and met the man's gray eyes, started to say how she didn't trust a man she was working with, how she'd spoken to another agent. But he didn't. Instead he said, "She was packed to come to me when she called. I told her to stay, to wait. I could be out here in about four to five hours and I was. I didn't want her traveling after . . . after she told me."

The agent nodded, and only stood there staring at Ella. He'd also called her Ella.

"Lisa. That helps, and her house? She said her house?"

"No, I don't think so. She said Lisa, talked about drugged tea and being packed to leave. Mostly . . ." He sighed and traced her cheekbone with his finger. "She cried for the baby. Our baby girl. Does any of that mean anything to you?"

The man's phone vibrated and he checked the ID. "I'll be back," the agent said and left.

Quinlan stared after him and then he hurried to the door. He wanted answers, damn it. The doctor was in the hall clicking information into a computer beside her room, but no Agent Jareaux. Where the hell did he go?

"Yes?" Dr. Forrester asked.

Quinlan swallowed. "Her voice. Her voice is wrong, hoarse like someone with laryngitis or something."

The doctor just looked at him and took a deep breath.

Quinlan hurried on, "She said she screamed and screamed for help but no one . . ."

The doctor nodded. "Makes sense." He shook his head and rubbed the bridge of his nose. "I don't know what all she went through. Frankly, she may never remember what all she went through, and if she screamed herself hoarse and voiceless, maybe that's a good thing, Mr. Kinncaid."

Quinlan couldn't look away from him and he nodded. Then he nodded again before he turned and went back to Ella. He took her hand and sat back down.

He continued to hold her hand, rubbing the back of it.

"Why? Ella," he whispered on an exhale. "Why didn't you call me months ago? Just pick up the phone and call me? Ella, why didn't you . . . God, Ella, how could you be that cruel?" He rubbed his face with his free hand.

No answer came.

He heard her words again from their conversation Friday, and her words from earlier. So many words practically choking on them, stumbling, and tripping.

She twitched, her hand fisting in his as her head shook back and forth on the pillow.

"You're safe now, Ella," he said softly. "You're safe with me, and this time I'll damn well make sure you stay that way."

He pulled the blanket up, tucking her arms under it—her bruised arms. So many bruises, some dark already, others just red. Her wrists were probably a mangled mess since he could see the swelling and the bruises above and below the bandages. Bruises and cuts, blood loss. The hemorrhaging.

. . . you'd be speaking to the medical examiner . . .

A shiver danced down his spine.

He carefully put her hands beneath the covers, not wanting to mess up the bandages or IVs.

"I almost lost you." Another shiver iced his stomach. "I thought I had lost you, sort of, you know. And that doesn't matter right now, does it?" he asked, though he didn't expect an answer. "But this . . . this is too dammed real. My brothers, they all had to worry about wives and girlfriends getting hurt. I thought I would not have to worry about all that, you know? Yeah, you do, I remember that conversation as we walked to Magnolia Grill one night. But I did worry. I do worry. I worried about you, all the damned time. What you were doing, who you were with, if you needed anything, if you were safe." He blew out a breath and watched her face, lax now again that the sedatives swam through her system. "If you were safe. I told myself that of course you were, or I would know. Somehow I'd know if you weren't. How, I have no idea. Stupid, I guess. I should have found you, at least made sure you were all right."

And why he hadn't, he didn't really know, had no answer.

"You wanted your space. I finally gave it to you, as I respected you and wanted to respect your stubborn choice. I should have done what I really wanted to do," he admitted quietly. "I should have followed you to New Mexico, or worked harder to just keep you in New Orleans. If you don't want to live in D.C., we didn't have to. I don't know if I ever said that before. Yeah, I should have followed you and tried on the whole stalker scenario. Should have told my family sooner. Hell, I don't know, Ella. I don't know. I just know I made the wrong choices too. I fucked up. I'm sorry."

Nothing made sense anymore.

The air felt heavy, and too still, too quiet, too . . . tight. Like a storm waiting to unleash its fury.

She muttered something. He rubbed his hand over her arm and she stilled.

Intense. It was all intense and messed up and it wasn't just him that felt it either. Ian was currently in his scary-focused mode. Then again, it was family and it was a child. Ian would be intense anyway, but it was as if he was hunting prey. There was no other way to describe that focused energy. Just like before when his brother had returned.

Someone in the hall laughed again and he wished they would all go away.

He didn't want to hear laughter just now.

He stood and leaned over her, brushing a strand of hair away from her forehead. Quinlan took a deep breath and realized she didn't smell the same, sweeter somehow, with a tang of medicine attached. He kissed her forehead.

Quinlan paced back and forth across the room. Nine steps one way. Checking Ella again, noting she hadn't stirred, he needed a bit more room to pace. The hallway was silent now as he stepped outside and left the door cracked.

Postpartum wing of labor and delivery.

Who had done this? When would she wake up so they could talk to her . . .

Too many questions.

The thought of never having *known of* his child, the fact that he might never know his child if . . . Panic sank its poisoned teeth deep. No, not going there.

He shoved it aside.

They'd find her. They *would*.

He walked the hallways. Only one nurse stopped him and asked if he needed help, and who he was visiting.

"My wife." He froze and stared at the nurse. Shaking his head, he said, "My wife. I just need some air."

As he walked away, the long block-patterned carpet muffling his footsteps a bit, he saw and heard another nurse speak to the first quietly. He wasn't far enough away not to hear the first's, "Oh, those poor people!"

He ignored them, walked to the end of the hall around the corner, through the door and finally back. At the nurse's station, he asked, "Can I see the nursery?"

For a moment, the middle-aged nurse behind the desk just looked at him, then jerked her head to the side door that he thought led back to the waiting room. No, the stupid sign hanging from the ceiling clearly said *Nursery*.

The Nursery . . .

He took a deep breath and followed the nurse through the doors. It was still a hallway; others stood in front of the glass. Three others actually.

"Most of the time, the babies are with their parents," the nurse told him.

He didn't answer, just looked through the glass. It was old glass, still had the little wired lines in it from decades past.

Clear—what were those baby things called?—bassinets held a few babies. The others were empty.

He stood there staring at the sleeping infants. One moved, jerkily. That had always amazed him. So tiny, so fragile, and they moved like automatons to him. Little jerks and starts as if the gears weren't quite working yet.

All babies looked the same to him.

Even the one clearly awake and moving, her tiny head covered with a pink-striped cap.

Where was she? Where was *his* daughter? Was she that tiny? How much had his daughter weighed? The girl safely bundled and wrapped behind the glass had a place card in her little unit. Even from here he could read that the baby had been eight pounds and three ounces.

Was his daughter smaller yet? And she'd been early. How early?

What if she needed medical attention? Preemies did, he knew that. How early was too early?

He could count. Nine months. It was almost nine months to the damned day he'd met Ella. Yet, he didn't know enough yet to know if the baby was only a little early or way early or . . .

God, he was going nuts.

The baby's little old face scrunched up.

Tiny old faces.

Did his daughter look like her, all pink skin and wrinkly? Or was she smooth like the baby next to that little girl?

Did she have a lot of hair? Red hair. Ella had said she'd had red hair during her hurried speech.

An innocent baby. Who did she look like? What of her eyes? Did she have his dimple? His father's eyes? Her mother's eyes?

Where was she?

And how did he even begin trying to find her?

Chapter 23

Sunday afternoon

Dark . . .

Sounds . . . a quiet hiss.

Ella slowly came to.

She heard a slight beep and then the tightening of the cuff on her arm.

No.

No. They'd found her. They had her.

She gasped, jerked, and opened her eyes. Where was she? Where was . . .

Her chest felt heavy, her limbs funny, cold and aching. She was cold. Where was she? Her hands went to her stomach. Where was her baby?

Her baby?

Panicked, she glanced around. No bassinet waited beside her. No nurse came to see her. What was this place? She'd been in the clinics and knew the color scheme. The labor and delivery at the local hospital was pastels, yes.

The walls here were a soft green, but not pastels, more . . . something. She didn't recognize where she was precisely, but she knew she was in a hospital. The scents, the feel, the fact she was hooked up to a blood pressure cuff and the IVs running into the back of her arm where the blood IV was taped down.

But where?

The door opened and she jerked at the sound.

They were coming. They were . . .

He stood in the doorway looking at her. Straight green eyes studied her, and a muscle bunched in his cheek. He took a deep breath, stepped into the room and let the door shut behind him. Still tall, still muscular and fit, still too . . . perfect.

A baby cry pierced through her. She started at the sound of it and realized it came from another room, maybe next door. Maybe across the hall.

It wasn't her baby.

"Quinlan?" She looked around again. Hoping to see. Hoping to find . . .

He sat beside her and reached for her hand.

"You're in the hospital." His voice was the same as she remembered. Calm, cool, soothing.

She did remember it otherwise, a couple of times.

Images flickered in her mind. A house. A bed. Her breath came faster. A policeman and red lights. Another cop . . . a detective? Quinlan talking to her.

His eyes locked onto hers. "You're safe now."

She shivered, ice skittering beneath her skin.

"The baby? Do you—do you have her?" she asked, hoping, praying, hoping. *Please. Please. Please.*

He took a deep breath. A muscle jumped in his jaw. "Ella." He sighed and looked away. "No. No, I don't have her. No one knows . . . No."

His eyes, always green, seemed to almost glow in the light. His features were not as smooth as she remembered. Instead they stood out, his skin tight over his cheekbones, the muscle still bunching in his jaw.

She realized his hand held hers and his fingers were softly rubbing the back of her hand.

"How—" She licked her dry lips. "How did I . . ."

Her heart fluttered and thundered in her chest. Panic clawed closer.

"Would you like some water? Or ice?"

Ice? She shook her head. "Water." What was wrong with her voice? She put her hand to her throat, which hurt.

He picked up the plastic pitcher beside her bed and poured it into the glass. Some sloshed out and puddled on the little rolling table. She remembered him doing this at some other point, but couldn't quiet wrap her mind around it.

Something hissed and the blood pressure cuff tightened on her arm. Ella struggled to sit up and took a long drink from the straw he bent toward her, her throat hurting more as she swallowed.

Silence roared between them.

What did she say? She'd thought he'd known. She'd written to him, given the letters to Jareaux to mail. She'd worried he hadn't known, but she'd written to him, and even if she had doubts about Jareaux, she'd always thought deep down that Quinlan *knew*.

"Why didn't you write me back?" she suddenly asked, picking at the blanket.

She'd been so scared. So very, very scared and all alone she realized now. Perfect for them. Perfect.

"You never wrote to me." The words bit out.

Her eyes jerked to his. "Yes, I did. Several times! Three letters. I never heard back. I told you about the baby. What I was doing, what I wanted. How when it was over . . . I wrote you."

He opened his mouth, closed it, opened it again and then took a deep breath. "If you wrote me, I never received any letters," he finally said, calmly and quietly.

Anger bit through the fear at his *if*.

She searched his eyes, then looked past him to the wall. Jareaux. Jareaux who hadn't wanted her to call his office, his office who acted as if they didn't know what she was talking about. Jareaux who had said he'd mail her letters. Jareaux who had blown her off because she wasn't getting him proof quickly enough.

Jareaux who hadn't wanted her to contact Quinlan because it might compromise the investigation, though he had offered to send her letters. She realized with sudden clarity the agent had never specified when he would send them. With a man like Jareaux, he probably hadn't, she realized.

"I really am stupid." Had she ever . . . No. And why hadn't she just emailed him? Because she'd thought it was a chickenshit way to let him know. Always griping about the gadgets, gadgets she could have used and . . . And the Nursery had fed into her quirk as well. Living off the grid, a more natural way of doing things. Healthier for the baby and whatever other crap they had fed her.

"He never mailed them. I gave the letters to . . . someone . . . to mail," she whispered. Stupid. She'd known it was stupid. Why hadn't she given the letters to Mr. Richardson? Or his wife? They were nice. They would have mailed the letters. And she had already explained the situation to her nice grandparently neighbors. They still wondered and asked her why she had run. She was always running, wasn't she? But she was helping the *FBI*, doing more, helping others, and of course she had given Jareaux the letters so that they could make certain she hadn't said anything to compromise the investigation. Of course she had because she had naïvely trusted the bastard.

God, where was her baby?

"To whom?" he asked softly.

"What?" she asked.

"Who did you give the letters to?"

"It doesn't matter, does it? He, they never mailed them, did he? Jareaux. Probably him. He lied. You never knew . . . Agent Jareaux . . . was it was all lies?" God, and the others. So many others. Who did she trust? Because she clearly trusted the wrong people. She thought she'd been helping . . .

"It matters to me. Why didn't you just mail them?"

She shook her head and tried to sit up, her head pulsing with pain.

"Oh, no, lay back down."

"I have to find her. I have . . ."

His hands on her shoulders held her down and panic spider-webbed over her skin. "Ella, you almost died. People are out looking. The letters matter to me, who?"

"Jareaux." She didn't elaborate.

"Fine." He only cocked a brow and shook his head. "We can get into all that later. Or again. The FBI wants to talk to you."

"Agent Jareaux? I don't want to talk to him."

He sat on the edge of her bed now. "Yes, and another agent . . . Sabino. You know them?"

"I don't want to see him. Jareaux, I don't want to see him." He'd lied, led her, used her just as much as . . . "He lied . . . before. I tried to tell him. He . . ." Everything was so messed up. She rubbed her forehead.

"He's the FBI, they are trying to learn what they can with you, to find our baby, and apparently there is some sort of investigation and . . ."

"*Now* he's worried about the investigation? He didn't seem concerned a few days ago, or hell, even last week. He was too busy with another investigation. Too busy to help me get out of the mess he put me in. I didn't find the proof quickly enough for him. Said he didn't have time to babysit me or hold my hand. On second thought, yeah, maybe I will talk to him."

"Ella, it's the FBI, they look for missing kids. Right now, that's our priority. We need all the help we can get to find her."

Anger flamed through the panic she was shoving back, but like a rising tide, she could feel it building.

"I know that, Quinlan," she whispered. "I know what they do, or say they'll do. I was helping them—him." She closed her eyes and admitted, "I listened to Jareaux when he said I could help them. When he said I was in the perfect situation to help them."

She felt him still, could feel the tension tighten around him. She opened her eyes and met his, glittering emerald green and just as hard.

"You were what?" he asked quietly.

She licked her lips. "Helping them—the FBI—or trying to. I did what he said. Jareaux. I tried . . . But I think he lied. Maybe about all of it. I wrote you letters telling you about the baby and how when the investigation was over I wanted us to be a family. I was sorry. Am sorry. Doesn't matter now . . ."

She dropped her head back on the pillow.

"You were helping the FBI with some sort of investigation because Jareaux asked for your help and he didn't mail the letters you wrote to me?"

"Missing babies, missing women from the place where I worked."

He nodded, the skin across his face tight, a muscle bunching in his jaw. He opened his mouth, then shut it. He took another deep breath.

They didn't have time for this. Again she tried to sit up, if she could find Lisa she might . . .

"Lie down," he told her.

She shook her head. "I have to find her, Quin. I have to look. Lisa . . . I have to . . ."

Again he put his hands on her shoulders and gently pressed her back down. "Ella," he said, his voice quiet steel. "You almost died, and if you think I'm going to let you get up and waltz out that door so you can finish the job, you can damned well think again."

Her eyes filled.

"I have to find her," she whispered, felt the warmth of tears trickle down her cheeks.

"We will. You have to heal, though."

The panic she'd been holding back crested and broke over her, sending chills quaking through her body. "She's so little, Quin. So little. Early, she's early."

"How early?" he asked, trying to keep her calm.

"Over three weeks early. You can check with Dr. Merchant or Radcliffe, though I don't know if they'll be honest. I don't know anything anymore, Quinlan. I just know I want my baby. I have to find her. I have to—" Again she tried to sit up, but he pressed her down again.

"Calm down. Please, look at me, Ella. You can't help by leaving and collapsing, but you can talk to the FBI, or whoever. They have questions about the baby, the locals have questions, the state police. Ian, my brother, he's talked to them, he and his wife are great at finding things and are here in New Mexico right now."

"They are? Really?" She thought back to their time together.

He grunted. "If there's anything to find, he'll find it. You need to concentrate on helping us at this end."

"She's so little, Quinlan. And she's early. What if something was wrong. How will anyone know? How will we find her? What if whoever has her isn't nice? What if she's . . ."

"No ifs. We'll find her. Now, look at me."

She met his gaze. A shadow dusted his jaw.

"How did you get here? Do you remember?"

Exhaustion slid through her veins. What drugs were they giving her?

She took a deep breath. "Journal . . . I have a journal. I wrote it all down who I thought was behind it, not Lisa though," she muttered.

"Who?"

She shook her head. "I don't know exactly. One of the doctors, I think. The midwife? I don't know. I don't know!" The image of her friend holding her baby. "Lisa, Lisa helps them." She gripped his hand. "I wrote it all down, not the Lisa part!"

Fractured and broken images skittered through her brain. The couch in her living room, the other room with gray walls, a hallway.

"Where's the journal?"

"I started one for the baby, but added other stuff. I think they took it, I don't know, it was in my bag. There was another on my laptop, but that was in my bag too. Where's my stuff?"

He shook his head.

"I made a copy of my journal and a few other things on a flash drive. I gave it to my neighbors to keep."

"Flash drive?"

"To keep stuff safe, in case anyone looked." Because someone always seemed to be watching, trying to talk her into giving up her baby.

Someone is very interested in your child, Ms. Ferguson.

"*I haven't decided yet and I don't believe the father will ever sign them.*" *She used the same excuse she'd always given them.*

This time though . . .

"*That can be gotten around,*" *the woman said, smiling.* "*Just leave that to us.*"

Her heart was racing. Racing.

. . . A quarter of a million dollars . . .

Her chest tightened. Panic roared. They took her. Took her precious little angel.

"I think you should rest," Quinlan said to her as a machine started to beep.

A nurse came in. "Is something wrong? Our monitors show . . ."

"You have to get the journal! Quinlan, you have to get the journal. I just wanted to get away, but I knew, I knew they could stop me and they did. I told you. You have to get it!"

"Mrs. Kinncaid, you need to calm down."

Calm down? Her baby was out there somewhere and she was stuck in the damned hospital.

She shook her head and tried to sit up, but the room spun and tilted. She pulled at the IV needle.

"No, I need to find my baby. I've got to find her. We have to find her. We have to . . ."

A hand on hers stopped her. "Ella."

She shook her head. No. No. She couldn't stay here. "Quinlan, help me. Please."

The nurse said something, and from the corner of her eye Ella saw her inject something into the IV line.

"No. No, don't! I don't need it!" She shook her head. "Please, not yet. I have to find her. I have to . . . Where . . ." God, she wanted to yell, to scream, and yet she barely managed whispers. "Please."

"You need to calm down, Ella," Quinlan told her. "Take a deep breath."

Her eyes locked on his green ones as he gently pushed her back down.

She took a breath.

"Another. Come on."

She listened to his calm voice.

Another voice came through the fog of panic.

"How much did you give her?"

"Half a dose. I know the FBI want to talk to her but she was becoming too agitated again."

"Mr. Kinncaid, I told you to keep her calm," the voice said.

Ella turned and saw a tall, dark-haired, blue-eyed man in a lab coat. She frowned.

"Hello, I'm Dr. Forrester."

The doctor.

She ignored him and looked back at Quinlan, who sat on the edge of her bed. "I want my baby . . . The journal will explain. The journal. I gave it to Mr. Richardson to keep it safe in case they looked through my stuff. The flash drive."

"I know Mr. Richardson, I'll ask him, okay?"

"You could call them, they would come and bring it."

"We're not in Taos, Ella. We're in Albuquerque."

"Albuquerque?"

She tried to wrap her mind around that. "But how? When? I was leaving. Had the car packed and ready to go. Called you . . ." Ella shook her head. "Where is she? Where is she, Quinlan? Who did they give her to? Who did they sell our child to?" The blood pressure cuff went off again and she started to shake.

"Calm down, honey." He brushed a strand of hair off her forehead, the brush of his fingers warm to her. "You need to rest. We'll figure it out. All of it. And I swear to you, we'll get her back."

"I'll talk to them, whoever, to help. I'll talk to them," she told him, feeling the slide of calm that coated over her nerves. "Don't leave me with them, please. I don't know who to trust. Jareaux didn't have time to listen . . . Please don't leave. I don't know who to trust . . ."

Her eyes were heavy. She felt his hand cup her jaw, brush across her cheek.

"You can trust me, Ella. I won't leave," she heard Quinlan say.

"They'll kill me. I know too much . . . Too much . . ." She slid into a calm pool of whatever drugs they were giving her. "They killed others. They'll kill me too."

"No, they won't. I won't let them."

Chapter 24

Quinlan waited until Ella dozed off and then stepped outside the door to call the Richardsons. He knew they were coming. He'd talked to them earlier this morning. Mr. Richardson said they'd be there after lunch. He had expected them before now. And now, he needed the journal. The call went to voice mail. Perfect. Next he called Ian and told him about the journal and Ella's mistrust of Jareaux. Ian agreed they'd check him out and that he'd be up in a minute, he was just grabbing a drink from the cafeteria.

The doctor walked out of the room just as he got off the phone with Ian.

"Mr. Kinncaid, we've discussed this. She *needs* to remain calm," the doctor snapped, frowning.

"Yes, I know." He raked a hand through his hair and leaned on his cane. His leg was killing him.

"Look. New mothers can be . . ." Again his eyes narrowed. "Can often be fragile. Especially new mothers who have been traumatized as Ella has been. Are you *trying* to push her off the deep end?"

"What?"

Dr. Forrester narrowed his eyes. "I know you want to know what happened, that you want to know where your child is. I get that. I do. But you can't push her much more. She's stable now, but still shocky, and her blood pressure isn't where I'd like it to be. Too high, to be perfectly honest. And until her tox screens are clear, or at least clear of whatever she was given, I don't really care to have her shut down, or spiral into postpartum depression."

He agreed, he did. He got it. "I know, but she wants to help, and the police need to talk to her. These bastards, whoever they are, scared her, pressured her, terrorized her." He saw Brody and Aiden stroll around the corner with the fed and two other policemen. Just seeing Agent Jareaux pissed him off.

They stopped beside him and the doctor, who turned to the newcomers and said, "I will be present when you speak to Mr. and Mrs. Kinncaid, gentlemen. As I just told Mr. Kinncaid, she's not completely out of the woods yet."

Agent Jareaux and the others nodded. The two—state and local—followed the doctor in. Just as Jareaux stepped up, something in Quinlan jerked tightly.

Without another thought, he swung out and right hooked the son of a bitch, who then tripped and slammed into the wall.

"Fuck," Brody said, grabbing his arm.

Quinlan threw him off and pressed his cane across the bastard's chest. "You and I have a few things to get clear, Jareaux," he bit out.

"Quinlan, for God's sake," Aiden said beside and behind him.

"You put her in danger. You put *my wife* in danger. You didn't listen to her, didn't have . . ." He pressed closer. "Time, I believe she said, didn't have time to babysit her or hold her hand. Didn't have time for her or the investigation *you* threw her into the middle of."

Jareaux's eyes, gunmetal gray, stared at him. He made no move to defend himself. "Mr. Kinncaid, I get that you are upset."

"Oh, no, Jareaux, I'm far, far beyond upset," he said very quietly, very calmly. "You endangered my wife. *No one* endangers my wife, let alone my child. Where is my daughter, Jareaux?"

He heard other voices join his brothers, heard, "Mr. Kinncaid, step away from Agent Jareaux."

"You, Jareaux, are just as responsible for my wife lying in there hurt and broken as much as the bastards who put her there." He straightened back, felt someone's hand on his shoulder and shrugged them off, never taking his eyes off the bastard with the gun—which was still in the man's holster. "One more thing, you have property that doesn't belong to you or the bureau. I want them back. Or, if you prefer, give them to my wife, as she signed and addressed them to me."

The agent swallowed. "Mr. Kinncaid, the investigation—"

"Fuck you and your investigation." He raked the man with his eyes. He stepped closer again, or as close as his brother grabbing his arm would allow him. "Your investigation led to this mess. They kidnapped her, forced her labor and *stole* her child. My child!"

He jerked his arm away from his brother and gave Jareaux one last piece of advice. "You be careful with her in there"—he pointed to her room—"you be very, very careful with her."

"Agent Jareaux is no longer working this case," a voice said behind them.

Quin was watching Jareaux, caught the slight flash of something in his eyes, before they narrowed and slid to the side.

Agent Sabino stepped up beside Quinlan. "Mr. Kinncaid, Jareaux will have no further contact with Mrs. Kinncaid. It will either be myself or Agent Landry."

"Why? I thought he was in charge of this, she said he was the one she spoke to, the one that got her involved in all this."

He finally turned from Jareaux and faced the female agent. She smiled, though it didn't reach her eyes. "Agent Jareaux is needed elsewhere, we will be handling your wife's case. Don't worry." She turned to Jareaux. "Agent, you're wanted back at the office, should we send someone with you?"

Jareaux held her gaze for a moment. "No." He rubbed his jaw.

"Good." She turned back to Quinlan. "Mr. Kinncaid, it's time we speak to your wife."

"Fine," he bit out. He stepped closer to Jareaux again. "In that case, stay the hell away from my wife."

A muscle bunched in Jareaux's jaw.

Quinlan took a deep breath and turned back to the doctor. Both Aiden and Brody held his arms, he didn't remember them doing that.

"Perhaps your wife isn't the only one who needs some rest," the doctor said, slapping him on the shoulder. "One of you needs to be clearheaded, and we both know it's not going to be her. After this interview, get some rest, Mr. Kinncaid." They walked into the room.

Brody leaned in and said, "You know, with everything else going on, I'd rather not have to worry about bailing your ass out of jail for assaulting a federal agent."

He cut his cousin silent with one look.

"I'm just saying," Brody said and then moved to the back of the room. Before the door shut, Ian slid in.

"What did I miss?" Ian asked Aiden.

"Oh, our formerly laid-back youngest brother just decked the dick of the FBI agent in front of the cops and said agent's colleagues."

"Really? Did you take a photo?"

"Evidence is not what we need, guys," Brody interrupted.

Quinlan listened as the cops, the one with the state police, asked the first question. Quinlan moved up and sat in the chair beside Ella, taking her hand. She turned her hand and laced their fingers.

"I thought I heard Jareaux's voice," she said.

"No, he won't be talking to you," he told her. "Agent Sabino will be, though, and the other agent, don't know his name, can't remember."

She shifted. "I won't have to talk to Jareaux? Good. He lied."

"About what?" Agent Sabino asked, stepping closer, probably to better hear Ella.

"Probably everything," she said, hardly more than a whisper. "The letters, he never mailed them to Quinlan. He told me I couldn't tell anyone about the investigation and said you guys had to approve the letters I sent Quinlan so that the investigation couldn't be compromised. I just wanted Quinlan to know about the baby. But Jareaux never mailed them. After talking to you on the phone, I realized he probably lied about it all, didn't he? Was there even a real case?"

Agent Sabino cleared her throat. "How did you get involved with Jareaux?"

Quinlan stilled at the question.

"I wasn't involved with the man," Ella said. "I'm married."

Sabino chuckled. "I didn't mean . . . How did you start working with him?"

Ella sighed. "He kept coming to the studio wanting to talk to me, leaving a card. Finally, I called, to verify he was who he said he was. You guys confirmed he worked with you so I met with him at the coffee shop and he asked for my help."

"Help with what, exactly?" Sabino asked.

"He said you guys knew I was working at the Retreat, wanted my help in watching things, making sure things were okay. Missing women, babies," she muttered. "I was perfect to help you. I was working there and I was pregnant."

"Okay, we'll come back to how you got roped into it later. Right now, let's go forward, all right? Our priority is your baby."

Ella nodded against the pillows and kept hold of his hand.

More questions followed and she squeezed his hand tightly as more and more questions were fired at her.

He listened, nausea greasing his stomach as he listened to her tell of her friend Lisa showing up, of the tea on the couch, how she felt dizzy.

"What's Lisa like? Tell us about her," Sabino asked, making notes.

"Lisa Hammerstein." Ella told them what she knew of Lisa. "I know she has a place in Taos, but I don't know where, she never invited me over. We always went out and did stuff. Or I met her at the studio or at the Retreat."

"Okay, so you remember being dizzy on the couch," Sabino asked, easing them back to Ella's kidnapping.

She nodded. "I remember looking at her, at the tea she'd made for me. I knew she'd put something in it and was wondering why."

"Then what happened?"

"I woke up . . . I woke up and couldn't move," she said, her voice devoid of any emotion. "I couldn't move."

"Why?" someone asked.

She shook her head, her eyes glass. "Tied down, I think. Plastic. Tied with plastic."

"Zip ties," Ian muttered.

"She left me," she said, her voice barely more than a whisper.

"Who left you, Ella?" Sabino asked.

Quinlan bit down at the way she trembled, and yet her eyes were so flat. Bastards.

"Lisa. Lisa was there, she said they needed the baby, my baby." She laid her hands on her stomach. "Or I think she did. It's such a blur. Some things are clear and jagged, sharp. Others are just foggy, smooth, and I don't know if they really happened or not. Like . . . like . . ." She shivered. "Fran. Like Fran. I think I know, but I'm not sure anymore."

"It's okay," he said, rubbing her arm gently. "Just tell them what you can."

And she did, painting pictures in his mind he didn't want, even as he'd wondered what the hell had happened for the last day or so.

"I was so tired by that point," she said. "But for just a mo-moment." She blew out a breath, tears running down her cheeks. "She was perfect. It was like the world stopped for a minute. I felt her on my stomach. Red hair, like Quin's, but brighter, lighter. So tiny. So little. And a birthmark on her inner arm. Like me." She held out her right arm and showed the little skin discoloration the size of his pinky nail that rested near her elbow. "All her fingers and toes . . ." She closed her eyes. "I could smell her, that perfect, absolutely perfect scent of baby. I kissed her head."

No one said anything. She swallowed and opened her eyes.

"She took her. They took her."

"Who else was there, Ella? Who else was with her?"

Her eyes glazed over again and she began to tremble. "I have to find her. I have to find her. They took her." Tears flooded her eyes and rained down. "I need to get out of here. I need—" She strained to sit up, but even as she gripped his hand with hers, he knew she was weak.

"Who else was there, Mrs. Kinncaid?" the other agent asked, stepping closer.

Her eyes locked on the agent and flashed with aquamarine fire. "You. You didn't help me. Jareaux said he was too busy with a new case. He got mad because I didn't get him proof quickly enough after he said I was established and settled. He—"

Her breaths came faster.

"He promised me I'd be safe. I told him they wanted my baby! I told him! I told him! And they did, didn't they?" She tried to yell, the muscles in her throat straining, but no more than a fractured whisper emerged.

"Enough," the doctor said.

"I. Want. My. Baby. Find her! You have to find my baby!" she tried to scream. "My baby!" The doctor took a syringe out and attached it to the IV in her arm.

"Doctor," the agent started.

The other cop put his hand on the agent's arm. "We can start looking for Lisa again."

"Ella, did Lisa say anything about the buyers?" the agent asked.

The doctor watched her monitors as she strained against Quinlan.

"Buyers? Buyers?" she asked, shaking her head.

"Not another word!" the doctor snapped. "Get out. Everyone out!"

The others filed out, clearly not wanting to piss off the doctor.

Ella cried against his chest until he again felt her relax. For several minutes he didn't let go, his mind swimming with what she'd told them.

A blessed time had become a horror.

He closed his eyes, kissed her hair, and realized the doctor was talking to him.

"You can lay her down now," the doctor said. "I think, considering everything, the nurse and I will check her over now. Why don't you go get something to eat, Mr. Kinncaid. She'll be out for a while. She needs rest and I think the cops have more than enough information to work with for today."

Quinlan gently eased her back and touched her cheek. "I'll be back," was all he could manage.

He took a deep breath when he stepped out of her room, but that didn't really help either.

Aiden and Brody stood there, leaning against the opposite wall. The nurse smiled at Brody as she passed.

"Where'd Ian go?" he asked.

"Followed the cops out. He seems pretty tight with the state guy, the local didn't have much to say and the agents were in a hurry. Ian said he'd be back later. Lieutenant Ruiz, the state boy, said he wanted to cheer you on earlier but that wouldn't have been appropriate. Apparently no one really likes Jareaux, who is always trying to get ahead. Ian was asking them questions."

He frowned and then nodded, realizing what the man had meant. He raked a hand through his hair, trying to dispel the thoughts and images there.

Tied down. Trying to get away . . .

Quinlan blew out a breath.

"You okay?" Aiden asked.

"No, but I'm not about to crumble into a heap on the floor and into a fetal position," Quin muttered.

Aiden scoffed. "I should hope not. I'd deny you as my brother if you did anything that weak. Kinncaids don't fold. We stand. We fight."

"And we damn well protect our own," Brody added.

"If given the chance, you're damned right we do," Quin said. "How are Mom and Pops?" he asked Aiden.

"Well, neither are in the hospital. Gavin's keeping an eye on them. Mom's pissed and still ranting, he said. And Dad hasn't said much." Aiden grinned and licked his lips. "You were always so perfect and quiet." He chuckled. "You just shot that all to hell. Mom just might not ever forgive you. And you did good with that federal asshole."

Quinlan turned and leaned back against the wall, closing his eyes for just a moment.

"Come on. I'll get us something to eat and drink. You didn't have any lunch." Brody motioned toward the elevators. "Doc's right. Running yourself straight into the ground isn't going to help anything. Nor will ending up in jail, just for the record."

"I'm not hungry. Though I could use something to drink." What, he didn't know. He doubted there would be an energy smoothie here, and though coffee would help, if he drank another cup he just might get sick. His stomach could only handle so much. "Got any antacids?" he asked.

Aiden dug some out of his pocket and passed them over. "As Brody said, food."

Quinlan looked back at the door and shook his head. "I shouldn't leave her alone."

Aiden jerked his head down the hallway a bit. There sat another man, vaguely familiar but Quin couldn't place him.

"One of Ian's men. Sent him over a bit ago to guard her room. If we're not here, then he is. We've already cleared him with the admin and with the feds, state, and local boys, so come on. Sleeping Beauty will still be here when you get back." Aiden slung his arm over Quin's shoulders and pulled him along.

They passed the nurse's station and the nursery. Another father stood there looking in, a tired smile on his face; even in profile his face held awe. He looked up and met their gazes. "Never gets old. This is our third, but it never gets old."

Quin wouldn't know and was past his patience limit. His leg was hurting, fate had his guts twisted and his air supply cut off, and someone had reached in and stopped his heart, or that's what it felt like. He didn't talk as they rode the elevator down and traversed the labyrinth of the older hospital corridors to the cafeteria.

"Why do they all smell the same?" Quin asked. "School lunches, college cafeterias, hospitals. It's like . . . sour food and something. I don't know what. But it's hardly appetizing."

"You want real food, too bad. However, it's not that bad here, so order something," Brody said.

He didn't care what they ordered. "Just get me something. I don't care what." With that, he thumped his way over to a table and eased into a chair, rubbing his thigh. In a couple of minutes his brother and cousin joined him. Aiden set a bowl of soup and half of some sort of wrap in front of him, along with a cup with a bendy straw.

He picked up the wrap and bit into it. Whole-grain flatbread with crunchy veggies inside, and some sort of cheese. Worked for him. Without realizing it he downed it.

"Did you even chew?" Aiden asked him.

He nodded and opened the soup container, blowing on the steam.

"So," Aiden said, biting into his own wrap.

"So," Brody added.

"What?" Quin asked.

"So, Brody let it slip on the way over—"

"—confessed under duress is a more accurate description—"

"—that he'd known you were married, but your assets were protected as much as he could protect them." Aiden took another bite. "We always knew you were quiet, but damn, Quin. You married her and just, what? Left her?"

"No! No, I did *not* just leave her. We might have started off married in a stupid, impulsive moment, but so what? She was the first woman I wanted to be with after . . . after. She's funny and bright and though I don't remember every detail, I'd do it again. She left me. I did not kick her out, I did *not* leave her in Vegas, well, technically I did. Left her a note and enough cash to get her back home if she ever went back to the hotel. Why do you think I was so damned late. She disappeared. Left me with the expensive ring and a lovely note the morning after. A damned note letting me know that I could get an annulment or divorce or whatever I wanted or needed to." Just the thought of that note. "I went back. I fucking went back after I dropped you guys off at D.C. I went and changed clothes, talked to Brody and flew the hell back out to Vegas looking for her. I didn't find her. Went back to New Orleans to make sure she made it home, though I didn't talk to her. Took me two weeks to get the courage up to go back.

"We hit it off. I saw her every damned weekend for almost six weeks. Sometimes I just flew down midweek just because I . . . I don't know. I had to. We talked on the phone every day. I thought . . . I thought . . . Then I thought I had her, that we'd worked it all out, that

I would talk her into coming to meet the family and we were going to tell them." He shrugged. "I waited too long. She'd applied for the job before we met, took the job when it was offered and put the house up for sale, which I . . . Never mind."

"And you never said a word to anyone?" Aiden asked, shocked.

"Technically, I told you *all*."

"When?" Aiden narrowed his eyes. "That crap on the way back from New Orleans when you finally showed up?"

Quinlan shrugged. "Not my fault you didn't believe me. I never once said I *didn't* get married."

Aiden looked from him to Brody. "You've been hanging out with the lawyer too long. Splitting hairs, Quin, and again I say you never told anyone."

"He told me," Brody said.

"Because he was covering his ass." Aiden shook his head.

Quinlan nodded. "Yeah, I guess. I don't know. If I'd told the family, I might have had a chance of keeping her. But I hadn't, you see, and she thought . . ."

"You didn't want to tell us?" Aiden said. "Can't imagine what she might have thought about that."

He leveled a look at his brother. "I fucked up. I know. She thought she wasn't good enough or that the family would think that and I must have agreed or I'd have told everyone already. I hurt her by keeping quiet. So she moved to New Mexico, where she'd be in charge of her own studio eventually. Wanted enough space to think and see . . ." He shrugged. "I had flown down to New Orleans, she basically told me thanks, but no thanks. We had a huge fight, she was already packed up and really wanted to try the job. Never made sense to me—her moving. Being hurt I didn't tell anyone or introduce her to the family, I get that. I left pissed, though I told her if she needed anything she knew how to get ahold of me. I asked her to please contact me when she got to New Mexico so I'd know she made it. She did. I was still pissed. I went back a few weeks later and . . ." The house didn't matter. "When I hadn't heard from her in a week and then two I figured she was as angry at me. I figured, fine. Let her go, if she didn't want me, why the hell was I trying so fucking hard to keep someone who clearly didn't want to be married to me. I tried her old number, but it was disconnected. I let go," he admitted, and shook his head.

Finally, he met his brother's eyes. "I let go when everything in me said to find her. But I didn't. Pride. Ya know." The plastic spoon snapped in his hand and he tossed the pieces on the table.

Neither Brody nor Aiden said a word.

"I've been selfish in the last couple of years. All I saw after the hospital was me. Me and what I'd lost, or thought I'd lost, what I couldn't do as well anymore. Poor me. Then one day in New Orleans, I bumped into this amazing, quirky, beautiful woman with blue hair and I didn't care about me. Not really. Not like I did. I only cared how she saw me. After a day with her, my ideas of things were changing. After a night, I only wanted her. She felt so . . ." He shook his head and looked at the tabletop. "*Right*. She felt so damned right. Beside me, holding my hand. Laughing. We laughed so much." He remembered that the most. The laughter. The simple joy in anything. "I was shocked as hell to wake up in Vegas with a ring on my finger, but I'm not going to lie and say I wished it were different. The only thing I wished was different was that she didn't have some stupid idea in her head that I or my family wouldn't approve. And I wish I had introduced her as my wife right away, to everyone." Anger swirled along his spine and had him shifting again.

Aiden sighed and leaned his elbows on the table, just listening.

"I know she's scared, I know she's confused and has been through a lot. I get she was helping that damned fed and the letters, but I also know she *denied* me my child. *My* child. I know *now* she didn't exactly intend to deny me, but damn it. I didn't get to find out I was going to be a father. I didn't get to go to the first doctor's visit, or hear the heartbeat or see the sonogram. Pick out stupid furniture." He leaned up. "I can't understand *why* she just didn't pick up the fucking phone! Screw the investigation and the fed or whatever."

Silence settled between them, grew red and thick to him. He rubbed his thigh again.

"I just don't understand . . . I don't . . . I know in the scheme of things . . . *Why?*" he asked his brother.

Brody shrugged. "Maybe she couldn't."

"Bullshit," Aiden said, taking a drink. "I was beyond pissed, and worried and terrified when Jesslyn finally told me, close to two months after the damned fact. Alone in Texas, worrying and scared alone until she finally picked up the damned phone."

"Yes, but she picked up the damned phone."

Aiden tilted his head. "My point is that I get that mass of confusion and rage and . . . and that's all but boiling under your skin. Add in the feds screwing with her, these people, the missing baby . . . Look, I get part of that chaos, knowing you can't snap at the person part of you really wants to. That would make you a real bastard and we'd all beat the shit out of you if you did."

"I'm not going to hurt her, for God's sake!"

"No, but you can cut quick with words, almost better than any of the rest of us, other than Ian maybe. My point is that I get where you are with the not knowing, but . . . But you have to be there for her now. You guys can work through this later. Marriage counseling or whatever. You still love her."

Yes, he still loved her.

"You could always divorce her and file to keep the baby," Brody added. "I've had the papers ready to draw up since you told me."

Aiden punched Brody's shoulder. "Not helping."

Quinlan jerked and looked at his cousin. "I *never* told you to draw up any divorce papers."

"No, you didn't. But if you did, then they were ready."

"Screw you. Ella's *mine*. I'm not about to let her walk out of my life again. If I have to put a fucking tracking device on her ass, I'll do it."

"I'm sure that will endear you to her," Aiden said. "Perhaps something less . . . drastic. Though I'd feel the same."

Quinlan simply stared at Aiden for a moment. "I haven't been able to find that joy in almost a year, and then for just a moment when I heard her voice, it all came flooding back. All the fun, all the laughter, all the . . . everything. You know? I told her I'd call her back, had to call Roger to fuel up the jet. Never got her again. Just for a moment the world seemed full of possibilities again before everything went so fucking wrong."

He closed his eyes and took a deep breath, wished he hadn't as the hodgepodge of cafeteria scents filled his nose. Then he remembered something else she said. "She asked why I never wrote her back. She wrote me letters at some point, but the feds wanted them before he'd mail them to make certain she didn't compromise the investigation, or the wonderful Jareaux convinced her of that. Surprisingly, the letters never made it to me. And the journal. So maybe we'll finally find out something when we get the flash drive from the Richardsons." He pulled his phone out to see if the Richardsons had returned his call yet. Nothing.

"They wanted her alone. All of them," Aiden said.

He nodded. "That was my take on it as well. If she'd been able to contact me, or had contacted me sooner, then I could have gotten to her, we would have . . ." Who knew? "She wouldn't have been alone then. I'd have talked her out of the investigation, or tried like hell to."

"Which is why Jareaux didn't send you the letters," Brody pointed out. "Because if you did that, then the Nursery wouldn't have had a shot because then she wouldn't have been so easy to isolate," Brody added. "If she's right, and the feds seem to give her credit as they are all but chomping at the bit to ask her more questions, then what is the Nursery exactly, other than a high-end adoption agency? If there are others, then how many and what happened to those babies and mothers?"

Chapter 25

The elevators finally opened on her floor and Quinlan stepped out. Something was wrong.

Hurrying down the corridor, he rounded the corner and saw a group of people outside her room. Scrubs, cops, the feds. His phone rang. He ignored it and hurried to the group, cursing his leg.

He shoved past the people there. Ian was standing in the door and met his eyes. "She's fine."

Quin pushed past his brother and saw the doctor and nurse checking her vitals and hanging a new IV bag. Ella was still out to the world.

"What the hell happened?" he asked.

Dr. Forrester looked from Quin to the crowd behind him to Ella. Then he jerked his head to the door.

Ian said, "I'll stay in here." He put his hand on Quin's shoulder. "She's fine. No harm done."

Quinlan wasn't buying that. He walked over to the bed and touched her. He just had to make sure. Her chest rose on a deep inhale. He leaned over and kissed her forehead.

"Quin, I'll be here. You need to talk to the cops."

"Why?" he asked his brother. "I'd rather hear it from you."

His daughter. Oh God, they'd found his daughter. Ian's face was set, his eyes bright and hard.

"The baby?" he asked quietly.

"No. No, we still don't know. It seems someone tried to administer something to your wife," Ian said.

"Administer?"

Agent Sabino stood in the corner with a baggy. Inside was a syringe. "A scuffle, the guard chased after him." She jerked her chin toward Ian. "His man. Guy who tried to give your wife whatever is in this?" She shook the baggy. "Took a swipe with a rather sharp blade to the guard."

Quinlan shook his head. "What?"

"We've switched out the IV port and line, and are running her tox screens again," Dr. Forrester said.

Quinlan looked from one to the other, then back at his sleeping wife. He walked to the door and waited while the others, sans Ian, joined him in the hallway.

"Explain, please."

Agent Sabino leveled a look at him. "Apparently, a man in scrubs was seen going into her room."

"Where was the guard?"

"Just down the hall, helping the older couple who had just come to visit her. The woman was really upset. He was helping them down the hallway when he looked back and saw someone go into the room. He went back." She shrugged. "Good thing too. The man's name didn't match the nurses or CNAs written on the whiteboard in her room. Then the guard noticed the syringe. He knocked it out of the man's hand. There was a scuffle, the assailant ran out and both went down the stairwell."

"Where is he?"

"Who?"

"Whoever the hell just tried to give my wife whatever is in that bag."

Sabino took a deep breath. "We're working on it."

He didn't say anything for a minute, just reminded himself that she was fine. His wife was fine. He speared the doc with a look. "When will her tox screens be back and when will we know what he tried to give her?"

"Not long," the doc said. "For her tox screens. I have nothing to do with what's in the syringe, but I'd appreciate a speedy update to compare to her blood work just in case he managed to get some of it in her."

Agent Sabino nodded. "You'll be the first I notify. I'm off to the lab now." She touched his arm. "Your wife is one lucky woman, Mr. Kinncaid."

He watched her walk down the hallway. To the doctor he asked, "You're sure she's fine?"

The doctor sighed. "For now, yes. As I said, I'm waiting on blood work and it shouldn't be long. We put a rush on it."

He nodded. "Thank you. How often, how easy is it for someone to do this?"

The doctor shifted. "Well, can't say I ever remember something like this happening in the years I've been here."

Quinlan let him walk away and ran a hand over his face. He knew he shouldn't have left her.

Aiden whistled down the hallway and jerked his head for Quin. He walked to his brother. "What?"

"Older couple, came to see Ella. They're really upset. I take it they're the Richardsons." He cut his eyes to the waiting room.

Quinlan sighed and walked to the elderly couple.

"Is she okay? What happened? No one will tell us anything," Mrs. Richardson said.

"She's fine. She's resting. They're running some blood tests to make sure, but they believe she's fine."

"What was all the excitement and cops and everything?"

He took a deep breath. He wasn't about to tell them someone had possibly just tried to kill his wife. Instead he said, "I don't know all the details, they're working on it. I was in the cafeteria."

Mrs. Richardson started to cry. "This is just all wrong. All wrong. We told her and told her to call you and tell you the truth. She was so worried and—"

He didn't know what to say to them. "She did call, Mrs. Richardson, that's how I knew to come."

The little old lady blew out a big breath. "I'm sorry we weren't here earlier. We would have been, but when we were almost here, we remembered something and had to go back."

Mr. Richardson said, "I have something she gave me. A computer flash drive or something. We wanted to bring it. She told me weeks ago that if something happened to her to contact you and to give you this. I should have given it to you yesterday, but honestly, I forgot about it. She gave me your number." The older bald man shook his head. "Just figured it was between you two and to stay out of it. Now I wish I hadn't."

So did Quin, but he didn't say that. Aiden stepped in and thanked the man, even as Brody said, "I'll let Ian know we have the flash drive."

Quinlan introduced his brother and his cousin as he took the little purple stick with peace stickers on it. He looked at it and wondered what was actually on it and if he was ready to see it.

"Thank you," he told them.

"We saw her for just a minute, the man by her door let us in when we told him who we were, though he stayed in the room with us. Walked us back out here. Nice man. Took off after someone though."

"Carmine, they don't care about that," her husband told her.

"She's so . . . she looks so . . ." The woman sniffed hard. "We were going to go back this evening, but I told Herb earlier we were going to wait here until she's a bit better."

He smiled and nodded. "That's very kind of you. She spoke of you earlier." He took the older woman's hand and patted it. "Thank you for looking out for her when I couldn't, didn't . . . was just too stupid to come after her."

Herb snorted. "I'm really starting to think you're a better sort than I'd originally thought you were."

"I don't know about that. Look, if you do stay, let us know. I think it might help her . . ." He shook his head. "We've got rooms somewhere." He looked to Aiden, who nodded. "You can stay with our crew, if you want."

Mrs. Richardson smiled and patted his arm. "I think we'll take you up on that. For now though, I'm just going to sit right over here and finish knitting the baby blanket."

"Let us know if you need anything." He left them in Aiden's capable hands, took his brother's laptop with him and went back down the hallway to his wife.

Chapter 26

Albuquerque, Sunday, late afternoon

The papers were signed and passed on to the parents. The DeSaros were all smiles and excitement. This was why he did this. Why he kept doing this. There were so many couples that couldn't have children. Children should be loved and from two-parent homes. Parents that could love them and raise them the way they were meant to be raised and loved. Parents were meant to nurture and teach, to guide and lead their children.

So many that came through here were not able to do any of those. And when it was clear that the baby would be better off without the birth mother, then one must step in and fix that problem.

Problems.

One of the latest problems was the fact the cops were already sniffing at them. He had several messages from his partner wanting to know what the hell was going on, that the Retreat had been invaded by the feds and their headquarters in Albuquerque had been shut down, as has their outlying clinics.

Didn't really matter. At least not to him just yet. He'd had this private office for years just for these sorts of transactions and meetings. Enough to give a personal touch, but nothing that couldn't either be left behind or moved very quickly.

He focused on the couple in front of him.

The DeSaros smiled at the baby in the car carrier. "She's so precious and . . . oh . . . and look at all that red hair!"

Mr. DeSaro laughed. "My mother had red hair. One of my siblings does as well."

Another packet of papers was passed over for signatures between the lawyers. His own, who always worried—or at least until the bank deposit cleared—and the DeSaros' legal representative. Everything must be legal, after all. Private adoptions could be sticky points.

Or at least look that way.

The baby mewled and squirmed.

"Can I pick her up?" the woman asked.

"Of course."

Mrs. DeSaro, dressed in a Chanel suit and enough diamonds he lost track of calculating, reached down and unclicked the harness and picked the baby up, cupping her perfectly manicured hand around the tiny head.

"Ohhh. Oh my. Oh my, Vincent. Look. Look at our beautiful baby girl." Tears trembled in her voice and her eyes. The woman simply sat on the floor and held the baby.

This was what it was all about. This was why it was so important to find the right ones. The ones that really wouldn't be missed.

Though this last one didn't quite fall under that umbrella.

Time to move this along.

Papers were quickly signed and finally the money was passed over. Quarter of a million dollars.

That was how much a precious bundle could cost.

Or at least that's how much this little doll was sold for. The auction had lasted for almost two days. And at the end, the DeSaros were the ones that won.

It had been a bidding war the likes of which they'd only seen twice before. He'd planned to take care of Ella himself, but thanks to his ever-greedy partner, the option to use her child—the child he'd actually had up for auction—or replace it with another, had been taken from him.

"We want to stay a few days here in Albuquerque to make certain there are no problems," Mr. DeSaro said, helping his wife stand and taking his own papers. Birth certificate, adoption papers, and medical records, changed accordingly.

And these records had to be forged on several fronts.

What a clusterfucking mess.

They needed to get it all cleaned up. First they had to be able to get to her and end her.

But she *knew*. The woman was still in the hospital. Of course, the cops had probably located the father and informed him. Who all had she talked to? What all did they now know, or wonder about?

Kinncaids—that family was going to screw this all up. He just knew it.

If only the stupid bitch had waited, he could have helped her, made less of a mess and cleaned up properly. It wasn't like he hadn't done it before.

He'd planned and waited for a child like this little one.

In no time, the DeSaros were laughing and crying and leaving. They'd taken pictures. His assistant had taken pictures. His secretary.

Everyone was very happy for the couple.

Most thought it was as legal as could be.

He, his lawyer, and Mr. DeSaro knew it might not be.

Mr. DeSaro stepped up to him, clasping his hand.

"I don't want any trouble from this."

He looked at the new father. "Do you think there could be trouble?"

"I know and you know, I bought this child."

He merely looked at the man.

Mr. DeSaro didn't so much as blink. Instead Mr. DeSaro pulled him closer. "I'm not a fool. None of us should have a problem. However, should one arise, do not think for a moment that I will let you take this child away from us. She's ours now. My wife is smiling and happy as I haven't seen her in years. If anyone comes looking and it's between doing right and feeding you to whatever law enforcement agency might be inquiring, don't for a second think I won't serve you up myself. And then when you're sitting in a cell, I'll make certain you won't have to worry about a long prison sentence."

He cleared his throat, saw his lawyer rise from his chair. "The total amount of expenditures might be shocking to some, but to us, we know you get what you pay for. Those were just to cover medical costs and child care, along with our exclusive prenatal care in such a caring and peaceful environment."

Mr. DeSaro nodded his salt-and-pepper head. "So long as we are clear. I will have my attorney double-check the paperwork with his firm to make certain there are no problems."

He smiled at the man and now wished he'd chosen the other couple, as the hair on the back of his neck stood up. But no, watching Mrs. DeSaro with the little girl, he knew he'd chosen right. It wasn't all about the money, after all. Just mostly.

Mr. DeSaro nodded and followed his wife from the room. Another man was with them and headed out.

He stood watching and smiled.

Who the hell did the bastard think he was? Really? He'd done them a favor. A godddamn favor and that was the thanks he got?

Then again, a quarter of a million was excessive, he supposed, but that was what the bidding reached.

The other family came in second at two hundred thirty-five grand. Apparently Mr. DeSaro wanted a baby girl for his wife. One from a good birth mother and father. Those were rare in his experience. The normal average Joe babies? Those were a dime a dozen. Babies born to impoverished teen mothers? Single mothers? More than he could keep up with. A baby born of an intelligent, beautiful woman? The father an affluent heir to a great family? A long line of looks and intelligence, of prosperity?

Those were very, very few.

So Ella hadn't exactly *wanted* to give the child up, and the process had been rushed, he knew. Though with her on the edge of running, he supposed there was little choice. They just needed to deal with her once and for all. He needed to deal with Kevin and Lisa.

• • •

Ian closed the door and walked around the SUV, shutting Rori's door. He knew better than to wish she would wait on him to help her from the car. He grinned at the thought.

"What has you smiling?" she asked as they crossed the street to the pueblo-style office building. The sun was already sinking against the peak of the mountains.

He'd learned there was another office, held by the corporation that kept cropping up in his search for buried information on the Nursery of Dreams.

"I'm surprised they'd meet us on a Sunday evening," Rori said. "Aren't they curious about someone wanting to meet on a day like today?"

Ian shook his head. "No. The fact I had this number seemed to be enough. He said they'd be in the office this evening anyway. It's all relative, darling."

She rolled her eyes.

Just as they reached the sidewalk he checked both directions and saw the car parked at the corner. Limo, dark tinted windows.

"That's interesting."

"Possibly."

A man stood beside the door handing a diaper bag into the depths of the car, then he straightened, grinned and turned.

Ian stopped, he knew him.

What was the man's name . . . Sicilian. Chicago man, in the hotel business as well. Wasn't he?

De something.

Saro.

DeSaro.

The man merely tilted his head and climbed in, then the car drove away.

"What?" Rori asked him.

He stood there, wondering . . . The DeSaros were a powerful family in their own right. What was that man doing here? Other than adopting a baby.

He'd find out. For now, they had a meeting. Shaking it off, he said to Rori, "Not sure. Maybe something, maybe nothing."

The DeSaros were as wealthy and prominent as his own family. They were out of Chicago, he thought, but he'd look them up. He'd recognized the man, as his family had done business with the DeSaros in years past, but it was unlikely that the other man recognized him. He'd been away for a dozen years and still kept a low profile.

Granted, it might be nothing. Might be. Then again, might not.

If the DeSaros had adopted a child and that child turned out to be Quin's . . . well, no matter how powerful the DeSaros were, the adoption wouldn't be legal, no matter what the Nursery officials and their lawyers said. Ella was his legal sister-in-law. Even if she lost her fucking mind and gave the baby up, Quinlan didn't. They were married, the baby was his.

"They were leaving with baby stuff, bags and whatnot," Rori said. "Coincidence has never been big with either of us."

"No, it hasn't."

"I got the plate of the limo, just in case."

He grinned. "So did I, but I know who it was." He took out his phone and called Johnno. "Look up Vincent DeSaro, his wife, and what they are doing in Albuquerque at an adoption agency."

For a moment there was silence.

"Fine."

He hung up and looked at Rori. "Ready to go see about adopting a baby?"

"Think that was the couple that got Quin's baby?" She still looked at the corner.

"Don't know, love. Even if they are, we'll need a court order. I can promise you that man will not let anyone take a child from them. And even with a court order, if that baby turns out to be Quin's, we might start a war with the DeSaros."

She quirked a brow. "Like that would concern you."

He just looked at her.

"Okay, it does concern you, but still. With a name like DeSaro, I'll assume they're Italian."

"Sicilian, I think."

"Then if the chap understands anything, he understands family."

"Oh, we all understand family. Our own. Everyone else's can go to hell."

With that, he turned and walked them into the building and to the elevators. Both were quiet on their ride up.

"I'm going to want to kill whomever is up here, won't I?" Rori whispered.

"Probably."

"But we can't."

He put his hand on the small of her back and kissed her cheek as he led her out and into a well-furnished reception area. "No, not yet."

Two men were standing there. One way to find out what was going on.

"Hi, we're the McGregors," he told the man he knew was a doctor with the Nursery.

"Dr. Merchant, and this is one of our lawyers, Mr. Hernandez. Nice to meet you, and I'm glad you found us." He ushered them into the office and the lawyer left. Hernandez. Another one they'd need to check out. Rori held out her hand and shook the man's. Ian could tell from her look that she was going to have more fun questioning this bastard than he was. And they couldn't even really play since the feds and cops knew they were here.

Damn, sometimes he missed his old life.

He motioned to a sitting area with photo albums on the coffee table and sat, shifting in one of the leather armchairs.

The man shifted again. "If you don't mind, how did you hear of us?"

Ian gave the man a small smile. "I'd rather not say. A previous happy couple that used you when no one else would help them. And I have my own ways of finding out information that is hard for the average individual to obtain."

For a moment no one said anything.

"I saw someone leaving downstairs who I recognized. Mr. DeSaro is an acquaintance. I believe we met at a party at his villa in Italy. Or was it Morocco, darling?"

She shrugged. "I thought it was the castle in Scotland."

And just like that, he felt the change come over Dr. Merchant. People said those with money were different. They smelled different, acted different, looked different.

Well, perhaps. He didn't really know. All this was just an act.

But greed?

Greed he knew and could recognize a mile away. He'd rolled and swam in it for years. He leaned back and laced his fingers. Yes, for this bastard, he was sorry he wouldn't get to play the game the way he used to. If he could, he'd know everything he needed to in half an hour, tops. Legalities be damned.

He glanced to Rori and knew she thought the same. Sometimes being good was nothing more than a waste of time.

Chapter 27

Sunday night, the hospital

Quinlan settled in a chair next to the bed and pulled up the journal from the flash drive. He should probably sleep, as he honestly had no idea the last time he'd slept in the last day . . . two? The attempt on her life earlier in the day killed any tiredness he'd had. Whoever had been in her room had tried to attach a syringe of potassium chloride to her IV. Thanks to Ian's man, Ella was fine. Her blood work was clear.

She was alive. He glanced at her. Sleeping again, but alive.

He sighed and opened the drive, found the folder marked *Journal* and opened it.

The first entry was weeks after she'd moved to Taos.

I'm starting this journal because . . . well, I'm pregnant! I'm so excited. So scared too. So . . . so . . . everything . . .

He read on, living through her experiences, practically hearing her voice in her words. At first he got lost in her words, smiling at phrases, expressions, things she'd experienced, said, hoped. There was a photo embedded of the first sonogram. As he read, he saw her change. Watched as she waited for his letters, to see what he thought, if he was excited too.

But he'd never gotten the letters.

Her exuberance gave way to fear. He read on. He read how those she worked with tried to talk her into considering adoption. How they told her that someone like him wouldn't want a by-blow, a love child. He took a deep breath and continued, growing more and more angry. He read of her worries about women she met, those she came to see as friends. He knew her, when something happened to one of the girls — like Nadia — she'd feel responsible.

I watched today. The girl that was worried? She's not here anymore. Another one gone . . .

Another passage stood out to him and he felt like maybe, just maybe he'd be able to breathe again at some point. She'd missed him, missed them.

I should never have left New Orleans. I know that now. I can feel it deep in my bones. I wish things were different. And why, oh why did I think I could make a difference? Could help these girls or women? Pride is a terrible, terrible sin and now I realize that.

I just want Quinlan, my Quinlan. Maybe he'll never forgive me. I know this. I never thought it would take this long. Regrets and whatever . . . I can't think.

My choices to run when life suddenly was too real, that will be on my tombstone someday: Here lies a woman who was afraid.

And after moving here and learning about the baby . . . even more real. Until I ran, Quin and I just sort of floated. He came down every weekend and it worked without being too difficult. Or I think it did. Maybe I'm wrong. I probably am. I know he wanted more. He wanted an us, in the same city, same bed, with the same names on stuff. Or at least the same last name. I ran and created more problems by running.

More problems than I understand. And I don't even know when it all happened. I was teaching yoga. These people in Taos are serious about yoga. Not the regulars or rich housewives I'm used to or the health nuts . . . but it's just different here. The new job at the Nursery of Dreams seemed perfect too.

I missed Quinlan.

And then . . .

The two pink lines.

Several of them.

And the class at the Nursery and talking to the doctors there and the feds. It's all such a blur tonight. But I agreed to help them. My choice. Not to contact anyone, except for those letters to Quinlan that Agent Jareaux said he'd take care of.

Why didn't Quinlan write me back? Why didn't I hear from him. I know, I know. What was I really thinking? Some great guy married me. I ran. Secret baby. Please, there were shelves of books with this plotline.

He knows I'm in Taos, and I know he's in D.C.

Then again, maybe he's pissed still because I left. But we talked so much before. Talked and talked and talked and I just knew that things this time were different.

And it would have been.

A voodoo priestess once told me I was my own worst enemy.

I see now what she meant.

I don't know myself, do I? I wouldn't be here if I did. If I don't know myself, how can I help myself, let alone anyone else.

Let alone my own child?

Her thoughts went from cohesive and flowing to jagged and skipped.

He took a deep breath and rolled his neck. Her worries that these bastards fed her, that he wouldn't want the baby, wouldn't want someone like her. That if he did want the baby, he and his family could hire better lawyers and take the baby. He read through arguments with herself that he would never do that, that she knew him. She wrote how she could understand if his family did take that course, if she had to battle them, how they would break her in a month. His chest felt tight seeing how she went from vivacious and his Ella to someone full of doubts and fears. He saw how through the weeks they tried to wear her down, tried to get the child legally through fear and coercion.

I'm worried.

They're still talking to me about adopting, but I don't want to give her up. She's MINE!

MINE!

I'm not giving her up. Even Lisa hinted at it. My doctor asked me if I was sure I wanted to keep the baby. It feels like they are all against me. Am I going crazy? It feels like I am.

I don't know who to talk to about things anymore. I feel like I'm being watched. I told Jareaux this, but he told me not to worry, they'd look into it. He's not the one with a child kicking him awake from the inside, is he? He said I worried too much and if I focused more on evidence than on myself this would be over.

Is he right?

I don't know anything anymore.

Or I feel like I don't.

I need help, but I don't know who to trust. I don't know if I can trust Jareaux or not. I wish Quinlan had answered my letters. Why didn't he answer them? Maybe Jareaux never gave him my letters.

I don't want to do this anymore.

The last entry. He rubbed his eyes and was glad it was done. He'd save a copy of the flash drive to the PC, get another one and give a copy to the cops, feds, whoever.

I'm in over my head.

I'm scared . . . I'm scared that they will just . . .

What if they just take her? What if they just take my baby?

I know that sounds crazy. I even mentioned it to my therapist at the Retreat. She said I needed to reevaluate the root of my fears. That I really feared Quinlan and his family taking her away and I was transferring my fears into a scenario that I would rather deal with. Well, that sounds good. And maybe Quinlan would take her away, but these people . . .

I know Quin. I know what he'd want. He wanted me. He wanted an us to make us work and if he's with the snooty Brit chick, then I have no one to blame but myself.

Snooty Brit chick? He smiled. Rori answering his phone. He glanced over to his sleeping wife. Then he forced himself to follow her now convoluted entry.

The other girl, the one that was staying at the Nursery and working in the kitchens — Amber — I haven't seen her in a couple of days. No one knows where she is.

She wanted to keep her baby. Amber had already signed papers though. She didn't know what to do. I told her to get a lawyer. People change their minds all the time. People change their minds about keeping kids. Sometimes they give them away, sometimes they give them back.

Sometimes they hold on to their kids until someone has to pry them away.

I'm so scared and nothing makes sense anymore.

Girls missing, but they aren't anyone who can be traced or missed. No family. It's the ones I know that worry me, the ones who talked to me, who worried about exercise and what they ate, who had no one else to turn to. They trusted me to help them.

Another girl who gave up her son told me she didn't want to talk to me after it was all over.

The other two?

Well, one went into labor and was yelling through it that she wanted to keep her son. I caught the look one of the nurses passed to another. Then something went wrong and they took her away. I haven't seen her since. I haven't seen the baby.

I've asked. Demanded to know. But I get the line that her medical information is protected and private and I'm not on her list of people to tell. I tried to find out, I snuck into Dr. Radcliffe's office, but Lisa saw me. She covered for me when Sally showed up as well. I looked through his files, try-

ing to find. There was one file I just caught a glimpse of before I heard some-one coming . . . a black file that only said "Others" on it.

Other whats?

Girls here, then suddenly not. Why? Because they left, just up and left without saying good-bye to friends, to people who were going through a life-changing experience with them?

Not a lot. Most were said to have changed their minds. They left the Re-treat to go home, or because of another job. And it's girls who were changing their minds anyway, or claiming to. Girls and women I knew.

I have to get out of here. Place is messing with my head. I can't find level ground. I so want to talk to Quinlan, want him to hold me and he won't. He'll be so angry. I know this. I know. I also know I need to get away. Get away from the Nursery and my friends here. From the girls before any more are hurt.

I just want Quinlan. I just want Quinlan. He can help, I know it.

I want us in the house in the Quarter. But I already sold it.

I don't know what to do.

I wish I knew what to do.

Quinlan stared at those words and wished he did as well. Finally he copied the files, saved them to Aiden's laptop, zipped and emailed copies to Ian and himself. Sighing, he stood and stared out the hospital window. It was quiet this evening. They still hadn't heard from Ian and he was trying not to pick up the damned phone and call his brother.

Why didn't they know anything yet? Why was it he was always left waiting.

Sunday night. He cursed and remembered what he'd forgotten. He pulled his phone from his pocket and made a call to the shelter in D.C. and made arrangements for the rest of the week for someone to cover his art therapy class with the kids.

He was tired. Still so pissed she hadn't told him the minute she knew; even as he knew why she hadn't, her fears, worries, the inves-tigation. And it didn't matter.

"I'm sorry," whispered behind him.

He didn't turn. "So am I."

For a minute nothing moved. He heard someone laugh out in the hallway and he ignored it.

Who the hell wanted to laugh?

His daughter was missing. A daughter he didn't even know existed until two days ago, or was it three? He rubbed a hand over his face.

He heard the rustle of the bedding and turned to help her. She waved him off, but he ignored her and helped as she climbed out of the bed. She still had an IV in her arm and rolled the stand over beside him. She looked out at the city lights; he watched her.

She was different.

But then why wouldn't she be?

There were shadows beneath her sunken eyes. Her skin was still pale, not golden like he remembered. He still couldn't get over how her hair, darker and longer, was just . . . wrong. He missed the spark, the flash of blue or purple or whatever that she wore in her hair, or all of her hair.

The tattoo was still on her wrist. He'd seen it when the nurse had changed the bandages. Her left hand was devoid of the band he knew she'd kept.

He rubbed his finger over her ring finger without realizing it.

"I wore it around my neck, but I think they took it. Or I lost it at the end. I don't know. I don't remember it all," she said, not looking at him.

She'd kept it. "You wore it?"

She turned to him then. "Yes, every day. Only when I was asked to help . . ." She stopped. "Anyway, I kept it on a chain, and—"

He put his finger against her lips and pulled a chain from beneath his shirt. His hung on it, as it had since he'd returned the first time from Vegas.

Her eyes narrowed. "You too?" She shook her head. "I've been so, so stupid. Oh God, Quin, what have I done? You came back for me, you did and I didn't . . . I didn't . . . I thought you'd . . ." She started crying and he sighed, reaching for her, pulling her close.

For a minute, she just cried against his shoulder, against his chest. Her arms came up and he felt the IV pull tight across his chest.

He pulled back and sat in the chair, settling her gently onto his lap. "It's all going to be all right, Ella. You're here now. I'm here now. Granted, you should have told me, but then again, I shouldn't have given up. None of my brothers would have."

"You're not your brothers," she muttered. "You're you."

"And look where that's got us."

She pushed back and stared at him. "I got us here more than you."

"Let's just settle on we both fucked up," he said. Then he kissed the top of her head. "We can fix it, though."

For a moment, she didn't say anything, then, "If it had been your brothers I wouldn't be married."

He scoffed. "That's the truth. None of them would have gone for the blue hair, or Elvis."

"Neither would we—Elvis, that is—had we been sober."

Again they lapsed into silence. God it felt good to have her in his arms, even as angry as he was, it felt right. Angry at her, himself, the world, he didn't know, and it didn't matter.

"I'm sorry. I should have ignored my pride, my fear, and jumped on the plane with you, then none of this would be . . ." She shook and he tightened his arms. "I don't understand anything anymore. You. Me. Us. They said they'd keep me safe. What have they done to her? Who has our baby? Quin?" She cried again. "I want my baby. I just want my baby."

"I know. I know. We'll find her. We will."

"I want out of here. I can't stay in here. I want to help. I have to help. We have to find her, we have to . . . Where's Jareaux? I'll even talk to him again."

"I've no idea where the man is," he said, angry all over again at the fact the idiot had put Quin's family in such danger.

"Ella, shhh. Shhh. Baby. We'll get through this," he said against her hair.

"I want out of here. I want out of here, Quin. Please . . ." She looked at him, her eyes watery and red, tears tracked down her face. "Please." Her voice was still broken and her pleas, shattered whispers.

He couldn't deny her.

"In the morning, I'll see what we need to do to get you out of here."

She sighed against him.

"I'll get you out of here on one condition, well, two actually."

She didn't say a word, only nodded.

"The doctor has to say it's okay. I'm not going to put you at risk."

He swallowed. "You almost . . ." He bit down. "They almost . . ." He remembered her so pale and lifeless, her lips without color. He'd spoken to the patrolman who had found her. "You could have died, Ella."

Her eyes held his, and though he tried to read them, there was. . . nothing. A flicker, but that was it. Her bandage caressed his neck just before she cupped her palm around his jaw. "But I didn't. I don't know why, I thought I would, you know."

He shook his head. He couldn't . . . Not right now . . . He just couldn't hear it.

He swallowed and tightened his hold. "I won't put you at risk, so first he has to agree. If he says tomorrow — or later today, as it's now after midnight, then fine. If he says Tuesday, then Tuesday it'll be. And then you have to come back for whatever appointments they think you need."

She nodded. "Okay, Quinlan."

He blew out a breath and tucked her close again. "You should be in bed."

She shook her head and settled closer against him. "I'm safe right here. This is the safest place in the whole world, I just wish I'd realized that sooner," she whispered.

"Hell, honey, I do, too." He kissed the top of her head again and just held her. They'd get through his. They would. Somehow. Some way, they'd get through this.

Chapter 28

Quinlan stopped, frozen in the doorway as all the air sucked from his lungs and his blood iced.

The room was shadowed in the fading light.

He took a deep breath, or tried to, and smelled something sour, decaying. Crime scene tape had been across the front and back door, not that his brother had cared. Ian had cut the tape and opened the door as if they owned the place.

The cops had informed them that the house in Albuquerque where Ella had been kept had been processed. Ian found the address, so here they were. Quin knew that whether the cops had cleared it or not, they'd still be here. Ian had been busy on the computer and phone all day. Quinlan had overheard him talking to a Mr. DeSaro about recommendations for the Nursery.

Quinlan knew of a DeSaro family; he'd asked Ian after the phone call, but Ian only told him that he was working an angle and when he knew something for certain, Quin would be the first to know.

Ella was still in the hospital, much to her annoyance. He hadn't wanted to leave her, but he wanted to see this, to do something. To help find his daughter. Rori said she'd help Ella if needed. Aiden and Brasher were there, as well as Brody. He still didn't like to be away from her for too long, but he had to come here. The Richardsons were still there as well.

Ian had pulled him aside and told him about the house. The house where she'd been held. He knew, from what they'd told him, from the fact his daughter was missing, that the baby wasn't here. He'd known Ella had been held against her will somewhere, and from what she remembered, vague and fragmented as it was, he knew she'd been bound. Damned if her wrists didn't still have the bandages on them.

But knowing all those things and standing here . . .

There were bolts on the bed, eyebolts screwed into the sides of the wooden bedrails of the small twin bed.

He stared at those eyebolts, and from here saw the rust on them.

Blood. Her blood stained the chrome and even the wood. The sheets were gone, but the bloodstained mattress was still there.

He bit down, felt the muscle bunch in his jaw.

"I told you, you didn't have to come. I told you I could check this out," Ian said softly from across the room.

Quinlan speared him with a look. He had no idea what his brother saw, but Ian held up his hands. "I get it. I'm not the enemy."

He took another deep breath. The room was small and dank, the window shuttered, bolted in place. Someone had cut the bolts because one of the shutters hung open, allowing the fading light into the room.

Soundproofing foam covered the walls.

"No one could hear her," he said, looking at the patchwork of different-colored impressioned foam.

He all but heard the giant clock slowly ticking away empty minutes. Minutes where he felt he wasn't any closer to finding his daughter than he'd been when he learned she was missing.

The room was sparse. A tray with food remnants sat in the corner of the dresser, spoiling. Looked like part of a sandwich. The top of the dresser was covered in a fine black film. He trailed his fingers through it and rubbed them together.

"They were dusting for prints."

Now that he'd thought of it, he'd seen the dust in the other part of the house, on their way back here. He'd just thought the house needing cleaning.

He walked to the window and looked out, pushing the shutter back with his cane. "What do you hope to find?"

"Who the hell kept her here."

Quinlan wanted that as well. "And then?"

Ian stopped and caught his gaze. "Then I'll question them."

He only nodded. "Let me know what I can do to help."

Ian sighed. "Then or now?"

"Both. Either."

Ian held his gaze for a long moment before nodding once. "Fine. For now, look around and see if you notice anything."

"Other than the bloodstains?" he mumbled, turning back around.

"Yes. Other than the bloodstains. I seriously doubt we will find anything, especially since the cops were already through here. This was a drop house, for want of a better term. Merchandise was dropped here," Ian said.

His words grated along Quinlan's nerves. He listened.

"Or in Ella's and the baby's case, merchandise was held here and then taken—"

"My daughter is *not* fucking merchandise," he bit out.

Ian was silent as he opened several drawers on the dresser. Quinlan looked in the nightstand. A few medical supplies, as if leftovers. A piece of bandage, wipies, a lid . . . alcohol?

Anger beat into fury and Quinlan stood wishing he'd . . . wishing he'd . . .

"I should have come out here for her. I should have . . ." He took a deep breath. "She wanted space. I gave her her damned space and look what happened. Would you have given Rori space?"

Ian sighed again and shook his head. "I thought we were here to look, but fine. I'd like to say no, I'd have followed her wherever the hell she went." Ian stared off into space for a moment and shook his head again. "But she's her own person, a strong and independent woman. Fact is, if she had really wanted some time away from me, from Darya, to decide if we were what she really wanted . . ." Ian nodded. "Yeah, I'd have given it to her, otherwise she would have been forced to stay, wouldn't she? And then I'd never know if she stayed because she wanted to or because I'd cut off all her other choices. Then again with Rori, if she wanted to leave, really leave, she would have no matter what. Thankfully, she, *we* decided we both wanted the same thing—an us."

"See."

"Should've, could've, would've doesn't matter, Quin. Beat yourself up later. You shouldn't have let her go in the first damned place, or at least should have checked up on her. And she shouldn't have kept the pregnancy from you. You're both at fault."

Quinlan turned to his brother. "Sometimes you are a right pain in the ass."

Ian smiled, but it didn't reach his eyes. "It's why you like me best. Go look in the other rooms."

Gladly. He couldn't stay in there another minute.

"Fuck it." He stalked from the room and walked down the hallway to the next door. The house was not that complicated. Not big. A normal house in a normal neighborhood. Not run-down, not upscale. Simple middle-class. Living and dining room at the front of the house. A sprawling kitchen in the middle and bedrooms in the back and to the side. Her room had been in the back of the house. If the room Ella had been kept in was such a nightmare, what the hell would he find in the other rooms?

He took a breath and turned the knob, silently pushing the door open with the flat of his hand.

The room was bright and cheery. Yellows and blues. Three cribs sat in front of the window. A dresser with one of those changing pad things on top. Or he thought that was what his brother Gavin called the one in their own nursery.

Three cribs. Three.

Chills danced over his skin.

How many more babies were out there while their parents looked for them? Then again, maybe those were legitimate adoptions. Or maybe those mothers weren't lucky enough to get away.

He walked to the cribs and gripped the pale wooden rail of one. The beds, of course, were empty. No child slept in them. The sheets had been stripped from the mattresses here as well. Lifting his hand, he realized that here too the crime scene guys had been busy. He wiped the dust off onto his jeans.

Had his daughter been kept here? In one of these beds? There was no way to tell, he supposed.

Both he and Ella had already provided DNA samples to match with anything anyone might find. They'd provided it to both the state boys here and the feds. Ian had also taken samples and sent it off to a private lab operated by a friend. Quin didn't ask, didn't care as long as they got the results quickly and their daughter was found alive and well.

The late day light slanted into the room, casting shadows. He gripped the rail of the crib again.

God, please, please, let them find his daughter. *Please.*

He gazed down at the mattress. Where had they taken her? If this was their drop house, as Ian called it, then where was his daughter?

The police checked all the hospitals and there was no child there who could be his.

Please, God . . .

He didn't know what he could possibly find that the crime guys would have missed. A sound in the doorway had him whirling around and then cursing as his leg caught. He gripped the crib behind him as he stumbled and cursed.

Jareaux stood leaning in the doorway. "I figured one of you Kinncaid boys would show up sooner or later."

Quin merely stared at him.

"You really shouldn't be here, Mr. Kinncaid."

"Where else might I be, Jareaux?"

The agent shrugged, bit down, and something shifted in the man's eyes. "I don't know, maybe with your *wife*?"

"She's resting."

"In fact, she's not. She called my number, wanting to know what all I know, wanted to know if I knew this address so she could help by coming here. Apparently the agents she was talking to earlier wouldn't bring her here."

No. Fucking. Way. Quinlan pushed away from the crib, stabbed his cane into the carpet and walked to the doorway. "She's *not* coming here. She barely got out of here alive."

Agent Jareaux stared at him. "I'm well aware of that fact, probably more so than you."

Movement out of the corner of his eye had him turning toward the room from hell. Ian's dark head leaned out. "Oh, it's you. Took you longer than I thought it would. Sneaking around, Jareaux? Word is you're rogue. Though I'm glad it's you that showed up and not the locals, they don't like me much," he muttered before going back into the room. Then he poked his head back out and said, "Might want to watch what you say to the kid, he's got a mean right hook. Always had one."

"She's not coming here," he repeated, looking slightly down and into the eyes of the fed.

Jareaux's eyes were flat, and yet there was something else hidden in the depths. Anger?

"Mr. Kinncaid, this is not the place for you."

"And did you tell her the same thing?"

Jareaux nodded. "In fact, I did. The crime guys tore this place apart. They found nothing. Well, a few things, but nothing that said where your daughter was. Nothing that said, bad guys, this way."

Smart ass.

"Perhaps I should ask what you're doing here, Jareaux? Agent Sabino made it clear you were off this case, if there ever was one."

"You're standing here and you're questioning if there's a case?" Jareaux asked him.

Quinlan didn't like him. He remembered the words Ella had spoken, the ones written in her journal.

She'd trusted him. That idea alone pissed the hell out of him. That his wife would trust this son of a bitch. He tried to shove it aside, but just the sight of the man set his teeth on edge, even knowing the man was trying to help them find their child, even if it was only to serve his own purpose—whatever that might be.

When he was even with the damned man, he used his cane to sweep the man's legs out from under him. He put the top of his cane on the fed's throat and leaned down, his knee on the bastard's chest.

"I'm getting tired of this," Jareaux bit out.

"Are you? I don't really care what you're tired of, Jareaux. You used *my wife* as bait. Our *unborn daughter* as bait because you couldn't do your job. I knew that, but seeing the bed, the eyebolts. Her fucking blood . . ." he said quietly.

He ignored Ian's, "Quin."

He leaned a bit more on his cane, watched Jareaux's eyes widen. "No one puts my family in harm's way."

"Where were you?" Jareaux gasped out.

"Right here if I'd followed my gut. I damned well would have been here and ruined your golden opportunity if I'd received her letters. But you knew that." He leaned onto his knee, until they were almost nose to nose. "I. Want. My. Letters."

Ian grabbed his shoulder. "Enough, Quinlan."

One last look into the fed's eyes. He stood and stepped back. "Not nearly enough."

"Yes, well, I thought Brody discussed this with you. Assaulting federal agents, even when clearly warranted, regardless if they are about to lose their jobs, is rather frowned upon."

He leveled a look at his brother, who only raised a brow before Ian looked down at Jareaux and offered the man a hand.

Jareaux sat up and rested his arms on his knees, looking from one to the other. A muscle bunched in his jaw. He stood, taking Ian's hand.

"Are you both going to stand out here continuing this entertainment, or are you going to help me flip the bed?" Ian asked.

With one last warning look, Quin walked passed Jareaux and into the bedroom, where Ian had already pulled all the furniture away from the walls. They pushed the heavy-logged frame from the wall and lifted it, flipping it to its side. There was nothing stuck to the back of the headboard, nor anything under the bed frame. They did find older, worn holes on the headboard.

"Stripped the anchors here. So they put in new ones on the side," Ian said, pointing to the eyebolts about halfway down the bed.

"We're still waiting on blood analysis to see how many times this place might have been used," Jareaux shared.

He could picture it all too damned clearly. Ella tied to the bed like a fucking animal, trapped and scared, screaming until she lost her voice.

Quinlan could only shake his head. "I need some air."

He walked out of the house and into the early evening. The air was cold but he didn't care. He started walking. The streetlights flickered and finally came on.

She'd been trapped in that fucking house. And what had he been doing? Flying out here, sleeping at the Richardsons, talking to police while his wife had been in hell.

He'd heard the doctors say what she'd gone through. Heard the police talk and question.

But the reality of being in that room. The bloodstains.

Her raw, almost nonexistent voice.

She'd screamed long and loud for help that never came.

Because he'd been too damned proud to fly out here and try just one more time. And one more time after that.

If he had, he'd have seen. There had been the phone call, but there was no way to trace it. He could have had Ian look after she'd called and Rori had answered. Why the hell hadn't he?

Pride again.

He was pissed. He'd freaking waited for her to call him back, to leave a damned number, and there had been nothing until she called on Friday.

If he'd just . . . If he'd only . . . He could have found her, could have had Ian find her in probably less than five minutes if he'd wanted to badly enough.

He'd have *known*. Never, never would he have left a pregnant wife, especially not one that he was crazy about, not one he was in love with.

Just a nonpregnant one who claimed she didn't want a life with you?

If he'd just *been* here!

She wouldn't have been alone. Alone and scared and bound to that damned bed cutting her wrists on zip ties she couldn't break.

So how had she gotten out? The ties had been cut, or had to have been? Maybe sometime during the labor and delivery they'd cut her loose, knowing there was no way a laboring woman could escape when far enough into the labor?

That made sense.

Then they'd taken her baby . . . *His* daughter.

And Ella.

Ella had been left for dead. She'd been left to bleed out on that damned mattress. Alone. Scared. Terrified and waiting for help that never came.

He stopped and threw his head back, wanting to yell . . .

But that would accomplish nothing. Not a damned thing. He looked up at the sky, the colors vibrant and screaming.

Why?

Why did this happen to us? he wondered at the sky, at God.

"What do we do?" he whispered. "What did I do?" Because surely she hadn't done anything for this sort of punishment.

Which was just a stupid-as-hell thought.

A breeze touched his face.

So what did he do now?

Go forward. That was all there was.

They'd find their daughter, and then? Then, he had no idea.

An image of Ella flashed in his mind. A before-and-after picture.

Before, her smiling, her dimples winking at him, her eyes dancing with laughter while her blue hair had blown in the breeze. Now? Now her hair was a shade darker than his own and a bit too brown. Her eyes didn't laugh. They didn't see anything. And the only thing he saw in them was fear.

He'd fix it. Somehow, some way, he'd fix it all.

• • •

Ian had talked to Jareaux for a few minutes to give Quinlan some time, but not too much time. He'd seen the look in his brother's eyes and on his face. Guilt. Guilt and fear and worry and . . .

No telling where the idiot would walk to if given too much time. Ian strode toward the front of the house and waited for Jareaux before he shut door.

"You shouldn't have brought him," Jareaux told him.

"Probably not, but then you shouldn't be here either, should you?" Ian said.

Jareaux sighed and raked a hand over his head. "Probably not. Look, I know he's against it, but I honestly think it'd be a good idea to get Ella over here. Seeing the house, the room, might jog her memory."

He'd thought the same thing, but then again, Ella wasn't Rori.

"Or it might just break her."

"I don't think so. I could be wrong, but any woman whose blood loss was to the point hers was, who still made it outside and found help . . . that woman is stronger than those around her might realize. The people who took her and did this, they underestimated her. I'd hate to think you guys did the same thing. I know I did."

Ian grunted and looked over at Jareaux. "Normally, feds only annoy me, and people only out for themselves, to make a name, to make the next collar, whose mistakes endanger innocents—they piss me off."

Jareaux shrugged. "It's okay. Normally, you mercenary types only piss me off."

Ian reached for his front pocket before remembering he'd quit smoking. He watched as his brother stopped a couple of blocks away and threw his head back. Kid was on a high simmer.

"My brother is usually . . . easier," he settled on, "than the rest of us." He looked back at Jareaux. "But this? All of this . . . He rather hates you. You put his family in jeopardy. We Kinncaids are rather touchy on that fact."

Jareaux put his shades on, even though they weren't needed. "Sometimes we all make mistakes."

Ian stilled. "See, my brother's laid-back, he might take a swing at you, momentarily cut off your air supply, think about other things he could do. Me? I'd just kill you."

"Threatening a federal officer, Mr. Kinncaid, is also frowned upon."

"I've a feeling you won't hold that title for long, Jareaux." Ian only smiled, and knew it held no humor. "I never threaten, Mr. Jareaux. I simply take care of matters."

Jareaux jerked open his car door. "I'll just bet you do." He fingered his tie until it loosened. "I wish I'd never heard the name Kinncaid."

Chapter 29

Albuquerque, Tuesday, after midnight

Please forgive me. I don't know why I did it. Maybe being around adoptions all the time let me see that there were more out there to help. I only wanted to help. I sold the Kinncaid woman's baby to a wonderful couple. The way I went about it was wrong. I know. Now, he knows too and he doesn't want me anymore. No one will understand. No one will ever forgive me and I don't blame them. I don't know why I did it and there's no way to undo it. I don't know what else to do. Please tell Ella I'm sorry. I'm really sorry. She really was my friend, I didn't lie about that.

~ Lisa

He read back through it and realized there should be another *really* there at the end. With a black-gloved finger, he typed the rest of the note. Yes, that would work. Perfect.

He wondered again if the man he had hired had accomplished what he'd set out to do, if he'd managed to kill the stupid Kinncaid woman. Really, how hard could it be? She'd been released from the hospital earlier today. Whether that would make it easier or harder, he wasn't yet sure. Either way, the bastard better do what he was paid to do.

At this point, though, it would hardly be over. If only it were that easy. Best thing to do is to clip the ends and hope things did not continue to unravel.

In the end, hopefully, his ass would be covered, but something told him he'd always be looking over his shoulder.

Walking to the bathroom, he cut off the faucet before the tub overflowed, felt the water and then wondered why he cared. It wasn't like she could feel it.

Wiping his hands on his pants, he stood and strode back into the bedroom. Carefully, so as not to touch anything, he stripped her down to her underwear. "Not long now, dearie. Don't worry, you won't feel a thing. All those Ambien pills I put in your drink and blended with the fruit and alcohol, it won't be long anyway."

He slipped his gloves back on. It really worked great knowing what her scripts were. Sleeping pills and alcohol, one of the oldest tricks in the books if one wanted to off themselves. Personally, he had never wanted to, never truly understood when people did, but then most people would never understand why he did what he did. That was fine with him. He hardly needed approval. He just didn't want to get caught.

This was another loose end to clip off.

He carried her to the bathtub and gently placed her in it. Then he put the knife into her own hand and studied it for a moment. No, wait, that's not how she would hold it, is it? He placed her fingers a bit more naturally against the hilt of the sharp kitchen knife. Then he sliced it down her left arm. He frowned. Probably should have done the right first. Did a person who was right-handed slice their left wrist first? If tendons were severed and nerves, then how did they then hold the knife to cut the other wrist?

He'd never thought about it before. Maybe he should have just let the pills take their toll. Of course, he could just drown her in the tub, but that could leave bruising.

She'd wanted to sleep with him earlier and he never passed up a chance to fuck the woman. She knew her way around a man's cock and he was more than happy to oblige. If anything came of it, it wasn't like their affair wasn't known about. He knew two of his nurses knew and Kevin had known.

There would be a reason his DNA and prints could be found here. It was a place they had frequently met. This time, though, he'd found out what she had done and was so shocked they'd fought and he left, telling her it was over.

Despondent over what she had done, over losing him, she'd swallowed her pills and alcohol. Or so he hoped it would be believed.

The note was already on her laptop, and would be found when the time was right.

The water was already red. He set the knife on the rim of the tub and tilted her head to the side; dropped to her chest as it was, she looked uncomfortable.

The earth-tone tiles hid the bright scarlet of the blood that had spurted from her opened veins. He stood and stepped back. Everything was as it should be.

He walked back through the apartment and stripped his gloves off, checking his scrubs. So there was a little blood on them, what else was new? He'd toss them and no one would think anything of it.

Had he thought of everything? He'd moved the money yesterday from the dummy corporate account he always used for delicate adoptions. He'd transferred it to hers. Of course the trail was now there. How to explain the money away?

Perhaps say she had access to that account?

After all, she was going to be found in this town house the corporation owned. Some of the deposits in her financial background would be traced back to the same company. The house the stupid woman had used was owned by the same.

He should just cut and run. The cops were looking for him. He knew because he'd checked his voice messages from a pay phone after he'd dumped his cell. His wife was a bit irritated at the police, their questions and insinuations. She'd wanted to know what was going on. He hadn't returned her call.

He'd run the background on the McGregors, which turned up nothing, but they still didn't feel right, felt off. Maybe he was seeing ghosts in shadows. Mr. McGregor had been too intense to his way of thinking.

Knowing his luck, they were probably working with the feds or the Kinncaids or something.

He glanced back down the hallway toward the bathroom. Damn Lisa. At least her death should buy him enough time to get out of the country.

Going away for fraud and kidnapping was one thing, murder was a whole other kettle, wasn't it? And he wasn't about to go down because the woman currently bleeding out in the bathtub where they'd made love a few days ago had been greedy and stupid. She'd wanted to return to her house in Taos, claiming she needed to check on her cats. He probably should have checked it himself Saturday evening when she'd called him after seeing the cops in the street. But he hadn't, and then it was too late. He hoped to hell she hadn't had anything incriminating at her place. Be like her, though. Stupid and impulsive she might be, but she was damned shrewd and greedy.

Greedy he could handle. When greed bred stupidity and the stupidity thrived . . . that he couldn't tolerate.

How long it would take the cops to find Kevin he had no idea, and it probably didn't matter. Charred remains were charred remains and at least Kevin wouldn't be able to tell all his secrets.

Checking to make sure everything was as it should be, he eased out of the house and down the stairs, staying to the shadows. In the lot, he climbed into a car he'd bought with cash off a used lot yesterday morning with a fake ID.

He fisted his hands on the steering wheel and knew it was all falling down. He needed to leave. Maybe he could catch a flight out to California and then . . . Thailand. Or Brazil. Hell, Mexico would work too. He had a couple of fake passports and had set up places in the two previous locales and Mexico . . . well, many got lost in Mexico. His wife though . . . and daughter?

They could never know. If it all came out, his own family would never forgive him.

Too much was at stake to leave any loose ends hanging. It wasn't the affair he was worried about. His wife knew him well enough that would not come as a surprise. They had an understanding.

But there was understanding small lies she didn't really care about and understanding lies that impacted their lives forever.

Some lies could never be discovered. He'd do whatever he had to to keep some secrets buried.

Chapter 30

Quinlan walked down the hotel hallway with its plain colorless walls. There was great art if you were an O'Keeffe fan, or loved *Koko-pelli* and the damned flute. He freaking hated New Mexico. It had taken too much from him. At any other time, he might have admired the hotel they were staying in, but honestly, he couldn't care less. What he wanted was answers. There were yet to be any.

What he had was only more questions.

Dr. Merchant was now missing. No one could find Lisa Hammerstein or some guy named Kevin who had worked at the Retreat.

Ella had rested for most of the day. She'd been released yesterday afternoon and between the Richardsons and his brothers, they'd gotten everyone here. The Richardsons had left this morning, wanting to check on things at home. They said they'd be back, probably tomorrow. He was both glad and nervous that she was out. But they were close to the hospital if anything came up. She had answered a few questions, a few and far too many for his way of thinking. Even when speaking to the police. She'd answer some and then it was like someone pressed the pause button and she'd shut down for a minute, staring off into space. Then she'd ask a question and the process looped all over again.

He didn't know what to do to help her.

They talked. They whispered. They danced around the issues that needed to be resolved.

She was his. If he'd wondered about it months previously, of letting her go, he knew now how futile that was.

She. Was. His.

However, like Ian said, if they really wanted space, you gave it to them . . . even when you didn't want to. Though when space led to nightmares, then what did you do?

He walked into the dining room, the wrought iron chandelier hanging from the beams of the *latilla* ceiling adding to the macabre feeling he seemed blanketed in.

And there she sat, near the kiva fireplace.

When space led to nightmares you helped battle them.

Ella. Just seeing her had him wanting to pull her into his arms, and yell at her at the same time. He didn't do either.

He'd told her she was coming out here to eat with his family, if he had to drag her. He knew she didn't really feel like it. Hell, he didn't feel like it, but that was just too damned bad. She'd hidden in their suite since yesterday, room service bringing her whatever she wanted, which was nothing. He felt like he was force-feeding her.

She didn't eat, nightmares ripped apart what little sleep she managed. She hardly spoke at all. She would sit staring off into space with tears streaming down her face, as if she wasn't aware she even cried.

He wanted Ella back. His Ella, bright, vibrant Ella.

Even if they hadn't taken his child, hadn't tormented his wife, he'd kill them for putting that broken look in her eyes.

He paused and just watched her as she watched the flames. The scent of wood smoke mixed with the scents of grilled meats, spicy peppers and alcohol. Someone cleared their throat and he looked over to the large dining table. He wondered if she'd eat anything tonight.

Agents Sabino and Landry lounged back against the chair listening to something Ian and Rori were saying. John Brasher was also there. Aiden sat jotting something down on paper. Man had every gadget currently on the market but he still preferred pen and paper. The normalcy of that small, stupid act settled something in Quin.

Ian looked up and quirked a brow at him.

He walked over to his wife and wondered yet again how the hell to reach her.

Squatting down beside the log chair she sat curled in, he reached out to take her hand. Just the brush of his fingers and she jerked her hand back. Her eyes flashed to his, and in them he only saw fear.

"Hey," he whispered.

She swallowed. "Sorry." This time, she reached out and gently settled her fingers on the back of his hands. He looked down at her hand as he laced his fingers through hers. White bandages still wrapped around her wrists. The zip ties had bit deep enough, often enough, the doctor said there would be permanent scarring. They'd met with a physical therapist yesterday before her release who worked with them on exercises for her to do. Mostly finger and wrist movements. Which reminded him, he wanted to get her a keyboard. One, it would be great physical therapy, and two, it might help her — somehow. Woman loved music, maybe it would help her deal with all of this. He knew she played, had played in the past.

He bit down and took a deep breath, shaking off the thought.

"What do you want to eat?"

She opened her mouth and he quirked a brow at her, narrowing his eyes. She was damned well going to eat.

Ella shut her mouth.

She looked at the man on his knees beside her. The room was dark; the murmur of voices rumbled from behind her, everyone trying to figure out what to do. She didn't know what to do. What did anyone do? She'd talked to the police, several times. Hell, she'd even spoken to Jareaux alone when Quinlan had left to check on her discharge papers and Jareaux had shown up. Granted, they'd only talked for a bit before some guy claiming to be her guard showed up and ran Jareaux off. What did she *do*?

Everything in her was . . .

Broken.

Just broken.

She couldn't find even ground. Didn't know which way to turn. Nothing sounded right. Nothing smelled right. Nothing was the way it was supposed to be. Drowning, she was drowning and had no idea how to get her head above water. If she could do something, anything, maybe then she could . . . could . . . breathe.

The fire flickered shadows onto Quinlan. His hair, still damp from his shower, held a scent she knew. She leaned over and kissed the top of his head. He smelled right. He felt right.

He lifted his head and their eyes met. She saw the questions in his, the fear. The fury. And the hurt.

She'd hurt him.

Again, he lifted his damned brow. "What do you want to eat?" he repeated.

Nothing. Nothing. She wasn't hungry.

Then again, she knew him well enough to know there was no way in hell he'd let that go. He'd ordered food for her for the last two days, had tried to get her to eat in the hospital.

She wasn't hungry then. She wasn't hungry now.

Empty. Everything was empty. Everything hurt. Her wrists, her stomach, all her muscles—from fighting, the doctors had told her. And her breasts. She should have been able to feed her baby, but there was no baby to nurse.

Who was feeding her child? Were they feeding her? What if she was hungry? What if she wanted her mother?

Four days. Four days, she thought, but maybe it was longer. The time in that room was fuzzy.

The cops had found the house she'd been kept in. They'd gone door to door in the neighborhood. No one had told her at first, but she'd heard Quinlan talking to an agent—not Jareaux—and his brothers last night. Glass had shattered out in the living room. She'd walked in and listened as they talked. Apparently he had gone with Ian on Monday. She'd never seen him that angry. She asked to go and no one had listened to her. Quin had and he'd told her over his dead body. She dropped it.

She hadn't asked again.

Tomorrow they were supposed to go back to the doctor.

"Hey. You've got to eat. We're going to find her, and she'll need her mom strong when we do, Ella." His words jerked her back. His fingers rubbed across the back of her knuckles.

"I know," she said and nodded.

She had asked constantly at first what they knew, what they had found, but hearing the same things was grating, so she didn't ask.

Eat.

She'd eat.

Sighing, she pushed herself up from the chair, startling again when Quinlan moved to help her.

He muttered something under his breath.

She stopped and stood, staring at him. "Sorry."

He shook his head. "No problem."

What a lie that was. There were so many problems strangling the two of them, so many on top of everything else. "How can you be nice to me?"

The words were out before she realized it.

He sighed and raked a hand through his hair. "We'll talk about this later."

Part of her, a large part, agreed. But then . . . "No. Now."

"Now isn't the time. Now, we're going to eat."

"I'm not hungry."

"You're going to eat, damn it," he snapped.

"Why won't you be honest with me? I know you're angry and —"

His eyes widened. "I'm not the one who wasn't honest, Ella. That was you."

Well, she had asked. She'd open this damned door. But she was tired of this ugly black ball between them, wrapped in barbs and trip wires. She couldn't deal with Quin too. Not this way. Not as though everything was fine. As though nothing had happened. When they both knew it was far, far from fine. He could go through the motions, but the truth beneath was eating away at her.

"Quin," one of his brothers said. She didn't know which one.

She held up her hand. "No, he's right. He's absolutely right." She nodded. "I wasn't honest with you."

She sighed and raked a hand through her hair. "I know that. But you're . . . you're . . ."

"What?"

"You! A damned Kinncaid, for God's sake. I did the rich boy marriage before, remember?"

"God, I'm so sick of that damned excuse! That's all you've ever said, 'I've done the rich boy before, and it didn't work.' What the hell does that have to do with anything?"

How to make him understand? She looked at him. "Look at you and where you come from. My mother was a stripper in the Quarter! And I don't care about that. She was great, I was lucky to have her. Others, though, have a problem with it."

"I don't," he said, his hands on his hips.

"I have a tattoo and I want another." She waved toward her hair. "I like to have weird hair."

"So? You don't have one tattoo, you have three, and I love each one. And? That's all who you are, who I want."

"So, I'm not right for someone like you. That was what I had tried to tell you. *Then.* Then I believed all that. Or thought I did. I tried to convince myself of all the differences between us and soon they were all I saw. It was easier that way, ya know? Easier to see the differences and convince myself it would never, ever work. Not really, not in the long run. After all, it didn't before. I know that's not fair. I know it was stupid, but it was how I felt then. There were too many parallels to my before and I . . . I just . . ."

He raised his brows.

"Freaked. Got scared and freaked. And ran as fast as I could from a wonderful man that I loved so much it scared me. I'm my own worst enemy."

He shook his head. "Why? I get I should have told my family and I'm sorry, but what did I do to make you think—"

"Nothing. God, nothing, Quin. That's what's so messed up." She walked to the window. "His name was Lance. Before, I was young and stupid and naively in love. College. I was on scholarship to Tulane. My mother had died before I graduated. Then I met Lance. Lance was . . ." She smiled, remembering . . . "We fell in love. That first hard, true love. Ya know? We spent all our time together and I weaved all sorts of happily-ever-afters in my mind. With my liberal arts degree and my marketing and his business we'd work together. Then I found out I was pregnant." She felt him start beside her. Turning, she saw the question in his eyes. "He was ecstatic, or said he was. Asked me to marry him, told me I'd be meeting his parents. I bought a dress and everything. I was so nervous, so excited. I so wanted to make a good impression." She sighed. "But I didn't meet his parents. He showed up and said that something had come up, but not to worry, I'd meet them later." She rubbed her arms. "I should have known then. But I was busy living in a fantasy world of my own making. We went to the justice of the peace a couple of weeks later. I asked about his parents. He told me they were in Europe." She shook her head again. "I never, ever questioned him. I guess I should give the man some credit. He tried to do the right thing. He did try."

Quinlan shifted beside her. "Trying is an excuse p— losers give when they didn't go all or nothing. Then again, I never should have walked out that door."

Of course, all or nothing as he was.

She focused on the dormant aspens in the courtyard. "We got an apartment. A really nice one, nicer than anything I had ever lived in. I was busy with school and wondering how I'd finish and be a good wife, and mother, and I was so scared. I remember being scared. I noticed he was quieter a bit more than usual, withdrawn. Then one afternoon, when he wasn't home, the knock came." She didn't turn to Quin. "His parents. Mr. and Mrs. Montinaire were *not* happy. They'd met him earlier that day, I was told. I knew he was wealthy, but had no idea who he really was. Why did I care? I just loved him. He loved me, or so I thought. Maybe he did, it hardly matters. They didn't believe me." She looked to Quin. "Someone like me, and those were her words, was *not* good enough for their son. I was the wrong type of woman for their family." She swallowed and tried not to remember how much that had hurt. "I tried to be nice. My mother had always said that smiles get you more than scowls. But it didn't work on them.

"They owned real estate in New Orleans. A lot apparently. And an old family plantation or something. Someone with my background was *unsuitable* for their son. After all, a daughter of a stripper and bartender must only see Lance's money, and I and the bastard I carried were not going to derail the plans their son had worked so hard to achieve. His father wrote me a check for three million dollars to leave their son alone. I remember feeling so insulted and thinking how idiotic these people were. I told them I didn't want their money, or their son's money. To which his mother replied that as long as he was married to me, he had no money. I told them to leave. They left the check and told me to be smart and not to fight them or make it difficult for Lance."

She still didn't turn, even as she knew he stood just behind her, felt the warmth from his body.

"He didn't come home that night. I know; I sat up all night on the couch telling myself it would be okay. He came in the next afternoon, looking horrible. I was worried and scared. The damned check still sat on the counter." She remembered the mass of feelings for that stupid boy. And he had been a boy. "He was just a boy, I suppose, just didn't get it. I didn't see it until then. He walked to me and said, 'I'm sorry, Ella. I'm so sorry,' and then he walked back to our bedroom. I still thought, poor man. To have parents like that. I think maybe I even said something like that. He said nothing, just got the bag out of the closet and started packing. I realized at some point he was talking to me, telling me that he'd talked to his parents, that he'd bought the apartment for me and it was paid for. I could keep it. And he'd see about getting me more money, so the baby and I wouldn't ever have to worry."

"Bastard," someone said.

She just looked out the dining room window to the courtyard beyond. The setting sun painted the sky periwinkle and peach.

"For a minute, I remember I didn't understand. He just finished packing, his face a face I didn't understand. I asked him about the baby. How could he do this? In this century? It wasn't like we were in the fifties or sixties or whenever. People made their own lives all the damned time now. It was the freaking age of dot-commers, for God's sake." She shook her head. "He just looked at me and said, 'With my family, it would never work. I'm sorry.' He was sorry. He just left." She swallowed. "I was so upset. So upset. I remember shaking, thinking some way I could fix this. I could . . . Trying to figure out how I could be *better* for him. So that I'd be good enough." She shook her head, felt Quin's hands settle on her shoulders.

"He was a stupid idiot. And he wasn't even in the realm of good enough for you."

"Oh, I know that now, but then I didn't. The pains woke me up. The bed was bloody. I called an ambulance and Lance. I didn't have anyone else to turn to."

"Your mom?" Quinlan asked.

She shook her head. "No, she'd died my sophomore year of college. Left work and someone . . ."

"Killed her, you told me that. I'm sorry," Quinlan told her.

"Doesn't matter." She shrugged. "I woke up in the hospital and there was Lance. The doctors were kind, the nurses kind. He just kept saying he was sorry."

She frowned. "But then, I'd seen, hadn't I? He wasn't the man I thought he was. Just a boy who didn't want to disappoint Mom and Dad, and I wouldn't want him to, not if I wasn't important enough to him. I didn't care at that point. I'd lost my baby." She turned back to Quinlan. "His parents had the marriage annulled—quietly, of course. They didn't want anyone to know of his little indiscretion. I kept the money. Sold the apartment and then, later, went back to finish my degree. Bought the house in the Quarter and just . . . cruised along. Loved my life, was content."

She smiled at him. "Until you. You slammed into me, literally, and nothing was the same after that. I told myself I was stupid. Didn't I learn the first time? I guess I figured if I left first, then you couldn't leave me. What he did to me wasn't easy . . . I remember being so lost. Lance broke my heart. But you — you could have shattered my soul and I knew it from the first. So I left, before I got hurt. Though that was a lie, too. When I asked if you'd told anyone . . . Even though I knew the answer . . . I wanted you to be different, and then I saw, even as I knew and it hurt." She took a deep breath.

"When I found out about the baby, that was one hell of a surprise. I picked up the phone to call you I don't know how many times. But I always chickened out. I saw myself making the same stupid mistakes. A man, a hasty wedding, a baby he might not want, a rich man, a woman his family wouldn't approve of."

"To us, family is sacred. You don't know my family. And clearly you don't know me."

"Oh, I believed my own BS for a while. Then," she said on a shrug, "I don't know, I got caught up in the Nursery. I realized there were bigger things out there than me. I wanted to help. I wanted to be me and make something of myself, make a difference, be someone not only I was proud of, but maybe you would be too," she finished, noticing how soft and fractured her voice still was.

Quin had leaned closer to hear her. His eyes met hers. "I was proud of you. I loved everything about you. I kept going back to New Orleans, Ella. We were married."

"I know and I almost . . . but I didn't. Then when I moved here and found out about the baby, I didn't call you. If I came to you then, you'd always wonder if it was only because of the baby, when as soon as I drove away from New Orleans I knew I should be going to you and not leaving. I just didn't trust myself."

"You'd be better off not thinking for me," he said, his eyes intense on hers.

She nodded. "I know. Now. Now, though, doesn't do us any good. Sometimes, now is too late."

He wrapped his arms around her. "Now is not too late. It's simply now, Ella, and what we make of it, or what we let go."

She tightened her arms around him. "There's so much more, though. More that has absolutely nothing to do with us or me or the baby. It's the Nursery. I'd planned to tell you, even helping them and then everything went to hell. I saw . . . I saw . . ."

The bag being drug across the ground . . . She shivered.

"Then things got complicated and I didn't know what to do. I thought maybe I was imagining things. But I thought they were watching me. Thought maybe . . .

"Look, I know it sounds crazy. And I don't have any proof. I know that!" She pulled away and looked around him to the men at the table, to the agents, then back to Quinlan. "They'd tried to talk me into giving the baby up too many times." She shivered again. "I knew what that meant. I knew. I knew," she tried louder, but her voice broke again. "I tried to get away and I trusted the wrong person, Quinlan. I trusted the wrong person and look what happened. Look."

Images slithered through her. Sharp, jagged, cutting and slicing across her chest.

She couldn't stop the trembles. "I don't blame you for being angry at me. I was her mother. Her *mother!*" *The baby soft on her stomach, her wrists aching, reaching, begging . . .*

She felt his hands on her arms, but she couldn't bear to be touched. She jerked away. "Her mother, and what did I do? What could I do?" Tears shattered her words as she held up her hands. Her wrists were wrapped. "I tried . . . I tried so hard to get . . . I could hear her crying, Quin, she was crying and I couldn't . . . I couldn't . . ."

She took a shuddering breath even as he stepped closer to her and cupped her face. "Look at me," he said, his voice firm.

Her eyes locked to his. *Look at me. Right here. Eyes on me, Ella.*

"I'm so glad you came," she whispered, tears trailing hotly down her face.

His eyes narrowed. "Ella, what the hell, do you think I wouldn't? I'm telling you right now, you better damned stop comparing me to that bastard Lance, or you might not like the consequences. I'm not him. You were scared, terrified, that was all I knew at first, all I cared about. That and you'd dropped a huge fatherhood surprise bomb on me. The baby . . . I can't . . . I didn't know. All I knew was that I had to get . . ." His hands tightened on her arms. "Damn it, Ella."

Emotion clogged her throat, and she tried to swallow around it, tried to rein in her emotions that were all over the damned place.

"She was mine. Mine and I didn't keep her safe. I didn't protect her! They just . . . Oh God . . ." Tears choked her and this time she didn't pull away as his arms came up around her. "Oh God, Quin. I'm sorry. I'm so, so sorry. I didn't . . . sooner . . . I should have . . ."

Sobs wracked her body and she didn't try to hold them in any longer. There was no reason she'd had to go through all this alone, other than stupidity and some idealized notion of helping others. Who the hell was she to lend a hand when she couldn't even breathe?

She felt him lift her, settle her down on his lap as he sat somewhere. His words were lost against her, but the timbre, the fact he was holding her . . .

"It's going to be okay, Ella. We'll find our daughter. We'll get through all this . . ."

Chapter 31

"Jock," she said, pulling him out of his musings.

"We are not rushing over there, Kaitie. The boys will take care of it and let us know. You'll only worry yourself into a damned heart attack."

She narrowed her gaze on him, stupid, stubborn man. The man she'd fallen in love with so many, many years ago and yet it seemed just like yesterday. So much had changed and yet stayed the same.

"You are not listening and I will damned well win this argument. I talked to Aiden." She shifted on the bed, trying to get comfortable. "Poor girl didn't think we'd like her."

"Apparently our sainted youngest thought the same thing."

She punched him in the arm. Propped up in bed, they were both wondering about tomorrow. The house was quiet, too quiet. Since Brayden and Christian married, they'd found their own place not too far from here, but she—and Jock, she knew—still missed seeing their granddaughter every day. It just wasn't the same, but life moved on. She loved it when Ian and his family had lived here for a bit, but she knew that wouldn't last longer than her son could stand it. The house might be stupidly large—she'd always thought so—but it was still Mom and Dad's, and what son really wanted to live with them? None of them, and that was as it should be. The only reason Brayden had moved into the west wing was because of Tori, and she was glad they'd had the years with their son and granddaughter that they'd had. But he'd finally left home, thank goodness. Granted, she'd wanted Quinlan to stay a bit longer, she worried about him, but she'd known, too, he'd hate to be seen as weak. He always did. Even as a boy. He always felt like he had something to prove.

"Did you know, Quin asked me once if you were his father?"

Jock didn't look up from his ereader. Instead he grunted. "Asked me the same thing years ago, think he was about ten. Said he looked nothing like me or his brothers." He waggled his brows at her. "Something you want to share, Kaitie?"

Again she hit him in the arm. "Don't be an idiot. I just can't for the life of me figure out why the hell he didn't tell us. What was he trying to prove this time? And nothing makes sense to me."

"Kaitie lass," he said, setting the reader down. "Nothing about the boys has ever made sense to either one of us. Half the time I just didn't get what they did or the why of it, and the other half you didn't. All in all, they turned out right and are good honorable men. We didn't screw up too badly."

She laughed. "No, I guess we didn't." She settled down onto her pillow and picked up her own reader, choosing the book she'd been reading. "We're still heading out to New Mexico tomorrow."

"Aiden asked us to stay here."

"And you are doing what one of the boys asked you to do? Since when?"

He looked at her over the rims of his glasses. "Since I don't want you to land in the hospital again."

She scoffed. "I'm the doctor, last time I checked."

He picked his reader back up. "Heal thyself, physician."

"We're going. I don't want her to think we don't want her as part of our family. I don't know why the hell Quinlan hid her away to begin with, which only added to her fear, and . . . ."

"I don't know as he hid her away so much as she hid away." He cleared his throat.

Jock worried about her, she knew that. She'd scared him a couple of years with all the stress with Quinlan and Ian and little Darya. She took a deep breath and laid her hand on his thigh. "Jock. He's our son. His child, *our* grandchild, has been taken by God knows who to God knows where. We. Are. Going."

He turned his head and speared her with a look he rarely used on her and one that she would completely ignore—when she normally didn't. Maybe she could talk him around to her way of thinking. He stared at her hard and finally sighed, setting the reader aside and giving her his full attention.

"I don't know that they'd want us there right now."

"I don't care. Quinlan will be angry, she must be worried sick. And with all she's been through . . . ."

Jock shook his head. "I know you said for us to stay out of the boys' lives time and time again. It feels odd for me to say it to you." He grinned at her and then continued, "Since Brice and Aiden, I have, thank you very much." He held up his hand. "What if she married him for his money, Kaitie? And this is all some ruse?"

She snorted. "Seriously? You think the poor girl knocked herself up by planning it perfectly? Then didn't tell him, kidnapped herself, held against her will and what? Paid people to take her baby?"

"Stranger things have happened. I just don't understand why, or how, he didn't know she was pregnant," he mumbled. "I damned well knew and I didn't let you run away."

She hummed, remembering way back when.

Oh, she could understand. Sometimes the Kinncaid men—including her darling sons—were just . . . She shook her head. "You know, I don't know why he ever questioned if he was your son. The others might look like you and Aiden takes after you all too much sometimes, but Quinlan . . . Quinlan has always reminded me of you the most."

He grunted.

"You both hide who you really are behind façades to keep us on our toes, always guessing. Were you the carefree playboy or the serious businessman? You come off as all gruff and territorial."

"I *am* territorial, in case it's escaped your notice all these years."

" —but really you're just . . . you just care about your family. He's the same way, just quieter and more reserved about it all. He might not have your bark, but he does have that cunning and never-give-up that you always have had."

"Kaitie, the boys—all of them—take after you, and me. I know that. And what that all has to do with us *not* going out there is beyond me."

"We *are* going out there. We are going to meet her."

He opened his mouth and she held her hand over his lips. "And if it turns out she is in fact a gold-digging . . . liar with something to hide, then fine. We can all hate her. Well, no, she's still the mother of one of our grandchildren and we will help them any way we can. However, I won't see Quin hurt either. I don't like when my boys hurt and neither do you."

He narrowed his eyes on hers.

"Which is why we will be leaving in the morning to fly out to Albuquerque, and while the others are all about looking and doing and whatever else, we will simply be there for them because that is what family does. That is what we both taught our boys and that is what we are going to do."

"Can I speak now?" he asked behind her hand.

He huffed out a sigh. "Kaitie," he grumbled under his breath. "Fine. We'll leave tomorrow *after* you see your cardiologist and he clears it. If he doesn't, we are *not* going, I don't care how upset you are with me. Period."

She bit her lip to keep from grinning.

His eyes narrowed on her again. "I swear there will come a day when I will deny you something."

"So you've said, many, many times, dear."

He pulled her to him and kissed her lips. So many years and still he made her heart race like that of a young girl. "I'll show you many, many times."

She giggled. "Promises, promises."

"Kaitie lass, if you ever learned anything about me through the years, you ought to know that any challenge, I'm more than capable of meeting."

"Thank God for those little pills."

"For that, I think I'll just torture you."

She laughed as he tickled her and the laughter soon died away into desire and into passion. So many changes and yet so much had remained the same.

• • •

Albuquerque, Thursday morning

Ian stood in the doorway of the bathroom looking in at the mess. That would really depreciate the value of this place. Great location, great view of the mountains from the living room. Tile, tall ceilings, clean lines, top-of-the-line appliances, lots of room and storage. Nice place.

The dead body in the tub rather took away from the prime bit of real estate though.

Agent Sabino had called him about an hour ago to let him know they'd found Lisa Hammerstein. Looked like she'd been dead for about a day, by his own guess.

Detective Hudson had nodded at him as he'd come into the town house.

"Kinncaid, figured you'd turn up sooner or later."

"Like an unlucky penny," he told the man. Ian didn't take it personally when the locals didn't really warm to him. He figured it was par for the course. Hudson, for all his irritation, wasn't a bad sort, just overworked and tired.

Hudson walked over to him and jerked his chin toward the tub. "That's a dead end."

"Leave it to Hudson to state the obvious," Sabino said.

"Leave it to the feds to complicate the issue and stay vague," Hudson returned.

"What have you got so far?" he asked.

Normally, he'd have brought Johnno along with him, but he'd left him at the hotel with the family. Rori was there but she was tired and worried about their own kids, even if she hadn't said as much yet.

Sabino shook her head. "Well, as you can see, appears to be suicide. And if the fabulous slice-and-dice job on her wrists didn't do the job, I'm sure the sleeping pills would have taken care of it."

A flash went off as the crime scene tech did his bit. Another young man stood. "I'd appreciate it, Agent, if you didn't speculate too much until I get tox screens back. Just because there are empty pill bottles does not mean they are in her system."

Sabino rolled her eyes. "Yes, Dr. Bainer."

"The doc on little sleep is as bad as my teenage daughters PMSing," Hudson said.

Ian smiled and Sabino shook her head. "He's right, though, shouldn't speculate, but really seems overkill to me." She stood and walked out of the bathroom, joining them.

She stepped into the hallway with them and motioned him over to a table where a laptop had already been dusted for prints, as has most things here in the town house. A fine layer of dust coated most every surface.

"How'd you find her?"

"Anonymous call. And look, there's a note." Sabino motioned to the laptop.

He shook his head. "Just missing a bow."

"Yeah, that's what I thought. Got agents and the state boys going over her place again in Taos with a fine-toothed comb. Sent them out there as soon as we got the call here, and that was about three hours ago."

Ian merely raised a brow.

Hudson grinned. "You didn't really think we'd call you right off, did you?"

"I've shared everything we've found," he said. "You should have called me earlier. I could have headed over to her house." He sighed and rubbed a hand over his face. "How far is that again?"

She grinned. "Too far for you to go and look tonight, Mr. Kinncaid."

"Call me Ian. There are too many Mr. Kinncaids."

She chuckled. "Yeah, well, this time our guys are going over everything. Found a neat little hidey-hole in the floorboards of her closet. Flash drive, some discs, and a couple of folders. Our guys are looking over all of them now."

"You need another tech guy? I've got a couple that are whizzes that could look at the drive and discs."

She smiled. "Mine already has the flash drive, which is apparently encrypted. Don't worry, he'll get it solved. Probably within a day, or maybe we'll be lucky and it'll be by tomorrow afternoon." She checked her watch. "I mean this afternoon. I swear the kid puts Red Bull in his Kurig. Maybe I should try that. Anyway, he's at the hotel and already started on it."

"Techies are just weird, great at figuring things out, but weird all the same," Hudson said. "And they're always twitchy. Like a crack addict waiting on another fix. Why is that?"

"Caffeine," both she and Ian answered.

"What about the laptop?" he asked, motioning to it.

"I'll get it to him as well. We'll see what's on it, but I'm doubting it will be anything like what she hid at her house."

"Because it wasn't hidden from whoever did this to her."

She tilted her head.

"What else was there?"

"The files appear to be docs of adoptions, photos of babies and couples. No idea what's on the disc or flash drive. I'll ask Bull when I get back, see if he got to them yet. I told him the flash drive was priority though."

He nodded and took a deep breath before he remembered not to and winced.

"Yeah, at least the heater was off, though. Small mercies and it's not July," Hudson offered with a grin.

True. Dead bodies and heat were not conducive to each other.

"Fine. I'd like to look around a bit more and then head back."

"You want us to tell her about Lisa?" Sabino asked him.

He shook his head. "No, I will when they get up in the morning . . . this morning, later. When the hell ever. Probably won't be long. She doesn't sleep much," he admitted, looking at the view and then back at the coffee table where the laptop set.

"Parents of missing kids never do, Kinncaid," she said. "We'll be over in the morning. Call me when she's up, or text or whatever." She handed him another card.

"I have your number and your partner's."

"And probably my boss's, but here's a card just in case someone else might need to call."

He tucked it into his pocket.

One person down who could have told them where his niece was.

"By the way, thanks for the tip on the DeSaros. We've talked to their lawyer and to Mr. DeSaro. We haven't been able to speak to Mrs. DeSaro as yet, or see the baby. We've had lots of leads to follow, call-ins. None have turned anything up. I'm getting a court order for the DeSaros in the morning, or at least as soon as the judge's golf round is done."

"Always waiting on someone."

"Guess you don't have to worry about that, do you?" she asked him.

He only grinned and walked out the door.

Chapter 32

Thursday morning

Ella opened her eyes, having dozed off earlier, but she couldn't sleep. She looked at Quinlan lying there beside her, facing her. His arm lay across her abdomen, as though holding her. Quinlan always held her.

She remembered the first time they met. The way he'd been so handsome, so . . . him. Though pain and frustration had danced in his eyes. Then the way it had slowly melted away the longer they spent together. The way he'd look at her across the kitchen as they were cooking and then make passionate love. The twinkle he'd get in his eyes. The way his chuckle would dance over her skin. Her heart still tripped just looking at him, just as it did when they first met. How had she ever thought she could get through life without him? Why had she wanted to?

Oh yeah, not to get hurt.

Life without Quinlan hurt, she knew that. She'd already been through it and had no one to blame but herself.

He'd lost weight, she suddenly noticed. His cheekbones were more pronounced. Even in sleep he looked stressed. There were dark circles under his eyes. She lifted her hand to brush across them, but paused. His hair was longer than the last time he'd come to see her in New Orleans.

She remembered running her fingers through the silky burnished strands when they made love, while they sat out on the stoop reading while jazz floated out of the neighbor's windows . . . the way the sun winked off the leaves as they walked to the market.

So fucking stupid, Ella, she thought. Why—who in their right mind walked away from this man?

Her head ached from her crying jag last night, and she still hadn't eaten.

Carefully, she eased out from under his arm, wanting to lean over and kiss his cheek, to say what she didn't even know how to begin saying.

But he'd had so little sleep, so little rest since he'd gotten here.

He'd stayed with her at the hospital, paced the room and the living room too often.

No, she'd let him sleep. She climbed softly from the bed and grabbed an extra pillow and blanket, settling into the window seat. That didn't last long either. Finally, she gave up and tiptoed out of their room to the living room.

Ella looked out the windowpanes of the balcony doors. She felt guilty for some reason for having left Quinlan sleeping in their room. He was so tired, and the dark circles under his eyes bothered her. He was never tired, not that she ever remembered, but then what did she know? She was so tired she could no longer think straight, but honestly? She didn't sleep. Never slept. Her wrists hurt, and itched. Which was apparently a good sign. She thought about doing yoga, just some easy stretches to try and ease the tightness in her shoulders.

Someone cleared their throat.

She whirled around.

The dangerous one. He was tall, maybe the same height as Quin, and with his short black hair, constant two-day beard, he could pass as one of the locals in Taos. The not-quite-kempt look. At least until someone looked into his eyes. He lacked the laid-back, no-worries-dude look that the locals had down great. He was as polished as his brothers, or so he exuded, but his eyes saw more than most ever did. This one was cold. And he scared her.

"I didn't mean to frighten you," he said, pouring a cup of coffee. "Want one?"

"No, thanks."

He kept his gaze on her after returning the carafe to the coffee-maker. "You're up early."

"So are you," she said, not taking her eyes off him. Her muscles tightened and her skin felt like it was slowly shrink-wrapping to her frame.

"Late night." He glanced to the hallway. "I should probably wait and tell you when Quin gets up."

"Tell me what?" she asked.

"Nothing to do with the baby, not really. But . . ."

"Just tell me."

"I'm not going to hurt you," he said softly, coming to stand beside her.

She didn't know about that. He probably wouldn't. After all, he was Quin's brother, but still . . .

"The authorities found Lisa last night, early this morning."

"Found her?" Relief slid through her. "What did she say? Did she tell you where —"

"She's dead."

The words fell between them and she just stared at him. "What?"

"She's dead. And as such, she can't help us."

Dead. She shook her head. "Dead? How?"

He sighed. "Does it matter? She's dead, so now, more than ever, I need your help. Quin needs your help. Your child needs your help," he said, his voice low and gruff. Reminded her of gravel over dry leaves for some reason.

"You think I don't know that?" she snapped.

"I don't know, do you?" he asked.

She looked at him, not sure what to say, what to . . .

"Look, you were given a raw deal," he said, leaning against the window ledge. "No one is arguing that. What my brother is pissed about, what the family will be pissed about, is that it could have been avoided if you hadn't been stupid."

She glared at him and took a step toward him. "You think I don't know that either? You think I didn't already figure that out by my-self?"

"I don't know if you have or haven't. All you do is mope about and cry."

She didn't know what to say, what to do, what to . . . Before she'd realized it, she'd balled up her fist and hit him. His head snapped back.

He looked back at her, working his jaw. "Not too bad, you hit like a girl though. Hurt yourself doing it that way. My daughter could hit better than that."

This time she punched him in the stomach, though she had the feeling he'd let her. He laughed. "Too easy. You're way too easy to read. Cry like a girl, fight like a girl . . ."

Anger, hot and bright, scorched through her, igniting within her soul and heart. She hit him again, her breath coming hard and fast.

"Weak. You're very weak, aren't you? Couldn't even save your own child."

Rage engulfed her. Without warning he turned, pivoted, and had her trapped against him. She struggled, fought, screamed a fractured cry, and still she couldn't get out of his hold.

"What the fuck is going on?" Quinlan asked.

"Doesn't matter, does it?" He whispered against her ear. "What you do? They'd have overpowered you. Stop blaming yourself, love. You want to fight, fight. I'll help you, Quin will most assuredly help you, but at least fucking eat. Otherwise, you're more a liability than an asset."

She struggled, gasping, and black spots danced in front of her eyes. Her wrists burned where he held them in his grasp, her vision wavered. She fought, tried to get her arms free, but he had them crossed over her chest and pinned to her. "You can fight until you pass out, and then what happens?"

Quin ripped her away from Ian. Yells bounced off her eardrums, the ringing growing louder, and she realized she was panting, hyperventilating. Deep breath. In. Hold it. Hold it. Out. Again.

"Don't you *ever* touch her like that again!" Quinlan yelled.

"I didn't hurt her. She's got a solid right hook."

"Fuck you," she bit out, as loud as she could—which was hardly more than a damned whisper.

Silence.

"What was that, love?" Ian asked, his voice tinged with laughter.

She pushed herself up from the floor by gripping the chair. Someone helped her but she shrugged them off. Who, she had no idea and didn't care. Looking straight into his ice-cold stare, she said, "Fuck. You."

"I don't think my wife would approve, or my brother. Not sure which would kill us first."

Without another word, she walked to the bedroom. She shut the door and locked it. She didn't want to talk to any of them. Didn't want to see them. Didn't want to hear what they had to say, or their damned questions.

She didn't want to be here. Didn't want to have to listen to more . . . more . . .

Why weren't they out looking? Wasn't that what Ian was supposed to be doing? He found things, Quin had told her. She'd told the cops everything she knew, again and again and again.

With a curse, she walked into the large master bath and turned the water on in the shower. She had a damned appointment today with an ob-gyn. Not her normal doctor. Because she didn't trust anyone anymore out at the Nursery. No. Someone else would be checking things. Fine.

She gathered what she needed and shut and locked the bathroom door as well. She heard someone knock on the outer door, probably Quin, but she needed and wanted some time alone.

. . . All you do is mope about and cry.

Had she been moping?

. . . you're more a liability than an asset . . .

He was right. She wasn't helping.

She unwrapped her wrists and tossed the bandages in the trash. She moved her hands one way and then the other. As she let the almost scalding water beat down on her, Ian's words circled around and around in her heard. Did he hate her? Blame her? Maybe.

Was he right?

Yes.

Yes, he was. Which pissed her off even more. She *was* moping, even if she'd been given a raw deal, as he'd said. She hadn't stopped crying since she woke up in the hospital. Granted, the pregnancy book she'd read way back when said that was common and normal. Nothing about this whole situation could be termed normal and she hated to cry. She hadn't been a big help to the authorities because she was just too numb. So what if she had to go over the same things again and again, maybe she'd remember something she hadn't even known she'd forgotten.

The numbness had protected her. She'd been too scared. Too frozen to feel anything.

Until a little while ago.

She stuck her hands out. They still shook from fury.

. . . couldn't even save your own child . . .

She'd tried. She'd fucking tried! Didn't he know that?

Rage still pounded through her at his words. Bastard. Even she agreed with him. Fury he'd pulled out of her taunt by taunt. No less than the truth, what everyone surely thought, but didn't dare say. He didn't really care. Not that one. He'd do whatever had to be done. Whatever had to be done to get a baby Kinncaid back.

Whatever had to be done.

Even if he pissed her off to do it.

Quin had coddled her and she was glad, that's what she needed from him. She'd wanted and needed a safe place, a haven, and Quin gave her that. He was her safe haven, God love that man.

His brother, though?

Ian.

She felt as if her head had broken the surface of a lake. No longer frozen, she wanted to get out. Wanted to hunt the bitch down that had put her in this place. This horrible, horrible, shell-shocked place, but Lisa was dead.

Her daughter was out there, and if someone had to be mean to her for her to pull her head out of her ass, then so be it.

She'd thank them.

She smiled. Quin's brother might be an ass, but he got things done.

By the time she got out of the shower, exhaustion pulled at her. So damned tired all the time and she didn't have *time* to be tired. She took care of matters and dressed in more yoga pants and a long-sleeved tee and a long sweater, pushing the sleeves up her forearms so they stayed off her wrists.

She towel-dried her hair and looked in the mirror.

"No more. No more hiding. No more whining. Whining gets nothing done."

It was time to *do*. Something. Anything. Her eyes glittered back at her. Not since Lance had walked away from her had she wallowed. And this was no time to wallow. Now she needed to *do*. As her mother used to say: Just do what needs to be done.

Chapter 33

Ella took a deep breath and walked back into the bedroom. It was quiet. The sitting area was still messed up from where she'd been earlier with her pillow and blanket.

Raised voices filtered through the doorway. Didn't matter. Not really.

She'd never hidden, never cowered before, why would she start now? Even with Lance she hadn't fallen this far into bleakness. What the hell had happened to her?

They'd whittled her down, almost broken her, by God, had almost *killed* her.

She opened the door and strode out, tired to the marrow of her bones.

Quinlan stood with his arms crossed, glaring at his brother Ian. Aiden stood beside Quinlan, saying, "Not everyone is like you or Rori, Ian."

"So?" Ian asked, calm as ever.

Man was irritating as hell.

"So?" Quinlan asked. His cane thumped as he walked to his brother. He rammed the cane into Ian's chest. "She's my *wife*. What the hell would you have done to any of us if we'd treated Rori that way?"

"Leave him alone," she said, coming into the room. Not looking at any of them, she sat at the table, wanting to lay her head on it. "I'm fine."

Someone snorted.

"All right," she snapped, or tried. "I *will be* fine. When I find my daughter, I'll be fine. After I've made them pay, I will be fine. Until then, I will tell whoever asks that I'm fine and if they don't like it, too damned bad."

No one said a word. She looked at Ian, caught the edge of his mouth kick up just a smidge. Aiden's brows were raised. She had no idea where anyone else was. Finally, she looked at Quinlan. "I'm okay, Quin. He didn't hurt me."

Quinlan walked to her, his gaze narrowed. "No one, not even one of my brothers, has the right to treat you that way. *Ever.*"

She thought about that, and smiled, a small smile, but a smile. "You are a really good man, Quinlan Kinncaid. But sometimes you miss the point."

"What the hell was his point then? Because from where I stood, it wasn't good, whatever it was."

She started to stand, and instead he sat in the chair beside her, their chairs facing each other. She looked at Ian. "I'd like some tea, please."

"And some breakfast." He crossed his arms over his chest and held her stare.

She narrowed her gaze. "You are a pain in the ass."

"So everyone tells me."

"Fine. Whatever."

"Waffle and eggs?"

"Fruit. Maybe some bacon."

The edge of his mouth definitely kicked up.

She looked back at Quinlan, who took her hand and was looking at her wrists. "I am fine. Did I like what he did? No, but . . ."

"But what?" he snapped, looking at her wrists.

She took a deep breath. "You remember when you told me about your time in the hospital and all the visitors and everyone being so careful with what they said and what they did?"

He nodded, and brushed a hair behind her ear. He was always touching her. Holding her hand. Even if she started or jerked away, he simply waited her out and then he reached again. Perseverance. Always proving he could because . . . just because.

"Yes, so?"

"So, out of all the visits and all the words, who was the one that made you see the clearest? That brought you back to where you were and what was really important?" She laced her fingers through his.

"You," he answered without hesitation.

She felt a grin pull her mouth. "Not me. Then. When you were in the hospital after the shooting."

His mouth twisted. "Ian, damn him."

She smiled again. "Yeah. Well, that's what he did."

"I don't care." His eyes narrowed on hers. "He can do whatever the hell he wants with me, with anyone else, but he will not treat you that way. Ever."

She brought their hands to her mouth, kissing his knuckles.

"You, Quinlan, were what I wanted most, what I needed, ya know? So much so, I couldn't breathe or sleep for way too long, and when I woke up in the hospital and saw you standing in the doorway, I thought I was dreaming. But at the same time, being safe with you . . . all the fears came crashing in, swirling around, just waiting."

"You don't have to be strong all the time," he told her quietly. "I'm here. I've always been here."

She nodded. "I know, I've just been alone for so long, that . . . With you there, I trust you, I could fall apart." She cupped his jaw. "With you, sugar, I could be scared because I had someone to say it would be okay, even if I didn't know if I believed it. But the fears, once let out . . . I couldn't get ahead of them, or out of them, or just enough away to breathe. It was like being frozen or something. Ian . . ." She cut her eyes to the side toward the kitchen, where she knew Ian had gone for her tea. "Ian just sort of microwaved me in less than a minute."

He shook his head.

"I'm pissed," she said, no longer smiling, no longer making her voice light. "I was so busy wallowing I wasn't thinking. So scared of what-ifs, I wasn't even *helping* in any way I could to find my own daughter and—"

"Our."

She stopped.

"You always say *my* daughter. She's *ours*." He leaned in so their noses touched and she saw the anger in his own gaze. And the hurt. "She. Is. *Our*. Daughter."

She nodded. "Yes. I know. Our." Something in her warmed. She had no idea where they'd go from here, but right now, she really didn't care. He was Quinlan. Always there. Always steady. Just . . . always.

She swallowed, cleared her throat and said another silent prayer.

"So, I went from the fear chewing me up to being pissed off. I'd rather be pissed. I can think when I'm pissed, you know? I can see things a bit more clearly. I have to do everything to find her, to help others find her, to stop them. We have to stop them. And if Ian's tactic this morning, though a little surprising and maybe a bit brutal, knocked me back into my head, then I'll thank him."

"Not necessary," Ian said as he set a mug on the table in front of her. "I'm just glad you're more with it. We can use all the help we can get, you know. Don't be so hard on yourself though. You've been through hell and they almost killed you."

She nodded.

"Well, he can question all he wants to, but after breakfast you are not missing your doctor's appointment. Rather, we are not going to miss it."

Quinlan didn't miss the way her hands tightened in his, didn't miss the way she seemed to pull into herself. "I don't want to go."

He had to change the subject from Ian and the morning incident to something else or he would hit his brother.

"Well, you're going. They're just going to check you out and make sure everything is okay." He pulled himself back and looked at his brother. "Breakfast?"

"Should be here in about twenty minutes, they said."

"You know, we ought to look into purchasing a hotel here in Albuquerque," Aiden muttered. "They are in need of better—"

"Don't even think of it," Quinlan snapped. "I do not want a single piece of Kinncaid property anywhere near here."

No one said a word.

He shifted. "Look, I just meant—"

"Understood. I wasn't thinking," Aiden said.

"Well, you can all do what you want, but once we have her back, I don't ever want to step foot here again," she muttered.

"That's the spirit," Ian said. He hurried into his own room down a short hallway in the suite and returned with an iPad and paper and pens.

"Do you mind working while eating?"

Someone knocked on the door.

"Great. Probably the feds already. Don't they ever sleep?" Ian muttered.

But it wasn't the agents. It was Mr. Brasher. She didn't understand what they were all doing here, not really. She hadn't really paid all that much attention.

Just as the door was about to shut, the federal agents showed up. Sabino and Landry paused in the doorway, looking in. She'd talked to them before, several times, but so much was a blur.

Breakfast arrived and everyone ate. More than enough food had been ordered that the additions did not go hungry. She wondered for a moment how normal this was with kidnappings. Was this the way it always went? She pushed her food around her plate. It had no taste and landed like paste in her stomach.

Had she asked that question at any point? She couldn't remember.

She wiped her mouth and looked at the agent who she had to trust. "Agent, what exactly is being done?"

"We're working on finding your daughter," Sabino said.

"And a few other people," Landry interjected, taking a bite of some sort of omelet or something. "Don't worry about things being fuzzy, it isn't uncommon to forget things in such situations. It's why we have you go over and over things."

"Where's Jareaux?" she asked.

"He won't be joining us," Sabino said. "He's not working this case, Mrs. Kinncaid."

"Yes, well, after contacting him for any of this it just seems weird, even if lately he wasn't interested in what I had to say. At least you guys are listening to me." She nodded again and licked her lips. "Of course you all are. Now. Now that you have a case. I was an idiot to have trusted you guys."

Sabino held her hands up. "I get you're pissed, and I would be too if someone had used me the way you've been used."

"Yeah, well, nice to know someone in your office has time for me now. Maybe I should have mentioned exactly who my in-laws were earlier. Granted, I never should have trusted Jareaux to begin with."

She'd been played. Played and used and . . . "I'm starting to think Jareaux is no better than they are."

Sabino shifted. "Look, I get it."

"No, you look."

Sabino stayed quiet, but Landry spoke up, "I know you're upset and you've every right to be."

She didn't remember standing, didn't remember leaning over the narrow table, but someone had their hand on her shoulder. "I have the right to be upset? My daughter is missing! Taken from me! And what the hell did you *do*? I tried to get in touch with Jareaux, several times."

"Yes, well, that was the problem," Sabino said. "I'm not condoning Jareaux's methods of your involvement, but he was seriously busy with another case last week when you were trying to contact him."

"For?" she asked. "Another baby?"

"A coyote."

"He was looking for a dog?" Brody asked. "You might want to just be quiet now."

The agents both shot Brody a look filled with disbelief. "Not a dog," Sabino said, running a hand through her short dark hair. "A person who brings illegals over. In this instance it was a shipping container of kids, left in the sun without adequate air or water or . . ." She stopped. "That's not important. I and the office apologize that you were not helped when you should have been. That you were not safe, when I'm sure Jareaux promised you you would be."

"He promised I'd be safe, that the baby would be safe."

"I know," Sabino said and nodded. "But he messed up."

She swallowed.

"I talked to Jareaux, he claims he only told you to keep your eyes and ears open, Ella. That he never told you to do more than that."

"Excuse me?" Quin asked very quietly beside her.

"I never should have listened to him." Ella shook her head. "He lied to you too, because yes, he told me that, but he also pressed for evidence. Told me to bring him something concrete. He even gave me a little point-and-shoot digital camera in case I could use it." She shook her head. "I should have just called Quinlan and gone home. But I thought I could help. I believed Jareaux. I listened to him when he gave all the reasons why I couldn't tell Quinlan. Now? Now I think he, your office, whoever was just bullshitting me to get me to do what you—he wanted . . . and I did it. Stupid, naïve me! I played right where you wanted me to. Still, girls went missing. What did you actually *do*? I tried to help and I could only hope it was enough."

"Did Jareaux ask you to stay in contact with him?"

She nodded. "Yes, but lately, the last few weeks he started blowing me off, said at one point that if I couldn't get him any useable evidence, I was wasting his time."

Sabino took a deep breath. "I'll tell you now, at some point Special Agent in Charge Inez, who runs our regional office, will want to talk to you herself. Just a heads-up."

"About what?"

"Jareaux," Ian answered her. "He crossed several lines."

"So?"

"Lines that weren't meant to be crossed," Ian told her.

Sabino nodded. "He's been suspended."

She shook her head and took a deep breath. "Good, can we just get this over with?"

"Yes, let's go through it again. Dr. Merchant was your doctor the whole time? You said you saw Radcliffe as well? Did another one show an interest in you?" Sabino asked.

"Merchant. Dr. Merchant mainly, which I've already told you. But they all see the patients. It's more a rotation thing. However, since I worked there, I realized who I preferred and scheduled my visits to hit his rotation."

"Why him? Why did you prefer Dr. Merchant? Did you ever at any point feel threatened by the other doctors?" Landry asked.

"We've gone over this." She shook her head. "I don't know. He was just . . . comfortable. His nurses were comfortable. Lisa was one of his nurses sometimes, though she mainly nursed and midwifed for Radcliffe. He was older. I don't know, I felt more comfortable with Merchant." She looked at all of them here. Sabino across the table from her, Quinlan at the head of the table. Aiden and Mr. Brasher were at the other end of the table. The lawyer, Brody, was against the wall, and Ian, Ian paced.

"I can't answer all the questions at once. But I'll go through it all again. Maybe I'll remember something else."

Sabino nodded.

She looked at Ian, then at Quinlan. "At first, I thought Jareaux was wrong, and I told him so. Nothing seemed wrong at first, no one was threatening. It seemed a wonderful setup. All these pregnant women staying in this one place. Some were older and couldn't have more kids, they were going to give them up and they stayed to have the best medical care. Same for the teens that were there to keep things quiet." She shook her head.

"At first it just seemed . . . I don't know, weird but nice. A retreat. One of the new-agey naturalist, tree-hugger things, ya know? It wasn't until they started pressing me to consider adoption that I saw more. If they'd left me alone, I probably never would have questioned, never would have wondered. Never would have . . . seen . . ."

Seen . . .

The blood. The scent of it in the room where no blood should be.

"She didn't go for it, was very adamant that she was *not* interested in giving the baby up for adoption, or at least that's what Jareaux complained about in his notes," Sabino said.

She felt more than saw Quin relax beside her.

"I never, for one moment, thought of giving up my da—" At Quin's shifting, she amended, "*Our* daughter. I just thought they'd leave me alone." She turned to Quin. "They started asking me questions about you."

"About Mr. Kinncaid?" Agent Sabino asked, pulling her gaze from her husband. "When did they start questioning you about the father?"

She shrugged and rubbed her forehead. "I don't know, near the end. Memories are sort of jumbled and confusing then."

"What sort of questions?"

She licked her lips. "What he did. Where he was from. If he'd want to be a part of the baby's life. I didn't tell them. I was vague on his details, but I did say that he'd be a very big part of our daughter's life regardless if we worked out our problems or not. Different doctors, my friend, the midwife. Or who I thought was my friend — her I told more, and now I realize I never should have trusted her. They asked questions. All of them, and if you put it all together . . ."

"They'd have realized they'd have a child from a creative, intelligent woman and an intelligent, highly affluent father," Ian muttered.

She shrugged.

"Lisa, my friend. She told me not to worry about it, I was being paranoid. But the counselor was always pushing too. Asking me how I planned to raise a child by myself. Even said that if I let the father know, he might take it away."

"You did *not* believe such bullshit, did you?" Quinlan asked her.

She shook her head. "Not really, no. Not at first, no. I mean, was it a fear? Yes. She was mine, I'd share her with you, but near the end, I was terrified of anyone taking her away, even you. I was scared of my own shadow."

She thought back, searched and tried to find the time, the exact moment she'd become so scared. "I don't know when it happened, exactly, or how . . . why I became so afraid. Or maybe I do."

"When? What happened?" Sabino asked.

That night. "I had this one girl in class. Fran. Bright, bubbly, always sharing joy, and she had no one. Not a single soul to care if she lived or died. No family she'd claim. No friends. So she made friends there at the Retreat. Bright red corkscrew curls. She had signed papers to give the baby up, but as it got closer and closer to the due date, she confided in me that she didn't want to. She knew it would be hard. She'd recently graduated. She was smart. She already had almost all her general requirements out of the way and she wanted to get into the radiology and sonography program. Had it all planned out. She figured with work she'd be twenty-one when she graduated and could get a job. She wasn't just talking, she had really thought about it all. Had student loans and a payment plan all drawn out. I told her I'd help her." She remembered more. The way the girl had simply looked at her, disbelief on her face.

"Always saving anyone you can," Quin muttered, reaching over and sliding his hand along the back of her neck.

"But I didn't save her." Jerkily at first, then more quickly, she told them of the storm, of the night they weren't able to get home. Of the dizziness, the heavy sleep, the disorientation.

"You stayed there?"

She didn't look to see who asked, barely heard them. "I sometimes stayed at the Retreat if the weather was bad. It was that night. I'd also passed out in class, so the nurses, docs, the girl were all concerned. My blood pressure was up a bit, okay, quite a bit. With the weather and that, the doctor talked me into staying." She walked them through the blurred memories she'd held on to. Told them what her doctors had told her.

"I know what they said, but I know what I saw." She sighed. "They made me stay there, to monitor my blood pressure. But I knew they lied. I knew it. I remember . . ."

"What?" Ian asked quietly.

She blinked. "The masks. I remember the masked people around her bed, all the blood. It was dripping onto . . . onto the floor.

"Another night, the next or the next . . . I don't know for sure. I stood at the window. It looked out back, just to the side of the walled courtyard. I saw . . . I saw . . ."

The moon had been bright. The first snowfall and it had started to melt that day, she'd heard it dripping off the eaves. The ground was still white mostly, the moon washing the world in almost daylight. And there she'd seen him. The figure pulling something long and black. Long and black to the pit that waited. She watched as he dumped the bundle into the ground and then laid the dirt over whatever it was . . .

"They buried her. They buried her. The body . . . The roses . . ." she muttered.

"Mrs. Kinncaid."

"Her hands are like ice."

She saw it all, the way the moon shimmered on the snow, glitter across the pale blue. She'd always loved the snow under a full moon.

And what else would they bury other than a body?

She had told no one. But she stopped sleeping, stopped eating, just went through the motions until she tried to leave.

"I know they do good in some lives, but someone there takes advantage of those they think no one will miss or if they're daring, just don't care."

Sabino's dark gaze pierced her. "Did you tell Jareaux this?"

"I tried. He blew me off before I even got through it all. He always asked for proof. There was no proof. They said it didn't happen like I remembered it. Someone went through my things because the camera's SD card was blank and I'd had photos on it. Normal ones, nothing he'd consider proof, but it was blank. I know they looked through my things. If anyone had bothered to look in her room, you'd have found traces of blood in her condition, so what? That would have proved nothing. And did I actually *see* them bury a body? No, I saw them dump something in a hole behind the courtyard, in the center of all the roses. They claimed I hit my head when I passed out, that with my high blood pressure and the concussion, I was disoriented. I was confused on what really happened."

Landry took a deep breath. "You should have called the police at least."

Whether she believed that, she didn't know. "Really? Because I was under the mistaken impression the feds were law enforcement as well. I tried calling Jareaux several times. He was always busy, always short."

"In his defense, we do have many other responsibilities, other cases too. I'm sorry this happened to you. It shouldn't have. He put you in a bad position and didn't follow through."

She just looked at Sabino. "No, it shouldn't have, but it shouldn't have happened to the others either."

"You're sure what you saw?"

She laughed, but it was hardly amused. "I'm not sure of anything anymore. Sometimes I look back and I don't know if something really happened or if it was a dream. For weeks I thought I was imagining things, or going crazy, but knew deep down they were going to take my baby and if I wasn't careful there would be nothing I could do about it. I knew if they got my baby, I was as good as dead." She looked at the tabletop. "Guess I was right. Lisa showed up and . . . well, you guys know the rest." She glanced to Quinlan. "I told her we made up on the phone and you were heading out here. I'd been charging my phone and she picked it up. I should have had it on me."

"I doubt it would have mattered, sweetie," Ian said. "She'd have found a way. I told her, by the way," he said to Sabino.

"Told her what?" Quin asked.

Sabino frowned at Ian. "We found Lisa earlier this morning, well, late last night, actually. Someone called . . . Looks like a suicide. She asked you to forgive her."

"But . . . the baby. Where's my baby? Did she say anything, leave anything? Are you sure?" Panic crawled through her again. "Please, she has to have left something."

"Mrs. Kinncaid, we're looking. We called Mr. Kinncaid, Ian, when we verified who she was."

Quinlan shifted and asked his brother, "Why didn't you say anything?"

Ian shrugged. "I told her this morning before she decked me. She was, at least to Ella's thoughts, a friend. I figured she should know. I didn't tell you because technically there wasn't anything to tell you yet."

"The woman who took our child is dead and you don't think that's anything to tell me?" Quin stood.

She grabbed his hand. "Was there anything other than the note?"

"Well, the apartment where she was found is owned by a dummy corporation or what appears to be a dummy corporation. The feds are taking her place in Taos apart again to see what else they can find."

Her baby. Where was her baby? She shook her head. "I don't believe she committed suicide. That wasn't Lisa's style."

"Honey," Quin said, "you've been all over the news, maybe she couldn't live with—"

She shook her head again. "No, no, I know I shouldn't have trusted her, but she was not the suicidal type. A note? She wrote a note?"

"Typed," Sabino said. "Did you know she had another apartment here in Albuquerque?"

"No, no. Oh God." Her hands trembled. "How will we ever find . . . How . . ."

"Well, we did find a flash drive hidden at her place, encrypted, and we're working on that now. My techie called just as we arrived and he thinks he's close to cracking it. Looks like accounts, he said, transactions."

"Babies," she muttered.

"Maybe," someone said.

"Transactions?" Quin said. "You mean babies? Other babies? Babies are bought and sold, aren't they?"

Transactions . . . Transactions, the word danced in her brain.

"For a quarter of a million, I'd imagine so."

"What?" several asked at once.

She blinked.

"What do you mean, a quarter of a million?" Quinlan asked her.

She sighed and frowned, rubbed her forehead. "Transactions. It's one of the foggy images. Sharp and foggy all at once, the between time. When I was . . . was there . . . I heard. I know I heard her say, 'a quarter of a million and change, little girl, that's what you're worth.'" She swallowed and swallowed again, but it didn't do any good. Shoving away from the table, she hurried to the bathroom and was sick. She heaved and heaved until there was nothing there, the wonderful breakfast a complete waste. "Oh God." She shuddered and sat on the tiled floor.

A cool cloth washed her face. "It's okay, it'll be okay."

She let him bathe her face. "Quinlan, they *sold* her, they sold our baby girl. How will that be okay? How can that ever be okay?"

"We have a trail to follow, honey," he told her.

"Money. You follow the money," Ian said from the doorway.

. . .

A place to start. Quin breathed a sigh of relief. He checked his watch. "Come on, babe. We need to get you cleaned up so you don't miss the doctor's appointment."

"I don't want to go," she whispered. "I hate the damned doctors. Clearly, they can't be trusted."

"I think Dr. Forrester is trustworthy," he answered her. So strong, and so scared. He'd caught glimpses of the woman he'd fallen in love with this morning at breakfast. What he'd seen before with Ian, that still pissed him off. He still had questions, and there were still things to do. Things that mattered more right now than them having the damned heart-to-heart they needed.

Scooping her up, he leaned against the wall.

"You can't carry me. Your leg," she muttered, though her arms wrapped around him. She was small and curvaceous, and weighed almost nothing. Shouldn't she weigh more if she'd given birth just a few days ago?

"I can carry my wife, thank you very much, or have you forgotten?" he whispered.

"No, I didn't forget. I just don't want you to hurt yourself."

He breathed deep and smelled his shampoo in her hair. Something about that wrapped inside him and unfurled part of the fear and whatever else had tightened in his chest.

They were going to get through this. He had no idea how, really, but by God, they were going to get through this if he had to drag them through it.

In the quiet of their room, he set her on her feet and watched as she went to the bathroom and brushed her teeth and washed her face. She tossed the towel on the counter and then joined him, sitting on the bed.

"What happened to us?" he asked her, brushing his thumb over her cheek.

She shrugged. "You wanted the Cleaver family and I got scared."

He smiled. "And I was mad and stupid and proud and let you walk away."

He leaned down and stared into her eyes. "I'm warning you now, Ella Kinncaid, never again. I'm never letting you walk away again. I'm never walking away again. I should have come after you when I heard you moved, but I was angry and so I let you be. If I hadn't . . ."

"If you hadn't, who knows. It doesn't matter."

"It does on so many different levels."

She leaned up and brushed her lips quickly across his. "I'm sorry."

He sighed. "I am too. I am sort of getting tired of us both saying it though. Instead of 'I'm sorry,' how about 'I love you'?"

She smiled at him. "Quinlan Kinncaid, I love you."

He had no idea how much he'd needed to hear those words until she said them. And she probably felt the same. He kissed her lips softly. "I love you, Mrs. Kinncaid," he whispered. "God, I love you."

She smiled, her dimples deepening. "We can see who can outlove who."

He chuckled. "Good try, but you're not getting out of going to the doctor. You want to change?"

She shook her head. "No, I'm good. I'm ready as I'm going to be." She sat and looked at him. "Please don't make me go. I hate hospitals. I hate the smell. I hate . . ."

"I know. But we need to know you're getting well and that nothing else is going on. If you get sick or land back in the hospital, you won't be able to help," he tried.

"Think you're smart, don't you?" she whispered.

"It's something I've tried to tell everyone for years, but no one listens."

She chuckled. "I love you, Quinlan. I always have."

He took a deep breath and another. He simply laid his head on hers and pulled her close. "I love you, too." Then he reached for her hand and laced their fingers together. "From here on, together, Ella. Everything's together. No more of one us doing it all. Got it?"

He felt her nod against his shoulder. "Together."

Chapter 34

Ian stood outside in the courtyard wondering if he was going off on a wild-goose chase. He'd told Brody already to get papers ready in regards to Quin's daughter. They really needed to name the poor girl. After all, if he was right, he didn't want to keep the parents from the baby longer than necessary. He'd also mentioned his suspicions to Sabino yesterday. She'd said they were still waiting for a court order from the judge.

He'd called and spoken to Mr. DeSaro Monday, when he found out they were still here in Albuquerque. He'd sent Johnno over to watch them as well on Tuesday when it looked like he wasn't needed at the hotel for guard duty. Mr. DeSaro had in fact recommended the Nursery of Dreams, since they had been able to obtain what he and his wife were looking for and had gotten around complications that other agencies had issues with. He did, however, caution Ian on meeting with them as he felt they might be in trouble.

"Perhaps a more private venue, yes?" he'd said. "I would hate to see a young man from such a good family get in trouble for wanting to give joy to his wife."

Sure.

He'd thanked the man and had promised to pass the hello on to his father.

A girl. They'd adopted a girl.

But if what he suspected were true, they were going to have hell on their hands.

"You think it's her, don't you?" Rori asked, coming out to stand beside him.

He shrugged and took a drink of the coffee that was too bitter for his liking. It worked though.

"Possibly."

"You know we could just sneak in, take the kid and bring it back here."

He had no idea what it said that he'd actually first thought the same thing—but that family. He understood the DeSaros. There was no way they'd just give up a child, any more than a Kinncaid would.

"Can't do that." He turned and sat in an iron chair. "You know that."

"Why the bloody hell not?" she asked, coming to sit on his lap. The courtyard was cool and chilly this morning with a hint of snow on the air.

"Because when little nameless Kinncaid comes home, I'm not leaving any legal loopholes for anyone to take her away again. I don't think her parents would deal well in that case. And, the DeSaros are a family not unlike our own, love, and if someone were to try and take any of our kids away, especially from either you or me after we'd adopted them . . ."

A fire flickered in her green eyes. "They might think they'd gotten away with it, but I'd hunt them down and more than likely kill them. Slowly."

He cupped her jaw and kissed her. "I'd love to, you'd want to, but with the heat that could bring down . . . we probably wouldn't." Damn, he was getting soft, wasn't he? Shaking off the absurd thought, he continued, "The point is that we will need all evidence before they will willingly hand over that little girl, and even then, I highly doubt it'll be willingly."

He bit down and a muscle jumped in his jaw. "A quarter of a million and change more than likely."

She took his coffee and sipped, grimaced. "Piss off, that's foul."

He grinned. "Yes, darling, I know, which is why I didn't offer you a drink as usual."

She thought for a minute. "A quarter mil and change off this baby. And I'd stake my rep there are more. Many more. They've done this before. So . . . where are the others? She'd have died easily if she hadn't gotten away. And why they let her get away is beyond me. I mean if it were me, I'd have killed her and gotten rid of the body."

"I believe they meant to. Fate, God himself, helped her get away."

"I always figured God's too busy, He sends angels. When He thinks about it."

He stopped his train of thought. Hers was so . . . unlike her. "You think God's too . . . Angels?"

"You know, like guardian. Patron saints and all that stuff."

A grin pulled at his mouth. "I thought you didn't believe in all that stuff?"

She shrugged. "Mum and Da — with my brothers, you know, they sent us to a school. And mass and all that. But after, back in the system, it strips the belief away. It was only after that that I didn't. 'Course Nikko's Catholic and a firm believer, so he was rather strict on some things, lax on others. Me, I saw too much to really believe for a long time."

"Didn't believe or still don't?"

She just looked at him and then shrugged. "Things have changed a lot since . . ."

"Since?"

"Since I watched you rescue a little girl from hell."

He cocked a brow, could feel her muscles tensing as they did when she was uncomfortable. He'd let it go. "Angels, huh? Well, fine, with some people I can see where it's the only explanation. Though it's more than likely, with Ella, they just thought she was too weak and didn't bother to restrain her again. Or they thought she was already close enough they cut the zip ties. If they had to do stuff with the baby and the mother died . . . that could have made things harder. Who knows the whys. Angels are as good an explanation as any." His contrary wife believed in guardian angels. He smiled. "Whichever. She's alive and they found the house, got all the info from it they could. She doesn't remember much, has no idea how far she wandered. At least she hasn't said thus far, maybe no one's told her."

"You pushed her really hard. I seriously thought Quinlan was going to go around with you."

"Might let him yet. He's got too much anger to focus effectively," he said, sliding her off his lap and standing. He supposed he ought to apologize. Again. Quin might not get it, but in Ian's experience, it was easier to be mad and productive than to wallow and wilt and hope for production. On the other hand, too much anger made you too rash. Quin's anger burned hot, bright.

Ella's.

Ella's anger he could use. And he would. Hers was beyond hot. Beyond burning. Hers was ice cold. That type he knew and understood all too well.

He'd seen the difference in her when she'd come back into the living room.

Sighing, he stood and said, "I should go talk to him."

"I doubt he wants to talk to you."

"Yes, but he has to." His phone rang. Aiden. "What?"

"Thought you'd want to know. Mom and Dad are on their way."

He pinched the bridge of his nose. "Where are you?"

"Out getting a bite to eat at this little hole-in-the-wall place. Huevos and pollo verde enchiladas or something. Great food. We'll have to eat here some other time. Two blocks west of the hotel. Maria's is the name of the joint."

He checked his watch. "When will they be here?"

"Not sure. Gavin just phoned and then Bray phoned and then Jesslyn. Anyway, Mom and Pops are on their way. If you're there, tell Quin and I guess Ella."

"Will do."

He hung up and looked at the woman who'd stolen his heart, a heart he'd thought dead and buried in more ways than one.

"Who's coming?" she asked him, tilting her head and stretching.

"Mom and Pops."

"Ian, I want to go home. I know you might need me here and I'll stay if you want me to, but I miss the kids and I don't like leaving them this long."

He didn't either, truth be known. His kids were safe though; his brother's family, not so much. He couldn't just go home . . .

"I'm not asking you to come with me," she said, wrapping her arms around his waist. "I would stay with you, but I know our daughter. She'll worry herself sick and into not eating if both of us are gone any longer. We've been gone days already. And Sebella mentioned the boys having nightmares."

He knew she was right. Didn't stop him from wishing she could stay. "I wish I could go with you."

"But you can't, so suck it up, bring her home to her parents and then come home yourself. Besides, I've a feeling it won't be much longer. Itchy near the end, you know?"

He nodded. "I love you. Thanks for going to check the adoption place out with me. And the apartment in the middle of the night. That was fun."

"You too. And of course I went with you. People like us have to play some or we get rusty, and if we get rusty—"

"We get killed." He brushed his finger down her nose. "You do know we are retired?"

"Said the pot to the kettle," she said, leaning up to kiss him. "Go make nice with Quin so he'll listen to you next time. I'm going to start digging more into Jareaux's background. I don't know as I trust his colleagues to fully vet him now, or punish him either."

He laughed. "Already on it, love."

"Figured." They walked back into the living room. Quin was helping Ella into a coat that someone had gotten for her. The bright blue jacket did nothing to help her pale complexion.

"Aiden called because others called to warn him," he said, pulling Quin to the side.

"Why? About what?"

"Mom and Pops are on their way. Will be here later today."

Quinlan grimaced and glanced to Ella, who waited by the door. "Great. I'll tell her. Get them another room though. I love 'em, but I can't handle them right now and all the questions and what all not."

"I'll see what I can do." Ian shifted. "I'm sorry I upset you earlier, Quin. That wasn't my intention."

"No? You accomplished it anyway." His brother's green eyes blazed at him as they had all morning. He knew Quin trusted him, or had.

"Look, we need her help. She needed a nudge to stop blaming herself."

"There's a difference between a nudge and a shove."

Kid was right. He nodded at him. "For what it's worth, I apologize for my methods."

"Can we all stop with the never-ending apologies?" Ella asked. "You're making me go to the doctor," she said to Quin. "I don't want to go, but I'm going, so let's go already. I'm fine. Stop being mad at him. I'm sure he's pissed everyone off at least once."

"Usually twice a day," Rori quipped from beside him. "For the most part, though, he's great."

"Rori's going to head home, as well," Ian told them. "Kids are getting restless."

Ella frowned. "I'm sorry. I didn't realize . . ."

"No worries, love," Rori told her. "When a Kinncaid's in trouble, the family descends."

"But I'm . . ." Ella's words faded.

"Glad you didn't finish that, or my mad would have switched

from Ian to you really quickly," Quin said. "Ready?"

"No, wait." She tilted her head and studied Rori, her eyes narrowed. "I admit, I've been out of it, and I haven't seen you much. You're quiet. But I think I know your voice, you're the woman on the phone. Quin's phone. Why did you . . . but I heard . . ." She looked from one to the other.

"Oh, not what you think," Rori said.

"Yeah, about my phone," Quin said, his eyes narrowing on the two of them. "Care to explain that?"

"That was me getting back at your husband," Rori explained. "A joke really. I am sorry. If I'd been a bit more . . . well, if I'd given you the time of day, as it were, we might not be here now. Or if I'd just answered it and passed the phone on like a normal person." Rori shifted. "For what it's worth, I am sorry."

Ella took a deep breath. "It doesn't matter, does it? Bless your heart."

Rori laughed outright. "I like you. You say the nicest thing, yet it sounds so 'fuck you.'"

Ella ignored that, knowing Rori was right. She looked at Quin. "At least you weren't actually screwing someone."

Quinlan jerked. "Wait, you mean . . . you thought . . ."

"Let's go," she told him, and to Rori, "Thanks for all your help here. Seriously. You ready, Quin?"

"No, but let's go. Apparently we have a few other things to discuss, like what loyalty means. Vows, that sort of thing."

Ella sighed and pulled her jacket to her. She was always cold. They walked through the hotel's corridors and down through the lobby. The sunlight was brighter than she'd been expecting.

"Here." Quin stopped her and pulled a pair of shades from his pocket. "Forgot to give you these."

"Do you know where we are going?" she asked him.

"Rental has GPS. We'll get there just fine," he said, settling the shades on her face and tucking her hair behind her ears. "I can't get over your hair," he muttered.

"Huh?"

"Your hair. I picture you the way I remember you. Wild, funky hair, either pale blue or purple. This dull dark brown with hints of red just isn't you to me." He frowned. "Sorry, it's your hair. If you like it plain, I'll get used to it. And either way, you're still beautiful."

She laughed, surprising herself, and grinned at him. "My hair? You miss my blue hair?"

"With the pink tips, or purple."

She shook her head and looked around. "Well, maybe we can stop on the way home and I can take care of that. I'd planned to go pink for the baby."

He sighed again and raked a hand through his hair. "Look, I thought about not telling you, but I don't think you'd want any surprises right now, but please don't freak."

She stilled, felt her muscles tightening.

Mr. Brasher was leaning against the car. Quin stopped. "I can get her to the hospital, thank you," he told the man, a slight edge to his voice.

Mr. Brasher shrugged.

"Why are you here?"

"I was asked," he only said.

"My wife and I want some time alone," he said, opening the passenger door of the silver SUV and helping her in. "Tell my brother we don't need a babysitter."

Mr. Brasher looked from one to the other. "That's what I told him you'd say. See ya." They watched him stride across the parking lot and back into the hotel.

Quin drove like he did everything else, confident and alert. When they stopped at a red light she asked, "What do you have to tell me?"

"Oh, sorry. My parents are flying in today. They'll probably be there when we get back from the hospital."

"What? You just now mention this?" Oh my God. She looked down at the clothes she was wearing.

He reached over and laced their fingers. "They'll love you."

"Oh, sure. I broke their baby boy's heart after I married him in Vegas after we only knew each other for a couple of days. Then I don't tell him I'm pregnant, and on top of all that someone took the baby. I'm sure they'll just love my ass. At least my hair isn't pink," she muttered. "When are they going to be here?"

He squeezed her hand and rubbed his thumb over the outside of hers. "Later today. Not sure what time. They wanted to come out much earlier, but I asked them to wait until we knew what all was going on."

"They are not going to approve of me."

He cut her a look from the corner of his eyes. "They don't have to approve of you. You're my wife. That's all that matters." He brought their joined hands up and kissed her knuckles. "You're worrying too much about them. They'll be fine. Granted, they may wonder and they'll probably think we're both stupid for walking away from a marriage. My parents are one of those solidly old-fashioned couples who believe in lifelong marriages, as long as everyone is happy and safe. But they also think you can work together and become happier."

"Really?"

"Really, not that they've ever said as much, that's just who they are. They don't think anyone should marry lightly."

"Mark against me there."

He shook his head. "Stop looking at faults. It'll all be fine. They'll all be so pissed I didn't say anything that it'll eclipse any wrong you could have done."

"Oh, you mean like not telling you you were going to be a father?" She raised her brow at him. "Uh-huh. Right. Bless your heart, you just keep telling yourself that."

He pulled into the parking lot of the hospital and found them a parking spot pretty close to the main doors. "I would drop you off, but I don't want you waiting alone."

"This is fine."

She started to reach for the door handle, but his hand on hers stopped her.

"Ella. My parents are . . . involved in their sons' lives, but only to a point. All of us have married where we wanted to, who we wanted to, when we wanted to. Mom's just bent because all the weddings were either rushed or hushed, as she said, and she never got to plan a big wedding."

"I don't even remember our wedding," she said. "Not really. I remember an Elvis. Which reminds me, what the hell did we drink?"

He thought back and remembered the bright green liquor in Vegas. "Absinthe, maybe. I think. I don't know. I only know I haven't drank since then."

"Me either. Well, the wine we had at the house in New Orleans, but that's it."

His gaze held hers. "So no worrying about Mom and Pops. They will be nice to you or they can get back on the damn plane and go home."

"Thank you for that, but you can't send them home. They're older and trips are harder on them than someone younger. Not to mention that if they raised such wonderful sons, they'd want to be there for one of you if you were in trouble. And this is their grandchild."

Her child, her daughter, had grandparents. A whole involved extended family.

"What?" he asked her.

"I just realized she has grandparents, and uncles and aunts." Why had she never thought of that before? Ian had mentioned kids. "Cousins?"

He smiled at her. "I know. Girl's gonna be spoiled rotten in no time when we get her back. Which reminds me, what did you name her?"

She just sat there. Her daughter wasn't alone. It wasn't just the two of them.

"What? What are you thinking, what put that look on your face?"

"It was just my mom and me growing up, you know? I don't even know if Mom had siblings, she never said. I know I didn't have grandparents, or she said I didn't. I just . . . for the last few months, it's just been me and the baby. I kept thinking of you too, and it's always been either the two of us or the three of us in my mind. I never saw beyond that." She smiled at him. "She has grandparents. And aunts and uncles who will drop everything to help find her."

He grinned back, a dimple winking from his right cheek. "Yes, she does. And enough uncles I won't have to worry about being the only one not letting her date."

She laughed. "Feels weird. Good, surprising, but weird too."

He leaned over and brushed his lips over her cheek quickly. "Get used to it, babe."

Quin climbed out of the car and hurried around the hood, opening her door and helping her out.

"I hate doctors."

"I imagine you do, but I'll be there with you."

Chapter 35

"Do you think she's too warm?" his wife asked him yet again.

DeSaro sighed and set the paper aside. "I don't know. I told you I didn't know when you asked me before."

"What if something is wrong with her?" she asked him, worrying her bottom lip as she bounced the little bundle in her arms. The baby had cried most of the night.

He stood, sighing, and wished again he'd researched the agency they'd used a bit deeper.

The news was filled with the story of the mother found wandering bloody and disoriented, looking for her baby.

The police and federal agents were looking for the missing baby as well. Luckily his wife had been too busy with the baby to notice the news, or to hear it, or to know that the baby the police were looking for had red hair and was only about a week old.

He'd kill someone at that agency. It didn't really matter that the baby was theirs; legally he was looking at a fucking nightmare.

And he knew Ian Kinncaid had not just called him out of the blue. He still wanted to know how the boy had gotten his private number. He knew Jock, remembered his boys. He had his guard look up the family and had a dossier on the entire clan.

Granted, Mr. and Mrs. Ian Kinncaid had adopted other children, but no babies. And he ran a high-end security firm.

Mr. DeSaro would bet the man was here to find that baby. If he was, then why? Had the mother hired him, and if she had, then the woman was better connected than he'd first thought. He wanted to look at the adoption papers again but his wife had them tucked away, and he didn't want to ask for them and alarm her. He hadn't really paid attention to the birth parents on the forms. He'd just signed the papers. If memory served there were no parental names other than theirs on the paperwork. It was a closed adoption. So there wouldn't be a birth mother's name or father's name on the paperwork.

God help anyone who lied to him. He knew that world was not a black-and-white place with readily defined lines. He knew there were varying shades of gray. The fact the damned agency did not return a single phone call he'd made to them, well, that was telling as well, wasn't it?

If they sold him someone else's child, and one not up for legal adoption, he'd make sure they never hurt anyone like that ever again. They wouldn't have to worry about the feds, or the cops, or the fucking Kinncaids. He'd take care of them himself.

His wife crooned to the baby and rocked her again. "What if she's sick, Vincent?"

She was so worried, already so attached to this baby. They could have just gone home immediately, but something had kept him here.

He couldn't tell her, though, what he was already worried about. He couldn't hurt her that way. She wanted a baby so badly and he'd made certain she'd gotten one.

The baby was beautiful, there was no arguing that. Bright red hair, pale perfect skin. She'd grow into a beautiful girl and woman someday.

As *their* daughter.

He'd always liked and respected the Kinncaids.

Could he keep their child? What if it were his child or grandchild, as the case could easily be?

He'd kill anyone who stood in his way of getting the baby back. Hell might be a furious woman, but a man on revenge, well, he knew all about that, didn't he? Women and their fury was one thing, but a DeSaro wronged was another thing altogether.

Vincent took the baby from his tired wife and felt the baby's forehead. She was burning up.

"How long has she been this hot?" he asked, worry icing through him, shoving thoughts of the Kinncaids and revenge away.

She sighed and put her hands on her hips. "Since this morning when she woke up. I gave her some Tylenol and the fever went down a bit, but it's still too high, she's too hot. Something is wrong. We need to take her to the doctor. I told you this but you just smiled at me like I was being over-worrying or something. I'm not. She's *sick*."

He thought about what that could mean.

"Sweetheart, maybe we should head home and have one of our own doctors look at her."

She shook her head. "No. No. We need to take her to the doctor here. If she needs something, then she can get it and then we can go home. What if we flew home and something horrible happened, I'd never forgive myself, Vincent." Tears filled her eyes. "Little Sophia needs a doctor now."

Sophia. They'd picked her name out weeks ago when the Nursery contacted them about the baby. Sophia had been his mother's name.

He looked down into the tiny red face and her coppery hair. Little ones should be protected. If the Kinncaids couldn't protect their own, it wasn't his fault.

He had no problem protecting his own and little Sophia had definitely become his own.

"Vincent, she's sick. She needs a doctor."

She was right. He could feel the heat radiating off the small defenseless body even through her onesie and blanket. She didn't even cry anymore, as if crying for the half hour before had completely worn her out.

The hospitals, though, would be looking for a newborn like this precious little one. He held her up to his neck, shocked again at how hot she was.

She wheezed against his neck.

"Vincent—"

"Shh," he told her, listening again.

Wheeze. Wheeze. Maybe she was snoring?

He pulled her away from him, cradling her head and looking into that tiny helpless face. Bright red cheeks. Her mouth was open and she wheezed again.

What if she couldn't breathe like she was supposed to be breathing? Didn't babies sometimes get that breathing disease? R something or other. He hadn't really ever paid attention, as all his other grown children had been perfectly healthy.

He swallowed and nodded. "Get her things, and the papers. We'll take her to the hospital."

They left with their guard and headed to the car. He knew, knew this was a bad idea. He should tell his wife what was going on, what he suspected. Worry lined her mouth and eyes. She hadn't gotten much sleep. He had a feeling she wouldn't be getting a lot in the days to come.

Damn that Dr. Merchant. He knew this was all too good to be true.

• • •

Almost an hour later, they walked back out the hospital doors. The bright day was still cool and Quinlan made sure she'd zipped up her coat so she wouldn't get cold.

He'd checked his phone. Texts from both Ian and Aiden. Their parents were here. Ian was pissed John hadn't come with them. Too damned bad. Quin wanted time alone with his wife. His overprotective brother could just deal.

"See, I told you everything was fine," she told him yet again as he helped her into the car. He quickly slid into the car and merged with traffic while she continued. "This was a waste of time. We should have gone to the house."

He didn't need to ask which house she was talking about. "No."

"I might remember something else."

He stopped her. "You. Are. Not. Going."

Her eyes narrowed on his. "I'm done wallowing. You might not like it, and I will hate it. I'll probably get sick and throw up, but I'm going. Not to is stupid, cowardly, and could cost our daughter her life. Something is wrong. I know it, Quin. I just know it. I have to help, and if looking at that house will help then I'll try it."

"It's not going to help with anything other than giving you more nightmares," he bit out. He didn't want her anywhere near the damned house.

They maneuvered through the late morning traffic.

Look, I know I haven't done much more than cry and lay in bed, but—"

"You almost fucking died!" he yelled and then took a deep breath, fisting and flexing his hands on the steering wheel.

She didn't say anything. For several moments silence weighed between them, but he wasn't going to speak until he was in better control. He was always in control. Or he used to always be in control, at least of his own emotions anyway.

"What were you supposed to do? Jerk out the IVs and search through Albuquerque in your hospital gown until you finished what they started and put yourself in a damned grave?" he said softly.

She didn't answer him.

He looked over at her and took another deep breath. "I apologize for yelling, that doesn't help anything and was uncalled for. Please, stop blaming yourself, Ella, for not doing more."

"I can't do that, Quin. I don't know if I'll ever be able to do that," she admitted quietly.

He took another deep breath, not having a clue what to say to her. Nothing came to mind. Nothing. They'd just keep going around in circles.

As they pulled back into the parking lot of the hotel, he thought about valet parking, but he didn't want to have to wait on them if he needed the car. Besides, no one in their crew had used the valet service thus far. Too many times the car was needed. And his brothers were like him. If they wanted something, they didn't want to have to ask for it, let alone wait for it. It wasn't like this was a huge hotel with a multilevel parking garage. It had one lot out front and to the side around the pueblo-style boutique hotel. He found a slot and pulled in near the back of the lot.

He realized the parking lot was nearly full and probably had been when they left, he'd just been too preoccupied to notice.

She'd leaned to the side, rested her head against the window. "Do you think she's okay, Quin?"

He'd tried like hell not to think of his daughter all morning. He'd been better at it after the doctor's appointment. He'd focused on traffic and on the surroundings.

He sighed and shook his head. Did he think she was okay? How the hell did he know that? He was scared, like he'd never been before, like he hadn't allowed himself to even contemplate. But he didn't tell her that, couldn't tell her that.

He reached again for her hands, which she had fisted in her lap. "She'll be fine. If you think about it, someone who would or could pay that much money for her must have wanted a baby very badly, Ella. They'd be able to see to her comfort and make sure she's not sick, that she needs for nothing."

"She's *my* daughter. *Your* daughter. She should be with us!" She hit her chest with her fist. "Ours! And someone else is . . . someone else is . . ."

He bit down. "I know, Ella. I know. But I can't think that way. I have to look at it as though she's just taking a break from us with people who will take care of her, and look after her. I can't think about what might be happening or I'll go nuts."

She closed her eyes, swallowed, and nodded even as a tear rolled down her cheek. He brushed it aside. "We. Are. Going. To. Get. Her. Back."

Her eyes met his. "How can you be so sure? So certain?" she whispered.

"I refuse to let it be any other way." He opened his door and walked around the car to help her out. His phone rang just as he shut her door. Ian. "What?"

"You back yet? Mom and Pops are here and Rori is about to head back. I didn't want to leave until you guys were back. Safely."

He shook his head. How his brother could make him feel like a kid so easily was beyond him. "Yeah, Dad, we're back. Did we break curfew?"

"You left Johnno here. The bad guys are still out there. They tried to kill your wife. You do realize . . ."

The rest of Ian's words were lost. Quinlan saw a man approaching with his hand in the pocket of his jacket. Dark shades hid his eyes but Quin sensed he was watching them. The hair stood up along the back of his neck.

He shifted the phone to his other ear with the hand that also held his cane and pulled Ella closer with his other hand, changing their course to walk between two cars. Why, he had no idea other than just a feeling.

"Hello?" Ian said in his ear.

He ignored him. When they'd rounded the front of the cars, he glanced back and the man was gone. Huh.

Paranoia probably wasn't a healthy thing. Probably. Could be a reporter.

He looked around, but the wall of pickup trucks and SUVs all but blocked him. Why did he park way the hell over there? He should have dropped her at the front door and —

The man stepped out from between two of the pickups.

"Ella Ferguson?" the man asked.

She stepped to the side of Quin. "Yes?"

The man smoothly lifted a gun. So fast. Too fast. Time slowed in some weird way to Quin, as it always did when things went wrong.

Quinlan shoved Ella away and swung the cane at the man in a clockwise spin, catching the gunman's right hand, hoping to bring the gun toward him, not toward her. "Run, Ella!"

Two shots pinged and fire blazed across his arm. He twisted the cane the other way as the man tried to leave. To hell with that. Quin took two running steps, pain screaming up his left leg, and brought his cane around in a hard sideswipe, catching the guy in the head. It was like striking the ground on a great golf swing, vibrations echoing up the cane into his arm. The man stumbled, tumbling down. He fell, his head smacking against the edge of the next pickup's metal grille guard.

The gunman crumpled before the truck, and its alarm now screamed in the lot.

"Quinlan?" he heard.

He whirled. "I told you to run! Damn it, Ella. Are you trying to get yourself killed?"

She held the gun and the look on her face was one he'd never seen before. No fear showed across her face and he'd seen it plenty in the last few days. There wasn't terror or even anxiety. He saw a cold finality in her eyes that he didn't like.

"I told you they'd have to kill me. I know too much. They tried in the hospital. I heard about that," she said softly, as if talking about the fact the sun was shining too brightly.

"Babe. Give me the gun."

He heard shouts and running feet. Quinlan only focused on her.

"He could have killed you!" This time there was more heat to her voice.

He opened his mouth to tell her he was fine.

"Then your family really would hate me!"

It was ludicrous. He could have laughed. "Honey, they love you. Come on. Hand me the gun."

She shook her head and walked toward him, pointing the gun at the man prone on the ground. "No. *No.* He could know something. He could tell us where she is," she said, her voice shaking.

He glanced away from her and saw his brother sprinting toward them, a gun in his hand, John Brasher and the fed bringing up the rear.

"Quin!" Ian yelled.

"Over here!" He still watched her. "Babe, give me the gun."

Again she shook her head. "No. No. I want to ask him where our daughter is. He was going to kill me, wasn't he?"

Ian burst around the edge of one of the vehicles, and he noticed the other two flanked them on either side.

"You two okay?" Ian asked, his gun down near his leg as he walked toward them, slowing down, his eyes still scanning the area.

"Ella," Quin told her, stepping closer to her. "Put the gun down. He can't answer you right now, he's unconscious."

"He'll wake up."

He heard Ian snort to the side of him. "I knew I liked her."

"If you hurt him, it won't make you feel any better," he finally said.

"And hitting him with your cane made you what? Sad?"

No, actually, it felt really damned good. He just had a problem watching her with the gun. He didn't like guns even though he'd become damned proficient with them in the last year, and he was an excellent marksman.

"Babe, please. We'll let Ian ask him all the questions. He's great at getting information out of people, even if they don't want to give it."

She cocked a brow down toward Ian. "Really?"

Ian sighed. "Normally, yes. And in this case, I just might enjoy it, however, he's dead."

"What?" Quinlan asked, whirling around.

Ian squatted beside the body. "He's dead or nearly there. Either your cane or his head connecting to the metal edge of this grille guard." He looked up and nodded to Sabino. "You might want to see who the man is and notify the authorities here." There wasn't any blood that Quin could see, though the man's face was now pale, blue veins spider-webbed from his temple.

He'd killed a man.

He'd *killed* someone.

Ian glanced up and narrowed his eyes. "Don't. Sometimes it's either them or you. Though this time it wasn't you. It was her." He jerked his head toward Ella.

Chills danced over his skin as he realized he'd almost lost her. Again.

He reached over and gently took the gun away from her and passed it off to John. Then he jerked her against him, breathing again the scent of his shampoo in her hair.

"I'm okay," she said, patting his back. "I'm okay, Quinlan."

"I can't lose you. I can't lose you again," he said, pulling back and kissing her, then wrapping her tightly in his arms again. "I can't."

"You didn't. You won't."

He didn't know which of them was shaking, him or her, and he didn't care.

"You're both all right?" Sabino asked them.

He pulled back and held her at arms' length. "Are you okay? The bullet didn't hit you?"

"How many rounds did he get off?" Ian asked. "I heard two on the phone when you yelled at Ella to run."

He thought back. "Yeah, two. One grazed my arm."

"What?" Ella asked, looking at his arm. "Oh my God! Quinlan, you're bleeding!"

"I'm fine," he told her. Ian had already stood and took his arm from Ella. "I'm fine. Both of you. Would you stop fussing." He jerked his arm away from the both of them.

"You need the hospital," Ella said, taking his arm again and carefully looking at the cut in his jacket from the bullet.

"I told you, it just grazed my arm, it's no big deal." Okay, that was a stupid-as-hell statement. They'd been shot at and hurt, but he didn't want her worrying. "You're the one we need to take back. The doctor said you don't need any added stress other than what you're already going through. Your body's had too much of a shock lately. You need to take it easy."

"I'm not the one who was shot," she answered back, not liking that he'd told her she needed the doctor again. He took a deep breath.

Ian stepped closer to him and led him a few steps away. Quinlan noticed that Johnno stepped closer to Ella as soon as he'd stepped away.

"You're going to the hospital to make sure she's okay and that you are okay because your daughter needs the both of you." Ian stepped closer. "Don't make me make you."

"I should have hit *you* with my cane." The idea had often appealed to him when it came to this particular overbearing brother. "I said I was fine."

"Probably you are, but you need stitches either way. And if you don't go there now, Mom will make you, as she's up in the suite now anyway. Worrying. Again. About you."

Hell.

"Why is it no one remembers I'm an adult?"

"'Cause you'll always be the baby of the family, kid."

He flipped his brother off, then stepped closer to Ella and pulled her into his arms again.

Sabino looked at John Brasher. "You drive them. I'll stay and smooth things over with the locals here. Though I'm sure they'll want your statements as soon as they can get them." Sirens sounded. "Go on, get them out of here."

"And this damned time," Ian told his friend, "please remember you carry the gun and my brother does not."

"He doesn't need a gun, he has his cane," Ella said. "I don't know if I want to laugh or cry."

She was too pale again. He brushed his finger over her soft cheek. For her he'd go. He hated hospitals as much as she probably did.

"Fine. Let's go so we can get back. Otherwise the others will gang up on us and haul us to the ER whether we want to go or not."

"Your family is . . ."

"A pain in the ass most of the time."

"Maybe, but it's wonderful too. You have people who care."

"We, babe. We have people who care. Now I have someone to help me battle them all back. They can be like zombies sometimes. They're always just . . . there."

She giggled, putting her arm around his waist, and he leaned over and kissed the top of her head. "I'm glad you're okay," he said softly, following John to the SUV parked at the back of the lot.

"You know, the hotel has valet parking," John told him as he helped Ella into the backseat.

"Just drive," he told him, getting in and pulling her into the crook of his good arm. His leg was hurting like a bitch. He was just glad it wasn't one of the times the muscle cramped or his leg gave out. He'd been able to save her.

They wanted her *dead*.

He pulled her tighter against him and swore they wouldn't get the chance again. He'd hire another firm if his brother didn't have another man to help guard Ella. He thought again of the sound of the man's head hitting the truck, of his cane hitting the man.

He shook the thought off, focusing instead on the fact if he hadn't, she — they could both be dead.

Quinlan wanted them. He wanted them all. For the fear he saw in her eyes, for stealing their child, for threatening and almost ending her life — twice.

Someone would pay.

Chapter 36

Ella sat on the table in the ER waiting. Her hands still shook. They'd already cleaned the abrasions on her palms where she'd stumbled and fallen when Quinlan had pushed her out of the way of the hit man.

She hadn't even been paying attention. When they were walking toward the building, she'd been going over how she was going to introduce herself to his parents. How she was going to explain to them. Quinlan might not be worried about them, and all of them meeting, but she damned sure was.

She'd been lost in thought, listening to Quin on the phone. Not once did she see the guy. Stupidly, she remembered what she'd been thinking of saying to his parents. "I love your son, it just took me a while to realize it." She'd worried that sounded cheesy and stupid, but knew that saying, "I promise I'm not a gold-digging slut," probably wouldn't go over any better. "Sorry I was trying to be superwoman and save some other pregnant women, they took my child instead of someone else's."

Then Quin had shoved her to the side and yelled at her to run. By the time she realized what was going on, the man was already on the ground. It happened so fast, blurring together, yet watching Quin take the guy out with his cane was very clear in her mind.

The image of the man holding the gun toward Quin seared into her mind again and again.

She wiped another tear away.

Please, please keep them all safe.

Another FBI agent had come in earlier and spoken to her, asking her to go over what she remembered three times and whether she knew the guy who held the gun on them. As if she was suddenly going to yell, "Oh, silly me. Of course, I saw him at McDonald's the other day."

She was done with the FBI. Done with the cops. A couple of cops had been in there as well when the fed was taking her statement. Then the doctors had come in. Two other cops whispered to both the agent and the other cops and they all left. To talk to Quin? No one would tell her how the hell Quin was doing, and if the nurse who went to ask didn't show up in a couple of minutes . . .

To hell with waiting a couple of minutes. She slid off the table and walked around the edge of the curtain, not wanting to draw attention to herself.

Which way to go? She peeked into a couple of rooms and around curtains. Finally she heard, "Where is my wife? If she's okay then why won't someone say that?"

"She's down in her own little curtained room waiting for them to say she's okay and can go," Mr. Brasher's voice said.

"So what the hell are you doing here then? What if some other idiot comes along and tries to kill her?" Quin bit out.

"In the ER?" Mr. Brasher answered. "She's got cops and feds around her."

She stepped into the room and saw Quin frowning from the bedside. "Actually they bailed on me, rather quickly too."

Mr. Brasher pushed away from the wall where he was leaning. "What? Where did they go? How long ago?"

"They left. I don't know. A few minutes ago. Maybe you can go find out," she said and slid onto the bed beside Quinlan. The attendant wrapped white gauze around his bicep. She'd forgotten how sexy his arms were.

How had she not noticed this before? Then again, she'd been so out of it the last few days, a herd of anything could have charged through their rooms and she might not have noticed.

Carefully, she fingered the edge of the gauze and took a deep breath. He was hurt because of her, because, she knew, for him there simply was nothing else to do than try to save her. Idiot, stupid, loveable idiot. "So, what did they say?"

"Ahh, it's just a scratch, honey."

She snorted. "How long have you wanted to say that?"

"I don't know, forever, I guess. What man doesn't want to say it to his girl?"

His girl. She liked the sound of that.

"What are you thinking? You've got a slightly shocked look to your face."

She shook her head. "Nothing. Your girl, huh?" She leaned into him and he wrapped his arm around her, pulling her close.

"Mine and no one else's. So what did you do to ditch the cops?"

She shrugged. "I really don't know. I was answering some fed's questions for the third time and some cop came in and pulled him to the side. They gave me a look and then lit out of my room, cubicle, whatever."

"You didn't scare them away? Threaten them?" he asked her, trying to cheer her up, she knew.

She shook her head. "Hard as it is to believe, I simply kept asking after you. I did hear some lady yelling that she wanted to know what was happening with her little girl, but other than that, it was quiet. Aside from all the hoopla our entourage caused."

"We're Kinncaids. We like to give our entourages things to do."

This time she snickered.

"Finally, a smile and a chuckle. I miss your laugh, El. I've heard it in my head for months, sharing different moments with me."

"They have meds for that."

"Don't need 'em. Got you, don't I?" He sighed and kissed the top of her head.

"I want her back, Quin. I want it all to just . . . just . . . stop. I want it all to just stop."

"I know."

"And I want us to be able to just go home, wherever that is."

"New Orleans," he said without thought.

She pulled out of his arms and looked at him, saw he wasn't joking. "New Orleans? Not D.C.?"

"You're happy in New Orleans. I honestly could never really envision you sitting pretty in the hotel or just touring the museums. Granted, you could always start another studio and I guess you could help out at the shelters in the D.C. area. I do, but I still never could see you there."

She just looked at him, waiting to see what he meant. If he really meant it. Not that she wouldn't move. "I'll live wherever you want. I've spent the last few months alone and I know that no place, no job, no stupid fears are nearly as important as you, as our daughter, as our family."

He looked over her face, touched the tip of her nose. "That all may be true, but—"

"*May* be true?" She stood beside his bed, bumping into the tray where supplies were still scattered.

"All right, that all *is* true, but honestly, I fell in love with a girl in the Quarter. Life is just . . . different there and that's where I want to live." He frowned. "For now at least. When the kids get in school, maybe we will revisit moving, but for now I like the Quarter better than my penthouse in D.C. or an old brownstone or whatever. Real estate in the capital is insane."

She huffed and leaned back against the wall. "I miss my house. I don't know what in the hell I was thinking to move, let alone sell it."

His eyes, green as emeralds, glittered at her. "You, my darling wife, were running scared."

"Yeah, and then I moved and tried to convince myself that I loved New Mexico and the artistry of Taos and my new job. When in fact I missed you, I missed looking forward to you showing up on my stoop on Thursdays or Fridays with some little stupid gift of fattening beignets or a crystal from the voodoo shop or some something. I missed you in the mornings and the way the sun would stream through the little window and shine in your hair." She reached over and ruffled the russet locks. "Or seeing you flustered in raggedy jeans with paint splattered everywhere. I missed talking to you and hearing you and I just missed . . . us. I missed us, and that was before I even learned I was pregnant, and then it all just went down a damned rabbit hole."

He opened his mouth, shut it, opened it again, still keeping his eyes on her. She swallowed. So serious. No grin, no . . . concern she'd become accustomed to seeing in his eyes. A muscle bunched in his jaw. He took a deep breath. "We have so much to make up for, you and I and . . . our little girl. She needs a name." He rubbed a hand, his free hand, over his face. "I don't like calling her 'little girl.' What did you name her?"

She sighed and looked up at him. "I didn't, actually. I mean, I thought of her as mine, but honestly, I couldn't pick a name until I had talked to you. I knew your mother's name was Kaitlyn, so a few times I called her Kaitie, but . . ." She shook her head. "I wanted to do something with you. My stupid need to help cost us too much, cost you precious little moments that we can never get back. God, what if we don't . . . what if I can't . . . what if no one ever knows . . ." She stopped, not wanting to go on.

He said, "I'll admit, I'm still a little mad I missed out on all the stuff, the heartbeat, the first time she moved, or feeling her kick against my hand as we were curled up on the couch or something. But in the whole scheme of things, Ella, that's not what's important." He stood and placed his hands on her shoulders. "There are many men who know about their wives' pregnancies and don't get to experience that. Maybe their job sent them overseas. Maybe they are deployed. Maybe they were just stupid asshats and walked away. But they all make it work. We'll make it work, and we *will* find her. Okay, unless we come up with something else, I'm going to start calling her Kaitie because I can't stand the thought she doesn't have a name."

She didn't have the heart to tell him that the little girl probably did have a name, that someone else had named her and . . .

"A name, Ella. Come on."

"I was thinking . . . I don't know. Hope, maybe. I thought of it last night," she admitted, looking down. Hope. Hope.

"I like Faith, actually, I think. We are going to have faith we'll get her back, so Faith fits her, doesn't it? Or Grace."

"Quinlan, I know you say to have faith, but she was early. She was early and early babies often have issues. What if she does and they don't know, what if . . ."

"What if whoever adopted her is a wonderful family and they take care of her until we can get her back?"

"Like they'll want to give her back to us?"

He shoved a hand through his hair. "I feel bad for them, I do, but she's ours. She's a Kinncaid, and if it takes the rest of my fucking life I'm going to find my daughter and bring her home where she belongs."

"I'm not arguing with you, but I also know that there are going to be issues to deal with."

"Like what? Whoever adopted her, it wasn't a legal adoption so there isn't going to be a legal battle. The only thing we may have to do is to run a DNA test to verify she's ours."

"That's it? That's all?" Relief slid through her. "You're sure? I've been worried we'd find her and whoever had her wouldn't give her back, or she'd be in foster care until the courts ruled or . . . That's all?"

"I talked to Brody, to the feds, to a judge here and that's all, Ella."

Quinlan looked at the woman standing against the wall. So pale.

He hated her pale. She'd actually had some color back in her cheeks earlier before the entire mess. Now her face was as pale as it had been in the hospital. He didn't like it.

"When this is all over, I'm taking my girls someplace, so figure out where you want that to be."

"Home. I just want to go home, wherever that is with you." Tears trembled in her eyes. "I never cried before I was pregnant and I haven't stopped since I read all those pink lines and the word 'pregnant.' I swear pregnancy hormones are for the birds."

He chuckled and wiped a tear away. "But it's kind of adorable."

She shoved at him, but then stopped and ran her finger over his bandage. "Sorry. Forgot for a minute. I love you. I'm hanging on by a very small thread."

"It's okay, I'll catch you. Besides, you would have just found another way to keep going. As you said, I let you settle, let you breathe, and I always will, Ella, because the God's honest truth is that you are my life. I don't like my life without you in it. I've tried that for months and I don't like the person I am without you. That doesn't mean that I'm going to sit back and allow you to be hurt, not ever again. You're stuck with me," he said, leaning down into her space, noting the way her eyes widened just a bit. "You are *mine*, Mrs. Kinncaid. We tried things your way, now we do them mine."

She smiled, stood on her toes and kissed him quickly on the mouth. "I really should have more of an issue when you get all . . . domineering, but . . ."

"But?" he asked, kissing her lightly back.

"But I don't. Or I'm just too tired to care." Her eyes widened and twinkled. "Hormones. Has to be the damned hormones."

He opened his mouth to say *he'd show her the effects of damned hormones,* but he didn't. He decided he'd just show her when the time was right.

Running footsteps sounding down the corridor had him moving slightly in front of her just as Ian burst into the room.

"We need to head over to the children's hospital," Ian told them, his jaw tight, his eyes bright. "Now."

Ian tossed him a jacket, which he caught and tried to pull on over the bandage.

"You found her?" Ella whispered. "Did you find her?"

• • •

Vincent sat holding his wife's hand. Cops surrounded them, along with federal agents and his own bodyguard.

As soon as they'd brought the baby in downstairs and he saw the nurses whispering, looking at him and then asking him and his wife again for the adoption papers, he knew. He knew it was only a matter of time.

His wife sat shaking her head. "She's ours. We adopted her from a reputable agency."

The federal agent . . . what the hell was his name? Landry nodded. "I understand you believed that, ma'am. But by your adoption papers—"

"The adoption was a closed adoption," DeSaro said.

"Yes, but this child fits the description of a missing baby who was not legally available for adoption. The mother did not want to give her up, the father never signed the papers. If there are papers stating otherwise, the papers were forged. Thus the adoption isn't legal."

"There is more, isn't there?" DeSaro asked.

Agent Landry just looked at him. "Mr. DeSaro, we found records of the adoptions by the agency you used, not all are legal. Yours is one of those. The records indicate this baby, the child you adopted, is in fact the legal child of someone else. Someone who has been moving heaven and earth to find her."

She jerked her hand from his and stood. "That baby is mine! Her parents weren't married, they didn't want her and—"

"With all due respect, Mrs. DeSaro, that isn't true. The baby's mother and father are very much married. The baby was forcibly taken from the mother, and honestly, both mother and daughter are damned lucky to be alive. I'm sorry for you and Mr. DeSaro, but the facts are facts."

"The papers said . . . the papers . . . they told us . . ." She turned watery eyes to him and Vincent could only shake his head. He stood and pulled her into his arms.

Looking at the federal agent, he said, "How do you know the adoption isn't legal?"

"First off, our techs have cracked encrypted documents, you are not the only couple this happened to—given a child that was not up for adoption. However, you are the first we . . . that is to say, with this case being what it is, everyone is looking for this little girl."

He knew, he already knew. Names could be forged and who would know the difference?

"We know, Mr. DeSaro. I apologize. But the family of this baby has been working with us to locate her. The parents never even considered adoption. They never signed the papers."

"But there are signatures, there have to be on the papers," his wife said, sniffling. "It was a closed adoption but they have to have signed something. Little Sophia is ours!"

"Ma'am, I'm sorry."

"I don't care. I don't care. She's mine." Her hands gripped his arm, her nails digging in. "Vincent, she's ours. Tell them! They can't just take her away, they can't." Her eyes, so blue, so watery and shiny, begged him.

He closed his own and kissed her forehead. If both he and his wife didn't end up in a pile of legal tape and charges, they'd be damned lucky. Or jail. Quarter of a million. All they had to do was trace the money, but maybe . . .

He took a deep breath. He wanted that little girl as badly as his wife did, but he'd be damned if he would spend time in prison, nor would his wife, for someone else's fuckup.

Clearing his throat, he said, "We met with them, the agency . . . they said . . . We paid for prenatal care. The best there was," he told them. "The Nursery came highly recommended and we paid for the best care for the mother and our child," he told them. "Was it all a lie? They just took our money and stole some poor woman's child to give to us?" He'd have to call his lawyer back. The man had flown out two days ago for another client.

Anger churned hot and thick in his gut, tightening into a cold ball as the elevators at the end of the NICU dinged. He glanced over and saw Kinncaids emerge.

It was over then. They'd lost. He knew it was all too good to be true. And could he fight it?

Not if the adoption wasn't even legal to begin with. He knew that. No matter the state, and he'd checked when they'd started this mess. New Mexico had to have both birth parents agree to the adoption. Not just the mother. And chances were DNA would confirm Sophia was a Kinncaid. He'd like to know what files they'd found, what all had happened.

There was no way a Kinncaid would give up one of theirs. No more than he would. He knew it.

His wife sobbed in his arms. "She's mine. She's my baby. The mother gave her away. She just . . ."

"No, no, I didn't. They took her. They just took her and no one is taking my child from me ever again," a woman with one of the Kinncaids stated fiercely.

Chapter 37

Quin stopped beside Ella and saw the man standing there. An older gentleman, not quite his father's age. A man he actually *knew*.

"Mr. DeSaro," he said, offering his hand.

For a moment, the man looked like he wanted to hit him, but then he took a deep breath and held out his hand. "Mr. Kinncaid."

"I want to see her. I have to see her. Now." Ella pulled her hand from his before he could grab her.

"Ella, wait."

"No. I want to see my daughter *now*."

Landry stepped up to her. "You will. But first there are some things you should know. She's sick, you'll have to ask the doctors for the particulars."

She whirled on the DeSaros.

"No," Landry said, grabbing her arm. "Listen to me, Mrs. Kinncaid. These people, they didn't do anything to her. You, and she, were very, very lucky. They believed the adoption was legal. They've only taken the very best care of your daughter. When she was sick, they brought her in. Luckily she was still in the area, Ella, or this reunion might have been much longer in coming."

She opened her mouth, closed it. Then opened it again. Finally she swallowed. "I. Want. To. See. Her."

Quin stepped up beside her. "We. We will see our daughter. Now."

Landry stepped closer to them. "You'd be wise to get your lawyer or brother to do a DNA test with the docs here and make sure the chain of evidence isn't compromised. I can put a rush on it with a local lab we use sometimes. We'd have the results sooner."

"We've already—"

"Just a precaution."

He nodded. "Fine. Whatever. How sure are you this is our daughter?" He glanced at Ella, who was looking toward the doors at the end of the hallway. "I can't have her broken again because this turns out not to be our daughter."

"Red hair and the birthmark matches. Blood type matches. Plus the tech called when you were shot, he'd cracked the encryption and the records show that the DeSaros adopted your wife's baby. Lisa kept a lot of records. We're going to be very busy for the foreseeable future."

He didn't care about that right now. He sighed. "So it's really her? Really our daughter?"

Landry smiled and slapped him on the shoulder. "Yes, Mr. Kinncaid. DNA is just a precaution, but yes."

A doctor stood to the side and nodded. "That's fine. Parents only."

He and Ella followed the doctor. Quinlan tried to ignore the other woman's cries and moans. "She's ours! Sophia is ours! Tell them, Vincent. Tell them!"

He stopped and turned back to them. This man he'd done business with previously. He'd always respected him and he'd never in a million years thought they would be standing where they were today.

"I'm sorry," he told the other couple. "I'm really sorry."

He turned and hurried after his wife and the doctor. He was going to see his daughter.

His daughter . . .

In one room, they stopped and followed the directions the doctor gave them about washing and scrubbing before putting on scrubs to enter the neonatal unit.

He could hear the doctor talking to them, telling them about tubes hooked up to their daughter, but it all faded. Something about respiratory distress due to her lungs not fully developing and an infection.

Ella's movements were quick, precise. When they were dressed he took her hand in his again and realized his were shaking.

As they walked through the door, the first thing he noticed were the machines. So many machines, quietly beeping, softly hissing. Little mewls and cries could be heard, but not many.

Which one was she?

He took a deep breath and another.

The doctor led them over to one Isolette where a baby lay on her back, an oxygen tube strapped to her little head, EKG patches attached to her chest and an IV in her arm.

Red hair. She had red hair and she was so pale, even as her fat little cheeks were flushed pink. Her little mouth was open as she panted.

"Oh my God. She's so little," he whispered. She was his.

Mine. She's mine.

Ella put her hands on the outside of the plastic. "Hey, sweet girl. Momma's here. I'm right here. I found you. I found you." She started to cry then, silent tears streaming down her face. "By the grace of God," she whispered. "We found you."

He bit down and swallowed, tried to rein in his emotions. His hands shook so badly, he took them from her shoulders and tried to shove them into his pocket, but the scrub gown didn't have pockets. Instead he fisted his hands and crossed his arms for a moment. He just needed a moment. He tried to swallow past the lump in his throat, but it didn't do any good. Looking back, all he could think was, *She's so tiny. So little to be sick.*

A beep went off behind him and he looked over to see more Isolettes. More babies. The one next to them was much, much tinier than their own daughter. The little baby would have fit into his hand and she—he?—was buried under tubes and wires, an eye patch thing covered its eyes. He really looked around then and noticed that in comparison, his daughter looked healthy.

He looked up, blinked, blinked again, but it didn't do any good.

Then Ella started to sing. An old Irish lullaby he vaguely remembered from childhood, from Grammy. Grammy who'd always told him that the good kind Lord worked things out. He smiled even as tears streamed down his own face.

His daughter moved at her mother's voice, soft and lilting in the old words.

The doctor stepped up to them. "I'll leave you in the nurse's hands."

"She'll . . ." He cleared his throat. "Sh-she'll be all right?" he finally managed to ask.

The doctor clapped him on the back. "Considering all that little girl has been through, to be born before thirty-six or seven weeks, I'd say she's doing wonderfully well. Her O_2 levels aren't exactly where I want them to read, but I know they'll get there. We've got her on meds and she's doing wonderfully with them. When she's a bit more stable, when her numbers are closer to where I want them, you can hold her. Might be a few hours."

He nodded.

The doctor left and Ella continued to sing, her voice soft, breaking, and still hoarse as she cried. "Look at her, Quinlan. Look."

Quinlan stepped closer to his wife and kissed her on the head as he looked down at that amazing little bundle.

"She's really ours?" he whispered.

Ella nodded.

"You can both touch her, if you want," a soft voice said beside them. "She's okay and will only get stronger. Babies like to hear their parents' voices."

But his daughter had never heard his.

Ella's hands immediately went into the holes on the side of the Isolette. "It's warm inside."

The nurse nodded. "We need to keep the babies warm. They can get cold really quickly. They're used to a different environment, aren't they? Mommas' tummies are nice warm places." The nurse said to him, "You won't hurt her, Dad. You can touch her too."

For a moment, he could only stand there. Dad. He was a dad.

He looked at his wife's small capable hands, one lightly resting on the baby's little chest, her other caressing the little head. Bright red hair.

That alone made him smile. He put his hands in the lower entrance and touched the softest skin he'd ever felt in his life. Her feet were perfect and he counted the toes, noticing that her heels were small and narrow, all her toes stubby and curled tight. He cupped the tiny, tiny foot and could only marvel. "Look at her, Ella. She's beautiful."

She looked up at him and they laughed together, crying together.

He leaned over and kissed her. "Look at our girl."

"I love you," she whispered. Then back to the baby, "I love you. Momma and Daddy are here and we're not going anywhere."

"This I'll defend," he whispered.

"What?" she asked him, looking up at him.

He swallowed and then swallowed again. "Our family motto. It's *This I'll defend*." He shrugged and tried to think how to explain. "Did I ever tell you that?"

She shook her head.

He ran a finger over the miniature fist, seeing how perfectly trimmed the nails were. "In our family, things like that are . . . well, we learn them young. Until you, I didn't get it. I did in theory, but in reality?" He took a deep breath. "This last week's been hell. I'm supposed to protect my wife, my family, that's what we do, and to see you—what they did." He felt his eyes fill again.

"Quinlan, you didn't fail me, or us, you know that, right? You did defend me, this afternoon, in fact." Her eyes narrowed. "Or have you forgotten the bullet wound in your arm?"

He waved her off. "You scared the hell out of me this last week, and then today . . . Today I was pissed at that man, irritated at you for not running." The tiny fist opened under his caress and the miniscule fingers wrapped around his pointer finger, squeezing slightly. He grinned. "Defending you, us, that's huge and scary. But she's so little, Ella. Kids . . . protecting a child is monumental. What if I screw up? Hell, I've already screwed it up. What if . . ."

She reached over their daughter and wrapped her hand around their joined ones. "Together, Quinlan. Didn't we just promise that today?"

He nodded.

"Together we'll defend her and protect her and just . . . love her."

His watery chuckle had him wiping his eyes. "This *we'll* defend," he amended. To his daughter he said, "Your mommy is very stubborn, but I love her. I love you too, little one."

• • •

He checked his watch. Just a few more minutes and he'd be able to board. He'd taken care of all the loose ends. Lisa was dead; he'd heard on the news they'd found her body late last night. Kevin's body would be found eventually near Espanola. Charred remains were in the burnt car.

He'd heard on the news as well that remains had been found under the rosebushes up at the Retreat. They'd announced that earlier today. That should keep the authorities busy.

He had a new identity, a passport. He'd be home free in just one more flight.

LAX was horribly packed and a madhouse, as always. Just a few more minutes. He wondered if they'd found the body of Kevin yet.

He hadn't heard of anyone finding the charred remains, but he knew they would. Probably.

Not his worry anymore.

He watched one of the airline personnel answer a phone behind the desk.

Please, not a delay. Not a damned delay.

She scanned the area and then nodded. Finally she hung up and picked up the mike. "We're going to have a delay, folks. Not to worry, we'll be boarding momentarily. Please . . ." The rest of what she said was drowned out by groans and complaints of passengers.

Why the delay?

Again he checked his watch. Maybe he should grab a bite. He stood up and turned and saw them.

Cops and suits. Suits were feds.

Were they looking for him?

One of them made eye contact and he knew.

Damn it.

He could run. But to where? He turned and saw another group approach from the other direction.

Could he make the exit? No, he'd have to dart by one of the groups and he'd probably get caught. Better to go peacefully and hope his lawyer would know what to do. He raised his hands and met one of the suits' eyes.

"Dr. Merchant," the man said.

"Yes?"

"You're under arrest for kidnapping, human trafficking, and murder. You have the right to remain silent . . ."

He let the words wash over him as they took his carry-on and laptop case, and cuffed him.

So damned close.

He should have killed that bitch months ago and then all this would have been averted. He'd be free. His family would never know.

And now?

Now it would all come crashing down. They'd have his computer; if they didn't already have it all figured out, they'd find his files. He'd tried to shred everything he could, tried to delete files that he knew would implicate him. But it all happened so fast. So damned fast . . .

As they walked him through the airport, he wished he'd never heard of Ella Ferguson . . . No. Kinncaid. Ella Kinncaid.

She'd brought the whole operation down.

He tried not to panic—after all, panic never did anyone any damned good. Not a bit. He didn't like to be confined but he wouldn't think about that.

One secret had to remain a secret. Had to. He'd do anything to make sure his wife and daughter never learned the truth.

His palms were damp as they helped him into an unmarked car parked at the curb of the terminal.

"I want my lawyer," he told the feds as they both buckled up.

"Don't worry, Dr. Merchant. You'll get him, I'm sure," one of them said.

He stared out the window and wondered what would happen if the whole truth ever did come out.

He'd helped people, damn it. He'd given people hope when they didn't have any. He'd provided wonderful loving homes for kids who would otherwise not have had them. He'd *saved* children and given them bright, promising futures.

Nothing else could be proven, he thought, nothing.

Chapter 38

The waiting room was full to bursting with Kinncaids and law enforcement officials. The Richardsons were even there, so someone had contacted them about her baby being found. Sadly, she hadn't thought of it.

Ella didn't want to leave, but Quinlan had finally made her go get some water at least.

"How is she?" Ian asked, leaning against the wall.

She stopped and could only look at him. "She's . . . she's fine. She'll be fine, or so they tell us. Her oxygen levels are better and she responds to our voices."

"Of course she does, you're her mother," he told her. An older couple had stood up when she'd come in. Quin's parents. She looked back at Ian. "She knows her father's voice. I saved all his voice messages to my sim card, so I still had them when I got my new phone. I played them to her. And a video I made of him back in New Orleans when he came to see me and he was singing," she admitted quietly.

"You're smiling."

"Just remembering."

"Does he know you played his voice for her?"

She shook her head. "No, I haven't told him yet. One day I will."

Her hands started to shake and she rubbed her forehead. "I'm not dreaming, am I? Please say I'm not."

Ian, always so serious, laughed. "No. You're here, she's here, he's here. You're all here together. With most of our interfering asses as well, and I'm told the others will be arriving later tonight."

Taking a deep breath, she stepped closer to him, noticed when he stiffened and then quickly leaned up and kissed his cheek. "Thank you. Thank you for everything."

"I really didn't do much, you know."

"You were there for him when I couldn't be."

"I'll figure out a way you can pay me back," he told her, grinning. "Maybe babysitting sometime."

She laughed.

The older couple stepped forward. The woman had graying red hair and looked familiar.

Quinlan, Ella realized. The woman resembled Quinlan.

"Welcome to the family, Ella. I'm Kaitlyn."

Ella swallowed, looked from the woman who was neatly dressed to the man beside her with his bushy white hair, back to Ian.

"Yeah, they made it, were actually at the hotel when the excitement happened in the parking lot. We've all been waiting to hear about the baby, and I'll warn you now, they're dying to see the newest addition to the family." Ian nodded behind. "Where's Quin?"

"We don't want to leave her alone and he said I needed to get some water or something. He's being bossy."

Kaitlyn handed her a water bottle. "Here. We've all had the water bottles for a while. Jock keeps shoving them on me. I told him I'm not thirsty, but he doesn't listen."

"That's what I told Quin."

Kaitlyn stepped forward and hugged her. For a moment, Ella stiffened and then slowly hugged her back.

"Yes, well, in case you haven't figured it out yet, dear, Kinncaid men like to get their way."

For the first time in way too long, she laughed. "I've sort of noticed that about them. *All* of them, or at least the ones I've spent time with, and I honestly thought Quinlan was the most laid-back of the bunch."

"Oh no, dear. That would be Brayden, or maybe Gavin. The twins are more laid-back than the other three. Ian's too intense and will end up with high blood pressure if he doesn't slow down. Aiden worries about everyone, like Ian and Quinlan. Quinlan's always tried to prove . . . well, something."

She just looked at this woman who was talking to her when she had every right to hate her. "Quinlan has nothing to prove." She met her mother-in-law's eyes. "Not a thing to anyone."

The woman smiled, and it was Quinlan's single-dimpled smile. "Oh, I know that. I'm glad to see you do as well."

For a minute they just stared at her. Ella looked at the man behind this lady and sort of nodded to him before she uncapped the water and played with it for a minute. Finally, she asked, "You want to see her? I'll ask them to raise the blinds so you can see her."

The older man cleared his throat. "Does she have a name? No one knows it if she does."

She gave him her attention. Must be where all his sons got their height. Dark blue eyes like Aiden and Ian, intense eyes that he trained on her now. She tried not to squirm. After everything, it wasn't like this man could hurt her. "We haven't decided yet."

"Well, don't wait too long," Ian said. "Dad's likely to give her some deplorable nickname."

Kaitlyn chuckled. "That's the truth."

"I resent that remark." The older man winked at her. "I only give nicknames that are deserved, Kaitie lass."

Her look said, *See what I mean?*

Ella drank some water and said to Ian, "Where are the DeSaros?"

Ian jerked his head to the side, where the gentleman was talking to the cops. Where was the woman?

Ian leaned over and whispered, "She's in the chapel down the hallway, I believe."

Nodding, she said, "I'll be right back, and then you guys can see her, okay?"

Without waiting for anyone to say anything, she asked a nurse at the station where the chapel was and followed the hallway down to a little room. For a moment, she stood staring at the door. Probably a dumb thing to do, but she had to. Inside sat a woman on a pew staring at a stained-glass window. Or she supposed it was supposed to be a window. Merely glass in front of a light so that it gave off a calming effect.

The woman didn't move, and Ella wondered if she should just leave well enough alone.

She turned around to the door, her hand freezing on the handle. Then she turned back and walked down the little aisle. Ferns stood on either side of the stained-glass angel.

She sat down in the pew beside the woman.

Taking another deep breath, she tried to think of what to say. Finally the woman looked to her.

"Is Sophia okay? Please tell me she's okay. They won't tell us anything, won't tell me any—"

"She's doing well, they said. Her oxygen levels are climbing and that's good."

The woman nodded. "Thank you for that." She blew out a breath. "I've wanted a baby for so long. I thought . . ."

Ella could only nod.

"I know. I know I can't have Sophia," she whispered and wiped a tear away. "That's what we called her, you know. I've all her stuff with us too. Or most of it. The diaper bag with her diapers and the formula and the—" She waved the words away. "It doesn't matter."

"I am sorry for your pain."

"Are you?" the woman asked, her blonde hair coming out of the ponytail it had been in. Her blue eyes were rimmed red from crying.

"I am. I know what you're going through." She looked down at her wrists, the skin red and marred. "I know what it's like to watch someone take your child and not be able to stop them."

Neither said a word for a long moment. "How do you get through it?"

Her jaw trembled and finally she reached over and took the woman's perfectly manicured hand. Mrs. DeSaro jerked away but then slowly placed her hand on top of Ella's. "What happened to your wrists?"

"They tied me to the bed with zip ties and the plastic cut my wrists when I tried to get away." She shrugged. "I tried so hard to get to her. So that helpless feeling you're feeling . . . I get that. And I wouldn't wish it on my worst enemy. And I'm sorry. I'm so sorry you're going through it. That you're hurting."

The other woman nodded and wiped a tear away. "I know you don't want to hear this, but to me, she's mine. She's my baby and I'm her mother. That's what we were told and . . ." She shook her head and took a deep breath. "Vincent doesn't know what to do. He's always got to protect, to fix things, and this time . . . there's no way to fix it. To stop it, to protect."

Ella shook her head. "You're wrong. You both protected her when I couldn't. That was the only thing that got me through. I prayed. I prayed and prayed and prayed that whoever had her would know. That God would have someone who really cared watch over her. That if I couldn't be with her, that someone else could love her just as much. Would feed her if she was hungry." She swallowed past the tightening in her throat. "I was terrified that whoever had her wouldn't hold her, wouldn't care for her, wouldn't—wouldn't know if she needed something. Or if she was sick."

Wiping her own tear away, she looked at this woman who had to hate her. "You saved her. You and your husband kept her safe. You were the answer to my prayers."

"What's the answer to mine?" she asked brokenly.

Ella shook her head. "I don't know."

The woman started crying, leaned over and cried on Ella's shoulder, and all she could do was mumble sweet nothings because there was nothing else to do.

• • •

Ian looked down the hallway to the chapel.

Landry walked up to him. "Thought you might be interested in Jareaux."

"I hear he's under investigation, and will probably lose his job."

Landry just cocked a brow. "I probably don't want to know how you know that, do I?"

Ian smiled. "No, you don't."

He left the agent there and strode down the hallway to look in on the chapel, just to make sure Ella was okay. No one was about to let anything happen to her now. Ella, for all her faults in helping people, wanted to help people. He didn't know about Mrs. DeSaro.

Mr. DeSaro didn't like that his wife was hurting, even as he understood the law and the right thing to do.

But sometimes right had different views on each side.

"Is she still in there?" the very man asked from behind him.

"Yes, they're . . ." Ian shook his head. "Hell if I know. Women baffle me."

The man peeked in, started to step in and then shook his head. "All she wanted was a baby. She can't have any, or I'm too old, I don't know, but either way I'd do just about anything to see her happy."

Ian nodded. "I get that. I do." He took a deep breath and thought about what he was about to say. He hated hospitals, the way they smelled, the way he had a constant itchy feeling between his shoulder blades. "Look, I know someone."

DeSaro only arched a brow at him. "Thanks, but no. I'll be lucky if we don't face prosecution for this." The man rubbed a hand over his face. His blue eyes were weary and angry and hurt. "So, no."

Ian looked down the hallway and then motioned to the doors at the far end of the hallway. "Take a walk with me."

DeSaro stared at the door that led to the chapel. "I need to get my wife out of here. The police said we could go."

"Yes, but I might have an answer to your problem. Just a walk. And a talk and if you're not . . . interested, fine."

The other man raked a hand over his face again and then finally nodded. "Okay. Five minutes."

Perfect. Ian led him to the elevators and then through the lobby and finally outside.

"Look, I used to work for someone who wishes to remain anonymous. He's widowed and apparently his late wife's sister and brother-in-law never changed their wills after her death. They died in a car accident recently, about a month ago. Both were lawyers in Georgetown. Their nine-month-old twin girls have no home and my old boss isn't interested in becoming a father. A guardian, or a godfather, maybe, or at least that was his stipulation to me."

"To you?" the other man asked him.

"He wanted to know if my wife and I wanted the girls. We have three other children, all adopted. Of course, we'd love to have them, but I haven't told her yet. If you're interested . . . well, I would have to talk it over with him. He'd want to meet you and your wife, I'm sure. But he might go for you guys adopting the girls instead."

For a long moment the man just stood there. He blew out a breath and shook his head. "I don't know."

"Actually, I already mentioned it to him," Ian admitted. "If you don't want them, fine. Rori and I will take them."

The man stared out over the parking lot. "Twins?"

Ian pulled up their photo on his phone and turned it so that DeSaro could see the smiling cherubs on the screen. Big blue eyes and almost bald heads, chubby cheeks.

"Cute kids," the man said. He blinked, studied them, then huffed out a breath. "When?"

"Tomorrow if you want. We can fly out to D.C. Or I can see if he'll meet us in Chicago."

"After this, I doubt a judge would agree."

Ian just looked at him. "Mr. DeSaro, I think we know that . . . how did you put it . . . men in our positions overcome complications? He's not looking for judges, it would be a straight private adoption. Your lawyer, his lawyer."

"What is the catch?" DeSaro asked him, his gaze narrowed on Ian.

Ian smiled. "Always a catch, isn't there? That's the thing. He's . . . let's just say he works behind the scenes. Though he doesn't believe he's conducive to giving the girls a proper, safe home life, he's not so keen on never ever seeing them either. He takes his responsibilities rather personally. So he'd want to know they're safe."

"You think they won't be?"

Ian smiled. "I think you'll keep them as safe and happy as I would."

The other man tilted his head. "I could truly hate your family. Little Sophia is an angel."

"But not your angel, DeSaro. Sorry. And you can have two new angels. It's not the same and I know Sophia isn't replaceable. Up to you, though." He tucked his phone back into his pocket.

"Children are not interchangeable, Mr. Kinncaid."

"No, they are not, and I apologize if you believed that was my intention." Ian merely looked at him. "Our family knows you are hurting, and nothing will take that pain away completely. However, this is an opportunity that is open to you now and might alleviate some of your wife's hurt. I wasn't attempting to swap children, DeSaro. They'll be part of our family if you don't want them. And if I didn't think you deserved them, I wouldn't offer these angels to you."

The man looked away and out over the parking lot. Finally, he sighed and nodded. "Give me tonight. I'll let you know in the morning. I need to take my wife to the hotel so she can rest."

Ian nodded and they went back inside. Neither said another word.

He'd be hearing from them, he knew it. And he knew enough about the DeSaros to know that the girls would have a great home. Might be almost too protected, but then with a family like the DeSaros, that was expected. He understood that.

Upstairs he found the family circled around the window into the neonatal unit. The blinds rose and there stood Quin and Ella in their scrubs. She handed the bundle of blankets and pink skin over to

Quin. Grinning, he walked to the window and held up his daughter so they could all see her.

"Oh, Jock! She has my hair!" his mother said.

His father tucked her under his arm and kissed the top of her head. "She'll be a beauty like her grandmother."

Rori bumped Ian's shoulder with her own. "Everything good with the DeSaros?"

He nodded. "Think so."

"Good, I'd hate to have to—"

He kissed her, often the only way to shut her up.

Aiden and Brody were betting on how obnoxious Quinlan would end up being as a dad. But then again, he had every right to be. Aiden was busy taking photos through the glass on his phone. Grinning, he said, "Got it, finally. Now Jesslyn will be happy and everyone else. I'll just send it to Gav and Bray as well."

Looking in through the glass at his brother's happiness, Ian was finally able to take the first deep breath he'd taken in since he'd realized how lost Quin had really been.

In there, in that nursery . . . there was their brother and his family.

Ella puffed on the glass and wrote *Sophia Grace*.

"Aww. What a lovely name," his mother said.

"Our Gracie is beautiful, isn't she?" his dad asked.

"Gracie? Really?" His mother chuckled.

"I like Gracie," Jock said.

"He's so happy, Jock. They're so happy," his mother said, wiping her eyes.

Ian jerked his head to his brother and cousin.

"Like we were," his father whispered.

"Thank you for our family, Jock."

He left his parents looking in at the new generation as he joined in on the betting about his youngest sibling before the others got here.

Epilogue

Chicago, January

Vincent DeSaro bounced one twin on his knee in the study. His wife had taken the other up to change her.

Two were a complete handful.

His Leah was already walking. Her sister Bianca still scootched all over the place and picked up everything. They'd already made a trip to the ER when she'd swallowed some plastic from a damned Christmas ornament.

It had been an eventful and happy Christmas.

New Year's had come and gone and they'd only had more blessings than he could count.

But he still missed Sophia. His wife made the best of it, often saying that God worked in mysterious ways.

Maybe.

But DeSaros worked in ways too and the DeSaro way wasn't that mysterious.

His private line rang. He picked it up. "DeSaro."

"Problem resolved."

He took a deep breath and set the baby on the floor. She immediately grabbed his pants leg and pulled herself up, grinning up at him and cooing as she steadied herself.

"How?"

"Heard the problem had an unfortunate incident with a sharp object."

He nodded. Good. He'd hated the fact that the bastard doctor who had caused so much pain might get away once he was out on bail. No one had paid his bail yet and it was set extremely high. Not even the man's wife, which was interesting in and of itself. Though the news had reported that the doctor's own daughter had been adopted as well, and no one ever knew.

Whether or not the wife had known was probably a moot point. Time would tell. If she'd known what was happening the authorities would find out.

Then he'd decide.

Until then?

"Thank you for letting me know. Now what about the trip to Sicily?" He wanted to take his family, surprise his wife.

"All set. You can leave at the end of the week."

He smiled at his daughter. "Good."

The line clicked and he set the phone aside, picking up Leah, kissing her cheek. Life was interesting, wasn't it?

• • •

New Orleans

Quinlan stood in the doorway of the kitchen just watching as Ella bustled around, switching pots and bowls. She even had an apron tied on. He didn't know she'd even owned one of those. Scents of garlic and spice wafted on the air, the heat from the kitchen fogging the windows. It was cold outside, but January was cold even in New Orleans on occasion.

She was stressed and worried.

Why, he had no idea. So his family was coming to visit. So what? She'd met them already. Spent part of the holidays with them in Seneca. They all loved her.

So beautiful was all he could think. And she was his. Finally, completely and wholly his. She was muttering to herself about his father's diet and if he should have spicy food or something.

"Marry me," he said softly, surprised that the words had just blurted out. He'd planned to ask her again, to beg her again if need be.

". . . maybe it would be better —" She whirled around. "What?"

"Marry me, Ella."

"I'm not in the mood for jokes, Quin. Your family is coming and I'm cooking and the baby's asleep for a bit and —"

He stepped closer and stopped her with his hands on her shoulders. "I'm not joking. I'd already planned to do this. Some night after Grace is asleep, maybe some wine or champagne out in the courtyard or up on the balcony. Hadn't decided yet. Some music, some romance and propose. Properly. I don't remember asking you before and I want to remember."

"Maybe I asked you," she said, grinning up at him, even as her brow furrowed.

"As fast as you ran, commitment-phobics have nothing on you, so I doubt it."

"Hello, Pot, I'm Kettle."

He ignored her. "And I realized you never had the whole pretty dress, the planning for a big or little wedding, a cake, a celebration with photographs and what all."

She just stared up at him as whatever was on the stove boiled.

"I love you, Ella Kinncaid. I love us. I want to give it to you. All of it. All . . ." He took a deep breath. "So, will you? Will you marry me?"

Still she just stared at him. Finally, she licked her lips. "You do know we are already married, right? Are you feeling okay?"

"That's not the point, and yes, I'm feeling fine."

She tilted her head and the lights flashed in her purple hair. He loved her hair, no matter what color it was. "Did I do something to make you think—"

"What? No! That's just it. I don't ever want you to look back and wonder. I want you to *know* you were it for me. I took one look at your blue hair with pink tips and your sassy Southern drawl and that was it. Once I met Ella Ferguson . . . Kinncaid, no one else came close. After swearing to anyone and everyone I'd never marry, I spent one memorable—" He stopped, winced. "Okay, and forgettable wild weekend with you and I was . . . fascinated. I want you to never, never wonder if or why or how come. But to *know*, simply know, what is."

Tears shimmered in her eyes.

"I love you, Ella Kinncaid, and I want the world to know it. So . . . will you marry me . . . again as the case sort of is?" Strangely, his heart was thrumming in his chest and his palms were damp.

"This isn't going to be a yearly thing, is it? A wedding?"

He hadn't thought of that. They'd met in February and here it was January.

"Maybe not the wedding," he said, pulling her toward him and dancing her back. "Maybe, maybe the proposing . . ."

"Hmmm . . ."

"Hmmm? You realize that isn't an answer, Ella." God, what if she said no. What if she were only with him because of Grace? What if . . .

No. No, that wasn't the case.

"Hmmm . . ." She leaned up, pulled him down to her and kissed him.

"El-la."

She grinned. "Quin-lan. Bless your heart, I've been your wife for a year."

"I know, and an absent wife at that. You're supposed to be *with* me. I don't like it when you're not beside me."

"I never slept right after leaving you." She laid her head on his chest. "I don't ever want to be there again. I could finally breathe again even if I was afraid to when you walked into my hospital room. I'd watch you sleep, afraid I'd wake up and you'd be gone." One tear trickled over and slid down her cheek. "I was so thankful, hopeful and . . . I don't even know when I realized we were still married and then . . . then . . ."

"Shh . . . it's okay now. We're okay now. We're a good team now, right?"

For a moment he just held her. "Yes. Yes, you tenacious man. We're okay now, we're a good team now and we always will be. Yes, I'll marry you." She leaned back and looked up at him. "Again. Today. Tomorrow. Next week. Next year." She put her arms around his neck as he picked her up. "Again and again, I'll marry you."

"Thank God. I was starting to worry I'd have to resort to extreme measures. Be a deceptive man. Seduce you quickly, spend a lot of time with you, whisk you off to Vegas for a secret wedding. Get your pregnant."

"Smart-ass." She kissed his cheek and he caught a whiff of her shampoo, sort of minty with flowers or something.

"You're a smart-ass."

"Just so you remember who you belong to, sugar."

He chuckled. "Same goes, honey."

"Like I'll ever forget."

"And I won't ever let you, not ever again, Mrs. Kinncaid. You're mine."

She kissed him, giggling. "Like anyone else would put up with me?"

Grace began to cry from the other room. He let her slide down and said, "There is that. I'll get her."

"Bring her in here," she said, turning back to the stove.

Quinlan hurried to their bedroom, where the cradle rested beside their bed. The nursery still wasn't finished, and frankly neither of them would ever sleep with her upstairs just yet. It was all still too new, the fear still too new for them to let her out of their sight for long.

Little fists thumped jerkily in the air. Encased in her pink and turquoise sleeper thing, the legs only half filled, the footsies dangled uselessly. She was still so tiny. She'd spit up enough yesterday, and her diapers had leaked enough, that most of her clothes were in the laundry. This size was for zero to three months and it was clearly too big.

"Hey, sweetie." He picked her up, careful to cup the back of her head. "Daddy's here. It's okay." He tucked her up close to him and patted her as he walked back to the kitchen. "Your momma is busy, busy. Grams and Pops are coming to see you tonight."

She stopped crying as she always did when he talked.

"That is so unfair. She never stops crying for me like that."

"Ohh," he cooed. "That's because she knows who her daddy is."

He looked up to see Ella biting her bottom lip. "I need to tell you something."

"What?"

"I used to play your voice messages to her. I saved them all." She'd never told him that. "So I'd play them, sometimes through the phone, but I also made a recording." She shrugged and turned back to the stove. "Sometimes I played that video of you singing 'My Girl.'" She glanced at him over her shoulder. "You remember? When you were being silly at the shelter? And you sang?"

The past was still a touchy thing for them to talk about sometimes, but they talked about it and worked through it.

"You did? I didn't know you'd recorded that."

She nodded. "Yep, and I played it for her, the phone against my big ol' belly." She stirred something on the stove. "I wanted her to know your voice. So that's what I did. And she knew you the first time she heard your voice."

He could only stare at her. She still surprised him. He'd often laughed at the baffled look on his father's face through the years when dealing with their mother.

Now he had more sympathy with the man. He knew, without a doubt, that forty years from now Ella would still surprise him.

Grace moved her head in the crook of his neck.

"See how smart your momma is, Gracie? She's brilliant, isn't she? And she loves you very, very much." He bounced and walked and patted his daughter's back until Ella had turned things off on the stove so she could feed her. They'd seen a lactation specialist and had been lucky that little Gracie liked her mother and nursing so much, even as the whole experience wasn't easy and completely foreign to him, as he'd been unable to help at all.

Ella turned from the stove. "I love you both very, very much."

"But Daddy loves his girls more," he said, kissing the top of Gracie's head. "My girls."

He hummed a few bars of the song and his daughter stilled against him. He grinned.

"No, Momma loves you guys more." Ella washed her hands and used the hand sanitizer.

"But Daddy loves his girls the mostest of the mostest of the mostest."

"Well, Momma loves y'all the mostest of the mostest of the mostest estest." Ella reached for Gracie.

Quinlan laughed. This was the life. A life he was beyond blessed to have and thankful for every day. A life he'd give his own to defend.

He leaned over and kissed his wife while holding his daughter. "Perfect."

Keep reading for an excerpt
from the story that started it all in
***Deadly Beginnings**!*

Jaycee Clark is best known for her series of romantic suspense novels featuring the very sexy Kinncaid brothers. But before Aiden, Ian, Brayden, Gavin, and Quinlan there was Jock Kinncaid, the charismatic patriarch to the Kinncaid family, and Kaitlyn O'Reilly, the woman who captured his heart forever.

Kaitlyn O'Reilly, an RN, believed she'd found love with the charming and well-liked surgeon she'd met at work. Landon Goldburg was kind, attentive, and she thought they had so much in common. Now engaged, the good doctor has quickly become the man of her nightmares. As he grows more controlling and violent, Kaitlyn wants her freedom.

Jock Kinncaid can't stop thinking about the quietly beautiful – and engaged – redhead he met at a fund-raising gala months ago. He knows a spitfire lurks beneath the surface of this woman who's invaded his dreams, and he knows she's exactly what's been missing from his otherwise ideal life. When a chance meeting throws the two of them together again, Jock swears he won't let her get away this time.

But even as Jock vows to protect the woman he loves and Kaitlyn struggles to trust Jock and the passion between them, the deranged doctor is bent on destroying them both, even if it means killing the only thing he loves.

Chapter 1

Summer 1969
Baltimore

There she was. The woman he was going to marry.

Her red hair was pulled severely if neatly back from her face, and what a beautiful face it was. Perfectly sloped nose, eyes a bit wide-set and slanted. He'd bet green.

Jock Kinncaid ignored the conversation going on around him but nodded and made appropriate noises. The guy was a bore, some doctor or other who was completely full of himself.

The people were here to write checks for whatever cause was deemed important by the evening, or rather whoever was hosting this event.

At least the food wasn't half bad.

He pulled at his collar and watched her as the doctor made some sort of motion and Jock's woman came over.

Jock watched her. Her long black gown draped over her perfectly, yet it seemed too harsh for some reason. Wrong.

She was still beautiful.

And she did have freckles, across the bridge of her nose, on her neck, her collarbone.

He caught something flash through—he was right—amazing green eyes as she walked closer, though he almost missed it.

The doctor waited until she joined the group and then he leaned down and said something in her ear. She stilled and looked down.

The doctor then commenced answering another man's question while he ignored the beautiful redhead.

What. The. Hell.

The band started up a song.

One Jock liked.

Well, if the doctor didn't give her attention, Jock would take care of that.

He reached his hand out to the lovely woman.

"May I have this dance?"

She looked at his hand, her eyes meeting his on a quick blink before she looked up at the doctor.

The man beside the doctor leaned in and whispered, "Kinncaid."

Jock didn't smile. "A woman as beautiful as you hardly needs anyone's permission."

Her eyes widened as she quickly met his stare.

Jock had been born with a name, one he'd always respected and one he garnered respect for. Mainly, he knew, people just wanted his money.

The doctor nodded and said to the woman, "Don't go far."

She swallowed and Jock took her hand, placing it on his arm, and led her to the dance floor where others had already gathered. He felt her fingers' slight tremble. Was she afraid to dance with him?

The trumpet sounded.

He wished Louis Armstrong were singing this.

"So, you enjoying this party?" he asked. Probably not with the doctor who was full of himself.

She looked up at him, her eyes darting to the side.

"Umm."

Jock laughed and twirled her to the music.

"What is this song?" she asked him, smiling shyly up at him.

"This song? You don't know?"

She shrugged.

"'A Kiss to Build a Dream On.'" He sang a few words of it.

Her brows arched.

Her gloved hand slid against his palm as he turned them in another circle, a bit farther away from the watching doctor.

Her left hand held in his right, he could easily feel the ring on her finger.

Damn.

"You married?"

Her eyes rose to his, wide. "Do you ask all your dancing partners that question?"

"Only the ones whom I want to keep dancing with."

She took a deep breath. "No."

"No? The ring?" He rubbed his fingers over the back of hers, on the ring beneath the long white gloves.

"It's his." She glanced to the side of them.

"Ah. Soon to be Dr. and Mrs. —"

"Perhaps."

"Oh, trouble in paradise. I'd say I'm sorry, but my parents taught me not to lie. So in that case, run away with me. I'll make you smile. I'll make you laugh. We'll get into all sorts of trouble," he told her, leaning close and whispering in her ear.

She smiled and pulled back, the smile dancing into her eyes, or almost. She pulled farther back. "You are probably enough trouble all on your own, Kinncaid, you don't need my help."

"You know my name. I have hope." He twirled them again. "So do you have one?"

"One?"

"A name." He grinned.

"Most people have them, yes."

"What's yours?"

She grinned a one-sided, one-dimpled grin at him. "What's the fun in giving you all the answers?"

He chuckled. "Ah, so it begins."

"What begins?"

"The challenge."

Her lips pursed. "Maybe."

They danced a bit more, and he kept his eye on the doctor. The man had issues, too tight, too stiff for this woman in Jock's arms. She was full of passion, he just knew it. Maybe it was the red hair, or the impish look he caught like sunlight shifting through clouds, there for just a minute before shadows moved in.

He didn't want shadows around her.

Didn't want that damned doctor around her.

Sure as hell didn't want the pompous ass's ring on her finger.

He pulled her just a bit closer as the jazzy song swagged on the air. She smelled like . . . lilacs? Lilies? A sweet flower, and that seemed wrong for her. Wrong like the dress and the damned doctor and the doctor's ring on her finger.

"You want to leave?" he blurted, leaning back to meet her gaze.

She smiled. "I didn't want to come in the first place."

"Then let's get out of here." He glanced to where the doctor had been but the man wasn't there.

She smiled, started to say something, and then stopped as her doctor stood just beside them.

"Excuse me." The man looked to his fiancée. "Katherine, there's someone I'd like you to meet."

She glanced between them and then licked her lips. "B-but the dance isn't over."

"That doesn't matter, Katherine. Come." She winced and pulled her hand from Jock's.

He reached out and grabbed hers again. "Thank you for a lovely dance."

Her eyes were once again shadowed. She swallowed and nodded even as she pulled her hand away and placed it on the doctor's damned arm. Jock watched as the man put his hand over hers, leaning close to whisper something into her ear. She stiffened, and even from here Jock could see the chills on her arms between the dress's sleeves and the tops of her gloves, but she kept walking. He noticed the man's hold tighten on her hand.

Jock took a deep breath. Katherine.

She didn't really look like a Katherine to him. Maybe a Kay or a Kaitie. Katherine was cold. That woman would not be cold in any way, shape or form.

She'd smiled. At him. A real, or almost-real, smile. He wondered how pretty she'd be if she really, truly smiled. As it was now, he figured she rarely smiled at all. But he had gotten one true grin out of her, half, mischievous, and dimpled. He wanted to taste that dimple.

Jock watched them make their way across the dance floor back to the doctor's group. There were few people he disliked, but that man . . . there was just something about him. The man's dark eyes were . . . cold. Empty.

She stood just a bit behind the man.

Jock shifted and caught a flash of green as she darted a quick look his way. He merely jerked his chin up.

He needed to learn more about her, about them both.

Now, though, wasn't the time. He'd had enough of this place.

He turned and strode to the doors that opened onto a terrace. Many people mingled outside and on the lawns. He spoke to a few. Promised some contributions and then decided it was time to go.

Jock looked around for the burnished copper hair but didn't see it. Another study of the attendees and he didn't see the doc either.

Well, he might not get another look at her tonight, but he would sooner or later.

Jock Kinncaid always got what he wanted.

• • •

Kaitlyn—her name was *not* Katherine—O'Reilly carefully took a deep breath and slowly let it out while they waited for the valet to bring Landon's car around.

Landon Goldburg III, a handsome, charming surgeon at Baltimore Sinai Hospital, was not happy. It had become smart to learn his moods—and what those moods could entail.

She'd known he wouldn't be happy the moment Landon interrupted the dance, though if she were honest, she knew it before. The moment Kinncaid had asked her to dance.

She shouldn't have smiled at Kinncaid.

Shouldn't have laughed, but Kinncaid was . . . easy. Smooth. Probably too smooth. Men, she was learning, were not what they appeared.

. . . *A woman as beautiful as you hardly needs anyone's permission* . . . Kinncaid thought she was beautiful. Kaitlyn almost smiled at the thought but caught herself.

Landon had seen she'd been having a good time, so of course he'd stopped it. She realized she was fidgeting with her glove and stilled, her stomach tightening. For just a moment, she'd dared to relax. She should have known better.

Would he be quiet all the way home?

Would he demand answers, all of which would be wrong? Landon was confusing at best, scary at worst.

There was a time when she'd thought he was a wonderful man, someone she had things in common with, someone she'd always admire and respect. She knew now that wasn't true. Landon could lie so well. His charm and smiles hid who he really was until she felt trapped.

She just didn't know how to get away from him. He was always there. At her apartment, at work, always at work, and now in her head. That's what scared her the most. The man was in her head and she—

"Did you have to make such a cake of yourself?" he asked, interrupting her thoughts and startling her.

There it was. She almost sighed. Landon quiet was still better than when he demanded answers, wanted to talk about whatever else she'd done wrong. And she always did something wrong. "I didn't, Landon."

He leaned in close to her. "You damned well did. It was embarrassing. Others remarked on it."

She looked down at the sidewalk and wished again she hadn't come tonight. Who, if anyone, had said anything and what was said? Had she made a cake of herself? She hadn't thought so.

"I sim-simply danced with the man."

"You *flirted* with him."

She knew better than to argue with him. He hated if she talked back, and she'd learned the hard way not to.

She glanced up at him out of the corner of her eye. A muscle twitched in his jaw and the line between his brows deepened.

Her stomach tightened even more, burning. Maybe she could get another ride home? But with whom? All those inside were his friends so she wouldn't ask any of them.

Cabs weren't stopping. Though if one showed up before the valet brought Landon's car around . . .

Tired, she turned to him. "No. I did not flirt, Landon. I merely danced and talked with someone. There is no harm in that." Something flickered in his dark eyes and she swallowed. "I'll—I'll get a cab home until you're in a better mood."

Quick as a snake, he reached out and grabbed her arm, jerking her to him. How could handsome be so cold?

"Are you calling me a liar?" he asked her, his voice slithering across her skin, his dark eyes glittering at her.

She froze. Stupid, very, very stupid. She knew better, but a part of her was tired of Landon and all his restrictions and his quick temper. She'd learned, though, not to be herself, not with Landon.

"I don't believe I said that at all, Landon," she said calmly. She tried to twist her arm away, but he tightened his hold on her and pulled her even closer, leaning down into her face.

"Either you're mine or you're not, Katherine. You do *not* flirt with other men. Ever," he hissed. "And you never, *ever* make a fool of me."

Her arm would be bruised tomorrow.

"You are my fiancée," he bit out, "and you should act like it."

"I didn't—"

"Ah, the darling affianced couple of the evening," a voice drawled.

She knew that voice. Closing her eyes, she took a small breath and jerked her arm away from Landon's hold. Surprisingly, he let her go.

"I'm sorry, was I interrupting?" Kinncaid asked as he nodded to the valet. "Richie, good to see you again. How's your mom doing?" he asked the young valet attendant.

"Good, Mr. K. Thanks for asking."

"Tell her I said hello, and if you get tired of working this gig, call. Your old spot's always open."

"Thanks, sir." The young man took off smiling.

Kinncaid turned back to them just as the valet brought Landon's Mercedes to a gentle stop near the curb.

Damn.

Landon stepped closer to her at her back and chills danced over her skin.

"I had meant to tell you, Doc, thanks for allowing me to dance with your lovely fiancée. You're a lucky man." His dark blue eyes rested on her, then dropped to her arm, where she realized she was rubbing it through her glove. She stopped.

Landon snorted. "Yes, well, she's learning."

Shame warmed her cheeks. Couldn't they just go? She wasn't a bone to be snarled over.

Something flashed in Kinncaid's blue eyes as they rose from her arm to meet her own eyes before he looked over her shoulder. "Something so beautiful should always be cherished, never mistreated."

"I completely agree, Mr. Kinncaid," Landon said. "But sometimes the treasures must learn how to shine."

Kinncaid made a noise in his throat. Some sort of growl or grunt. A cab pulled to the curb behind Landon's car even as a shiny blue Stingray pulled in behind the cab.

Kinncaid shifted as she did.

She'd had enough.

"Good night, gentlemen. I'd say it's been enjoyable, but I was taught not to lie."

Not daring to look back, she jerked her hand away from Landon when he reached for her, walked to the cab and climbed in. Both men were staring after her.

Kinncaid's lips were tilted up at the corners.

Landon's lips were pressed together and the muscle bunched in his cheek.

Her hands trembled as she climbed into the cab and gave him her address.

She'd pay for leaving Landon standing there. She knew it, she just had no idea how to get away from it. With her work, her job she'd worked hard for, she didn't want to give it up. Giving up meant saying Landon had won another part of her. If she quit, she'd be giving him what she knew he'd want, though he hadn't said that. Sighing, she leaned back and met Kinncaid's eyes as he grinned and tilted his head at her.

Kaitlyn closed her eyes and wondered when and how her life had become so complicated.

The Kinncaid Brothers Series

About the Author

Jaycee never really grew up—she still enjoys playing with imaginary people on a daily basis. Sometimes those people are nice, sometimes they're not, but in the end the girl gets the guy, so all is well. Jaycee earned her degree in Elementary Education from Eastern New Mexico University. She lives in Texas with her family, who puts up with her when her characters demand more of her time and appreciates her weirdness—or so they claim. There are also the cats and the corgis, who, in truth, rule the family. When she's not chained to her keyboard, she's doubling as a parent, a teacher, a maid, a chef, a chauffeur, a therapist, and promoting her education in human development while finishing her masters in plant elimination.

You can learn more about Jaycee by visiting her website at www.jayceeclark.com or emailing her at jaycee@jayceeclark.com. Her newsletter and blog subscriptions can be found on her website, along with links to follow her on Twitter, Facebook, and various other sites.